HAWTHORN ACADEMY

HAWTHORN ACADEMY

YEAR ONE

D.R. PERRY

DISRUPTIVE IMAGINATION

LMBPN Publishing
PMB 196, 2540 South Maryland Pkwy
Las Vegas, NV 89109

First US edition, February 2020

ebook ISBN: 978-1-64202-737-2
Print ISBN: 978-1-64202-738-9

GLOSSARY

People

- **Changeling-** A mortal child of either one or two faerie parents. Most changelings choose a monarch sometime in their twenties, although some do it earlier than they have to.
- **Dampyr-** The mortal offspring of two vampires. They aren't as rare as many suspect, although because their blood is exceptionally sustaining to vampires, they keep their status secret. Dampyr sometimes have magic or psychic powers that work unreliably.
- **Faerie-** A term used to describe either a changeling who has tithed to a monarch and spent a year and a day in the Under or the pure creatures such as Gnomes and Pixies who were created by the king and queen.
- **Ghost-** A dead person with unfinished business becomes a ghost. If a mortal makes a contract before death, that gives them unfinished business and lets them linger. When ghosts finish their business, they move on, but no one knows where they go from here.

- **Magus**- A mortal who can use magic. Magic comes from energy in the world. Most magi can only use one type of magic. However, a rare few can do more than one kind. Those are called extramagi.
- **Merfolk**- People who can live on land with legs or in the sea with fins and tails. They only emerged from the ocean after the Big Reveal and are still extremely rare outside of harbor towns.
- **Psychic**- A mortal with psychic power. Psychic ability comes from a person's own body and mind.
- **Vampire**- An unliving person who drinks blood to survive and enhance their abilities. Only regular mortals, psychics, and magi can get turned into vampires. Shifters, changelings, and faeries won't turn, and most of those won't survive an attempt.
- **Shifter**- A mortal who can take an animal's shape. Shifters have one form, with coloring similar to what they have while human. They usually have an enhanced sense while human-shaped, which goes along with their animal. For example, an owl shifter might have keen eyesight and a wolf shifter, a great sense of smell.

Shifter Varieties

- **Dragon**- The only shifters who can see both magic and psychic abilities, though only while shifted. The most powerful ones can partially shapeshift. Dragons are immortal and reproduce infrequently. There are so few of them since the Reveal that they've started taking other magical shifters as mates.
- **Kelpie**- A magical shifter who gets their abilities from an enchanted faerie pelt that bonds with their soul. The Kelpie pelts were created by the Goblin King, so they have Unseelie energy and restrictions. A Kelpie's animal form is a horse. Families pass the pelts down through generations,

and part of each ancestor lives on to help their descendants. The ancestors can get distracting, however.

- **Selkie-** A magical shifter who gets their abilities from an enchanted faerie pelt that bonds with their soul. The Selkie pelts were created by the Sidhe queen, so they have Seelie energy and restrictions. A Selkie's animal form is a seal or sometimes a sea otter. They can use water magic as long as they wear the pelt. Families pass the pelts down through the generations, and part of each ancestor lives on to help their descendants. The ancestors can get distracting, however.
- **Tanuki-** A magical shifter with enhanced speed and the ability to see all types of magic while shifted. They are also the only creatures who can manipulate luck, causing it to turn from good to bad or the other way around. They stop aging if they own a charm infused with luck from humans. Very few of those charms exist, having been either used up during the Reveal or locked away.

Powers

- **Air magic-** The power to conjure, control, and banish wind or air.
- **Earth magic-** The power to conjure, control, and banish earth, sand, or rock.
- **Empathy-** A psychic power to sense and influence emotions in other people.
- **Fire magic-** The power to conjure, control, and banish flames.
- **Ice magic-** The power to conjure, control, and banish ice.
- **Lightning magic-** The power to conjure, control, and banish lightning.
- **Poison magic-** The power to conjure, control, and banish poison. Each magus has a slightly different type of toxin they produce. Some are even antidotes to others.
- **Precognitive-** A psychic power to foretell future events.

- **Spectral magic**- the power to conjure, control, and banish light.
- **Spectral Affinity**- A trait some spectral magi have that makes them charismatic and believable.
- **Summoner**- A psychic power that lets the user make contracts with pure faeries, letting the summoner call them in times of need. Each creature has an anchor, some item symbolizing the bond. Mastery of summoning takes decades of study, which is why the most powerful are either vampires or past middle age.
- **Seelie**- The Sidhe queen's court. The Seelie way is about following the letter of the law, even when it's hard or cruel. They have a hard time reconciling faerie rules with the new mortal laws since the Big Reveal.
- **Solar Magic**- The power to conjure, control, or banish sunlight. Some of the most powerful practitioners can find hidden objects or discover long-kept secrets.
- **Solar Affinity**- A trait some solar magi have that makes them beacons for coincidence.
- **Space magic**- The power to move the self or objects instantly across distances. Some can even move other people.
- **Space Affinity**- This space power comes with an ability to locate people or things important to the magus.
- **Telekinesis**- A psychic power that moves objects.
- **Telepathy**- A psychic power to read minds.
- **Tithe**- The process of pledging to either the queen or king, making a changeling choose to be either Seelie or Unseelie.
- **Umbral magic**- The power to conjure, control, and banish shadows and veil or camouflage objects or people.
- **Umbral Affinity**- A trait some umbral magi have that makes them difficult to remember without psychic ability, faerie magic, or a shifter pack bond.

- **Undeath magic**- The power to conjure, control, and banish unliving energy.
- **Unseelie**- The Goblin king's court. The Unseelies bend the rules and often navigate mortal society more easily than their Seelie counterparts.
- **Water magic**- The power to conjure, banish, and control water.
- **Wood magic**- The power to conjure, banish, and control wood. It takes extreme power to influencing a living plant.

Creatures

- **Basilisk**- A venomous serpent that also has poison magic.
- **Dragonet**- A tiny dragon-like creature, always associated with one or more element which powers their breath attacks later in life. They have scales but are warm-blooded like birds. Most don't get much bigger than a small cat.
- **Familiar**- A magical or mythical creature who makes a bond with a magus.
- **Gryphon**- A chimera which has the head of a bird and hindquarters of a predatory mammal. They come in several combinations of base species, and habitat influences their choice in magi to bond with.
- **Karkus**- A crab that can change its shape. They're said to be the offspring of the crab that pinched Hercules as he battled the Hydra.
- **Lightning Bird**- A familiar from South Africa with an affinity for lightning. Its beak can jump-start a car.
- **Mercat**- A shapeshifting feline with fur for land and scales in the water. They can live in lakes, rivers, or in the sea as well as on land. They must never completely dry out, or they will die.
- **Moon Hare**- A magical rabbit that gets power from its particular moon phase. They commonly bond with umbral magi.

- **Pharaoh's Rat**- These natural predators of dragon shifters are the size of ferrets and resemble a mongoose with more fur. They have an affinity for space magic and can use it on occasion.
- **Pigeon**- Not as mundane as most think, some pigeons have an uncanny sense of direction due to their affinity for air magic.
- **Pricus**- An aquatic goat said to be descended from Capricorn. They can warp time even better than Gnomes.
- **Pure Faeries**- Creatures who spring to life from magical sources in the Under. They are genderless, and their type and ability depend on place of origin. They're associated with only one court, although they will work together to defeat a common enemy.
- **Sand Cat**- A feline that lives in the desert, able to go for weeks without water. Earth magic lets them do this.
- **Sha**- A magical desert dog from Egypt. Sha are the size of mundane toy breeds with short hair and small pointy ears. They could pass for mundane except for their blue tongues. They are attracted to anything undead.
- **Sphinx**- A magic cat with an affinity for fire. The reason they're hairless is that they're resistant to flames.
- **Strix**- A venomous owl with an affinity for poison. Female striges have rounded tufts on their heads, while males have pointed ones.
- **Sumxu**- A lop-eared cat found only in northern China. They are masters of camouflage and have an affinity for several kinds of magic.

Places

- **The Academy**—Something between a community college and a military academy for extrahumans, the Academy is geared toward helping extrahumans who don't play well with mortals get ready to join a blended society. It's got divisions for learners of all ages, though they are housed separately.

- **Cherry Blossom School**- A dojo geared toward teaching extrahumans self-restraint, meditation, and how to temper their enhanced physical abilities with more mundane skills. It's been around for close to a hundred years, run by the Ichiro family. Mundane classes used to be offered as a front but now are a separate division.
- **Ellicot City Magitechnic**- A prep school for magi and psychics specializing in magipsychic technology. It's located outside Baltimore.
- **Gallows Hill School**- Traditionally for shifters, this prep school in Salem recently opened its doors to changelings and other extrahumans not categorized as magi or psychics.
- **Hawthorn Academy**- A preparatory school for magi in Salem. Its campus is in the space between the mortal realm and the Under, giving it unrivaled privacy. They specialize in teaching familiar magic.
- **Providence Paranormal College**- A school founded just one year after Brown University and located right in its shadow. Providence Paranormal used to admit only magi and psychics, but it's been accepting all types of extrahumans ever since Henrietta Thurston became headmistress. There has been trouble since then for students and faculty, leading people to believe dissenters are sabotaging the school.
- **Trout Academy**- A prestigious preparatory school for changelings with magic, recently open to magi and magical shifters. Its campus is located in South County and has been operating in some form or another since Rhode Island Colony was founded.
- **The Under**- The faerie realm. It's been divided into two parts ever since the Sidhe Queen and the Goblin king split up thousands of years ago. Mortals don't age in the Under, but it's a dangerous place for them to be. Getting lost means

never being seen again, and it's easy to get indebted to something nasty while trying to get through or out of the Under.

- **Wolf Messing Prep**- An institute for psychics to learn to control their skills before heading to college.

Events

- **The Big Reveal**- The term used for the 1990s, when the world discovered magic was real and extrahumans existed. The decade was marked with fear as everyone adjusted to the changes. Since the 21st Century, law and technology work for both humans and extrahumans.
- **Boston Internment**- A reaction by Boston government officials to the disappearance and suspected trafficking in extrahumans, especially shifters. All registered extrahumans in Boston lived on barges for close to a month under guard by the Boston Police. The traffickers got their hands on some magical gadgets, rendering the protection useless. Few survived.

PREFACE

I'm Aliyah Morgenstern. I grew up on tales of my great-grandfather's magic bringing light and healing to the world. I bonded with my dragonet Ember on my sixteenth birthday, which means I'll be scary powerful someday. There's one problem.

Mom's kept secrets that everyone at my new school seems to know. Turns out, I've got an infamous criminal uncle, Richard Hopewell. Now everyone's waiting for me to do something evil, and my first day at school's so horrible, I'm convinced, too.

My biggest challenge this year isn't history, math, gym, or even the dreaded magiscience Lab. It's keeping a devastating secret from almost everyone, including my family. I'm an extramagus like Uncle Richard, whose incredible powers corrupted him.

Is evil my destiny, or can I fight it somehow?

CHAPTER ONE

"Beware the Ides of June." I lifted my hand and touched the back of it to my forehead, tilting my head back in a melodramatic pose. "They herald impending disaster!"

I wasn't trying to be a drama queen, only distract my friends from the boring news broadcast about the Federal Bureau of Extrahumans arresting that evil extramagus from Rhode Island. Not a good look for a television hanging from an arcade's ceiling.

"Aliyah, honestly. It's only your birthday." Noah rolled his eyes. "I'd tell you to grow up, but that's pointless." His familiar, Lotan, poked her snaky head out of my brother's collar, sticking her forked tongue out at me.

"Don't be a dick, Noah." Izzy shrugged. "Anyway, Aliyah's sixteen today, not six. And her magic's at least as strong as yours, so watch yourself."

"But I'm her big brother." Noah flashed us all one of his stage-perfect smiles. "It's my job to give her grief, after all. She can't exactly hold it against me."

I took my hand off my forehead, made a fist, then used the other hand to make a cranking motion as I raised just one finger in my brother's general direction. You can guess which one.

"Hey, Miss, please don't do that in here."

I dropped my hands, turning to face the speaker. It was a broad-shouldered, dusky-complected, blue-haired guy in a Salem Willows apron. Great. Just what I needed on my birthday—a seasonal employee on my case for flipping the bird. He seemed to be about my age on top of it all, with melty brown eyes, perfect ringlets, and a chiseled jawline.

"Sorry, yeah, I know." Salem Willows Arcade has always been an all-ages environment. "I'll watch my figurative mouth while I'm here."

" I'm sorry, it's kind of my job to be a jerk. My manager really doesn't like it when parental units ask to speak to him." He shrugged. "Them's the breaks, I guess."

"Oh, good gracious me, is it really so awful working here?" Cadence folded her pale hands, then used them as a pedestal to rest one side of her head on. She blinked, her turquoise eyes like the sea. Which makes sense, 'cause she's a mermaid.

"Yeah, this is the best and worst summer job in Salem. But what can you do?" He shook his head. "This job is sort of a requirement for me."

"I guess everyone wants more money." Cadence sighed, sounding sympathetic. Practically everything she says, whether word or noise, comes off sounding like exactly what you want to hear. It's all part of her mermaid mojo. "Easy come, easy go."

"She wouldn't know anything about that." Noah turned his head, pausing beside the Skee-Ball machine. "Cadence's family is super-important. Rumor has it, they've got mountains of clams."

"Noah!" I tossed my crumpled straw wrapper at his head, and for once, he didn't manage to duck in time. "It's my freaking birthday, and you weren't invited, so just leave already."

"Whatever." Noah rolled his eyes for the five hundredth time that day. "You'll have to put up with me and my attitude at home later." He faked a pout. "So there."

And with that, my obnoxious older brother flipped his jet-black shoulder-length hair to one side, slapped his last token on my table, and sashayed toward the exit.

"What's his problem?" Izzy scooped up the token, bouncing it in her hand.

"I don't know. But you'd think he was my younger brother, the way he tags along everywhere we go." I chuckled. "And that attitude."

"He's your brother?" The curly-haired guy blinked. "That guy there?"

"Yup."

"I'm sorry."

"Oh, it gets worse." Cadence sighed, batting her eyes.

Why was she flirting with this guy? It shouldn't have mattered to me. She was the flirt of the group. I'm awkward and gangly, and Izzy just isn't interested in boys. Or girls either, for that matter.

"Do you know they're going to the same prep school in the fall?" Cadence dropped this line while somehow managing to brush right past the heartrending elephant in the room.

Which was that we three besties would suffer social amputation from each other, come September. But I couldn't blame her. I'd have tried forgetting that too if I could. That was impossible because Izzy, Cadence, and I had an epic friendship history that had started in kindergarten. We thought it would never die, but Izzy didn't talk about it all last year. For a divination psychic like her, that silence was a literal bad omen.

The Arcade's newest summer employee stood there with his mouth open like Cadence had slapped him in the face with a fistful of minnows instead of dropping hints about our educational apocalypse. He stared at me with eyes like fancy cups of coffee on saucers.

"First you tell me you're Noah Morgenstern's sister, then I find out you're starting Hawthorn Academy right along with me this fall?" He grinned. It looked so good on him, I wondered whether he was using a glamour or something. But he couldn't be. Changelings didn't go to Hawthorn. "Hi, I'm Dylan Kahn."

"And that's important because?" Izzy snorted. I noticed her hand inside the little black backpack she always carried. She was probably about to consult her cards. My psychic friend Isabella Mendez always brought sass along with her predictions.

3

"Because I don't know anyone here in Salem." He leaned against the table, speaking to me instead of my friends. "It's one reason I had to get a job this summer. My parents won't let me be a total introvert anymore."

"That's the lamest pickup line she's ever heard." Izzy slapped the card in her hand on the table face up. Thank goodness she didn't mention how it was almost the first pickup line I'd heard.

"Or maybe it's not a total failure." My psychic friend parted her fingers to show us the Two of Cups. It wasn't even reversed.

"Oh, Izzy." Cadence clucked like a mother seahen. "I don't think your card has anything to do with this fellow."

Dylan's jaw eased, like the words were a refreshing sea breeze. But then, my merfriend continued.

"Even if he is trying to flirt with our birthday girl," Cadence said, winking, "I've got mermaid's intuition that something else is going on here."

"Uh." Dylan's hands wrung the hem of his Salem Willows apron.

"Why?" Izzy tilted her head, eyes on the mermaid.

"Because that's the same card Noah got when he found Lo—" Cadence emitted a squeak like a dolphin's.

"Holy—"

"Mother—"

They were all cut off as I bolted out of my seat. Something touched my shoulder, and not just any something. It felt cold and slightly sticky, like a spiderweb, but it wasn't one. It was too thick and had sinew in it; strength, direction, and purpose. I sucked in air, just knowing I'd let it out in a scream the next instant.

If Salem Willows management would chew me out over flipping the bird, they might ban me all summer if I cussed a blue streak in there, so I did the only thing I could think of.

I bolted.

The Salem Willows Arcade had wide-open doors, like an auto garage except there were Skee-Ball and claw machines and video games inside. That made it easy to flee the scene plus what- or whoever had me by the shoulder. I didn't even have to dodge too many people because elementary and middle schools were in session for another week.

Anyway, all this was beside the point because my attempted escape wasn't working.

The wind rushed past my ears, but behind me, something whooshed overhead. It was like getting dive-bombed by a seagull looking for errant tater tots, and the thing was still on my neck. I ran faster.

My feet just barely hit the pavement as I hightailed it out of there. I wasn't using magic. I conjure fire, not air. It was just a side effect of trying so hard to get away. The moment I reached the edge of the grass near the veterans' monument, I stopped, dropped, and counted on my friends to help me with whatever creepazoid had me by the shoulder. And also, the hair.

Except they didn't. Instead, I heard a trill from Cadence and wheezing snorts from Izzy. They laughed, which meant I wasn't in mortal danger, so of course, I lifted my heavier-than-usual head to see what was so funny.

And that was when I realized something was sitting on my head. Maybe more like perching. I almost batted it away when a red-gold scaled head, upside down, dangled in my face.

"Peep?"

"Sorry, I don't speak dragonet." I waved my hand. "Shoo!"

Yeah, that's right. A dragonet had goosed and chased me. And after all that, the little magical critter wouldn't leave me alone. The tiny winged lizard didn't shoo, scram, skedaddle, or get off my head. Just hung there, peeping in my face.

At least the critter held on with its claws retracted.

I waved both hands over my head this time. I didn't want to hit the dragonet but wanted its grip on my hair to release. The pulling sensation hurt a bit. I was rewarded for my effort by the critter plopping into my lap, strands of my obnoxiously brassy blonde hair dangling from the creature's toe scales. Both my pride and my intentionally messy bun were a wreck.

My friends had stopped laughing, at least. That was a good thing because I'd have told them to shut their traps. The dragonet sat up in my lap, tail flailing as one wing extended and the other dragged like a flag in a rainstorm. My stomach sank as I wondered whether this innocent creature had been injured because I'd freaked out.

"Poor thing, your wing's hurt." I reached out, offering it my arm because everybody knows you don't just grab animals or put your hands near their mouths. "Come on, I know just where to bring you."

The dragonet hopped up on my arm, favoring the injured wing. Rounding in the hindquarters suggested she was female and young— like me. I blinked my stinging eyes, hoping I could stop crying. I wasn't one of those super-expressive people, and I almost never tear up while reading or watching a movie.

Somehow, I practically felt the magical critter's pain and misery. No, that wouldn't do. Ember was her name. A wave of relief washed over me as I examined her injured wing, which was twisted, not broken, with a small red sore. Ember would recover if she got proper care.

"Where are you going, Lee?"

"To see Bubbe."

My friends followed as I headed toward my grandmother's office. None of us drive, and Salem Willows was a ways from downtown, but the dragonet's injury wasn't immediately life-threatening. Getting there in time would be a piece of cake.

We crossed Fort Avenue a block early to avoid Irzyk Park, also known as Tank Park because its main feature was a decommissioned military vehicle. The local shifter gangbangers hung out there, and Noah always told us to stay away. Cadence's parents agreed.

Cadence looked over her shoulder at the thankfully vacant area, something she'd never bothered with until just a couple of weeks ago. I hoped she wasn't thinking of introducing herself to the Tanks. That was what they called themselves. At least there was no such thing as a shark shifter, but you wouldn't have guessed that if you saw the way my aquatic friend stared.

"Cadence, quit it." Izzy, direct as ever, called the mermaid on the carpet.

6

"Just making sure the, um, unsavories aren't watching." She pointed out a crow perched on top of the tank. "Which maybe they are."

"Sure, whatever you say." Izzy snorted. She did that an awful lot, but I hardly blamed her. If she were a beverage, Izzy would be water. Direct, to the point, and exactly what you needed most of the time. Cadence was more like a cosmic coolatta.

Ember peeped again, clinging to my arm with little talons that were sharp like a baby's nails. I understood her renewed distress as we approached a busier area. Magical critters could camouflage themselves, but dragonets needed to fold their wings in order to look like mundane lizards. She couldn't, and that put her on edge.

Everybody had known about magic since before I was born anyway, so I wasn't worried about getting in trouble. Just about Ember getting nervous and hurting herself.

The only way I could help was by adjusting the strap on my bag so it hung partly in front of Ember's back and hindquarters. This settled her a bit, which was good because the last thing I wanted to do was drop her.

"Just a few more blocks, okay?" One corner of my mouth twitched, but I couldn't quite manage the reassuring smile Bubbe would have worn.

Ember blinked, then lowered her head to rest it on my arm. I took that as a good sign.

At the corner of Forrester and Hawthorne Street, we stopped for traffic and then crossed. Half a block down, we took a right after Izzy's house and headed behind it to number ten and a half. Bubbe's office was on the first floor, and my family all lived upstairs in the top two stories.

My arms were full, so Cadence opened the door for me. That was nice, even if she added in her signature flourishing curtsy to show off as I passed her. There was only one reason she'd showboat like this— someone was watching us. I looked over my shoulder.

All I saw was another crow perching on the awning of the antique shop across the street. Or maybe the same one; I know magical critters, not mundane birds. If it were a bad omen, Izzy would have said

7

something. There was no time to ask Cadence about her sudden-onset aviary obsession with an injured dragonet in my arms.

CHAPTER TWO

Bubbe was in the back when we got inside. I knew because I heard her singing to one of her patients behind the door separating the exam room from the waiting area. That was no problem because she'd see we came in on the magipsychic security system. My grandma was pretty high tech for an older lady who'd learned her magic decades before the Great Reveal.

I sat down to wait, Ember cradled in my arms, and a less on-key rendition of the same tune Bubbe sang in the other room coming out of my mouth. It was a good thing I didn't want a performance art career. Some extrahuman folk have had great success along those lines, but I'd never be one of them, and that's okay.

I didn't want to be Irina Kazynski or Lane Meyer. Instead, I wanted Bubbe's job, which was helping animals. I just had to get a B+ average or higher at Hawthorn Academy so I could get into Providence Paranormal after I graduated.

Ember got downright clingy, tail curled around my arm like a copper bracelet as she leaned against me. She used my breastbone as a pillow, and it was absolutely adorable.

"You've got a new scaly bestie." Izzy peered at me from behind one of her tarot cards. I had no idea which one because it faced her. She put it away. "Familiar material."

"Yes, Isabella, you soothsaid all of this at the Arcade if I'm not mistaken." Cadence nodded in a way I assumed she believed was wise. Her chestnut curls bounced, making her look about as sage as a sorority pledge. Maybe that was a bad analogy, and not just because my Mer-friend looked nothing like Barbie. The gal from that movie about the blonde law student was in a sorority, and she had a giant brain, right?

"Maybe." Izzy shrugged. "That two of cups might have meant something else, but this is a sure thing. You and the scaly critter might already have a bond."

"That is so cool!" Cadence bounced on her toes. She did the same thing with her tail when she was in the ocean.

But my seagoing friend was only this expressive with positive emotions. All her turmoil (which I suspected was vast) stayed hidden. For about the millionth time, I wondered how she handled life with a foot on land and a fin under the sea. I probably wouldn't manage going between an exclusively magical school and my regular townie life as handily.

I was very thankful for my friends. We always got through everything together, before. For a hot minute, I dared to think this year would be no different.

And then all my gratitude toward the universe and its ineffable movements crashed around me as I remembered how I'd barely have time to see them once this summer was over.

Before I got maudlin enough for Izzy and Cadence to notice, Bubbe stepped through the door behind the counter.

My paternal grandmother wasn't all arms and legs like my mom and me. Instead, she was built along the same lines as Dad, which meant petite yet comfortingly solid. Her hair was bobbed and curly, a trait she also shared with my old man, but unlike him, she dyed all her gray in a variety of punk-rock hues. That week it was bubblegum pink.

Bubbe was my role model in just about everything, though biology had dictated long ago that I'd be nothing like her physically when I'm fully grown. At that moment, I couldn't imagine stronger life goals than following her career path.

She carried a dropper bottle filled with pearly blue liquid, which meant the critter in the back was another magical reptile. Bubbe's always had a soft spot for the critters most people avoid, like serpents, salamanders, spiders, and of course, dragonets.

"Bissel, who have you brought in today?" She peered down at the dragonet in my arms. I couldn't bring myself to roll my eyes at the diminutive, which meant "little bit."

"Bubbe, I'm practically a giant nowadays." The weak protest was all I could muster. I leaned forward, giving my grandmother a better view of my little friend. "Anyway, she's a dragonet. I'm calling her Ember for now."

"It's the wing, I see." Bubbe turned sideways, gesturing toward the door she'd emerged from. "Come along, girls."

I walked carefully past my grandmother and toward the door. Izzy and Cadence glanced at each other, hesitating. They'd never been invited into the back at Bubbe's. When Cadence took a step forward, Izzy put out a hand to stop her, but my grandmother shook her head.

"Isabella, you're like family here. Cadence, too. It's about time you got a look at how all of this works."

"Wow, thanks, Doc Morgenstern!" Cadence clapped her hands. I would have too if mine hadn't been full of small, cute, and scaly. I'd always wanted them to see how awesome extraveterinary medicine is.

"Yeah, thanks." Izzy's bluntness came from being brought up in a psychic shop, watching her parents work while being seen but not heard Of the three of us, she always fought change the hardest.

In the back, there was a hallway with a series of half-doors. What I mean is the doors all had bottoms and tops which open and closed separately. Most were closed all the way, but a few had only the bottoms shut. Bubbe called them Dutch doors.

I turned my head to the right as we passed the first half-open door.

Inside was a Grim. Those weren't the sort of magical animals who can be familiars. Instead, they're pure faerie creatures who usually live in the Under unless they've got an agreement with a psychic Summoner. Some of them were totally sentient like Gnomes or even smarter than average humans and extrahumans like Brownies, but Grims were pretty much like regular dogs. Plenty of folks were scared of them, but I always thought they were awesome.

"Whose is that, Bubbe?" I jerked my chin at the shadow beastie.

"Oh, I'm just sheltering this Grim here today as a favor to a visiting friend." Bubbe reached out and pulled the top half of the door closed. "Just for a rest while my friend is sightseeing. Too bright a day for an Unseelie creature to be out and about comfortably."

"That's awful nice of you, Doc Morgenstern." Izzy smiled, then elbowed Cadence. "So, I guess having psychic friends runs in your family."

Cadence gave Izzy a stiff sort of nod.

"And merfolk, too, Cadence." I reached out to grab her hand, squeezing. Her smile widened as it eased. "Anyway, it's really nice of you to help like that, especially during the summer when it's busy, Bubbe."

"It's not quite so hectic yet." My grandmother dropped us all a wink.

As if to disprove her point, a tinkle of chimes sounded in the air beside Bubbe's head. She tapped one of the moonstone studs in her earlobe and the music stopped.

"Magipsychic earrings! Cool!" Cadence beamed again.

The merfolk had spent most of the last thirty years avoiding us landlubber extrahumans and all the integration we've done with the rest of the world's population. Her family was one of only a few who had living space on land. She said it was because her family did important diplomatic work with the land-dwellers.

My grandmother blinked three times, activating the device that let her see the waiting room. I was shaky on the details of how that worked because I was a future animal doctor, not a magipsychic engineer. Whatever she saw out there had her turning on her heel and power-walking back up the hall. Of course, I followed her all the way out into the waiting room.

Big mistake.

Standing at the counter was a gaggle of magi, all girls about my age. The two waiflike brunettes were identical twins, while the redhead in the middle looked totally unrelated. They had on enough makeup for a red-carpet premiere.

All three of them wore actual designer clothes, and I realized they were in town on vacation. From New York City, judging by their accents, and uptown, based on their hairstyles and jewelry.

The non-twin carried an oversized Hermes tote, its top level with the surface the girl leaned on. I saw a platinum luggage tag bearing an engraved Park Avenue address.

A sleek snout with a curving canine muzzle poked out of it, followed by the head of an Egyptian Sha disguising itself as a small dog. Its ebony and gold familiar's collar gleamed against its short dark gray fur, more ornate than it had to be but unmistakable all the same. It sniffed before I noticed its gaze fall squarely on Ember's busted wing.

The crested canine Sha tended to gravitate toward magi with undeath, umbral, or poison magic, which were all on the opposite spectrum from my own fire magic. So of course, the animals reacted to each other like oil and water.

As the Sha made a yappy racket, I sighed. Maybe my eyes rolled. The other girl started huffing and puffing and threatening to ask for the manager.

"How stupid can you be, bringing a dragonet around a Sha like that? That beast isn't even your familiar. Is this an extraveterinary office or an underground animal fight club? Honestly. I ought to take my business somewhere else."

"It'd be nice if you could, Miss Fairbanks. However, Hawthorn Academy's got its familiar licensing contract with my office. Here's the required form." Bubbe pushed a piece of paper across the counter toward the girl, shooting what I call "the look" at the Sha. It shut its mouth, of course. All critters did when Bubbe made that face.

"Whatever. Just have your moronic assistant get that scaly menace out of here." She turned her nose up. "Or I'll be back on our next long weekend up here with my father. And you're well aware of how connected he is."

Miss Park Avenue was threatening Bubbe.

Her words burned. And yeah, it started getting hot in there because that's what happens to fire magi like me when we're angry. I took a deep breath, about to tell this girl who she's talking to and why she should stop it.

Ember whimpered. When I looked down at her, she had the most miserable expression on her face, like Dad got when I let him down in some way.

And just like that, I banked all that shame and anger to the lowest levels I could manage. When I said "bank," I used the double meaning. One thing my mom taught me about fire magic is this: you can't just lock it up indefinitely. It's got to come out sooner or later, or that inferno will eat you alive.

But that day, with a hurt animal in my arms, was not the time.

I turned my back, striding with as much of my shaken confidence as I could muster toward the door Izzy held open. My upper lip was stiff, chin up, head held high.

It was all a show, but a good one, I hoped.

"That's what I thought." The alpha mean-girl scoffed.

"You showed her, Faith."

"True story." Faith laughed. I listened to the scratch of pen on paper as she filled out the forms for her Sha. At least she seemed to care about her familiar.

As Izzy stepped aside, letting go of the door, Faith Fairbanks delivered her parting shot.

"I'll show her even more at school in September."

I didn't return fire. It would have been literal, and I didn't want to burn down Bubbe's lobby. I had no idea why this girl had taken a few barks and hisses so personally, but as I headed into an exam room with Ember in my arms and my best friends at my side, I knew one thing.

I'd have to handle anything Faith Fairbanks decided to dish out on my own. Noah wouldn't get in the middle of a dispute between first-years.

Happy birthday to me.

CHAPTER THREE

In July, we were in the middle of the hottest week on record in Salem. Izzy, Cadence, and I had already seen all three movies at Cinema-Salem. None of our parents could drive us to the Danvers Mall, and anyway, they didn't allow dragonets in there.

There was one place left for us to go have fun: Salem Willows, of course. We were there half the week but didn't mind making another trip. It had Izzy's favorite game and people-watching for Cadence—and a future fellow Hawthorn attendee I really ought to try harder to befriend.

"So, you're back for more Skee-Ball, I see." Dylan Kahn waved as he approached. "You three are practically fixtures in here."

"It's an arcade, and we're still kids." Izzy chuckled, brandishing a ten-dollar bill. "Now, give me all your tokens!"

"Technically kids, you mean." Cadence examined her nails like she didn't want to be here. But I caught her stealing glances at the chrome-sided machines with their particolored flashing lights.

"Whatever." I shrugged. Ember gripped my shoulder tighter, struggling to keep her balance. "Oops, sorry about that, girl."

"Peep."

"What's that mean?" Izzy planted her feet in front of her Skee-Ball lane, preparing to roll.

"I think she said something like okay." I headed to the next row, where I helped the dragonet perch above the ball return so she could watch.

"So why isn't she your familiar yet, Aliyah?" Dylan leaned against a support beam. The Willows had plenty of those, and he made good use of them.

"I'm not sure?" I shook my head. "I think my parents expected me to bond with a Tallin like Dad and Noah."

The little split-tailed sun serpents dated at least as far back as the Old Testament days. The Morgensterns have been associated with them for just as long.

"Well, what about Bubbe?" Cadence grinned. "Doesn't she have one of those little snakies too?"

"She did until last fall, and her next one's probably going to be the same type." I put the token into the slot and listened to the balls roll down.

"So, either Ember's the anomaly, or you are." Izzy's bluntness hit me like a lead pipe to the head. She sank her first ball into the five-hundred-point slot, too. Skee-Ball was totally her game. Always has been.

"None of the above." I took a shot and managed one hundred points. "It could just be a dragonet thing. Maybe they imprint or something. Bubbe said she must have hatched the day we tangled, or maybe the one before."

"Wow." Cadence twisted one of her shell bracelets. "Ember's practically a baby, then."

"I can't believe your grandma lets you bring her everywhere." Dylan rummaged in his apron, collecting the tokens Izzy already paid for. "Lucky."

"The fresh air is good for her." I rolled my second ball, which landed in the gutter.

"How come we haven't seen your familiar, Dylan?" Izzy sank a ball for one hundred points.

"Uh, well." He cleared his throat. "You all get to come here for fun. I'm working."

"I see." Izzy snorted before glancing up at our scores. "Come on, Aliyah. Keep rolling."

I did, but no matter what, I couldn't catch up to Izzy that day. Cadence did better, but our psychic friend managed to squeak out a victory by a scant five points.

"Well, I'm out of tokens and money."

"And I'm practically drying up in this heat." Cadence fanned herself with a flier from the Engine House, where we usually went after a day at the arcade. But the mermaid had other ideas. "Let's go swimming. Dylan, too."

"Dylan what now?" He'd just come back from handing his apron to the manager.

"Come out with us." Cadence smiled.

"Yeah." I nodded. "You've been in town for over a month now, and I've never once seen you do anything just for fun."

"Well, that's because I've got to save my money and stuff."

"Swimming is free." I flashed him a grin. "Perfect for the teenager on a budget."

"Peep!" Apparently, Ember was happy with the choice of activity. Even fire dragonets enjoyed swimming, which made sense because in the wild, they'd catch and eat fish to survive.

"Come on, Ember." I held my arm out so she could make her way up to my shoulder. "And come on, Dylan."

"I don't have a swimsuit."

"I have brothers." Izzy tucked the tickets she'd won into the back pocket of her cutoffs. "They're younger, but Matteo's the same size as you."

"Okay, then."

We headed back toward downtown Salem and Hawthorne Street. Cadence led the way, a spring in her step as we passed Irzyk Park. Once again, I didn't see anyone hanging around, but the big black bird was back, cawing and flapping its wings.

"What's with that raven?" Dylan jerked his thumb at the feathered fiend.

Izzy scoffed. "Probably found something tasty in the garbage."

"Hey, don't assume." I shook my head. "Ravens can be familiars sometimes, especially for air magi." I glanced at Dylan.

"Yeah, no. Not me." His cheeks reddened. "I mean, I'm air but no ravens. After reading that Poe poem, they sort of freak me out."

"Huh." Cadence's voice had a lilt to it I'd only ever heard when she discussed boys. "I think they're cool. Mysterious, you know?" She fluttered her fingers at the bird, which stopped its hopping and stared.

"Well, clearly that one's intelligent." I made a mental note to remind Bubbe to check for nests. "Anyway, it's too hot to stand around here bird-watching."

"Yeah, I guess." Cadence flipped her ponytail to the other side of her neck. "Let's get the clothes and go swim already."

She hurried off, ending up on the porch at Izzy's house. The mermaid sulked on the porch while the psychic fetched Matteo's extra swim trunks for Dylan. After that, she headed back inside to change.

I beckoned to Cadence and Dylan, leading them up the driveway between numbers ten and eleven. I gestured at the stoop, and they sat. When he saw the number placard beside the door, Dylan chuckled.

"Wow. I didn't know half addresses existed stateside. Mom would lose her mind if she knew."

"Why not show her, then?" Cadence pointed back down the driveway. "Even my folks have come to see this, and they hate walking when they don't have to."

"Well, they're back in London, working." He stared at Bubbe's van, the fence behind it, and then his shoes. "I'm here by myself."

"Oh, I had no idea." I fumbled with the keys, all butterfingers as I tried to open the door I've used on my own for most of my life. "Where are you staying?"

"Down at the Y. The one for magi."

"Ugh, I heard their cafeteria sucks." I shook my head. "I'll bring down some snacks for all of us. Swimming is hunger-making."

Finally, I pulled the door open and headed up the stairs two at a time. Being too tall has some advantages. Ember clung to my shoulder, her tail wrapped under my armpit.

Once inside the apartment, I jogged through the kitchen and then up the back stairs to the top floor. Once Ember was perched safely on my headboard, I rushed through changing, whipping my clothes off and whisking them into the hamper.

Rummaging through my drawers, I found my trusty swimsuit, a royal blue one-piece with racerback straps and a built-in sports bra.

And I found it too short to pull the straps past my bust.

"Oh, come on!" I growled, frustrated by the fabric. "You fit last month! Ugh. It's not you, it's me."

"You okay, Aliyah?"

I turned, arms crossed over my chest.

"It doesn't fit, Mom. And everyone's going swimming." I sniffled. "Stupid teenage hormones being all—stupid."

"We'll fix this." She beckoned. "Come along."

"Huh." I snagged a tissue from the box on my dresser and followed her, dabbing my cheeks and wiping my nose. "With magic?"

"Not exactly." Mom pushed the door of the room she shared with Dad open. "With a belated birthday present."

She headed toward the cedar wardrobe that's sat in the corner for as long as I can remember. I avoided the thing whenever possible because one of my earliest memories is of Noah shutting himself in there by accident, trying to get into the Under and meet a Sprite.

And there I was, standing in front if its intricately carved and matte-finished surface, face all red and sticky from crying. The earlier incident had been a way better reason to cry because as hard as I tugged, I couldn't get the door open to let my brother out of there. And he kept saying he couldn't breathe.

This July day's upset was over a perfectly normal bathing suit I'd grown out of seemingly overnight.

Mom finished rummaging and turned around, handing me a bag from Queen of Hearts in Providence, Rhode Island. That was where my mother came from, even though she never talked about it. I knew more about my great-grandpa escaping Nazis than about Mom's childhood in the Ocean State. So, how'd she get something from there in a bag and not an online order box?

Since Mom worked from home almost all the time and I had been at Salem Middle School every day last year, she could have taken a trip pretty easily. It was two and a half hours on the commuter rail and less than two in a car from Salem to Providence. The jaunt was even shorter via magical conveyance.

I stood there staring at the bag and forgetting just about everything in an attempt to remember one shred of info about Mom. Had she mentioned going out of town without us over the spring?

"Would you like to open it?" She had one hand out, palm up and pointing at the bag. The other was in a white-knuckled fist by her side.

I heard her voice, but the words didn't register. It was the same as trying to hear Noah through the wardrobe door all those years ago.

"Peep?" The sound came with a red-gold tail waving near my arm, tapping the back of my hand like the dragonet was asking if I was okay when she was the one with the twisted wing.

"I'm okay." I looked down at Ember and back up at Mom. "And yeah. I'll open it. I just never heard of this store before," I lied. Everyone knew where it was. "Is it a new place? Maybe in Portsmouth or Boston?"

"Providence." Her lips turned up, but Mom's eyes weren't smiling. She wasn't happy that I'd caught her out, then. I dropped that subject.

I reached into the bag, pushing past gilt tissue paper. In seconds, my fingertips brushed smooth and stretchy fabric. I gripped and pulled, revealing a turquoise and royal blue tankini. The bottoms were horizontal striped boy-shorts, and the top was printed with a Celtic knotwork pattern featuring dragons.

I ran one finger along the outline of a wing, noticing how much it resembled Ember when she stretched.

"Mom, this is—I mean, thanks so much." My throat tightened, choked up by a silly bathing suit. At that point, I didn't care anymore whether Mom had gotten it on some day trip she'd never told me about. "It's perfect."

"Run along and change now." This time when she smiled, Mom's whole face lit up.

I dashed into my room and changed into the new suit. Ember followed, peeping cheerfully. It fit perfectly, and because it was two pieces, getting taller wouldn't be a problem. I threw a maxi dress over it and slipped sandals on, then I held my arm down for Ember to climb up. After a quick check in the mirror, I grabbed my beach bag and hustled out of my room.

"Love you, Mom!" I hollered down the hall.

"To the Under and back," she replied.

For the rest of the day, I only went to the beach. Dylan headed into the park's bathroom to change out of his work clothes. Izzy braided her thick acorn-brown hair into two buns, one behind each ear, as usual. Cadence gazed at the sky, so I pointed out clouds with interesting shapes, but she wasn't in the mood for chatter. Ember butted her head against my cheek, begging for chin scratches.

We spent some of our time wading down by the park. Izzy wore the same old triathlon suit, and Dylan kept on his muscle shirt with his borrowed trunks. I tucked my maxi dress into the beach bag, sauntering along without a care because my new suit was so comfortable.

Cadence, of course, didn't need to change clothes. The seawater turned her legs scaly wherever it hit them, something that didn't happen with rain or tap water. When we finally went in, she let her legs fully shift into a tail and then swam rings around the three of us.

Cadence always seemed so free in the ocean; water's literally her element. She never went out far enough to really get going. It was because her parents wouldn't allow that until she was older.

It was nice to get into the water and cool off, but the northern Atlantic temperatures meant most of us couldn't stay in for long. Dylan managed for longer than I'd expected. When he emerged, he shivered so hard I gave him my towel.

We sat in a line on the tide wall, legs dangling and bags between us like beads on a string. I was still puzzled by Dylan's ability to tolerate the chilly water, so I asked him.

"I'm an air magus." He shrugged. "My parents taught me that if I wanted to be any good with this element, I'd need to try tolerating both heat and cold."

"Well, if you need practice with the heat part, Aliyah's an expert." Cadence grinned.

"I bet she's getting rusty with magic." Izzy side-eyed Cadence like an onion ring that fell on the floor. "All that time babysitting scaly critters, you know."

"Am not." I snorted. "Not that I can give you a demonstration or anything."

"I wouldn't think of asking." Dylan nodded. "Not in the middle of summer."

Cadence watched me like a seagull over a picnic table. Izzy sighed and tapped one finger on the concrete under her hand, eyes wide and mouth small, like she gets while trying to solve a math problem. I wasn't sure what all the fuss was about. Dylan seemed as clueless as I was.

Magical creatures were so much easier.

"Peep?" Ember poked her head out of my beach bag, one of my hair ties sitting on top of her head like some kind of pretty floral bonnet.

Everybody laughed, even Ember, in a chirpy dragonet sort of way.

And just like that, the silence went from awkward to friendly. It stayed that way between the four of us all summer.

CHAPTER FOUR

A week into August, I paced my bedroom. That wasn't as easy as it had been last summer. I had always been gangly, limbs longer than they ought to be, but this year, I'd gotten extra tall on top of it. I bumped into people and things more than at any previous time in my life.

My ceiling was gabled, with slanting at the corners so the roof drained and let go of snow properly in the New England climate. As a little kid, I'd loved this. I'd made tents by tacking old sheets to the edges I could reach. But for pacing as a string-bean teen, it felt like courting a concussion.

I was about to give up when someone knocked on my door. Four quick taps, which meant Dad. Leaning slightly while reaching let me open it from where I stood.

"What's up, Aliyah?" He bent his knees a little as he craned his neck. My father didn't smirk about his dad joke, just showed a slight smile.

"Stuff. Things." I shrugged, feeling like a giraffe in a railway car. "Whatever."

"Why don't you come on downstairs and visit Bubbe with me?" He leaned on the doorframe, turning that smile up a notch.

I took a step before remembering my grandma had asked me to

run some errands for her yesterday. That always meant she wanted me out of her hair at the office. "Um, I thought she had a full house down there?"

"Mom and I talked to her last night, and that's not exactly the case."

"Well, what's the deal, then?"

"She's got a tricky surgery this morning."

"All the more reason to stay out of her way." I shook my head, not sure what my father was getting at. "What's your point?"

"You are. Look at you, worrying."

"I'm sixteen and going to a new school. Without my best friends. Of course, I'm worried."

"Are you sure that's what's got its hooks in you today?"

"Uh." I blinked. "No. Actually, I've got no idea what my problem is right now."

"Your mother's got a theory about a certain dragonet."

Mom's theories were no joke. That had been her college major, after all—theoretical magic.

"Ember? She's just an injured stray I brought to Bubbe. I've been doing that for years, Dad. No big deal."

"That may well be, but this surgery I mentioned is to fix her wing."

"Oh." I sat down on the edge of my bed.

"Your mother thinks coincidence had a hand in your finding her on your sixteenth birthday. We all think Ember's your familiar, Aliyah. It's time to test that, and if it's true, make things official."

As if to drive home his point, I got a twinge near my left shoulder. That might not sound strange since aches and pains happened all over the bodies of growing people, but it wasn't a spot on my body hurting. It was like phantom pain, except in a limb anyone who's not a flying shifter doesn't have. It was near my left shoulder, sure—off to the side, exactly where the first knuckle joint on a dragonet's wing would be.

"Ow?"

"I hate to say I told you so." My father shrugged. "But, well..."

"No, you don't, Dad." I smirked to show him there are no hard feelings. I didn't think my father hated anything.

"What else is new?" Dad turned his back, but not before I caught him smiling.

"Point."

I left my room and followed him down the hall toward the stairs that led down from the third floor with its four bedrooms and full bathroom. I didn't mind that Dad knew more than me. With Mom, it was a different story.

Mom was gentle and kind but always seemed sad somehow. And back then, nobody told me why. The handful of times I asked Dad or Bubbe outright, they said she'd tell me herself when she was ready.

I breathed a sigh of relief as we avoided her, continuing down the back stairs of the building instead of stopping on the second floor, which has our kitchen, dining, and living spaces, and Mom's office space. I heard her in there, talking to the principals at Salem High, Gallows Hill Hall, and Wolf Messing Prep on a clairvoyant device. One of her jobs was previewing the magical curricula for the schools around here.

Salem High wasn't specifically for extrahumans, but they were required by law to provide special courses for any students who weren't strictly human. Mostly, magical kids going there couldn't afford the prep schools and didn't have the grades for a scholarship. They spent a fifth year there, just for them, learning enough about their powers to do magical majors at college.

Izzy was going to Wolf Messing Prep down the road in Peabody. It was a day school for young psychic folks. They had some of the best courses in the United States for mentalists like clairvoyants and telepaths. Psychics whose powers were physically based, like teleki-netics, had to go all the way to Copperfield College Preparatory in Las Vegas if they wanted a specialized education.

Gallows Hill was the local school for shifters. They'd let Cadence in because technically she shapeshifts. She said it had to be better to be the only mermaid at a school full of folks who switched between skin and fur or feathers than kids who just didn't get it.

Gallows Hill had recently opened their admissions to include any rare type of extrahuman but also Changelings since the Seelie and

Unseelie courts had reconciled. That whole business had happened thanks to the students and faculty at Providence Paranormal College. I wasn't entirely sure what they did or how they did it, but the group of them managed to take down a few seriously powerful bad guys in the process.

You'd think rational adults would consider them to be awesome role-models, but Dad was ambivalent, while Mom seemed uneasy whenever I gushed about how cool they all were. Even the very first mundane human to ever attend college there.

Mom loves that I've got such great friends in Cadence and Izzy, but she always asked why I never seemed drawn to other magi my age. I always told her it was because the ones in town were either younger or older than me. Hiding my anxiety about fitting in wasn't easy, but that summer, I realized Mom was almost as nervous as me about it. But she worked in the education field. She must have thought starting a magical prep school was the most important thing in the world.

Good thing Bubbe didn't tell her about my brand-new feud with Faith Fairchild. I hoped to smooth things over once school started. "That doesn't seem likely."

"What's that, Aliyah?" His hand hovered over the latch at the back entrance to Bubbe's office.

"My inside voice being an idiot again, Dad." I rolled my eyes. "Sorry. It wasn't directed at you." I stared at my feet, inexplicably frustrated. Was this what Noah meant when he cursed teenage hormones? Or was Dad right about me experiencing Ember's feelings?

"I understand that the eye roll is part of the teenage nonverbal landscape. No worries." His smile was like a calm sea. "But you said something doesn't seem likely, which reminds me of that old Magic 8 Ball you and Izzy used to play with. Is there something you want to talk about?"

"No." I shook my head.

"Okay." He opened the door and held it, standing aside for me.

I silenced the growl that was trying to escape my throat. At that point, I was convinced. He was right; this fear and anger had nothing to do with the situation I was in. It came from somewhere else. Some*one* else. Ember.

We strode down the hall at Bubbe's. Scuttling around on the floor inside one of the boarding rooms was a pastel-blue dragonet, rounded scales shimmering like cirrus clouds in an otherwise empty sky. His hindquarters were decidedly triangular, unlike Ember's. Also, he wore a gold and silver braided collar that designated him as someone's familiar.

"Whose critter is that, Dad?" I always asked questions in here, but that time I was extra curious. Dragonets were uncommon, so seeing another one was rare, even in a magical town like Salem.

"I'm not entirely sure." He shook his head. "But he's a friendly little guy. His magus must be missing him terribly."

"Hmm." The one thing that could distract me from an animal in trouble was a second one in need of aid. I almost suggested that we head over to Hawthorn Academy to ask around about a lost dragonet, but it was too late for that.

Somewhere behind the door leading into Bubbe's surgery, Ember shrieked.

I pushed past Dad and barged in, slamming the door open so hard it nearly hit me in the face on the backswing. I wasn't usually that aggressive, and the look on Bubbe's face had me wondering if maybe I went too far.

"Aliyah." Her jaw squared, hinting at the smooth, angular line it must have made when she was a much younger woman. "This isn't a pleasant event. Are you sure you want to be here for this?"

Ember let out a wail so desperate I could do nothing but rush to where she sat swaddled against the surgical steel table. Her injured wing was exposed, sticking out of an intentional hole in the muslin wrap holding her captive. I saw what was wrong with her. The sprain had healed, but the small lump near the joint turned into a bulging cyst. It had to be lanced, or Ember might never fly again.

I knew better than to try releasing her from the restraints or even touch her since everything had been sterilized, but I knew for sure that she needed me here. The whole situation was confusing for her, and she must have expected more pain. Anyone familiar with dragonets would recognize that pleading expression on her reptilian features. But it was not just how she looked that clued me in.

I could palpably feel just how much my presence in the room, where she could see me, helped Ember.

"I'm staying, Bubbe."

"As you wish, Bissel."

"But Mom!" I blinked a breath before Bubbe interrupted my father. He almost never called her that.

"No buts out of you, Aaron Uriel Morgenstern." Bubbe turned toward the sink, where she finished scrubbing up. "This is still my office and my surgery. Your daughter stays, and if you've got an issue with that, you go."

"No issue, Mom."

"And as for you, Aliyah, sit there, on the stool near the table. Put on a mask. Don't touch the patient until I say so."

"Okay, Bubbe."

I got a mask and followed her instructions. Dad leaned against the wall behind me. As we settled in and watched my grandmother, it became clear that this would be different from the last time I'd sat in on a surgery.

This wasn't my first animal hospital rodeo. When I was seven, Bubbe started taking my desire to be an animal doctor seriously. She'd also let me into the business side of her office for the first time back then, too. Over the last nine years, I'd seen pretty much everything.

Including a handful of patients she wasn't able to save.

Mom didn't much like that. She said it was nothing she'd have wanted to see when she was my age.

"You're not me, Aliyah. Go your own way," was what she told me back then. Mom believed in different strokes for different folks. It was the one filament of coolness twisted around the rest of her too-serious nature.

I let out the breath I'd been holding. Yes, I was aware of not breath-ing, thanks. And I'd hydrated earlier too because self-care is important. So is taking care of those who can't help themselves, which was the main reason I tried to help keep a dragonet from wigging out.

Looking Ember in the eye wasn't easy from where I sat, so I pulled the lever on the bottom of the stool to lower it. Once I reached eye level, I gazed at her scaly, angular face until she noticed I was there, which was practically immediately. She was a bright little thing.

"Peep." The sound was low and dull instead of that first bright chirp on the day I found her. Or maybe it was the other way around.

"I know, Ember." I gazed at the eye she turned toward me, wondering what was going on on the other side of that coppery iris with its vertical pupil. "We'll do something fun after this, okay? Maybe visit your buddy."

"That's right. Once you're better, you two can have a playdate." Dad grinned.

Bubbe called on her solar magic with a few words in Polish. The energy felt like the afternoon sun in winter. She imbued a scalpel with a crystal blade, one of the few instruments that would work on a very young magical creature like Ember without doing more harm than good. Even magi could never be sure exactly what kinds of magic they had, so using any metal on them was a risk, considering the various supernatural and elemental weaknesses they might suffer.

Metals, especially alloys like steel, were like rubbing peanut oil on every baby in a human maternity ward. You couldn't possibly know which one was allergic to what.

"Ember, I won't lie." I held out a hand, palm up. "This is going to hurt. But my grandma's the best doctor around."

"Peep." Ember nodded, and I felt her comprehension. Bubbe took hold of the injured wing with her free hand. The little dragonet shivered briefly, and I got the impression that for her, fear was cold.

"I'm making you a fire." I squinted at my outstretched hand, concentrating. "This is just for you. Watch the flames, and before you know it, this whole thing will be over, and you'll get better. Okay?"

She blinked as orange and yellow lit up the hollow of my palm. The center wasn't blue since I wasn't that powerful yet, but that didn't bother Ember.

As Bubbe's scalpel met Ember's cyst, they hissed in tandem. Through my flames, I saw a gout of greenish fluid erupt from the incision.

"Easy now, almost through." Bubbe's voice was low but flat as though she didn't like what she saw in the wound.

She set the scalpel aside and picked up a bottle of saline to rinse the incision. Once that was done, she applied an adhesive bandage treated with an herbal ointment mixed specially for dragonet scales. I exhaled. Ember joined in. The flames in my hand guttered.

"There." Bubbe tidied the table, tossing some items in the trash and others in a basin of rubbing alcohol.

"Can I hold her now?"

"Let's get the restraints off her first."

I put my fire out and helped. Green liquid from the cyst stained the fabric. It had an odor like stagnant ponds choked with algae. Bubbe took a few swabs and set aside samples for testing later. Maybe someday we'd get an idea of what had caused the injury.

Ember peeped a few times before settling her head in the hollow between my collarbone and trapezius muscle. I cradled her there, marveling at how even with the bandage, she could fold both wings fully against her back. In the right light, she'd be mistaken for a mundane lizard, but warm-blooded.

In moments she was snoring, tiny tendrils of smoke rising from her nostrils and making a foggy haze around my head.

"I think that about says everything." Dad nodded at Ember. He'd been so quiet I'd almost forgotten he was there.

"Yes." Bubbe sighed. "Yes, it does." She turned her back, busying herself with the simple task of cleaning. I couldn't blame her for playing the stoic now. Bubbe's familiar had passed on just last year, so of course, this was hard on her. Her knuckles whitened as she clutched the trash bag. "Well, go on then, Aaron." And she headed out of the room.

As my father stepped forward, holding the gold and silver braided collar, I watched his hands go through the formal motions as he murmured his binding incantation. Each magus used the language most significant to them. Dad's was Hebrew. A soft glow of solar magic that felt like midday in an apple orchard surrounded his hands.

Comforting sunlit energy enfolded me and the dragonet like a warm hug. A thread of fire magic flowed between us like we were the filament in an incandescent lightbulb.

As he fastened the collar around Ember's neck, I felt closer to the little dragonet than ever. A tear or three rolled down my face, blazing a trail through the ashes smudging it. I hadn't even noticed my fire magic leaving traces, but for once, I had an excellent excuse.

One glance at Dad told me there was something wrong, but not what.

He was crying.

Not a few drops of relief like my own tears. This was grief, like the night I barely remembered when we got the knock on the door. An officer in dress uniform stood in the hall and told us Dad's father had passed. But this was different somehow. Farther back than that grief.

I had no idea what was so painful about my bonding with a familiar at an appropriate age. His Tallin, Lyssa, grandmother of my brother's serpentine familiar, was with him that moment, peeking out of his shirt pocket.

"Dad?"

"Peep?" Ember queried in her sleep.

"I'll be okay." Dad sniffled, raising his sleeve to his face. Lyssa hissed, waving a handkerchief at him with her forked tail. "You just reminded me of something. Someone. A long time ago. Thanks." He took the square of fabric and made use of it.

He left a load of information out, but until he was ready to talk about it, there was nothing I could do. That went double for Bubbe, who I heard sniffling on the other side of the door.

CHAPTER FIVE

"Aliyah!"

Someone called my name in the dark, the cozy warm dark where my feet weren't remotely cold for once. A repeat performance of my name told me who was hollering it.

"Shut up, Noah. Mmmsleepin'." I tugged at the down-alternative filled comforter, pulling it farther over my head.

"How can you sleep at a time like this?" My jerkface brother yanked my blanket in the opposite direction. The bastard.

"Whahoozit?"

I had no choice but to sit up, blindly flailing around for my now-out-of-reach bedding. I winced as my wrist made contact with my bedpost. Bedpost? Crap. I committed a sin against gravity and overextended. Again.

"Oww!" My hip smacked against hardwood as I fell out of bed. Even barely awake, I was a klutz.

"Peep!" The whoosh of wings past my head made me chuckle. Yeah, Ember totally dive-bombed my big brother.

"You've meddled in the affairs of a dragonet, Noah!" I snorted.

"Dealing with dragons is totally different from dealing with dragonets. Anyway, I'm not crunchy, and ketchup's utterly basic." He ducked and covered. "Even your winged monstrosity knows it."

"Peep?" Ember perched on top of his head, blinking.

"Let him go, girl." I flashed her a grin. "He's done his worst here."

My room was already a disaster area. That was what happened when I procrastinated and left packing for dorm life until the last minute. Ember glided back to her favorite perch on my headboard.

"Is this really all you're bringing?" Noah aimed a withering glare at the rolling suitcase next to the door.

"Why? Do you think I'll need more than that?"

"This would fit under an economy seat, Aliyah."

Noah clicked his tongue, making a beeline for my closet. After opening the door, he stepped back, mouth wide with shock. Even his serpent Lotan pulled back into a near-strike position, forked tongue flickering.

"Everything's still here!" He pulled a dress-swaddled hanger off the rail inside. "There's no excuse for not bringing this."

Noah shook the mint-green dress almost cruelly before dropping it at the foot of my bed. A purple and orange broomstick skirt that he'd picked out for me in the hippie shop down at the Wharf joined it. More dresses, skirts, and a few blouses I almost never wore finished off the pile. He even tossed in a cardigan, the kind with little fabric-covered buttons.

"That's more than what I already packed."

"You'll be wanting all of this."

"It's only five days of classes. I'll be spending most of this one in pajamas anyway. I plan to go straight to my room after the welcome assembly."

"You absolutely will not. I'll be introducing you to some upper-classmen, and then you may go and change. Not into pajamas, either. You'll want something festive." He snagged my other suitcase—the one we brought on long weekends to Bar Harbor—off the floor of the closet. He began folding each item in half, hanger and all, before stowing them in there.

After a moment, he glanced at my bureau.

"Hey, no rummaging around in there." I shook my pointer finger at him. "I already packed socks and underwear, thank you very much."

"Well then, where in the world do you keep your accessories?"

I jerked my chin at the inside of the closet door, where the handful of necklaces I own hang on hooks.

"You don't have any scarves?" He feigned shock. "Blasphemous! I'll lend you a few of mine."

Noah trotted across the hall into his room and returned in under ten seconds. The variety of scarves in his arms told me he'd been planning this wardrobe intervention at least all morning, and possibly even all week.

"I can't believe you're not letting me choose my own clothes." I rolled my eyes. "We're allowed to wear whatever we want under our school blazers, after all."

"Oh, but I did, for the most part." He chuckled, waving at my much smaller bag. "All of this is just for special occasions."

"Look, you might like parading around at every one of Hawthorn's social mixers like a peacock, but that's not my style." I crossed my legs and arms. "I intend to study more often than not, and you know it, too."

"I'm not trying to make you into my mini-me, but you don't understand." His back was to me, so I couldn't see his face. "You can ease back on them eventually, but the social events and mixers that they have these first few weeks aren't optional."

"Mom and Dad never told me that."

"Well, for whatever reason, neither of them bothers much with the grease on the wheels of extrahuman society." He chuckled. "Thank goodness that part of this apple fell farther from their trees."

"Hey!" I stood up, bumping my head but angry enough to ignore it. "You're my brother, so I expect snark and torment from you. But insulting our parents like that is going too far."

"Ugh. No." Noah waved his hand as though shooing a nonexistent fly. "I'm not insulting. Just saying that it's a good thing someone in this family can handle socializing. You should give it a try. Who knows, you might even be halfway decent at it."

I didn't protest. Instead, I left Noah in my room and went to brush my teeth. At least the bathroom had a high ceiling. As annoying as the ceilings were, I'd miss 10-1/2 Hawthorne Street.

I spat into the sink, running the water to rinse my toothbrush. While rinsing my face with water cold enough to feel abrasive, I wondered whether anyone in my family was as over the top as Noah when they were teenagers. He had to get that from somewhere.

Maybe it was Mom's side of the family. She never talked about, let alone to them. Noah and I hadn't found even a hint of her maiden name anywhere in the house, even though magi were better than Ancestry.com at keeping tabs on heritage.

What was curiouser was that we'd heard everything about Bubbe, plus her parents and how they came to Salem from London after World War Two.

I shuffled back into my bedroom, where Noah wrapped a selection of jewelry I barely ever wore in one of his scarves.

"Hey, does it ever bother you that we never see Mom's family?"

He froze, elbows bent and shoulders tense enough to hold the weight of the world.

"Bother?" He went back to his task, the slight tremor in his wrists the only sign this conversation disturbed him. "No. If she doesn't want to talk about them or have them around, that's her business."

"I seem to remember a chat we had a year back, the night before you went off to Hawthorn for your first year." I sat on my bed, shaking my head. "You told me that what you don't know can hurt you. What's different now?"

"You'll understand when we get there."

He tucked the silk-wrapped bundle of accessories into a pocket on the top of the oversized suitcase. I tossed my ragged old sheepskin slippers on top of all the party dresses.

"You've got subzero fashion sense, Aliyah, honestly."

"Haven't you ever heard of hygge, Noah?"

"Yeah, but the Danish aren't known for haute couture." He chuckled, leaning over to add a box containing my one and only pair of shoes with actual heels.

"Usually, Cadence helps me figure out what to wear." I stared at my bare feet. "But, well..."

"Good thing you've got a brother at your school with a decent eye, then." Noah's eyes twinkled. Lotan peeked out from his collar, rising up to bump my brother's earlobe with his nose.

I realized then what I should have figured out on my birthday back at the beginning of the summer. I'd wrapped my entire head and heart up in how badly I'd miss my friends when all the while, my brother had spent an entire year missing me.

"Yeah, that is definitely a good thing." I managed a smile.

Maybe everything would work out.

Downstairs, we had oatmeal. Again. Which I shouldn't have complained about, even though it's totally bland. A plateful of eggs or even a bagel with a super-basic shmear might not have sat well in my nervous stomach. Ember perched on the back of my chair, wrinkling her snout. I tried offering her a few grains of my breakfast, but she turned up her nose. After that, she gazed longingly at an apple in the basket on the counter.

"Really?" I reached toward the fruit, which elicited a series of excited peeps. "Okay, then."

Ember's diet was supposed to be omnivorous, and she'd already had some herring that morning. I snagged the apple and tossed it above my head. She launched herself into the air, chasing it down to spear it with the claws of one foot. As she perched to eat it on one leg at the counter's edge, I remember how I used to shave in the shower last year before I got my fire magic and used that to get rid of unwanted hair.

I glanced through the doorway into the living room, where our suitcases were piled in a stack. At least Noah had brought the most stuff. He probably had at least six pairs of shoes. Noah took his last bite of breakfast and headed to the sink to rinse his dirty dishes.

"Are you almost ready?" Dad cracked his knuckles, glancing at all the luggage.

"Mostly." I shrugged, scraping my spoon around in the bowl of half-eaten oatmeal. "But can't Mom come with us?"

Pregnant was a total understatement for the level of pause in the room after my question. She hadn't gone with Noah on his first day last year, but I'd thought it was because she had to stay home with me.

"Lee, I don't think—" Dad started.

"You know what, Aaron?" Mom stepped out of her office, slinging her handbag across her body. "I'll come along. If only to help with all that." She grinned.

I scarfed down the rest of my oatmeal, finally getting some of my appetite back. My mood improved so much, I even grabbed Mom's and Dad's empty bowls to rinse and load into the dishwasher.

After that, I put my Hawthorn Academy blazer on. It felt odd; not the kind of thing I'd have worn at my old school. Fortunately, the jeggings and tunic I had on underneath were part of my usual wardrobe staples.

As we hefted all the bags, preparing to leave the house and make our way toward Essex Street, my mood improved exponentially.

If only it had lasted.

CHAPTER SIX

Rolling a suitcase should have been easy, especially on a street for pedestrian traffic only. But with cobblestone pavement dating back to the 1600s, not so much.

That was what we did as we tried to find where the entrance to Hawthorn Academy was that day.

The headmaster was supposed to be one in a long line of famously powerful space magi. No, he wasn't an alien, just able to ensure the entire school existed in the space between this world and the faerie realm of the Under.

A lot of the more mundanely educated folks thought there was just a barrier there, like a wall. I guess it was easier to imagine it that way, but it was impractical when you were a magus who needed to pull energy out of or even through that space.

Plenty of schools didn't hide all or even half of their campus like this. Providence Paranormal College was one—those buildings were in plain old mundane space, even the ones with magically restricted access. That was one reason they'd had to deal with so much trouble a couple of years ago.

Hawthorn Academy was bigger on the inside and also safer. The pocket-school model did have one inconvenient feature, however. It was a mundane dead tech zone, along with most of Essex Street. Something about pocket buildings messed with wireless everything. Cell phones, wi-fi, satellite, and data didn't work there. No binge-streaming for the students at good old Hawthorn.

Wired phone lines existed inside the school, but they were for emergencies only. The worst part of all this was being unable to message Izzy and Cadence when I missed them, but I'd gotten a top-secret belated birthday gift from my friends. There was no way I'd be able to use it while looking for the migrating door, though.

It was supposedly for safety reasons that the school entrance moved up, down, and around Essex Street. After the Great Reveal when the entire world found out all the creatures of legend actually existed, people had started poking around, looking for places like Hawthorn.

Thing was, I had it on the best authority that the door had moved around back before Mom's and Dad's days here, too. Bubbe had told me, so I sort of hoped the headmaster just thought it'd be more whimsical this way.

"Oh no, my shoe!" Noah wailed because a suitcase just scuffed his Oxford. "We've got to stop." He pointed at a storefront across the street.

"Didn't you bring a kit with you?" Dad raised an eyebrow. "For your shoes and all that?"

"Yes, but everyone will see me before I unpack and get a chance to use it." Noah pouted. "Please let me go and see the cobbler?"

"You can get your shoe shined back up as soon as they finish the welcoming ceremony." Mom's always been firm with us, and Noah's tendency toward melodrama was never an excuse.

"But Mom—"

"I don't see Aliyah making a fuss, and she'll be meeting all those people for the first time." Mom sighed, maneuvering my larger suitcase plus one of my brother's. "We don't need to put on airs, not with Bubbe's place in the local community and you being third-generation legacy students."

Noah huffed and puffed and knocked his largest suitcase down. As he bent to stand it back up, Dad pointed ahead and to the left, dragging the third roller behind him.

"Found it."

I looked in that direction and concentrated. The faint tint of blue magic emanated from the alcove next door to the tinker's shop. We all followed Dad, heading in that direction slowly to encourage the suitcases to behave themselves. It was a good thing Mom had come along to help. How she managed those two bags without dropping either of them was beyond me, however.

As we passed the tinker's shop, I had a peek in the window. The place always fascinated me with its collection of magipsychic gadgets. Many of them were imbued and designed so anyone could use them. Because of this, every single item in there sat beside its official certificate of authenticity.

Magic or psychic services and devices always needed a license, at least when sold to the public. Magical animals needed them, too, which meant we saw the certifying board every year. The majority of licenses Bubbe issued came in August and September. That was because most of the magi studying familiar-based magic at Hawthorn had to bring their critters in no later than the first of October.

Not having one by that date meant you'd need to start the alternate program of study or leave school entirely.

I leaned my head to the side and gave Ember an affectionate bump. I was lucky to find her when I did, and not just because, as a fire creature, she was compatible with my magic. Dragonets are some of the rarest familiars out there.

I mean, sure, there were plenty of them around, especially in warmer climates than New England, but they were notoriously picky about who they bonded with. Usually this said something about the magus they chose. A dragonet was a sign I'd take after Mom, whose magic was all brute force. The Morgensterns tended toward finesse, one of the reasons three generations of them had bonded with serpentine Tallin.

Bubbe said dragonets picked either the strongest or the kindest person they could find.

I wasn't certain which of those categories I fell into, but as I stared into the light streaming through the door my brother already walked through, I figured I'd find out. That was half the point of a magical education—discovering your potential.

While heading through the door, I overheard something confusing.

"Are you sure, Angie?" Dad didn't often call Mom by her given name, usually opting for "honey" or some other term of endearment.

"No." Her sigh had more weight than the one she'd spared Noah. "But my setting foot in here can't possibly be an issue after all this time."

"That doesn't mean it won't be, especially after current events." I heard a rustle of fabric. Were they hugging? Why? "You'll be okay?"

"You're with me." Mom sniffled. She was almost never emotional, so why was she crying? "I'll be fine. It's her we ought to worry about. In here. Practically alone."

I stumbled on nothing as they followed me down the hall. There was only one person they could be referring to.

Me.

"Peep." Ember flapped her wings, talons clutched firmly in the fabric of my school blazer.

My familiar kept me from toppling over, but the purring sound of fabric ripping meant she'd also clawed at least six holes in my uniform.

Well, so much for making an impressive entrance.

CHAPTER SEVEN

I followed Noah into the brightly lit lobby. It was hard not to squint as I stepped into the glare. I also had trouble keeping my jaw from dropping.

Even though I'd seen photographs of the inside of Hawthorn Academy, the real thing was totally awe-inspiring. The walls were wood, stained a honey brown hue, and polished to a soft shine. The floors were herringbone hardwood in pristine condition. Noah's soles tapped on the surface like he was performing a soft shoe routine.

From the ceiling hung a chandelier. It wasn't what you'd expect in a place like this, having no crystal teardrops or gilt rods. Instead, it was a wrought iron affair fashioned in the shape of a spider, each leg holding a globe filled with solar magic. The spider's eyes glowed with the same light.

"Check it out, Lee." I forgave Noah's elbow to my rib cage as he pointed out the plaque on the wall.

"Lighting fixtures donated by Morgenstern Magical Creature Care," I read aloud.

"This is why we need to make a good impression," Noah whispered. "It's more than legacy; great-grandpa helped pull the school out of serious trouble when he came over from London."

"I didn't know that."

"Peep." Ember's tail curled around the shoulder opposite the one she stood on.

"Thanks for the hug, girl." I reached up to give her a chin scratch.

"Oh, yeah, familiars are good for that kind of thing." The voice to my right belonged to a girl about six inches shorter than me. Her hair was jet-black and her skin tan, with ruddy accents on her cheeks and lips. She held out her hand. "I'm Grace Dubois, by the way. From Quebec."

"Aliyah." I reached out, and we shook awkwardly because of Ember's weight on my right shoulder and something under her arm. "Uh, Morgenstern. From down the street."

We both had a chuckle over that.

"Don't worry, Lune." Grace finished the handshake, then put her hand on her hip, curling her arm around a rolled-up blanket in some sort of sling. "I won't drop you."

"Is Lune your familiar?"

"Yeah. He's a moon hare." She smiled, smoothing the collar of her blazer, which covered a threadbare flannel shirt. "You're really a Morgenstern?"

"Yes, she is. Just like me." Noah's tone was so icy I almost caught a chill. "Come on, Lee. You ought to meet some of the more well-connected magi here."

Grace giggled so hard she snorted. I instantly liked her because the goofy laugh reminded me of Izzy. As Noah led me away, I turned my head to look back, giving Grace a sympathetic smile before rolling my eyes at my brother. Grace winked back.

"Elanor!" Noah dropped my arm, extending both of his as he rushed toward a statuesque girl with a pink pixie cut.

"Noah, darling!" She reached out and took him by the shoulders, placing an air kiss on either side of his face. She was dressed like a jetsetter, despite the punky hairdo. Her makeup included way too much glitter, but her jewelry was straight out of Tiffany's.

"I can't believe your parents made you work in Vegas all summer."

Noah shook his head, clicking his tongue at what I assumed was his school bestie.

"Well, they couldn't let me traipse around up here for three months." Elanor's laugh was like broken glass tinkling on pavement. "I had to manage the act while they helped Logan train his dragon, of course."

Lotan sat up on Noah's left shoulder, his tongue flicking in and out as his forked tail waved on the right. I recognized that as a serpent greeting, and sure enough, a bird with brilliant plumage fluttered down from a rafter somewhere above to perch on Elanor's shoulder. It warbled at Lotan, then shook its tail feathers, which were pink and orange and yellow.

She had a firebird familiar, the sort that usually partnered with magi in musical or other performance arts. I wondered what kind of talent Elanor had and was about to ask when someone interrupted.

"Hi, I'm Logan." The boy grinning at me was drop-dead gorgeous, like a tall ship in the harbor at sunrise. That was the most stunning thing I could think of besides this fellow.

His shoulders were broad, his waist narrow, and his face could have been chiseled from marble. I realized my mouth was wide open, like a fish's or a frog's, which was kind of gross.

"Um, Aliyah." I stuck my hand out, hoping it didn't remind him of dead fish. It felt awfully clammy when he clasped it.

"Yeah, Noah's sister." His smile showed off teeth impossibly straight and white. "I know."

"You know?" I blinked.

"Elanor talked all summer about how her best friend had a sister my age starting here the same year as me and how we had to meet, of course." He shrugged, smiling again. "And here we are. She never mentioned you had a dragonet familiar, though."

"That's sort of a recent development." My voice came out more monotone than usual. "I just bonded with Ember this summer."

"Ember?" It was his turn to blink. "She's a fire critter? And you actually bonded with her?"

47

That statement was a bit odd, but I let it pass. Maybe Logan felt nervous and awkward, too.

"Yeah." I turned my head, intending to show her off, but my little friend had burrowed all the way under my collar and behind my hair. "Come on out, girl."

She didn't. Instead, Ember huddled in there. I got the feeling she'd hidden intentionally. I could hardly blame her since she'd probably picked up the jitters from me.

"Huh." Logan peered at the space between my blazer's lapels, or maybe just into space. I finally noticed one flaw—his hands. His fingernails and the cuticles were downright ragged, like he worried at them all the time.

"Um." My face felt as hot as a couple of years ago when I got the flu, except without all the phlegm and puffy eyes and nausea.

"Oh, sorry." Logan's grin was like an obvious backdrop on a movie set. "It's just that I thought I saw some tail there." His face went magenta.

He'd called me tail and then pointed at my chest. I took a step back, totally not used to guys dropping innuendos about me, even by accident. That was when I realized what was off about Logan— besides the social gaffes, I mean.

"So." My lips twisted into something between a smile and a grimace. "Where's your familiar, anyway?"

"That's hardly important." Logan flapped one hand dismissively. His lips went pale and thin, along with most of his face. "I mean, um, he's around—"

"Hey, Aliyah." The person behind me cleared his throat. "Is this guy bothering you?"

"Um, I don't know?" I turned away from blazing hot Logan to find relief in a familiar face—a literal breath of fresh air. "Hi, Dylan."

"Hi, yourself." He wore the school blazer with a black shirt and a green barista's apron. "Haven't seen you in a week. How's things?"

"Oh, the usual nerve-wracking experience of arriving at a new place." My laugh was way too high-pitched. "You know."

"Yeah, all too well." His smile was a soothing balm.

"So, what are you up to, now that the Willows doesn't need summer help anymore?"

"I'm working here ten hours a week." Dylan jerked his thumb toward the hall. "They've got an espresso bar in the main student lounge, and I've got café experience."

"Cool."

"Aliyah, I need to introduce you to someone." Noah tugged my sleeve like a toddler.

"Duty calls, I guess. See you later, Dylan." I let Noah drag me away, hoping it wasn't in the direction of another embarrassing boy.

"Later!" He waved, then turned his back on Logan, who looked like he was about to say something.

"Please don't push me at another dude, Noah." I shook my head. "And you didn't introduce me to Elanor back there, you know."

"Yeah, sorry about that." He shrugged, a gesture I recognized as apologetic only because he's my brother. "This time, it's someone in your grade I haven't met in person either."

"Oh?"

"Yes. We chatted online, and she's also looking to go into extraveterinary at college. Not a boy." He grinned. "Just someone I think you've got a lot in common with."

"Cool." I took a slow breath, hoping to relax a bit before having to shake another hand.

I couldn't exhale since he was leading me straight toward the last person I wanted to see—Faith Fairbanks. Yes, the girl with the yappy Sha who'd called me a "moronic assistant" last time we met.

"Aliyah, this is—"

"Uh, Noah—" I tried to pull away.

"I've met *her* before." The other girl gave me an icy stare. "And she doesn't look *one bit* like a Morgenstern."

Faith wasn't wrong. I looked like my mom, who was only a Morgenstern by marriage. I had no idea what to say, because I didn't know her maiden name or whether she was from a magical family. All I knew was she used to go here.

"Oh, but she is." The cool, collected voice behind me belonged to my mother—a tone I was used to hearing during her long work conferences through the office door. "I'm Mrs. Morgenstern, Aliyah's mother."

"Is that right?" Faith put a hand on her hip, tilting her head. The Sha inside her handbag flashed a canine grin I wasn't certain I liked. "Because to me, you look an awful lot like a Hopewell."

You know how sometimes in a room full of people, the conversation sort of pauses to the point where everyone can hear a pin drop? Well, that happened right then, at the exact moment Faith dropped that name.

Hopewell. The silence continued, stretching in anticipation of my mom's answer.

Now, where had I heard that name? On television. Finally, my fried brain let me remember.

Richard Hopewell, the extramagus murderer who'd tried to take over both Faerie Courts. My mom was a good person. She couldn't be related to that despicable man from the news. I'd never seen her lose her temper, and couldn't imagine her ever harming another person.

"Noah's totally a Morgenstern, but everyone who takes after the Hopewell family is pure evil," Faith continued. "So, are you one or not?"

"I was a Hopewell, yes. That criminal's sister, in fact. I married after attending this fine institution and stopped associating with my birth family." My mother put her arm around me. "And if you or any other student has an issue with that, I've already arranged for you to take it up with Headmaster Hawkins."

"Mother, you didn't have to make a fuss about—" Noah looked like he was about to take a step backward, but Mom put her other arm around his waist, stopping him.

"Apparently, I do." Her smile could have melted butter.

I thought it was strong, parental, and protective, but almost everyone else in this room took a step back, continued their silence as though they feared her. I couldn't imagine why.

"Come on, Angie." My father held out his arm, elbow crooked. "I believe we've overstayed this particular welcome."

"Yes. I agree." My mother hugged Noah and then me, both somehow warm gestures despite their rapidity. "Remember, we are right around the corner if you need anything."

"Thanks, Mom." I grinned at her, more than a little in awe of how unexpectedly badass she was.

As our parents escorted each other out of the lobby and through the door, it occurred to me that maybe taking after her wasn't such a bad thing.

But the fearful looks on all the faces around me drove home the idea that I might be wrong.

CHAPTER EIGHT

Noah pretty much abandoned me once the door closed behind our parents. There was nothing much to do except stand there with my two ridiculous suitcases. Unless I wanted to start crying.

I totally could have. I'm the niece of a man who tried to kill a pack of students at Providence Paranormal College. What would happen when I graduated and tried applying there? Would they reject me? Maybe the headmistress would spell me into orbit or something.

Legacy magi at a stuffy old private prep school are super-privileged. Noah's rubbed elbows with Fairbankses and their ilk. He didn't seem to care if they all acted like Faith, either.

I felt like a total outsider, and I didn't even have a good reason, like the end of the world or being some kind of foreseen chosen one. Nope. Instead, I was a privileged princess from one family I don't share magic with and another that's flagrantly abused its power.

All my problems were secondhand, with no way to counter them.

I had at least an hour before that required welcome assembly. At least I knew what to do next. The far wall was covered with pneumatic tubes, a way to send messages around the entire pocket-universe campus. I headed toward one of them, then fired up my hand with magical energy to touch it.

It lit up to a brilliant orange-red, and in moments, a slip of paper fluttered down to the little hatch in the plexiglass. The paper sailed into my waiting hand after it opened. I unfolded it and read the directions to my dorm room.

"Cool."

I was talking to nobody, technically. This message system wasn't run by ghosts. Hawthorn Academy didn't employ any psychics, not even a medium. Because it didn't exist in either world, the dead couldn't haunt this campus.

Instead, all the paper and the energy that moved it came from a magus working somewhere in here. So, it was them I thanked, even if they couldn't hear me.

"Thanks."

"Why?" It was Grace. She stood two tubes over, blinking.

"Because I was raised with manners and thanking people is part of that." I shrugged, jostling Ember, who was still tucked under my blazer. "Secret evil extramagus uncle or no."

"Makes sense." She peered at her dorm slip. "Well, it's off to the third floor for me."

"Same here."

"You wouldn't happen to be in 322?"

"That's the place." I sighed, shaking my head. "We're roommates, I guess. Sorry."

"Don't be." Grace grinned. "I should be the one apologizing. You're the one who's going to be stuck staring at a bunch of K-Pop posters, after all. So sorry back, from this here Canadian."

I covered my mouth to stifle the laugh, not wanting to draw any more attention to myself. Grace helped by padding quietly toward the wide set of stairs in the near corner. Once we both stood on the bottom step, she said our floor number, and they started moving upward.

The staircases didn't change positions or become some kind of tricky maze. What kind of monstrous headmaster would want a feature like that in their school? I mean, it was hard enough being away from home for the first time without dealing with something like that.

Of course, I knew all this because Noah and my parents had talked about good old Hawthorn for practically my whole life. But what about Grace? She clearly knew her way around, and her family was all the way in hecking Quebec, for crying out loud.

I kept my shirt on and waited to ask her. We were roommates, so there'd be plenty of time to chat in the future. At least I actually liked Grace.

Hopefully, she liked me too, and this wasn't all some kind of elaborate ploy to ridicule me for "social capital."

"Social what?" Grace stepped off the top stair and then moved aside to let me by.

"Oh." I tittered, hands going clammy. "Um, I have inside versus outside voice problems sometimes."

"Hmm." She nodded. "My cousin's a fire magus. He has that problem too."

"I'd say cool, but it's literally not." I hung my head, and Ember used that gesture as an excuse to headbutt me on the temple.

"You're right." Grace smiled. "Fire. The opposite of cool."

Our chuckles carried us down the hall to room 322, which wasn't far, actually. The doors were all artistically carved from wood with numbers worked into the designs, setting them apart from the plain old stained paneling on the rest of the walls. Grace apparently didn't know everything because she clearly blinked at the flat and unadorned area on the door where the doorknob would be.

"I got this."

I held my hand out, palm toward the small rectangle in the wood. Then I projected my magic energy toward it. There was a click and the door opened, swinging slightly inward.

That feature was one reason Hawthorn Academy will probably never accept mundane students; none of them would be able to get into their rooms. Without the correct type of magical energy, this door would stay shut.

Although I bet all of them responded to Headmaster Hawkins's space magic.

I shook off the paranoid thoughts. Noah said that Hawkins went here when Bubbe got the job after his own father retired. This place wouldn't still be prestigious if the headmaster was a creepazoid. Right?

Pushing through the door activated the magical solar lighting system, a feature I was accustomed to at home. I wasn't used to how ornate the walls were. They were the same wood as the door, with similar baroque carvings.

The walls must have been decorated so extremely to make up for the lack of windows. Not a single bare space existed for Grace to hang her K-Pop posters. Even the lights hung from the ceilings, mini versions of the downstairs chandelier.

"That's the most natural supernatural lighting I've ever seen." Grace strode toward the bed on the left. "Is it cool if I take this one?"

"Sure, go ahead." I grinned, heading toward the identical bed on the right.

She set her bundled familiar down at the foot of the bed and then slipped her arms out of an enormous backpack, a re-purposed hiking rig.

I heaved the larger suitcase up onto my bed, then wheeled the smaller one to the dresser on the right-hand wall. Unloading it was easy, especially with Ember flapping around, opening the drawers for me as I worked.

I zipped the suitcase up before it was completely unpacked, however; Grace didn't need to see that last item rolling around in the bottom. I stowed it under my bed, then got to work on the other suitcase, hanging each piece Noah had chosen on the rail inside the slim wardrobe beside the simple desk. At least the furnishings in here were unassuming enough not to be distracting.

"Ahh." Grace sighed, stretching her arms over her head. She hadn't started unpacking, but I wouldn't judge a person over something like that. "It's so good to be out of that stupid pack. You can come out now, Lune."

The bundle of blankets moved, rustling. Ember sat back on her haunches, looking down from her perch on top of the wardrobe. After a few moments, a whiskered nose emerged. It wriggled rapidly, and then the rest of the moon hare's head shook free.

Lune's fur was mostly gray, with a silvery streak down his back, which was what I'd expected to see, based on Bubbe's books. His ears were long, and he held them at a relaxed angle, which meant Ember's presence didn't alarm him.

This made more sense when he came all the way out of his blankety burrow. He was longer and stronger than my dragonet, outweighing her by at least five pounds. Also, Lune was a full-grown adult moon hare, while Ember was still a juvenile of her species.

When he stretched, I noticed a scar on his left rear flank, and when he took a few exploratory hops around the bed, I noticed his limp.

"He's a handsome fellow." I smiled, crouching by Grace's bed and holding my hand out for Lune to sniff.

"You think?" She sat on the edge of the bed. "Most people find moon hares a bit boring to look at, you know?"

"No, he is." I nodded at him. "Coat's got a healthy sheen, and his ears are nice and straight. He looks strong, too. How long have you two been bonded?"

"He showed up when I was eleven." Grace averted her eyes, then reached out to give Lune an affectionate pat. "I really needed a friend that year, and he pretty much rescued me. Hears trouble coming a mile away." I was about to ask her what kind of trouble, but she changed the subject. "Your dragonet's a real cutie."

"Yeah." I chuckled. "Ember's a lot of fun, but I'm still not sure what she's good at besides breaking awkward silences. I have a lot of those, though, so I'm lucky to have her."

"Well, I haven't heard any since we met." Lune stepped into Grace's lap, edging toward her knees to peer at the floor.

"Um." I winced. "I don't want to womansplain, but—"

"That particular incident wasn't your fault—which was why you wanted to escape, of course."

"All the same, I could have handled it better."

"Not really." Grace helped Lune down from the bed and he loped around, exploring the room. "I mean, she's a Fairbanks. Long line of mostly earth magi and mentalist psychics, and every one of them is a world-class pain in the ass."

"All?" I watched as Ember spiraled down from the wardrobe to the floor, where she followed Lune around, mimicking his movements. "Wait, there are more of them?"

"Oh, yeah. Aunt Mabel told me to watch out for them while I'm here." Grace shook her head. "Steer clear as much as possible."

"There's really more than one?" I blinked.

"Yes. Faith's a middle child. Her older sister's a senior, and her younger sister starts next year."

"Wow."

"How is this a wow moment, exactly?" She reached down to help Lune with an itchy spot on his shoulder, looking up at me out of the corner of her eye.

"Um."

I wasn't sure what to say next because this was more like the sort of conversation Noah would have about someone who's not present to stick up for themselves. Was it right to continue on a sour topic like this? Bubbe always said you attract more bees with honey than vinegar.

But I didn't want to say anything like that to Grace. I had to get along with her all year, regardless of whether she gossiped or not. So, I sat like the proverbial bump on a log, saying and doing nothing. That was at least a familiar enough course of action to feel comfortable.

"You're an oddball, Aliyah Morgenstern." Crap. She did think I was weird.

"I am?"

"Yeah. I mean that in a good way." She peered at the wall above the door, which was carved into a circle with hands and numbers, making a clock. "Anyway, we've got to go to that assembly."

"You're right." I stood, my knees crackling like a bowl of cereal recently introduced to milk. "My brother Noah thought I should wear something fancier."

"You go ahead and put on the dog if you want." Grace flopped back on the bed, throwing her arm over her eyes. "I'm strictly a flannel and jeans kind of gal."

"I totally understand."

Even though Grace practically copied my wardrobe manifesto, I couldn't follow it with her, not with the way I'd embarrassed my brother earlier. Grace unpacked as I put on the outfit Noah had selected this morning for the assembly. And I noticed something.

Grace Dubois didn't seem to own anything but well-worn or threadbare garments.

I'd complained about bringing too much stuff. My roommate seemed to have nothing.

Talk about a disparity.

I had to learn a ton from Grace and quickly because the only way to befriend a person from an entirely different set of circumstances is to stop talking and listen.

CHAPTER NINE

Back down in the lobby, the space was full of chairs except for the far end, where a podium sat waiting for someone to step up and speak. Most of the seats were already taken, which meant Grace and I had to walk all the way down to the front.

Normally in academic settings where I had my pick, I chose the row and column closest to the instructor. Maybe I overachieved a little, which wasn't usually a bad thing with career goals in a medical profession.

Socially, it was a nightmare.

Once again, this was a totally abnormal situation. At any other school, I'd have been perfectly fine with the mean girl hating me, with sauntering in at the last minute, or with sitting in front like the big giant nerd I am. At every other school I'd attended, Izzy and Cadence were with me, and I didn't care what other people thought.

Noah was a whole different animal.

As I settled myself in the front and center chair, a fire grew in my belly, one intent on fueling itself with the idea that my discomfort and shame were Noah's fault.

It would have been easy to blame him. I closed my eyes, trying to banish that thought. It was cruel and went against the way my family always stuck together. Bile rose, and a sour taste coated the back of my tongue. I couldn't do the right thing and let it go.

This wasn't garden-variety sibling rivalry, either.

Before I could process this any further or retreat to relative solitude somewhere to work things through, my escape plans were foiled by the start of the assembly.

A *POP!* along with the rush of displacing air blew my bangs off my forehead. Ember clung more tightly to my shoulder, and beside me, Grace gasped, holding Lune closer.

A chorus of whispered voices followed hers. I managed not to add mine, a testament to my anger and the herculean effort I'd made to hold it in.

A man stood at the podium. He didn't do anything so mundane as walk up to it. No, he used his space magic, something he was clearly proud of. A mirthful grin stretched across his round, dusky-skinned face, which was awfully smooth for a man my grandmother's age. His buzz-cut hair was dark brown, without a hint of gray in it.

Headmaster Hawkins had a sense of humor, and even with the deluge of information from my family, nobody had bothered to tell me this. Or maybe this wasn't Bubbe's old classmate, after all.

"Welcome, students!" He chuckled. The resonant voice carried farther than it should have with mundane acoustics. He was using magic for that, too. "I hope the summer left you refreshed and ready to work hard this year."

"My middle name, practically." It was Dylan's voice, murmuring behind me.

"Some of you have been here and done this in previous years. You were expecting my father, but he went on sabbatical and has left the job to me." That explained why he was Dad's age. He was new to the position that fall.

"I'll try going against the grain and be brief." Hawkins smiled, clearly having fun with this. "Welcome students, old and new. You'll get your room assignments at the pneumatic tubes if you haven't already. Your class schedules will appear on your dorm desks after lunch today, and once you have those, all first-years will report back here with them for an academic campus tour, guided by your home-room instructors."

He stood, gripping both sides of the lectern atop the podium with solid hands. I wasn't sure what he was doing at first but understood when he eventually made eye contact with me.

Not more magic. He locked gazes with each student, remembering us all individually. Headmaster Hawkins wanted to know us by sight even if he didn't have all the names to go with the faces.

I felt the tension in the room ease. Most of it, anyway. When people calmed down, the ambient temperature lowered, and that was the sort of thing a fire magus noticed, especially when she hadn't managed to cool her own hot head.

When he locked gazes with me, it felt eternal, although not in any weird emo way like how it was with Ember in Bubbe's surgery. It felt more like this man saw everywhere I'd been and maybe even some of the places I might go someday. It should have been a profoundly unsettling experience, but it was more a minor annoyance. That might have been because I was still angry about Noah giving me the cold shoulder.

"Peep." The dragonet's tail caressed my cheek, cool and soothing.

"Thanks." I reached up and gave her flank a pat.

Hawkins and I continued staring through this entire exchange. It lasted until the empty chair across the aisle to my right creaked.

"Sorry I'm late." The voice was male and cracked slightly.

He was very late since the headmaster had already clapped his hands and waved us off, dismissing us. This kid had missed the entire assembly.

"You've heard me practice that speech a million times, Harold." Headmaster Hawkins sighed. "Just go and get your room assignment, okay?"

"All right, Dad."

"Did he just say 'dad?'" Grace nudged me in the side.

"Yeah." I turned to look at the headmaster's kid.

Harold Hawkins had dark bronze skin and black hair, but other-wise looked very much like his father—stocky and solid. He was much shorter and on the pudgy side, maybe a year too young to be here. He had a long and furry critter curled up in his lap, and I'd seen one of them before, even though they're pretty rare in New England.

"Wow." I stood, taking three steps to cross the aisle and stop beside the boy. "Is that a Pharaoh's Rat?"

"Yeah, her name's Ningirima, but you can call her Nin for short." His face paled as he stared up at Ember, including her in the conversation. "She's friendly, I promise."

He said that because Pharaoh's Rats hunt dragons, the giant shape-shifting kind. And also dragonets if they're hungry enough.

"This is Ember." I held my arm out, and she sauntered down slowly. "She's way more confident than I am, I promise."

"Okay. And you can call me Hal. Harold's what my folks call me." Hal smiled. His eyes cut to my left, where Grace peeked out from behind me. His entire face lit up. "Oh, wow. You're Grace Dubois. I read your essay!"

"My-my entrance essay?" She blinked. "Um, I thought that was supposed to be, you know, personal?"

"Yeah, and it was really something else." He grinned. "The way you described what it was like living in—"

"Okay, um, thanks and all." Grace's eyes widened, and I felt the waves of near panic coming off her. Her stomach audibly churned. "But—"

"Hey, I think maybe we're all hungry," I interrupted. "I mean, Grace came an awful long way and probably missed breakfast, and I couldn't eat much this morning—nerves and all. So, when do they start serving lunch?"

"Oh, not for another half-hour or so." Hal stood, Nin running up his arm to stretch out along his shoulders like a fur stole. He turned to Grace, making a slight bow. "And I'm sorry about before, going on like that. I can get you a little something right now to make up for it. Do you like apples or bananas?"

"Um, either. Or both?" Grace blinked rapidly a few times.

"Half a moment." His brows furrowed. "Here you go."

A banana appeared in his left hand. A moment later, an apple rested in his right. Lune stood on his haunches and sniffed, his whiskers brushing against the back of Hal's right hand. Grace barked a surprised sound somewhere between alarm and laughter.

"Thanks, half-pint."

Just like that, Elanor sashayed by and snatched the banana out of Hal's hand. She giggled, peeling the fruit as she took a seat a few rows up, next to Noah.

"What the ever-living fu—" Grace's nostrils flared.

"You've still got an apple." Hal extended it toward Grace.

"Thanks, buddy." She shook her head. "But that was bitchy. And you just brushed it off?"

"I'm the headmaster's son." Hal deflated a little. "I've got to be a good example, or families might decide to send their kids to some other school. Anyway, I like being kind. It's practically a counterculture nowadays."

"There's a lot of pressure on some of us, for sure." I nodded. Hal and Grace were at least people I could understand. "Others, not so much." I gestured at Elanor.

She peeled the banana, making eyes at pretty much the entire room. Most of the boys stared, watching and waiting for her to eat it. A handful, including Hal and Elanor's brother Logan, averted their eyes. Even Noah looked on, though with an eye-rolling smirk.

I might have been a total newbie at flirting, dating, and the romantic side of socializing, but I'd been on the internet and watched television. Maybe the boys had some weird sex thing on the brain.

With a wolfish grin, Elanor turned the banana sideways and took an enormous bite out of it, cutting it neatly in half with her teeth. I should have figured she'd do that. Noah had told me a million times that she's gay like him.

The watching boys immediately found something else to look at. Some of them even left the room. Grace rolled her eyes and took an extra-loud bite of her apple.

"She's not into boys," Dylan said as he approached our little cluster. "Heard her chatting up my manager earlier. I mean, she didn't get far

65

because Kayla's twenty and doesn't want to lose her job over inappropriate relations with a student."

"So, you're saying she pulled that whole stunt just to freak everyone out?" Hal shook his head. "I don't get it."

"Probably only likes girls and doesn't want boys bugging her all year." Grace shrugged, her stomach rumbling again. "Okay, obnoxious internal organ, I get it. You need more food." She made quick work of the apple.

"I won't have Elanor's problem," I mumbled, but somehow my three companions all heard me because they let out a chorus of sighs. Well, two of them did, at least.

Dylan blinked. Hal shook his head, a wry grin twisting his full lips. Grace snorted. Clearly, my new friends didn't agree with my self-deprecation. Or they were being nice despite all the sarcasm. Or both. At any rate, I felt a bit better now.

"None of that innocent blinking, pal." I tilted my head to look up at Dylan. "You must have looked in a mirror recently."

"Peep!"

Everyone laughed. Nobody else in the room even noticed because all the students broke into clusters. Ours was the smallest, but at that moment, I didn't care. Bigger wasn't always better. As I introduced Dylan to my two newer friends, I realized something.

The fire in my belly was banked. It wasn't completely gone, but it was manageable now. All I needed to do was avoid another fight with Noah for the rest of the day, and it'd go away.

I hoped.

CHAPTER TEN

"So, you don't have a familiar yet, Dylan?" Hal dipped a piece of bread into his bowl of chicken soup.

"Nope. But don't tell anyone." He shrugged, twirling some noodles on a fork. "Mom wanted me to try bonding with one before I went stateside, but Dad disagreed. Said Customs was hard enough on a magus without bringing a familiar into the mix. By hard, he meant expensive. It's always money with him."

"What is it with your mother?" Grace arched an eyebrow, holding a double cheeseburger in both her hands.

"He's got a tiger mom." I waved a triangle of turkey on rye in his general direction. "That's what you said over the summer, right, Dylan?"

"Pretty much. She's hoping I'll get more interested in what she calls "actual medicine" instead of the extraveterinary kind." He rolled his eyes. "Dad doesn't care as long as it's something lucrative."

"Running this school is lucrative." Hal shook his head. "But I'd prefer not to do it when I'm older."

"Yeah, about that." I put my sandwich down, suddenly not so hungry. "Wasn't it supposed to be your grandfather and not your dad running things this year?"

"Sharp, Aliyah." Hal tapped his nose. "You're right. This is Dad's first year as headmaster and it's super last-minute. I wasn't supposed to start courses here until next year, but so it goes."

"Why?" I leaned forward, listening intently.

"I'm not supposed to talk about it." He glanced up, down, and around.

"Isn't, um..." Grace swallowed the mouthful of burger she'd tried to talk around. "Isn't your dad worried he's not ready?"

"Well, some of the faculty are helping him a lot." He waved his crust of bread at a table of four adults, all wearing staff lanyards. "See that lady professor over there?"

We looked. She was the only woman at the table, with long ash-brown hair in cornrows, light brown skin, and blue eyes. She dressed unconventionally for an academic, sporting a touristy Salem t-shirt over a pair of leggings printed with lightning bolts.

"That's Doctor Susan DeBeer. She came all the way from South Africa to teach at this school. She's been here since right after the Big Reveal. I met her one time before today, but Dad had meetings with her all summer."

"What about that guy?" Dylan jerked his thumb at a slightly built man sitting alone.

That fellow looked to be about my grandma's age. He had more salt than pepper in the hair ringing his bald olive-tone pate. A pair of spectacles was perched on his nose, horn-rimmed in a color that matched the owlish creature perched on his shoulder.

"That's Professor Luciano. Grandpa hired him last year." Hal finished the last of his bread, then reached for another roll from the basket on the table. "He used to teach at Academe Magica in the Italian Alps."

"How stereotypical." Dylan rolled his eyes, leaning in and lowering his voice. "A magic-school professor with an owl familiar."

"That's no owl," Grace whispered.

"You're right, he's a Strix, which means he's got four wings and venom." I leaned forward. "They're Roman, and commonly associated with poison magi."

"An astute assessment to be sure, Miss Hopewell. Hmm, perhaps I've gotten that wrong. It's Miss Morgenstern, yes?" An accompanying basso laugh rumbled like rocks falling. "And you've made one incorrect assumption."

I looked up to find Luciano towering over us. My mouth hung open, and I wasn't alone. We all sat there gawking like a nest full of baby birds.

He'd caught us talking about him and was now throwing insults like a student instead of a teacher. And Dylan had thought an owlish familiar was a horrible stereotype.

"Male Strixes have triangular tufts." He gestured at his familiar's head, drawing our attention to the rounded feathers at the crown, chuckling softly. "As you can see, my companion is female."

"Peep?" Ember fluttered to my other shoulder, craning her neck to get a better look, as if she also wanted to learn about the sexual dimorphism of magical creatures.

"Hoo." The Strix blinked. She was either sleepy or thought dragonets were no big deal. Probably the latter since she didn't bother yawning.

The only course of action was my fallback: what would Bubbe do?

"Well, thanks for the instruction, Professor." I stood carefully so Ember didn't get too unbalanced. "You might already know that I'm Noah Morgenstern's sister, Aliyah. It's good to meet you."

Behind the smile I showed, it felt like being encased in ice because for me, fear was paralyzingly glacial. Professor Luciano walking up like that, despite the chuckle, had me stone-cold scared—which was why I extended my hand anyway.

"It might be nice to meet you, too." The professor didn't shake my hand, only stood there gazing at each of us in turn. "However, I see one of your cohorts is lacking a familiar. Can you tell me why that is, Miss Morgenstern?"

"Well, that's not my story to tell." I looked at Dylan, who'd gone completely still. He'd asked us not to repeat his story. There was no choice but to introduce him, but I managed to give him an out. "This is Dylan Khan. He's from London."

"Customs, Professor." He stood, brushing crumbs off his hands. "You must be aware of how difficult it is to get a magical creature over here on a student visa. I waited instead of seeking one out at home."

"Fortunately, not a matter of concern with an instructor's visa, to be sure." Luciano inclined his head. "And no issue for Miss Dubois and her moon hare."

"I've got dual citizenship, Professor." She cuddled Lune, who was clearly not comfortable under the Strix's gaze. "It's not difficult for me."

"All the same, Mister Khan. I'm sure you're aware that if you have no familiar at the start of your second month here, you'll need to change your focus from Familiar Studies to Preparatory Academia."

Dylan nodded, staring down at his shoes. I would have too, in his place because only a handful of students ever ended up in Preparatory Academia. The only reason they even had an alternate course of study was that someone in the inaugural class had lost their familiar in an accident halfway through their first year.

Hawthorn Academy was all about familiars. It'd suck for Dylan if he didn't find one. As far as I knew, my mom was the only person who'd ever enrolled in Preparatory Academia voluntarily.

"Oi, Lucy. Let them off the hook for now, yeah?" Professor DeBeer came to the rescue. She flipped a long lock of hair off her shoulder, revealing a leather pauldron strapped to it. I wondered why until her familiar fluttered down from a rafter. It was a long-legged bird with stark black and white plumage, one I didn't immediately recognize.

"Kek," the bird said as it perched. I saw why she wore that contraption.

"Those are some serious claws, Professor." I grinned. "What kind of bird is that?"

"You don't already know, Miss Morgenstern?"

"Oh, honestly, Lucy." Professor DeBeer rolled her eyes. "She wouldn't be here if she knew everything."

"It's Luciano, Professor, as we've previously discussed. Remember?" Professor Luciano's hands clenched into fists, but somehow, he managed to look tense and exhausted at the same time.

"Right, right." She waved her hand. "Forgot. Terribly sorry, Professor Luciano. Anyway, this fine fellow is named Hammer and he's an Impundulu, more commonly known as a lightning bird."

"Oh, wow!" Hal popped out of his seat, stars in his eyes. "Professor, could I watch the next time you feed him?"

"Hmm, not so sure on that one." Professor DeBeer shook her head. "Feeding time's pretty gory. I'll have to run that by the headmaster. At any rate, I wanted to discuss lesson plans with this old sod right here, so if you don't mind, we'll just be dragging each other away for now."

She stepped to one side, gesturing away from us with one arm and wagging her eyebrows at Lucciano. He took a deep breath, exhaling slowly as he audibly counted to five. I wasn't sure whether to empathize with him or her at that point.

The four of us watched them go, Nin peeking out from her hiding place in the left side of Hal's jacket.

"The professors are the most confusing part of this place, in my opinion." I shook my head. "At least so far."

"Faith Fairbanks isn't?" Grace raised an eyebrow.

"Nah, just another mean girl." I grinned. "Every school has some of those. What's one more?"

Behind me came the chittering clatter of plastic on tile. Hal's eyes went wide and Dylan turned. I followed suit just in time to recognize Faith as she hurried along the food line and out through the entrance, leaving her dropped tray and all the food that was on it strewn across the floor. Her little Sha scurried after her, yapping.

I looked around, scanning the cafeteria for her mean-girl wannabe hangers-on. They sat with Noah and Elanor, plus one more young woman. This fifth individual bore a striking resemblance to Faith. In fact, I'd have thought it was her if you'd asked me a minute earlier. But I realized the other girl was older and pretty enough to be on a magazine cover. Her hair was a brighter shade of red, too.

It had to be her older sister.

Faith's fair-weather friends were clearly engrossed in whatever the three upperclassmen were saying. It included a heaping pile of pointing and laughing at the mess the unfortunate girl had left behind.

It was only then that I realized Faith had arrived alone, and although she'd surely overheard us talking about her, we weren't her main focus.

Noah's table was, of course.

"This is all wrong." I sighed, feeling my willpower crumble.

I should have felt relief that I wasn't getting picked on by the bullies my brother kept company with, and I did for a moment. But that emotion didn't stick, because I got angry at him for siding with the mean crew. That's not how we were raised.

"Yeah, I think so." Dylan's voice was strained. "But what can we do?"

"I'm going after her." Hal stepped around Grace, looking down at the floor to avoid slipping in the pasta. "Damage control is kind of my responsibility. See you guys later."

"Huh." Grace glanced down at Lune, who thumped the floor three times with his left foot. After that, she stared at the clock on the wall. "We need to go back and get our homeroom assignments, or we'll be late."

"Would you mind getting mine, Grace?"

"Why?" Her eyes widened.

"I want to ask my brother something." My hands clenched. He'd gotten on my last nerve because we'd promised each other years ago that we'd never be bullies. A low growl began near my ear. Ember was riled up too, apparently.

"If that's what you gotta do." She took a step backward. "Come on, Lune, let's go. Talk to you later."

Grace headed for the cafeteria's exit faster than I'd seen her move so far. My nostrils flared as I set my jaw and my resolve. I turned toward Noah's table, about to march over there and give him hell. Dylan's hand on my arm stopped me.

"Aliyah, wait."

"I've got sibling business, Dylan. Don't you have a homeroom assignment to fetch?"

"No." He stepped in front of me, blocking Noah from my view.

"Work-study folks get everything early. Anyway, let me come with you."

"Why? He's being a total tool. I have to get on his case about it."

"Because you're angry. That makes sense, but calling him out won't fix this."

"Maybe it will." I snorted. "Anyway, who died and made you the boss of me?"

"Izzy's alive and well, but last week she asked me to help you anyway." He crossed his arms over his chest. "Take a look over there and tell me he's the real problem—the ringleader—and then I'll let you handle it alone, okay?"

"Yeah, fine. Sure. Whatever." I stepped sideways as Dylan turned. We both had an unobstructed view of the in-crowd's table.

Noah sat back, mouth closed, with his lips pressed into a thin line. Elanor leaned one elbow on the table, her casual posture clearly well-rehearsed. The twins stared, eyes saucer-sized as they hung on every word Faith's sister said.

"So, I told the filthy bloodsucker I'd call the police if he didn't stop chatting up my sister and get lost." Her laugh reminded me of a hyena's.

"What did Faith say to that, Charity?" the twin on the left asked.

"Nothing. Everybody knows you don't make friends with diseased corpses." She wrinkled her nose, pantomiming a dry heave. "Even when you're an undeath magus like she is."

So, the oldest Fairbanks sister was an anti-vampire bigot, which went against practically all the values our family had taught us. And my brother was going along with it.

"Plenty of vampires follow the rules." Noah leaned back in his chair. "My grandmother even knows some who are doctors, helping the sick and dying."

"You know that's just one of the ways they manipulate people into giving them blood, right?" Charity narrowed her eyes. "Because that's all they want—to control the world and spread their disgusting disease."

I knew for sure that wasn't true. I'd met many vampires, living in a touristy place like Salem. They suffered every night of their unlives because the rules people like Charity put in place barely allowed them to survive.

"Ass. You. Me." My brother mumbled our old joke about assumptions under his breath like a mantra he'd practiced countless times.

"What was that, Morgenstern?"

"Nothing." Noah closed his eyes, his Adam's apple bobbing as he swallowed. He only did that when seriously stressed out. I watched all traces of protest die in his eyes once he opened them again.

"Good." Charity's grin was downright wolfish. "You don't want to be on the wrong end of this food chain, so don't make me put you there like I did with Faith and her fleabag Sha."

"What's wrong with her Sha?" One of the twins scratched her head.

"They're drawn to undeath magic." Charity wrinkled her nose. "Ugh."

And just like that, my anger changed its focus.

"You know what, Dylan?" I turned my head, looking at him.

"Hmm?"

"I don't want to kill my brother anymore." I set my jaw. "You're right, he's not the problem."

"Good."

"I'm going to save him from this bitch instead."

"Aliyah—"

Dylan was too slow. Seeing Noah cowed like that gave me wings. In a flash, I was beside the popular crowd's table, looming over them, gunning for bear. Ember extended her wings, hissing at them all.

"Mean people suck." I put my palms flat against the cherry-stained wood, narrowing my eyes.

"And losers get no action." Charity's smirk was light and airy like angel food poison. She rested a raw-silk-clad elbow on the wood. "Your point?"

Elanor's titter was too high-pitched, even for her, and her firebird ducked its head behind hers. Noah blinked, pushing back from the table's edge. Lotan reared up on his shoulder, his warning hiss louder than I'd ever heard it.

The twins guffawed, hands slapping the table. The pigeon familiars on their shoulders flapped, cooing along.

I held out my hand, palm up and cupped, calling flames into it.

Then I inhaled, Ember breathing in tandem. For a moment, it felt like we shared a body, that I had wings, and she was bipedal. The air changed around us, shimmering like summer heat rising off blacktop.

The solar lights in the chandelier above our heads flickered. I almost thought I felt them pulling toward my magic somehow, but that should have been impossible.

"Bailey, put it out," one twin shrieked, pulling her rapidly blistering hand off the table she'd been slapping. The other stood up so fast her chair toppled behind her.

"Shit! Hailey, I can't!"

Ember and I exhaled.

The table and everything on it burst into flame.

Including Charity's shirtsleeves.

From above, the chandelier blasted out an ear-shattering wail, counterpointed with a phrase on repeat.

DANGER: FIRE, LOCATION: CAFETERIA.

"Deluge!" The voice came from my left.

Rain poured down from overhead. The table was still on fire, trays and food charred husks. But Charity's sleeve was out, her flesh unscathed.

A spotted tomcat stood in her lap, back arched and tail straight up. He hissed, sand flying between him and the mean girl. Her familiar's quick thinking and their combined earth magic had saved them from being crispy critters.

I could have killed someone. All because of my temper.

It was raining in the cafeteria. And it was all my fault. I felt horror now instead of rage, but I couldn't stop myself. I still breathed fire, and even though I wanted them to, the flames wouldn't die.

"Pull 'em apart!" Professor DeBeer pointed at my dragonet.

"Yes." It was Professor Luciano behind me. Ember squealed, and I felt her grip on my shoulder loosen before it let go entirely.

"Vacuum!" That was Dylan, behind me. The air spell felt different from his summer cooling conjures. There was an absence along with it, something besides lack of oxygen smothering my magic. Ice cold. But how?

The fire died, and the rain stopped. Also, I couldn't breathe. I put my hands on my throat, trying to gasp, but the air around me just didn't exist. My knees buckled.

"To the infirmary with her." The professor pointed, her lightning bird gliding off her shoulder to lead the way. "Now!"

"Got you." A pair of arms caught under me.

I took a deep breath. The air tasted like burnt everything. My stomach churned and heaved. The supporting hands turned me sideways, lowering me to the floor.

Somehow, I managed to not vomit.

"Get her feet." My other rescuer was Logan. That's right, the kid who was so awkward he accidentally pointed at my boobs. Maybe he conjured the rain.

"On it." Dylan didn't literally lift me by my shoes or socks, thank goodness, but he got my knees.

Together the boys carried me out of the cafeteria, where everything was a blur of carved wood, wrought iron, and sickening self-loathing.

I was still struggling to catch my breath, and my body couldn't handle any more. I passed out.

CHAPTER ELEVEN

INTERLUDE

Harold of Change

I followed Faith Fairbanks because it was my duty.

She was nothing nice, but I couldn't fault her for that. All she knew was shock and snark after growing up Fairbanks, and I knew for sure she'd have it even worse when her little sister Temperance started here next year. So, it was my responsibility to make sure she had a soft place to fall.

I knew loads about the other students here, stuff they'd never have told me themselves. The week before classes started and I moved to this campus between worlds with my overworked father, I asked myself what would Grandma do.

Her example would always guide me, no matter what anyone said about her. And they said an awful lot of terrible things, especially Dad.

That was why I had looked through the files on all the other students in my year. I knew they'd think I didn't belong here. I was almost sixteen, just like all of them, although I looked younger. If things worked out the way I hoped, they'd look past that. Some of them, at least.

Anyway, knowledge is power—and when you had as much as the

people in my family typically did, you used it for the greater good. Hence the whole duty thing.

If only I were typical.

"Faith, wait up." Because my growth got stunted when my magic showed up, I'm on the shorter side, which made me feel like I was running to stand still most times. And the floor next to the window by the dishwashing station was slippery.

"No. Go away."

The sound of clanking plates filled the space between our voices.

"Okay."

My answer worked. She stopped and stared, her shock having the same ultimate effect as kindness would have. People without experience being kind needed to practice it inadvertently sometimes, just to start making good habits. Finally, I caught up and stood beside her.

"What do you mean, okay?" She froze, one heel off the ground, with wide, feral eyes. She could have drowned me in them, and I'd have died happy.

"I'll go away. But for now, I'm a bit out of breath. Give me a minute."

"Whatever." She still didn't move. "It figures the lamest kid at school's the only one who gives a shit."

"Untrue." I shook my head. Keeping my expression flat wasn't easy, but it was the only way someone who's been dissed that hard on her first day by her own sister would believe me. "I had to stop three other people from coming after you too."

"Why?" And just like that, she started coming out the shock. Faith's leg eased, her previously upraised foot now planted on the solid hardwood.

"Because we don't abide bullying." I let the corners of my mouth turn up. "Not even from your ironically named sister."

"Oh." The widening eyes that peered past me and then all around the small corridor told me more than the conversation. She wasn't scared of Charity. Faith was terrified, which confirmed my take on her file.

"Oh?" Sometimes, echoing a person can get them talking. Both my parents said it helped ease a coping mechanism some kids had, ones with more trouble than I had at home.

"Well, what are you going to do about it?"

"I'm the headmaster's son, Faith." I held a hand out. "He listens to me. And everyone here knows it, too."

"You can't be serious. I'm a Fairbanks. I know what everyone here says about my family. What if I sting you while we cross this river? Charity would do it in a heartbeat."

"If how she acts bothers you this much, you understand that the way they treat you isn't the only way to be." I took a deep breath. It'd been short an awful lot since I relied more on my magic, but I couldn't let my mysterious chronic illness bother me now. "You're not a scorpion, and this isn't the Rubicon."

"You're not a historian."

"No. Just another kid trying to be fair, and trying to be a friend."

She mulled that over. It was probably just a handful of seconds, yet it felt like forever. Life-changing moments are always the ones we get stuck in. It couldn't have been easy for her.

Ultimately, our familiars decided things for us. Nin peeked out of my blazer. When Seth noticed her, the back of the tote Faith carried him in swayed from side to side. He was wagging his tail, following up with a whine before he thrust his nose into her hand.

"Are you sure?" I'd have thought she asked the Sha if she weren't looking me right in the eyes.

Finally, I could smile at her because I absolutely was sure about befriending her—even if her gaze almost stole what little breath I had left.

"I chase you on these," I waved a hand at my short, thick legs, "then form an informal debate team next to restaurant trash, and you ask if I'm sure?" I grinned.

"Good point." She tossed her hair over her shoulder. "I've still got no idea why anyone would bother, let alone you. Nobody has before." Her shoulders eased down and back. "But I'm sick of that. The way things have always been."

"I believe it." I nodded. "So let's try something different. Walk back in there with me. Let's hang together."

My hand was out between us all this time, open, like my heart. Dad used to say it was too big. Mom's favorite counter to that was, "Of course, he's a space magus." They both had it right.

"Okay." She reached out, taking my hand. "Nobody wants to hang separately."

Her palm was cool and dry against mine. As her long, elegant fingers curled, intertwining with my short stubby ones, I felt something else. Our magic.

It's not unusual for magi our age to accidentally conjure small amounts of energy in our hands, especially at times of high emotion. But I'd only ever read about it before because I was weak in my magic, even for someone my age. That was par for my course, though, and it would only get worse with time.

Faith was strong in her magic, which was undeath. No wonder people feared her. She probably scared herself, too.

If I truly wanted to help, that'd have to change.

We walked together back toward the cafeteria. She let go, her hand slipping out of mine. I didn't blame her. Nobody wanted to be seen holding hands with the fat kid, but the connection was still there between us like the tether-projection psychics describe as linking them to their bodies when they're out of them.

My heart was full of hope, my head high and confident because I was almost totally sure I could make a difference at school, despite experiencing the most horrible year of my life right before watching Mom go her own way. No, not despite. Because of living through that. I needed to make every one of my moments count, and this was where I had to start.

I was going to help Faith Fairbanks save herself if it was the last thing I did.

"Oh, no." Faith stopped in front of me, her back stiff and her head shaking.

"What's wrong?"

"Look."

I stepped around her to see the half-burnt table in front of me. Paper napkins in sodden heaps dotted its charred surface. Dun-colored sand striped the floor. Clearly, this was the scene of an epic confrontation between an earth magus and a fire magus, with a water magus stepping in.

Charity and Aliyah, then. And probably Logan Pierce, too.

"That Hopewell girl's got no idea who she's messed with here."

"She's a Morgenstern. And maybe she doesn't." I sighed, shaking my head. "But the damage is done. They're enemies for sure now."

The silence stretching between us wasn't uncomfortable. There was tension, a sort I'd never felt before. Surprisingly pleasant, much like Faith.

"What do we do?"

I looked up at her, letting Faith see how she brought a faint smile to my face. Because she said, "We."

"Try hard. Run fast. But mostly, be kind."

"That's it?" She snorted. "Charity wouldn't do that for us."

"We don't have to be kind to her, just provide it as an alternative to everyone else."

"I'm not good at that. Actually, I'm atrocious." She clenched her fists. The remains of her energy lingered in my palm. Curious, that.

"Were you good at swimming right away?" I knew from her file that she'd learned that skill later than most people, and also that it wasn't easy for her. Trauma again.

"No. Okay, I get it."

Faith began walking away, picking her way past the burnt table toward the cafeteria's exit. She moved slowly this time, at least for her. For me, it was a brisk pace.

"Where are you going?"

"Class." She adjusted the strap on her tote. "Keep up, Harold."

Her voice and actions weren't much different than earlier, at least on the surface, but Faith's prickly veneer had started to crack. Maybe, sometime, it'd turn into something she could use when she wanted to, like putting on armor instead of it being her emotional default mode. How did I know this?

Seth turned around in the tote. The little magical canine couldn't stop wagging his tail, his eyes bright as he grinned doggily at me. And that was why I didn't take credit for this change. All I did was get a ball rolling. The Sha would be the one to chase it out into the sunlight. Nin would help more than I could. The other kids' critters, too.

For practitioners of familiar magic, there has always been one more factor in the nature/nurture influence on our personalities, compared with any other extrahumans.

Our companions.

CHAPTER TWELVE

ALIYAH

I woke with my cheek pressed against a flat pillow swathed in pilled jersey fabric that smelled of bleach. My right arm was asleep because I'd been lying on it, and my entire body felt warm and weighed down, so much so that I couldn't immediately sit up.

"Ember?" My next thought was for the dragonet's wellbeing.

"Be still." The voice was a warm tenor, like Izzy's cousin Eduardo but without his accent. "We've got you bundled in a weighted blanket. Your dragonet's perched at the foot of this cot. You need a bit more rest."

"What happened?" As the words slurred out of my mouth, I wished I could swallow them because I remembered it all. "Oh, no. I'm a monster."

"No, just a young and powerful magus with a newfound familiar." A cool hand pressed my forehead. "I'll tell you a secret. You're not the first new student this has happened to. He had a dragonet, too. You remind me of him quite a bit, in fact."

"Who was he?" I cringed, expecting to hear the name "Richard Hopewell." "What happened to him?"

"Someone very special." The voice lowered, like Bubbe's when she was talking about my grandfather. "He grew into his powers, and used them heroically after the Reveal."

I opened my eyes. The man on the stool beside the cot I lay on was pale, with wavy honey-brown hair and a goatee. Amber eyes gazed from behind the round spectacles perched on his unlined face. His thin and bloodless lips tilted up slightly, as though he had resting sympathy face. Or something else.

"Are you a vampire?"

"Nobody's perfect." He shrugged. "I'm also an ice magus, for what it's worth."

Out in Haverhill, Bubbe had a vampire colleague practicing extraveterinary medicine. Salem Hospital also employed several, with a vamp physician on their board of directors. They heard and smelled things wrong with living bodies that even the most powerful magus or psychic couldn't.

I blinked slowly. Vampires weren't allowed to be students here. I knew that already, overheard through years of Mom's conference calls, but apparently, there was no ban on them working here, as long as they were also magi. That wasn't something I'd have considered controversial as recently as yesterday.

"There's no way Hailey or Charity let you take care of them."

"And I didn't." He shook his head. "I'm merely an assistant at this time. But Nurse Smith is almost done with them. He'll be with you shortly."

As I lay there, opening and closing my right hand under the blanket to work the pins and needles out of it, I pondered who this guy was. It took some serious mental and emotional armor for a flammable vampire, even one with ice magic, to remain calm at a time like this.

He was alone in a room with the girl who'd almost burned the cafeteria down—and being so kind. I couldn't have managed a feat like that, so of course, I had to know more about him.

"E. Brown, CNA." I read his badge. "Can I sit up now?"

"Yes." He grinned again, turning down the weighted blanket and giving me a hand up. "By the by, E is for Ezekiel, but students here call me Zeke. They say it sounds cooler, which suits my magical element, I suppose."

"Well, thanks for taking care of me, Zeke." I smoothed my hair, which was messy but not matted, thankfully. "Where's Dylan? And Logan? The boys who brought me here?"

"They both departed to get their class schedules." He nodded at the door. "The one with the dark hair said he'd return right after that."

"That'd be Dylan. He's a good friend." I reached out my left arm toward where Ember perched. "Met him the same day I found her."

"I see."

"Is it going to be a problem?" Ember stretched her wings, as though testing them. She opted for hopping across the bed instead of flying over. "The fact that I missed the tour, I mean?"

"The headmaster will show you around, along with the other students who missed it."

"But isn't Charity Fairbanks an upperclassman?" Ember climbed into my lap and leaned against my stomach, resting her head on my breastbone. I cuddled her, of course.

"That she is. But I speak of her sister." Zeke nodded. "Faith."

There was a knock on the door before I could ask how she ended up missing such a crucial part of orientation. She wasn't with me.

I cleared my throat. "Come in."

The door opened, revealing a short man with a buzz cut wearing blue scrubs covered by an assortment of pockets. His neck was decorated with tattoos, black lines in peaks and whorls like ocean waves. He held up a round-bottomed flask filled with water, positioning it between him and me. The line where the water met the glass wavered slightly, then stilled.

"You're doing much better now, Miss Morgenstern." He waggled the flask in his hand. "I might be able to let you return to regular activities."

"Might?" I raised an eyebrow as Ember lifted her head off my chest.

"Yes." Nurse Smith pulled a stool over, rolling it on casters. "I just need to ask you a few questions."

85

"Um, can Zeke stay?" I was nervous. No, that's a lie. I was scared half to death that I'd get expelled, and if this was a psych screening, I wanted a witness, even if the only one available was a vampiric nursing assistant.

"Of course." He leaned forward, setting the flask of water on the bedside table. After that, he reached toward his largest pocket. A gleaming blue claw emerged, handing him a notepad with a pen protruding from its spiral top.

"Now, I heard that in the cafeteria, you got into an argument with Charity Fairbanks. How did it start?" The nurse flipped open the pad, pen poised over the empty page.

I took a deep breath, closed my eyes, and let it out. I was a bit hazy on that. I noticed that the water inside the flask rolled slightly like it had its own current.

"Peep." Ember nuzzled my chin, and it all came back to me.

"It started with Faith, actually." I told the nurse she ran off, and how I realized why. I stopped before getting to what I overheard. "Look, I don't want to repeat what she said, even though I sort of have to."

"Why not?"

'Because it's hate speech, Nurse Smith." I glanced at Zeke. "It's also total hogwash, and I don't want to repeat that pack of lies. It's nasty and might hurt someone."

"Like fire might hurt someone?"

Nurse Smith's words hit me like a breaker hitting the shore.

"I didn't mean to shoot the flames out, only conjure them."

"Peep!" Ember had my back, at least.

"Okay." He nodded. "So, was this hate speech against your Jewish heritage? Or perhaps against fire or solar magi?"

"No." I sighed, not looking at Zeke. "It was anti-vampire."

"Hmm." His eyes cut left, then he marked something down on the paper. "Charity told me that you said, 'Mean people suck.' Is that true?"

"Yes."

"And then you set the table on fire?"

"No." I shook my head. "That's not how it happened."

I told him about her insult, how I was pretty much struck speechless. How I wasn't even aware of raising the temperature around me while making the flame in my hand.

"So, it's a simple loss of control, then." Nurse Smith nodded.

"No. It wasn't simple." I swallowed. "I wish it was. But people got hurt, so it's way more complicated."

I left out the part where I felt like Ember and I had merged, and the bit about the lights. That had to be some sort of hallucination because I couldn't do solar magic. I'd have had to be an extramagus to affect those lights or even draw energy from them.

I shook my head again. The esteemed medical professionals might have thought I was trying to remember, not deciding whether to lie, but it was all too much for me to handle or even speak about when it might mean my expulsion. It wasn't even the first day. I said the only thing I could be sure of.

"This was all my fault." My shoulders drooped, and I cradled Ember. "I flew off the handle, and I'm sorry. Should have had better control."

"Miss Morgenstern," Nurse Smith said, patting my arm. "This is actually quite common with fire magi your age."

"Really?"

"Yes. In fact, your own mother struggled the same way when she was a student here." He made another note on his pad. I must have seemed confused because when he glanced up again, he said, "Oh, I see. She hasn't discussed that with you."

"No." I looked up at the clock, unable to meet the nurse's gaze. "All she did was teach me some meditation techniques. But those aren't so helpful now that I'm here. I feel like a total freak."

"You're in an unfamiliar place. It's your first day, and you stood up for what you believe in." Nurse Smith gave me a gentle smile. "It sounds like normal behavior to me."

"This wouldn't have been my kind of normal last year."

"Your magic wasn't as developed then. Remember, you and all the other students here are growing into their powers. It's going to take adjustment on everyone's part."

"Am I expelled?"

"Oh, goodness, no." The nurse tucked his pad and pen back in his pocket. "But I'm afraid you'll have an extra course for this first month of school. It's time-consuming, but it will help you avoid control issues in the future. It's designed for students who aren't fitting in for various reasons."

"What?" I blinked. My plans for afternoons off-campus with Cadence and Izzy would be foiled.

"Headmaster Hawkins will fill you in on all the details during your tour." He picked up the flask, which I'd almost forgotten about, and put that away too. "Now, if you'll excuse me, I need to go and write some reports."

Was he using the flask as some kind of lie detector? No, that was more of an air thing. With water as his element, the nurse probably used it as a way to gauge emotional states.

"Your roommate brought a bag while you were sleeping." Zeke pulled it out from under the bed. "You can freshen up while you wait for the headmaster."

"Wow." I took the bag, setting it on the table beside me. "Thank you, Zeke. For everything."

"It was no trouble." The vampire CNA grinned again, less sadly this time. "I would say I hope to see you again, but I'd prefer it if you stay safe."

"Be sure to come back here if you see heat warping the air again, Miss Morgenstern." Nurse Smith stood. Zeke joined him by the door.

As they stepped toward the exit, I spoke. "Thanks, Nurse Smith." For nothing.

At least I managed to keep my inside voice locked away this time.

They closed the door. Once I changed and freshened up, I exited the infirmary, on my way to take my second chance at a new beginning.

CHAPTER THIRTEEN

I wore the same old leggings and tunic again because that was what Grace had packed. She'd also stuffed my course schedule in the bag, bless her. A scrawl of handwriting told me to meet Professor Hawkins in the main lobby, where we had the welcome assembly.

On arrival, I was relieved to see Hal, Logan, and Dylan. Faith not so much, but I was prepared to give her a second chance.

But the twin I'd injured was there too. Hailey. Or was it Bailey? I wracked my brain because I wanted to go over and apologize, but it was coming up blank.

I froze.

"Peep." Ember twisted her head in front of my face, then knocked some sense into me by headbutting my nose.

"Thanks."

My feet moved again, and I was sure it was Hailey who got hurt now. I kept my eyes fixed on the girl I accidentally injured. More specifically, on the gauze wrapped over her wound, no doubt holding a magical compress in place.

"Hailey, I'm so sorry you got hurt." I looked her in the eye as I continued, "I just couldn't stop the fire I conjured from getting away, and I want to apologize for even using magic back there. I shouldn't have."

"Oh." She blinked, but whether it was from shock or to block tears, I don't know. "Well. Um."

"For Pete's sake, don't hem and haw." Faith snorted. "Accept her apology or not, but pick one before you drive us all batty." Her Sha let out a short bark from the tote slung across her body. "See? Even Seth agrees." The little canine licked her arm.

"Okay. Fine." Hailey tilted her head, her side-ponytail bobbing. "Accepted. But that doesn't mean we're friends. Far from it."

"I don't blame you." I nodded, then headed over toward the boys.

"You okay?" Hal stood, Nin dashing up his arm to twine around his shoulders. "I heard all about what happened in there."

"I screwed up." I shook my head. "And I'm going to make up for it. The nurse set me up with some kind of after-class activity."

"Oh, no way." Logan winced. "Not Familiar Bondage?"

I'd have heard a pin drop if Hailey wasn't snickering into her sleeve.

"What?" Hal scratched his head. Clearly, he'd never checked out Urban Dictionary or been anywhere near Snapchat.

"Logan, buddy." Dylan sighed. "It's 'bonding.' They don't have detention, but the next best thing at good old Hawthorn Academy is called Familiar Bonding. Drop the -age and add -ing."

"I'll bet fifty bucks nobody but the Firestarter over there is required to take it." Faith snorted as she idly patted Seth the Sha.

"Awesomesauce!" Dylan clapped his hands, then held one out. "I'm rich!"

"Fetch, puppy." Faith sighed, snapping her fingers. Seth turned around, his long, straight tail sticking out of the bag as he rummaged in it. He emerged with a crocodile-skin wallet.

"Wait." I shook my head. "Are you being punished because you helped me?" I blinked.

Faith whipped out a fifty, tossing it into the air.

"No." Dylan held out his hand, and the bill see-sawed down to his

90

palm. "It's the coursework for misfit kids. I don't have a familiar, so I don't fit in yet."

"That means you owe me too, Faith." Logan chuckled. "I'm taking it also." He jerked his thumb at his shoulder. "Familiar gone."

"Ugh, dropping adverbs is gauche." Faith wrinkled her nose but paid up anyway. "You're not funny, Logan. Like, ever. Go to the library and check out a joke book or something."

His face fell like one of Bubbe's soufflés. My grandma could bake anything but soufflés. Nobody's perfect.

"Never will be, either," Hailey chimed in. "Ya basic."

"I didn't say that." Faith swallowed. "Just that he's got a lot to learn."

"So do you." Hailey rolled her eyes. "You know what your problem is? You're too nice. And you can hardly call a boy that pretty a charity case."

"Seems to me that all of you need improvement."

We all looked up as the headmaster appeared out of nowhere. I suppose it was a good thing this family of space magi decided to open a prep school instead of an old folks' home because otherwise, they'd give everybody heart attacks. Teleportation is startling on the receiving end.

"Yeah." I took a deep breath. "I'm sorry about the fire in the cafeteria."

"Understood." Headmaster Hawkins nodded.

"Now, all of you missed the tour earlier, so this is the only way I can ensure you won't get lost tomorrow." The headmaster clapped his hands. I got a stomach-turning sense of rapid movement that only lasted a second. "Unfortunately, you can't make up for not meeting the professors who will be advising you during your education here."

"Bummer." Hailey rubbed her eyes, blinking, and I didn't blame her. The lighting was different all of a sudden. "Can we go see the classrooms yet?"

"You're already in one of them." He gestured.

We stared up, down, and all around like turkeys in the rain. The headmaster must have teleported us when he clapped his hands. This classroom was different from the dorms and common areas.

There were a few similarities, of course. The chandeliers were that same spidery wrought iron with solar globes, and the clock was just like the rest of those wooden ones, but it was hung on the wall instead of worked into the decor.

The walls weren't carved wood in here, they were covered with chalkboards. Not the mundane kind. These were magipsychic, which means they generated illustrations to go with what was written on them.

One wall actually had a window. It looked out on the Axelrod walking park behind the Peabody Essex Museum. I could almost see my house from here.

Checking the board at the front, I read a message beside a gorgeous multicolor chalked mural of a beach with a man in a Santa suit sunbathing on it. That had to be what Christmas was like in the southern hemisphere. I chuckled before reading aloud, "Welcome to Professor DeBeer's homeroom."

"Yes." Headmaster Hawkins nodded. "Dylan and Hailey will report here for class in the morning. Please feel free to explore the room and read all the messages left for you by your professor. You other four can follow me across the hall."

We left the classroom, all a bit dismayed that the seemingly fun Susan DeBeers wouldn't be the person we reported to in emergencies or come to when we had questions or concerns. She wouldn't be giving our lectures or running our labs either.

"Don't worry," Hal whispered. "You're not alone."

I nodded, then took the chance to look around the hall.

It was more wood, but bleached and polished instead of stained this time, allowing for a brighter though less warm feeling. It was brisk in there, giving the impression that it was designed for students to hurry through on their way to different places.

When we reached the room across the hall, we found it equipped the same way. However, the chalkboard illustrations were abstract instead of immediately recognizable. The colors and placement exuded a depth that was more intriguing than whimsical.

It was obvious that serious learning went on in here, but never in a boring way. This reminded me immediately of Bubbe. I headed directly to the front, curious to know the name of the person with this oddly comforting teaching style. I was too shocked to read it aloud. Faith did it for me.

"Professor Luciano?"

"Yes." Headmaster Hawkins leaned against the doorframe. "He's excited to have all of you in his homeroom this year."

"Interesting." I turned my back on the headmaster, using my impulse to examine the window in here to cover my disappointment. Outside was the roof of the Bridge Street parking lot.

"I'll be in the hall. You have five minutes."

"I'm not sure I can handle it in here." I glanced at Hal, who gazed out the window with me. "Luciano's tough, by all accounts, and he's in charge of all our academic testing."

"Oh, boy." Logan hung his head. "You're right. Poison owl man probably won't cut us any slack."

"If we stick together and study, we'll get by." Hal gestured at a diagram of different magics and how they interacted with each other. It was straightforward, while still containing new-to-me subject matter. "The way these look, it seems like he'll at least be fair, even if his assignments are challenging."

"Are you sure?" Logan's eyebrows rose. "I mean, I'm not horrible at tests on paper, but labs freak me out."

"So we stick together, like Hal said." Faith elbowed Logan in the ribs. At least we were in agreement. Better together.

The four of us circled the room like restless cats. It was hard to concentrate on reading all the messages, but we managed. Luciano's tone was what I expected—business casual. He'd expect decorum and following the rules, for sure, but all of that was stuff I'd done before.

"We don't spend all day in this room, I hope." Faith leaned against a desk.

"No." Hal pulled his schedule out of a pocket in his blazer, pointing out the blocks. "We'll get broken out in the middle of the day for lunch, library time, and our specials. See?"

"Gym before lunch and Health after." I peered at the paper. "And thank goodness for the library period before we go to Lab."

"Yeah, and Creatives is before Gym. We get to pick what kind of art we make or practice, and we're together with DeBeer's class in one big room."

"Awesome." I was relieved I'd get at least some time with Grace and Dylan during class days. Hal seemed like a good guy, and Logan was mostly harmless. I was still worried about Faith. She was intimidating.

"It's almost time." Faith jerked her chin at the clock. "What's next?"

"Not much." Hal smiled at her. "Dad's just going to show us where the specials are, and then we're done."

"Thanks, losers." She stood and hurried out, contradicting her gratitude by avoiding us like the plague.

"Uh, wow." Logan blinked after Faith. "She's dramatic. I'll just say thanks, I guess. You guys are nice." He grinned, then sauntered out of the room, tossing a wave overhead.

"I don't get it." Hal's frown surprised me. "She didn't talk like that after I followed her."

"She's been a mean girl, Hal." I sighed. "Maybe it's her default mode when people are looking. Old habits—"

"Die hard. I know." He hung his head. "I'm trying to change a few of my own, so I get it. But hope dies hard, too."

"Don't expect much." I chewed my lower lip, wondering whether Hal was one of those angry "nice guys" who think being helpful is money in some sort of twisted romantic bank. But I knew anger when I saw it, and Hal seemed more sad than anything else. Or tired. "Low expectations mean less disappointment later."

"All I wanted was to make some friends here." He winced. "Which is going to take a miracle. It doesn't feel like I fit in."

"Oh?" I blinked. Bubbe always says I ought to be a light in the world. Hal was so amiable I didn't understand how he would have a hard time making friends, but here we were. All I could do was try to help. "Well, you're not alone."

"Yeah. I guess Dylan and Logan not having familiars makes them feel weird too." He fidgeted with the sleeve on his blazer, staring down

94

at the silver buttons. I wondered whether he felt as lonely as me, even with a familiar who clearly loved him and his father in charge of the school.

"Don't forget the gal who set the café on fire." I rolled my eyes. "She's a literal hot mess. I hear she wants to be friends with you, for what it's worth."

"Thanks, Aliyah." He perked up. "It means a lot."

We had a chuckle as we headed out into the hall. Everyone else was there, so Headmaster Hawkins started walking as soon as we emerged. Following him, I thought maybe my second chance just might work out.

If only.

CHAPTER FOURTEEN

The Creatives room was locked, so we didn't get to see inside. Knowing its location was a relief, though, because there was no way I would have found it on my own. Professor Hawkins only told us it was directed study with instruction on request. As we walked on, he spoke.

"For those of you in Familiar Bonding, it meets in the infirmary after the last class block."

"The infirmary?" Logan's chuckle was a little too high-pitched. "Are we sick in the head or something?"

"No." Headmaster Hawkins shook his head. "Nurse Smith has all the knowledge and materials needed, however, and he prefers to assemble where he can handle any medical emergencies."

"Makes sense." I nodded.

The gym was open. In there, the walls were once again wood but stained like the academic hallways. It was interesting how something as simple as wood stain changed the sense of place. Izzy would say there was psychology to it, that certain colors helped the mind focus on different types of tasks. Cadence would disagree and say the decor's purpose was emotional.

I wished they were with me.

Bleachers stood against the walls, folded in on themselves. Unlike the ones at my old school, which were made of metal and plastic, these were wood. It was impossible to tell how they opened, but when I brushed the back of my hand against one, I sensed its magical energy.

Great. I was a barely controlled fire magus in a school made almost entirely out of wood.

"Peep."

Ember used her tail to give me a hug. Somehow, she always knew when I needed one, which reminded me of Bubbe and Mom. If they had gotten through education at Hawthorn Academy with solar and fire magic, I suppose I might make it too.

If only I could keep from burning the school down.

I dismissed the seriously unhealthy thinking and continued to check out the gymnasium. It helped take my mind off the idea that my academic career might literally go up in smoke.

The gym had three carved clocks, a scoreboard that was the second cousin of the chalkboards in the classrooms, and four magic chandeliers. I had to crane my neck to look at them because the ceiling was so high.

There were a handful of students inside, running laps on the track outlined on the hardwood. That was where I got what I thought might be a pleasant surprise.

"Hi, Noah!" I smiled and waved.

My brother ran by, totally ignoring me. Lotan didn't do the usual and wave his tail at me, either, and he was only jogging, not even close to his regular level of exertion when working out at home.

I had thought going to the same school would improve our relationship.

My words to Hal back in the homeroom felt more hollow than a collapsing log. A wave of homesickness washed over me. All I wanted right then was one of those long afternoons at the Willows, a time warp back to summer, before all of this.

Headmaster Hawkins moved on before my brother completed another lap and ignored me again. Thank goodness.

"Health is at the end of the hall closest to the infirmary, and like the Creatives room, it's closed." He spoke as he strode down the hall. "After I show you the way, you ought to prepare for the mixer. You're short on time."

He walked so fast, we all had to hustle to keep up, even me with my awkwardly long legs. A glance at one of the hall clocks told me why. It was late.

I wondered why the space magus wasn't using magic to move us around the school as he had on the way here. I was only momentarily puzzled instead of completely stumped by this. I worked it out quickly.

We needed to see how to get in and out of the academic wing, of course. That would be impossible if he teleported us everywhere during the tour. The corridor with the classrooms was long, but half of the classrooms were locked up and dark, unused. I didn't need to wonder why our class was so small.

Life as an extrahuman wasn't secret anymore. New laws, practices, and opportunities had developed before I was even born. This had led to lots of new freedoms for many of us, especially psychics and magi like me—including freedom of education.

Public schools offered so many more specialized programs for extrahumans than in the years after the Big Reveal. Enough to get average and above students into community and state colleges with majors in using extrahuman skills for careers.

Back in Bubbe's day, psychics and magi learned in secret, while shifters and changelings got pulled from mundane high schools to avoid revealing their true natures by accident. The latter often ended up as dropouts because expensive schools like Hawthorn or Trout and The Academy down in Rhode Island were the only places that could accommodate them. Post-Reveal, parents who couldn't afford to send their kids to any other school were now guaranteed public options.

Of course, legacy students like me and families like Dylan's wanted a shot at the best future for their offspring. So, plenty of us still busted our humps to begin and sustain academic careers at the old traditional schools, but we had become the minority.

There were even homeschool options now, online instruction with seasonal labs held in larger cities like Boston. I did loads of research on those, with the idea of convincing my parents to let me learn that way instead of having to stay on this campus.

Considering the day I'd had, I probably should've pushed that angle further, but it was too late for that. I'd gotten stuck being the hot mess in residence at Hawthorn Academy.

But things could only get better, right? I had to keep on hoping. It was only the first day, so even if I couldn't make up with Noah and fix all the problems, there was always tomorrow. And the day after that. But I wasn't sure how to manage.

My temper was a big problem. A fire magus in a school made almost entirely of wood could never be completely at ease.

I missed Izzy and Cadence in a big way. All I needed to do was get through the next few hours, and hopefully, I'd be able to talk to them without getting caught, because my means to do so was totally against school rules.

The headmaster pushed through a set of doors inlaid with stained glass. The cut and soldered pieces made a pair of pictures, one on each side. The first one showed the bay here in Salem, the sun rising over it in shards of orange, purple, and pink. The other depicted Gallows Hill at night, bare tree branches reaching to touch a full moon, all yellow, blue, and black.

The designs reminded me of the faerie courts, something I didn't expect to be confronted with here at school. There was only one family with fae living in Salem, the Ambersmiths. Which made me wonder who the artist was, and how these pieces came to be here. The act of making that art might have been pure rebellion.

I got so curious about them I stopped, not caring about having to jog to catch up with the group later. Like most other elements of decor here at Hawthorn, these doors had a plaque beside them.

"Long Division," I read. "Created by Gamila Hadaad-Hawkins." I closed my mouth, pondering the name along with the date, which I didn't read aloud.

The stained-glass artwork was about the same age as my new

friend Hal. The fact that the artist shared his last name made me wonder how they were related—by marriage with that hyphen there, perhaps. But there was no way Hal Hawkins was old enough to get married, even with parental consent. Also, that was only a common practice among magical shifters, so Gamila Hadaad-Hawkins must be some other maternal relative. Probably with faerie blood.

The sound behind me practically had me jumping out of my skin. Ember flew off my shoulder, propelling herself upward and emitting a roar instead of her usual peep. I turned on my heel and felt nearly instantaneous relief. It was just the headmaster.

"My mother made that, you know." He nodded at the doors. "She used to oversee Creatives. Do you like it?"

"It's sad, somehow?" And that was true. Something about the scene, its mood, maybe, or the title, nagged at my mind. "But I'm not sure."

"Well, come and see me in class when you decide." He nodded. "I'm in charge of Creatives for your year. But for now, there's a mixer everyone needs to attend."

"I'm sorry about everything." I held out my arm so Ember could land. "It feels like I've done nothing but ruin your day. And a number of other people's too."

"These things happen. What's important is that we don't let the hiccups define our ability to breathe." He shrugged. "Or some analogy more profound than I can come up with."

"You're not anything like I expected, Headmaster." I couldn't keep the smile off my lips without letting the laughter behind it out.

"Well, we can't all be wise bearded sages." He chuckled. "Although with a little luck, some far future class or other at this institution will get the chance to see me that way."

"Do I really have to be at the mixer, Headmaster?"

"Well, at least stay for a half-hour, through the presentation of faces and names." He gave me a sidelong glance. "Unless you're still ill and need to spend the night in the infirmary?"

"No, I'm just tired is all." The last thing I wanted was to get stuck all night away from my room and the contraband object I'd hidden in there. "I'll tough it out."

Instead of leading the way, Headmaster Hawkins walked beside me around the corner that led to the lobby. The place was packed with students and teachers, most of them dressed in cocktail attire. Noah was right—a varied wardrobe was a necessity here.

It seemed like everyone had gotten fancied up. Even Hailey had passable attire for the occasion, which I realized must be because her twin had brought clothes to the infirmary that'd fit her. I searched the room, hoping to find somebody—even one person—as dressed-down as I was.

Across the room, I saw her: Grace, my roommate. She was still clad in the same pegged jeans and threadbare flannel she'd arrived at school this morning wearing, with the school blazer, of course. As I stood in a corner, tugging at the hem of my blazer and hoping it covered the understated tunic atop my leggings, Grace guffawed with Dylan as though she hadn't a care in the world. Hal joined them, adding his quiet and grinning presence to the small group.

If I could have bottled my roommate's confidence and sold it, I'd be a millionaire.

As I considered my newfound lack of bravery, I scanned the room for more folks I'd met on my first day. Faith hovered at the fringes of her sister's group, saying nothing but molding her features into a resting bitch face that might just have had the power to silence Izzy's sass. I realized she must be trying to patch things up with her sibling. I couldn't blame her for trying because I'd made the same effort in the gym with Noah. But Charity was just awful, and I was surprised Faith wasn't trying to escape her orbit.

Until she did.

Logan sauntered through the archway I was standing beside. He saw me and started to head over. I waffled between wincing in anticipation of his social gaffes and relief that someone, *anyone*, noticed me flirting unwillingly with pariah status. At least he was smiling, and the sentiment looked genuine. But he was from a showbiz family, after all. I couldn't decide whether to take his goodwill at face value or consider it a veneer.

Faith intercepted him, hooking her arm around his. He blinked, then furrowed his brow, whispering something to her. She shook her head, giving him a look that'd wilt daisies. The pair of them headed back toward Charity's cluster of beautiful people. I suppose that was best for Logan. He certainly looked like he belonged with them, awkward or not.

I stopped people-watching to look for my brother. He hadn't arrived yet, but Noah loved being fashionably late. Even though he'd snubbed me back in the gym, I wanted to see him.

As I turned myself into a wallflower, leaning near the archway I came in through, I wondered how he did it. Fitting in here, I mean. Everything about this school was opposite to how home felt. Like alien territory, as though I came from another planet.

Hawthorn Academy is technically in another dimension, after all, one Noah's taken to like a duck to water. I watched him saunter in arm-in-arm with his bestie, Elanor. He'd never had a friend who carried on with him like that back at public school, and his entrance wouldn't have gotten such a positive reaction back then, either. People actually stopped, smiling or rushing over to say hello. My brother was Mr. Popularity. Watching his reception and his reaction to it, I understood.

This was Noah's home now. Had been for a year before I got here, and if he was a duck in this water, I was oil on top of it, unable to mix in or blend. Off in the opposite corner, I spotted someone I recognized from pictures Noah had shown me over the summer—Darren, his boyfriend. An introvert. But even he wasn't by himself. Another boy I didn't recognize was over there with him, leaning against the wall.

Suddenly, I couldn't even bear people-watching anymore. I turned my head, resting it against Ember's flank to hide my eyes. I'd wait this mandatory event out and go back to my room.

Because I didn't want anyone to see the tears I couldn't keep in anymore.

Somewhere in the haze of stomach-dropping anguish, I heard the chandelier loudspeaker apparatus announcing names in alphabetical order. That must have been what Headmaster Hawkins meant about faces and names, so I looked up.

A magipsychic display on one wall lighted up. It was like a mundane electronic screen in function, but completely different in how it operated. It was basically a giant HD device with a psychic source and magical power.

Faces of students with their familiars flashed on the screen, along with their names in both text and speech. My stomach felt even worse when I realized the images were generated directly from each person in real-time. The device was taking our pictures right then and there.

And I looked like a waterlogged albatross.

"GRACE DUBOIS: FAMILIAR LUNE," the magically amplified voice said.

As the alphabet moved past F for Fairbanks and on to H for Hawkins, I wiped my eyes on my sleeve. I managed to dab my nose with the hem of my tunic by the time Dylan Khan's face flashed on the screen. I thought I couldn't look too bad until the name Aliyah Morgenstern, familiar Ember boomed through the room.

The face on the screen was blotchy and tearstained, the eyes red-rimmed. And my cowlick stood up in full force, making one side of my hair nearly vertical like Bubbe's yearbook back when New Wave hairstyles were cool. At least Ember looked decent, even if her expression was more feral than usual.

"The new dark lord—"

"Should have said Hopewell—"

"Almost burned the school down—"

Fragments of conversation like shattering mirrors came from red supergiant it-girl Charity and her solar system of mean planets. I hoped she collapsed someday to turn into a supermassive black hole.

They even ignored the boy right after me, a fellow with some sort of serpent familiar.

Logan Pierce saved me, but not in person. His model-perfect mug appeared up on the screen next, and the voices switched to squeals and coos as they decided to fawn over him instead of laughing at me.

And the alphabetical listing went on. Judging by the number of first-year students, we'd have six in each class, which was about average for a magical prep school.

"LEE YOUNG: FAMILIAR SCRATCH" boomed out. A kid with windswept purple bangs over black hair flashed on the screen along with a lop-eared Sumxu cat, and the presentation ended. Finally.

I wanted to run—turn the corner as quickly as possible—but Bubbe always told me that running attracts attention. I took measured steps toward the arch, forcing my breath into a normal pattern instead of the frantic gasps my lungs wanted to take.

Finally, I made it to the stairs, just managing to mumble the number three. When the steps began moving, I knew I had made my escape.

CHAPTER FIFTEEN

"Is this thing on?"

It felt weird, sitting in bed while talking to a glowing glass orb, but I guess it was better than hiding in the corner on the verge of a panic attack. If it worked, I'd be able to vent to my two best friends. Maybe my only real friends in the world.

The device in question was made from a seaglass orb, one of those items frequently found in antique shops all over downtown Salem. Last week, after I bonded with Ember, my friends and I had bought three of them and spent the afternoon enchanting all the orbs together.

Without Dylan. We didn't want to involve him because it was against school rules to bring a device with a connection to the outside world. That seemed unnecessarily cruel, which was why we decided to break the rule, but if Dylan got in trouble for something like this, he'd lose his scholarship and have to go home.

"Testing? One? Two?"

Closing my eyes, I inwardly bemoaned the fact that it would have taken months plus help from an actual telepathic psychic to get the orbs to transmit thoughts instead of speech. That would also have required more education than we had to create. A simple magical voice device was easy at our level of skill.

After opening my eyes again, I stared into its center, only seeing the bottom of my suitcase through it, tinted pink. That came from the glittery substance Cadence had contributed along with her energies. The damn thing was supposed to light up and glow like a candle with an internal flame. That part came from me and my fire magic. And then we were supposed to hear each other's voices through the glass, a feature fueled by Izzy's psychic powers.

We tested it, so the device should have worked here. Maybe I wasn't talking loud enough.

"Izzy? Cadence?" I raised my voice as much as I dared.

"Leelee!" Cadence's voice was a bit muffled, but there, thank goodness.

"Psychics-R-Us, you say 'em, we sooth 'em." I practically saw Izzy's eyebrows waggling as she joked around.

"You guys, I'm so glad this works. You have no idea."

"Rough first day?" Izzy's words were snarky, but her tone was more comfortable than cozy socks in the middle of winter. "I mean, was it bad?"

"That's an understatement."

"Peep!"

"Aww." Cadence squealed. "Is that cute little dragony-wagony being a good little girl?"

Ember's tail thumped the headboard in response.

"Yeah, she's behaving way better than me." I hung my head even though my friends couldn't see me. I told them all about my no good, lousy, horrible, rotten day.

I told them everything down to the last detail, including poor Zeke Brown, the vampire CNA who had to live in the school every year with a bunch of bigoted magi. As a matter of fact, I started with him because said bigotry was part of the reason I got into so much trouble in the first place.

"Jeez Louise, Aliyah." Izzy clicked her tongue against her teeth. "That Charity person sounds like a total itch with a B in front."

"What's with the censor bar, Izzy?" Cadence chimed in.

"I'm watching the baby." Izzy means her youngest brother Ricky, who was six, not an infant. But that was what her family called their youngest member. "Gotta watch my language."

"So, how was the Open House at Messing, Izzy? I don't want to be a total time hog." I leaned back against the wall with my open suitcase on my lap. It was the only way I could use the seaglass without Grace seeing it if she walked into the room.

"Not as interesting as your first day at Hawthorn, but I do have a couple of annoying little tag-alongs. They practically followed me onto the wrong bus home."

"You guys are so lucky, going to schools where you don't have to stay overnight and swan around at a bunch of stupid mixers."

"That sounded heinous," said Izzy. "The way they put candid pictures up there without any warning. I mean, who does that to a room full of teenagers?"

"I don't know, Izz." Cadence sighed. "It's hard to remember every-one's name and match them up with their faces on the first day, so I think that's something I'd actually like. But I'm a mermaid, so..."

"Oh, you would have been totally at home in there, Cadence." I groaned. "You've never had a hard time fitting in." I grinned at the mental image of Cadence totally showing Charity's mean girl squad up with her amiable chatter.

"We'll see how that goes when I start my first day tomorrow." I heard Cadence take a puff from her inhaler, which told me she was more nervous than she let on. "It's easy getting along with mundanes, but shifters don't have the best view of mermaids since the Boston Internment. I'll probably hang out with the changelings."

"Well, if things go wrong and you need to talk about it, you know where to go." Izzy snorted. "Under the sea."

We all laughed at the old joke. Cadence gave up protesting years ago that she wasn't allowed anywhere in the ocean besides the shal-lows in the Bay. Something about her parents' agreement which enabled them to live on land.

"So, are you and Dylan dating yet?" Cadence tittered.

"No, not dating anyone." I cringed, forgetting they couldn't see me. "Nobody would want to, anyway."

"Oh, no." I heard Izzy slap a hand on some surface, imagining her family's kitchen table. "You're not going to get all boy-crazy like our merfriend here, are you, Aliyah?"

"I'm just trying to make friends, not influence people into dating me by mistake." I sighed, leaning my cheek against Ember's flank. "After today, I doubt anyone's interested. Which is good, because I've got too much to worry about right now."

"Speaking of you getting into trouble, maybe we shouldn't press our luck on this little conference call." Cadence was often silly, but any time she said something sensible, she was usually right. "I mean, I'm surprised setting a table on fire didn't get you kicked out, but you're probably on thin ice, so—"

"She's right. It stinks, but I think we ought to get going." Izzy agreed. "Are you coming home this weekend?"

"Yeah, I think so. Unless something else happens. You're the clairvoyant, so maybe you'd know before I do." I couldn't believe I was this unsure of myself, punting a decision this simple at my best friend's extrahuman ability.

"It's in the cards, yeah." Izzy chuckled. "And I foresee Dylan coming out with us for a little while, too. And from what you tell me, I'd like to meet Hal Hawkins, the space magus. Seems like a good guy to know."

"I'll ask." I shrugged. Hearing their voices made it easy to forget they couldn't see me. "Dylan will come out unless he has to work. And Hal, probably. But I can't say for sure until I ask."

"Cool," Cadence said.

"Hey, you guys, thanks." I closed my eyes, the weight of the day's events falling on me as I prepared to end my lifeline call. "I really appreciate you listening to me tonight."

"I'd say any time, but that horrible rule means you have to be careful." I heard the rustle of fabric on Cadence's end. "I'm gonna give you the biggest hug in the world next time I see you."

"Better make that a group hug," Izzy added.

"Thanks again. You're both awesome, talk to you later."

I took my hand off the glass, watching the light inside it fade as the call ended. The entire room felt darker, like it had closed in on me. As I zipped the suitcase shut around my only connection to the world outside Hawthorn Academy, tears rolled down my face. I barely had the presence of mind to tuck the case back under my bed. After that, I flopped back, displacing Ember. As she fluttered to perch on the headboard, I flung my arm across my puffy eyes.

"I wish I was anywhere but here."

I didn't know what I was expecting, but it wasn't my roommate walking in the door as if in response to my statement of misery. I felt my cheeks heat up and immediately took three calming breaths. The last thing I wanted was an embarrassment-induced firestorm right here in my room.

"I'd say that your wish is my command, but I'm no Djinn." Grace held the door open, letting Lune in behind her. "Are you okay?"

"Um." I removed my arm from my face so I could see hers. I expected sympathy at best, pity at worst.

Grace looked like she hadn't slept in days. Lune was even limping, and she had carried him half the day. I sat up immediately.

"That's a question I could also ask you."

"Aren't we like two peas in a pod, then?" She yawned, slurring some of her words.

"Maybe." I shrugged. "But you didn't almost burn down the cafeteria."

"No." Grace rubbed her eyes. When she took her hands away, they looked dull. "It would have been worse than that if I'd lost it."

Grace didn't sit on her bed so much as drop like a sack of potatoes. She pushed her shoes off with her feet, leaving them where they landed. After that, she turned her head toward the dresser, gazing as though it was leagues away.

"Do you want to talk about it?" I tilted my head to one side, trying to figure out if I should call Nurse Smith.

"Not really." Her head bowed like an invisible hand had pushed it down. "Just need darkness. And probably sleep."

"Okay, then. I was about to turn in. Just want to brush my teeth and put on pajamas." I stood. "Can I get you anything?"

"Dunno. Just do your thing. I guess."

I shuffled toward the dresser to grab some clothes, along with my bathroom bag. This was one of the items on the school list, to make using the dormitory restrooms more convenient. I hadn't been in one yet, but Noah had told me plenty over the summer.

"Come on, Ember. I'll be back," I said as I pushed open the door, which wasn't locked from inside. Her lack of response made me pause, staring at the palm-sized rectangle beside the door. "Do you want the lights off?"

"Yeah."

Ember glided toward me and sailed through the door.

I pressed my hand against that smooth surface on the wall and the solar globes went dark. I stepped into the warmly lit hallway and shut the door behind me, leaving my roommate in darkness, probably for the first time today. My familiar landed on my shoulder. Shuffling across the hall to the bathroom gave me a few moments alone with some new thoughts.

Grace hadn't told me what element of magic she has. Based on her bond with Lune the moon hare and her need for darkness, she had to be an umbral magus, but without the affinity that makes some of them totally forgettable. This place was brightly lit all the time with solar magic, and her energy's opposite. Maybe that was the cause of her extreme exhaustion.

Ember fluttered to a perch carved into the row of sinks, clearly there just so flying familiars would have a place to sit. While brushing my teeth, I began to wonder whether we'd both been cursed somehow, or perhaps unwittingly angered a luck-wielding Tanuki. This many unlucky events all at the same time felt like more than coincidence.

Extrahumans don't believe in fate. Magic is more complicated than it seems, and it's got patterns. Over millennia of recorded history, we've discovered that those can be tracked, and we called it coincidence. When the pattern has a net positive outcome, we call it good and try to repeat events, reinforcing the cycle. But when it's net negative, everything's on hard mode.

Maybe I could look for a pattern, something that would help me find a workaround.

After putting my toothbrush away, I washed my face, then headed to the back of the restroom. Ember followed, swooping behind me. Across from the sinks were toilets, of course, making this section look like a hall with plumbing. But past those, the room opened up. Space wasn't a problem here at Hawthorn Academy, so, of course, the bathing and changing areas were luxurious.

The layout was like a Roman bath, with a section for changing and tubs of three different temperatures, plus a steam room and a sauna. Most students wore bathing suits in the tubs because they're communal.

Plain old showers stood across from the changing section, which had curtained cubbies for privacy. I shouldn't have said plain or old. The showers were great, with three heads per stall and beautiful tiles that changed color with water temperature.

I ignored all that, stepping into a cubby with all my stuff. The wall had several hooks plus another perch for flying familiars. There was even a mat under the bench in there for the earthbound variety. Changing into my comfy pajamas and cozy socks was my only goal, so I did that quickly. I'd shower in the morning. Just as I sat on the bench and pulled on one striped fluffy sock, I heard a rustle of fabric followed by a sob. The sound pinned me down.

Who besides me would have come in here to have a cry at this hour?

CHAPTER SIXTEEN

The curtained cubby hid me from whoever was there. I realized this entire situation could turn into another disaster if I reacted without thinking. The girl out there didn't need that so I kept quiet, hoping Ember would do the same.

But of course, she didn't.

If there was one consistent thing about my familiar, it was that she loved rushing in. I reached up, trying to coax her on to my lap so she'd sit nicely instead of flying out there.

Because of our bond, I knew that was what she wanted to do.

On most days, that'd also be my choice. Today, nothing I decided to do went right. I waved, flapped my arms, and made silly faces, but Ember didn't pay attention. She craned her neck, turning one side toward the curtain. I watched her haunches bunch as she prepared to take off.

A moment later, she froze because Faith's Sha Seth whined nearby.

Finally, Ember noticed me and saw something in my posture that undid the tension in hers. The dragonet glided down to my lap, where she let me cradle her in my arms. Arcing her neck up so her mouth was beside my ear, she breathed two times, in and out.

"Peep?" she whispered.

I couldn't respond without being overheard, so I just patted her back, then scratched the ridge between her wings. She trembled, though whether in fear of the Sha or the desire to check on his partner was a mystery to me.

Usually, it was the other way around. Sha feared fire dragonets because fire is the opposite of unliving magic. In ancient lore, the doglike creatures used to seek out desecrated graves, guiding magi with that energy to right the wrongs done to final resting places. During wars between ancient peoples, some undeath magi used their powers to raise dead soldiers right on the battlefield. It was fire magi like me who fought back.

I'd read theories that the soldiers inside the Trojan Horse were in fact the risen thralls of an undeath magus. I'd also read that the very first magus with this power created vampires, but that was widely believed to be pure fabrication.

However, practitioners like Faith were compatible with vampires —not in a romantic way, although that was possible. From what I remembered reading on the subject, even a low-powered undeath magus could draw enough energy from nearby vamps to strengthen their powers exponentially. With a powerful enough undeath magus around, a vampire could go without feeding for months.

No wonder the older Fairbanks girl ostracized her sister. With the right help, Faith could overpower Charity with her hands tied behind her back. A Sha familiar certainly helped with that. Given the bigoted sentiments I'd heard earlier, sibling rivalry could lead down dark paths in the Fairbanks family.

And there I was, getting caught in the middle. Charity probably wanted me constantly on edge, about to fly off the handle because my mere presence in that state would scare her sister into keeping her head down.

My eyes, already sore from crying so much that day, burned again with impending tears.

It wasn't just me and Faith being pushed toward an inevitable conflict. The environment throughout the entire school made Grace sick. Dylan and Logan didn't have familiars but were both enrolled to work with them. Hal was so worried about being here, he had read everyone's entrance essays over the summer. I had no idea what was up with the students in my year who I hadn't met yet.

Why was everything so hard for the new students here? Decks stacked against us on our first day?

As I sat rocking back and forth with Ember, the tears finally came, silently. She hummed softly in my ear, a musical yet mournful sound. It reminded me of recordings I'd heard of dragon-shifter mourning days, the keening they did for hours after one of them died. Maybe in a sense, some part of each of us had gone away. If only the feeling of loss would "move on."

"No, you move." Faith sniffled on the other side of the curtain. "This is my bathroom."

"Oh, no." I held Ember protectively, crossing my arms over her. "That's not what I meant at all. And I'm only putting on pajamas. After that, I'm going to bed."

Seth whined again, much closer this time. I saw his muzzle bump the curtain's hem, pressing it in so it looked like a ghostly doggie nose.

"Well, okay then." Faith's voice came from my left now, meaning she was in the cubby next door. Seth whined louder and longer this time, almost a faint howl. The poor thing sounded almost as miserable as I felt.

Ember craned her head down at Seth's curtain-draped nose, then whispered, still trembling slightly, in my ear.

"Peep." She looked me in the eye, then moved her gaze to my arms and back again. She wanted me to put her down, but I didn't want her getting in a fight with a Sha. I'd have to trust her to do the right thing and avoid a fight.

"Are you sure?"

Ember nodded.

"Okay, then."

I bent at the waist, lowering my arms. And just like that, I let her go.

"Peep?" Ember's voice was louder. In response, Seth's whine took an inquisitive turn.

I hurried up and pulled my other sock on because the last thing two miserable teenagers away from home needed was injured familiars. I stood, turning as fast as I could to sling my bathroom bag over my arm, prepared to scoop Ember up and hustle her out of there. But when I turned back around, she wasn't in the cubby anymore. Pulling back the curtain, I saw the most amazing thing.

My dragonet and Faith's Sha sat quietly together, making small noises and looking for all the world like they were having a chat. Not a cozy one—it was too intense for that. But the sense I got was that they were commiserating.

"Are you seeing what I'm seeing, Morgenstern?"

I turned my head left to find Faith in a near copy of my stance, holding back the curtain in the doorway of her cubby. We stood there, blinking at each other.

"Yeah. Two magi so stressed out that our familiars, who are natural enemies, have to vent to each other."

"I didn't think the first day would be this bad." Faith leaned against the tiled entrance on her cubby. "My sister's a total bitch. What's worse, I think it runs in the family."

"Same here." I sighed. "Except mine's an asshole brother. And ditto on the family thing."

"This doesn't mean we're friends."

"That's not world-ending for me or anything."

"Whatever." She crossed her arms, sniffling again.

"Look, if they can get along, can we maybe have a truce?" I gazed at the unlikely pair of critters as Ember patted Seth's head with the thumb claw on her wing and he headbutted her chest. I know Faith saw that too. "For their sake?"

"Also because our siblings are out to get us, but yeah." Her glare softened as she gazed at her familiar. "For their sake."

"Deal." I stepped out, crossing the tile floor. "Come on, Ember. Let's go to bed and finally end this day."

"Peep!"

She gave Seth one last pat, then sprang up from the floor, heading straight for my shoulder. As I reached the sink and toilet section, the Sha let out a single short bark. It didn't quite cover Faith's voice.

"Thanks."

I didn't look back. Maybe that made me a bad person, but I was about to cry again and wanted to hide it. I echoed the word of gratitude back at her, then opened the door to cross the hall.

When I entered my room, the light tried to come on. Grace's breathing was even and deep enough to tell me she was probably sleeping. But Lune's rear leg moved, thumping near the foot of the bed.

I shut the lights down before they turned all the way up. A fire magus like me will never have trouble getting around in the dark. I called a flame to my hand and used it to light my way.

That one familiar act reminded me that I needed to get a grip as soon as possible. The school wasn't a powder keg, but it was the next best thing. If I ended up igniting it because I'd never bothered to learn temperance and tolerance, I'd be no better than my evil Uncle Richard.

Ember settled in the space between my pillow and the wall. Once she curled up, I extinguished the flame and got into bed. After pushing my feet between the sheets, I turned my back to Grace. I bundled the blanket over the top and back of my head and stared into the dark.

I had no idea how to improve things.

But I could start trying the next day.

CHAPTER SEVENTEEN

Mondays sucked.

The worst thing about them was how, no matter how much purpose and hope I wanted to start the week with, everybody else was going through the motions. Students in the cafeteria milled about, listing from side to side like extras in a zombie movie. We bridged the gap between the end of elementary in sixth grade to prep schools with middle school, which went from seventh through tenth. Magic academies went to thirteenth grade, while Mundanes only did twelve. At any rate, everyone had shuffled through breakfast back then, too.

The morning shamble was universal, probably.

"Peep." From her perch on my shoulder, Ember pointed with one wing at the cereal station.

Rows of containers sat on the counter against the wall, and just looking at them had my stomach growling like a pack of angry were-wolves. Somehow, I had forgotten to eat dinner last night. This was why, when the person ahead of me finished shoveling raisin bran into her bowl, I went hog-wild.

If I'd already gotten a reputation as the class weirdo, I'd better have fun with it.

"Ember, go!" I pointed a finger straight ahead, then set my tray down.

"PEEP!" The little dragonet had a big voice when she wanted to use it.

She also had an enormous sense of adventure, which was one reason my little stunt worked beautifully. A mashup of gasps and other expressions of surprise sounded from various points behind me.

Ember pulled off her stunt, a series of divebomb attacks on the most important meal of the day. She got me one scoop from each cereal container, using both feet, deposited them into bowls on my tray, then headed back for more.

I planned ahead for this by covering my tray with as many bowls as it could hold, which was five, incidentally. I didn't care that the cereals got mixed. In fact, that was part of the idea. Some people were corn puff purists. Me, not so much.

Corn, rice, wheat, and oat bits rained down like manna from heaven—if heaven produced cold cereal, that was. I grinned, chuckling softly to myself. Ember had a blast, as well as getting some early morning exercise, but she was clearly done with that by the time the bowls were full.

"Peep." Ember settled back down on my shoulder, stretching out across them so her feet fell to my right and her neck was on my left collarbone. I happily let her rest there; she'd earned it.

"I know, right?" With a wide grin, I picked up my tray and headed for the beverage section to get some kind of non-dairy milk.

On the way, I saw Elanor wagging a finger at her brother Logan.

"You'd better figure it out fast. Mom and Dad are gonna be pissed as hell, and I'm not covering for you anymore."

"Yeah, okay." Logan stared down at the floor.

That made it impossible to catch his eye to see if he needed a rescue, so I continued on my way to the counter with all the drinks and saw another familiar and much friendlier face.

"That was, er, something." Dylan was there, but not for breakfast. He was restocking the coffee urns from a rolling cart, swapping out full insulated containers for the empties. "Are you really going to eat all that?"

'Why not?" I set my tray down and lifted a bowl, holding it under the oat milk dispenser and letting it rip.

"Because it looks good." He reached one hand toward my unconventional breakfast feast. "And I'm a hardworking growing boy, you know."

"Bad magus!" I swatted his hand away. "No biscuit!"

We laughed together. There, so close to the scene of yesterday's drama, that felt like a righteous protest.

"Mondays don't get you two down, apparently." Hal stood nearby, empty glass in hand as he held it up to the juice dispenser. He clicked it off halfway through filling it with orange juice, then moved it to the cranberry. "It's inspiring."

"Thanks, my dude." Dylan smiled.

"When do you get to have a bite?" I waved a hand vaguely at the various food stations.

"After I bring the empties back to Kayley." Dylan heaved the last two full urns off the cart and set them beside the others. "Professors need their coffee because I don't want to risk them dropping letter grades."

"Okay, well, you can sit with us when you get back, then." Hal smiled.

"Awesome. See you in a few shakes." Dylan put the empties on the cart, then pushed it toward the exit.

"Us?" I blinked. "Figured I'd be alone after yesterday."

"No way." Hal set his two-toned juice on his tray, picked it up, and beckoned. "Hawkins family honor code says nobody has to sit alone."

"Oh."

I followed him, passing the roped-off table that still had scorch marks. I shouldn't have looked at it, but it was as compelling as that time a tour bus fell on its side down by the wharf. Disasters were magnets for attention, so, I wasn't surprised when heads turned. My presence might have that effect for a while.

Everybody stared. Even the familiars spared me a glance. I refused to look away, keeping my head up and my eyes open. I owed it to myself to just keep going. Even the biggest disasters were recoverable to some degree with time and effort. If I gave in, I'd be a hot mess for the next three years.

Hal led us to a booth and sat on the outside of the bench. I saw this for the strategic move it was. He knew that random people, whatever their intentions, couldn't sit next to us unless we allowed it. I followed his lead and took a seat on the opposite side.

After I took about twenty bites of cereal, I looked up to find Hal playing with his food. Half his juice was gone, so at least he'd gotten some fuel for the morning. Before speaking, I washed down a mouthful of crunchy goodness with water.

"Aren't you going to eat?"

"Dunno. I'm not that hungry to tell you the truth." Nin poked her sleek head out of Hal's sleeve and deftly snatched a sausage off his plate. Instead of wolfing it down, the Pharaoh's Rat held it up in one paw and pointed it toward her friend's mouth. "Well, I guess my familiar disagrees."

He smiled, cooing at her and patting her head. Then he took a bite of the sausage but passed the rest to his familiar. It occurred to me that in this battle against my reputation and the strictures of magus society, Hal Hawkins was a good ally.

"Do you know what we're supposed to do in there on the first day?" I gestured with my spoon toward the doorway. "In Luciano's homeroom, I mean?"

"Not really." Hal shrugged. "I don't read the curriculum, just watch and listen."

"You don't read, huh?" Grace stood at the side of the table, bearing a plate piled high with home-fried potatoes and a side of ketchup. A smaller plate with something green lurked beside it. "Could've fooled me yesterday."

I moved over to let her sit. As she settled in beside me, Grace left extra space at the end of the bench, patted it, and helped Lune hop up beside her. Picking up her fork, my roommate stabbed some potatoes, then shook her head and set it down. She reached out and picked up the side plate full of carrot tops, leafy green strands trailing off its edges.

"There you go, Lune." She set it down in front of him, then picked up her fork again to dip the home fries in ketchup. "Are you two going to be okay in Luciano's class?"

"Well, at least we're not going it alone." I shrugged, taking another bite of cereal.

"Yeah, but you can't copy off me." Hal chuckled. "You aren't alone either, Grace." Hal waved his nearly unused fork. "Hey, Dylan!"

He slid over to make room for our friend. Dylan had four paper-wrapped packages, which he dropped on the table before sitting. Unwrapping the first, he took a quick bite and chewed, leaning back and closing his eyes like this was the best food in the world.

"I guess I wasn't the only one who was starving this morning." I peered at my five bowls. A few stray oat rings and flakes of bran floated at the edge. My stomach audibly growled.

"Maybe you should go and get more?" Grace lifted her tray, displaying her now-empty plate. "That's what I'm gonna do, anyway."

"In a sec." I began pouring dregs of oat milk from four of the bowls into the fifth. After that, I picked it up and chugged.

"Where do you two put it, honestly?" Hal blinked at our empties. His plate of sausage and cantaloupe was still almost totally intact.

"Oh, yeah, I got a hollow leg." Grace quipped, then moved Lune's now-empty plate back up to her tray as he hopped down to the floor. She got up, grabbing it and moving aside to let me by. "Should have written that in my essay and then you'd have known, yeah?"

"Um." I set my bowl down, exchanged it for a napkin, and dabbed my lips. "Growth spurt this summer."

"Peep!" Ember held her head up, swung it in front of mine, and nodded. She swayed slightly as I stood to move out of the booth.

"Are you sure you're not part-giant?" Hal slouched on the bench, craning his neck up at me.

"Not sure about that kind of thing, really." I stared down into the five empty bowls, reminded of that tarot card Izzy sometimes pulled for me. The Five of Cups, about loss and leaving things behind. "Mom left an awful lot out."

"Oh, crap." Hal sat up, peering past me at something on the other side of the room. "Sorry, didn't mean anything by it."

"Okay." His joke had attracted some unwanted attention, and I was all too glad the excuse of second helpings let me make an escape.

Grace was shorter than me but managed to be faster on our way to drop the empty plates and trays at the dish window. The middle-aged woman who took them nodded. Grace looked her straight in the eye and said thanks, which I echoed.

"Could have been me," she said. "Still might if I don't keep my wits about me here."

"How do you mean?"

We headed toward the pastry and toast counter, where Grace put two slices of bread in the toaster and turned the dial to eleven. I snagged a plate and added a trio of banana-apple mini muffins. There was also apricot rugelach, my favorite, so of course, I took five.

"If Lune hadn't found me at such a young age, I'd be doing a job like that instead of studying here." She snagged a butter knife and stood there, brandishing it at the toaster while she waited. "It's important to count blessings."

"Sounds like something my friend Izzy would say."

"You've got a good friend, then."

"Yeah, known her since kindergarten."

"Is that grade one here?" Grace gathered a heap of jam packets, setting them on the tray beside her plate. "Your schools are different from ours, right?"

"That's the year before what we call first grade."

"Peep?" Ember wasn't trying to agree. When I checked, she was looking down at Lune, who stamped the floor.

"Okay." She wrinkled her nose, then popped the toast early, wincing as she put it on the plate with her bare hands. "I think we need to go back to the table."

We hurried, Grace taking three steps to each of my strides. We must have looked silly, like some scene out of Tolkein with the height difference. But when I came around the corner, all trace of humor faded. Charity stood at our table, flanked by the mean twins. Her cat perched on the edge next to Dylan, whose mouth was full of egg and cheese sandwich. The sandy feline hissed at Nin, who was trying to hide in Hal's blazer.

"Better teleport that deformed rat before it's cat food." Charity sneered.

Hal couldn't. He'd had trouble teleporting fruit the day before. If someone didn't act, Nin could end up in the infirmary or worse.

Fortunately, Bubbe had taught me how to deescalate magical critter confrontations, and my reputation ought to do the trick on Charity too. If I played things right, she might leave us alone for good. At least, that was my plan. But first, I set my tray down on the table.

"Hey!" I put my hands on my hips, standing as tall as I possibly could.

"Oh, look," Charity drawled. "It's the wannabe evil overlord's favorite niece."

Hailey and Bailey tittered, the matching pigeons on their shoulders cooing in counterpoint.

"Yeah." I narrowed my eyes and flared my nostrils, leaning on their expectations to stop them from noticing the tremor in my voice. "Get away from my table. Or else."

"What? You'll burn this one, too? With your little dingleberry stuck in the corner there?" She jerked her thumb at Hal, more than once. After that, Charity tilted her head, dropping a wink at Dylan. "You're too good-looking to get stuck associating with these people, so I'll let you leave if you go quickly."

Dylan's mouth was almost comically full, and he was probably too shocked to swallow half-chewed food. But he shook his head and sat up straight, setting down the remains of his sandwich and placing his hands palm-down on the table.

"Suit yourself, then." Charity put one hand on her hip, leaning into it, and held out another. "Your fire's nothing against my earth magic, little Miss Moldyvort."

I refused to stoop to her level, and I refused to prove her right about my heritage, either. Bubbe had said that kindness is the most powerful magic in the world. I wouldn't become a bully to overcome her. What was it Mom always said?

Justice takes time. Anything instant was only vengeance.

"Ember, go!" I shrugged, concentrating hard on what I wanted my familiar to do. She got the message immediately.

On gilded wings, she swooped down, snagging the sand cat by the scruff, making the swipe she was taking at Nin fall short. Flapping like she was trying to set a record, my dragonet lifted the sputtering feline off the table, high enough to brush against the chandelier.

"How dare you?" Charity growled. "Make that beast put him down this instant!"

"Leave us alone, then." My hands stayed firmly on my hips as they curled into fists. It was the only way to stop myself from flying off the handle again with my magic.

"I do as I please." She smirked. "But if your familiar can't control herself, she'll be put into confinement."

I had nothing to say to that. There was no way I could prove Ember didn't act on her own. Nobody would take my word for it after yesterday, either. Charity was way more experienced at confrontations like this. I shouldn't have tried to out-thinking her. That was why I had no choice.

"Ember, down."

My dragonet flapped, circling until the airsick feline had all four paws on the hardwood floor. At least Ember managed to let the cat go a safe distance away from Hal and Nin.

"You must be such a badass, messing with a bunch of first-year students." Grace stepped up next to me, rolling her eyes. "I mean, really? Don't you seniors have tons of homework plus college entrance exams to worry about?"

"Ugh, the rabbit speaks. Let's go, girls. Leave the future crime-lady and her thug minions alone for now." Charity slapped her hand against the table, letting out a small shower of fine sand. It landed all over our trays and plates, ruining every last morsel of food there, even though it was barely detectible to anyone who didn't see it fall. "This isn't over. I'll make sure everybody here sees your true colors if it's the last thing I do."

With that parting shot, she stalked off, the twins flanking her.

"Well." Dylan finally swallowed the food in his mouth. "This has been a strange repast. But we'll have to hurry to class, or we won't make it in time."

"Yeah." Grace nodded.

"The sand will ruin the dishwashers back there." Hal narrowed his eyes, cheeks going a darker shade. He picked his plate up, dumping its sandy contents on the tray. After that, he repeated the process with the rest of the dishes, stacking them. "Put it all together."

I start helping, getting all of the sand-coated food on the now empty tray. In moments, it was all in a single heap.

"Here goes nothing." Hal put his hands on the pile and stared at it, his brow furrowing. Nin draped herself over his shoulders, letting out a high-pitched trill that gave me the impression she was helping.

Sweat beaded on his temples, forehead, and upper lip. Nin's tail stuck straight up, trembling. The dirt started fading, going pale. Once it was gone, Hal leaned back, gasping like a fish out of water.

None of us knew what to do.

"Oh, shit!" The voice behind me was the last one I expected. "What happened here?"

"Get lost, Faith." Grace rounded on her. "This is your fault."

"No," Hal managed. He couldn't say more, but I understood what he was doing.

Because I was living it.

"Don't blame Faith for something her relative did." I turned to look at the other girl.

Faith's face was pale, one hand pressed against her breastbone and the other outstretched. She only had eyes for Hal. Seth the Sha sat at her feet, looking in the same direction, whining pitifully.

"Get him to the nurse." Dylan got up, moving aside to give Hal room.

"To me?" There was Nurse Smith, striding over.

We all got out of the way, letting the medical professional handle this. He took Hal's vitals, a regular enough course of action, but after that, he got the dreaded emo-detection flask out of his pocket and set it on the table.

"Now tell me," Nurse Smith glanced at me. "Whose fault is this?"

"Mine." Hal shivered like it was below freezing in there.

The water stayed flat. I already knew what that meant.

"Bullshit." Faith leaned over the table, putting her hands on it as though she didn't dare touch Hal but wanted to show support. "We all know who's responsible for this."

"From what I see here, he's being honest." The nurse stowed his flask back in his pocket. "But Hal's coming with me. I refuse to let him go without a full checkup after overextending himself that much."

A bell chimed, signaling five minutes before class started.

"Totally unfair." Faith crossed her arms. "He'll miss his first homeroom."

"Said it was my fault." Hal let Nurse Smith help him off the bench. "Gotta go."

We all watched as they left the cafeteria.

Without another word, we exited, turning toward the hall leading to our first day of classes.

CHAPTER EIGHTEEN

Professor Luciano took attendance. When he got to Hal's name, he looked up and around the room, searching.

"Ah, yes, I remember." He cleared his throat. "Mr. Hawkins is in the infirmary. I've been informed, thanks to Ms. Fairbanks. Moving on."

The first thing he did was give us a pop quiz—ten questions, simple. The only one in the room who seemed to have any trouble with it was Logan. He took the entire ten minutes to finish, occasionally scratching his head and punctuating his many erasures with a series of hems and haws. But he managed to get through it, flipping the paper over and dropping the pencil like comedians drop mics.

When the professor collected the quizzes, he shuffled through them as he walked around the desks. A series of numbers appeared on the board as he checked them over, displaying each of our scores without names to match.

Nobody failed. One person got a perfect score. I was unsure who, but I knew it wasn't me. Another one barely passed, by one correct answer. Judging from my memory of the questions, I was among the nine out of tens.

A lecture on ancient magus society followed, one more interesting than I'd expected. The beginning wasn't about magical creatures, so there was plenty I hadn't heard before. I took notes like almost everybody else. Once again, this was an area Logan seemed deficient in. He listened, head cocked like the RCA dog. He either hadn't heard of taking notes or forgot something to write on. I tore a sheet of paper from my notebook and offered it to him.

"Oh, no, thanks." Logan leaned away from me, not much but enough. Either he bought what the mean girls said, or he had OCD and ripped-out spiral pages freaked him out.

"Are you sure?"

"Ms. Morgenstern, while I appreciate your efforts to assist your classmate, it's unnecessary." Professor Luciano stood in the center of the class, which put him right in line with my desk.

"Taking notes is important, though, and I don't want Logan to—"

"Trust me, he'll get the information he needs." Professor Luciano waved a hand dismissively. "Now, as I was saying, when magi from Rome invaded the British Isles, they discovered an entirely different style of magic being practiced there."

I didn't have to listen to this part of the lecture because I knew it already inside and out. The Pictish people living in what would eventually become the United Kingdom had practiced a form of familiar magic similar to what Hawthorn Academy taught to this day. Being a legacy student was good for something unexpected. I began doodling on the paper absentmindedly.

As I glanced out the window, I noticed that Logan's head was down, his face red. Somehow, I had embarrassed him, but I wasn't sure why or how.

I should've understood from the beginning because my mother dealt with this sort of thing all the time in her job. He had magicpsychic accommodations to help him with lectures, and he probably wanted to keep it a secret.

It was bad enough having people bully me with the whole evil magus angle. Poor Logan had to be just as self-conscious about his unconventional learning style as I was about the Hopewell side of my family.

Professor Luciano moved on in his lecture to a less familiar subject. I took more notes, finally noticing what I'd been drawing earlier.

It was an apple tree, with all the windfalls littering the ground nearby. In defiance, I paused for a moment to draw one more, this time almost all the way at the edge of the paper. "Take that, genetics."

"Is there something you'd like to share with the class, Miss Morgenstern?"

"Um." I peered at the last words I'd jotted on the paper, scrambling for a relevant answer. "I was just wondering what ancient magi thought about genetics. There were so many restrictions back then, more than now, it feels like. I wonder whether people our age had more trouble in that regard than we do today."

"That is an interesting topic, Miss Morgenstern, but a bit digressive." Professor Luciano leaned against his desk and continued, "You'll hear more about extrahuman genetics next year in Health. For now, suffice it to say that the complex social structures of the faerie courts and the coincidental records of magi often prevented paramours from marrying whom they chose. Such remains the case in dragon-shifter families to this day."

He continued to detail how, in magus society, the more things had changed before the Great Reveal, the more things stayed the same. His lecture took us around the world, the magical chalkboards illustrating places and faces to go with the subjects he discussed.

As I wrote my notes, I found myself wishing I could copy all of the chalk illustrations from the lecture as well. The visual references would come in handy while studying, besides being beautiful.

As he ended his lecture, I raised my hand to ask Professor Luciano about getting a copy of the drawings. Faith did the same thing. He ignored both of us but still managed to answer my unspoken question.

"All illustrations are in the books under your seats. You may take these anywhere on campus, but if they leave school grounds, everything in them will be wiped clean." The professor pulled a book from the top of his desk and held it up for us to see.

"This is a copy here." He put it back down. "Incidentally, I have one of these for Mr. Hawkins. If he hasn't returned in time for lab, I will pass this and his notes along to Professor DeBeer, and Mr. Young will bring it to him in the room they share. Homeroom dismissed. Proceed next to Creatives, which you share with the other class."

The sound of paper rustling and bags opening echoed through the room. I stretched in my seat, holding both hands overhead before bringing them down. Ember fluttered off my shoulder, perched on the desk, and mimicked me.

"Um, Aliyah?" Logan stood beside my desk, shuffling his feet and looking at Ember instead of me.

"Logan, I'm sorry. About earlier."

"Oh, that? That's got nothing to do with this." He glanced from side to side. "It's just, can I walk with you to Creatives? I've got a problem."

"I'm happy to help with whatever might be bothering you, Logan." I got up and slung my bag over my shoulder. "Come on, Ember."

The dragonet finished her stretching and took a spin around Logan's head before landing on my shoulder.

"Peep?" Her nostrils flared, and her tongue flickered in and out of her mouth like a snake's. I knew that behavior meant she found something interesting about Logan, but I had no idea what. All the same, I sensed her curiosity.

We headed out of the room together, taking a right to get to the Creatives room. I noticed Faith following Dylan and Grace, who had just exited Professor DeBeer's class. She jogged to catch up with them. There was only one reason I could think of they'd have to leave the academic wing on such a short break.

To visit the infirmary. But I already promised to help Logan. I settled for hollering after them, "Tell Hal I said hi!"

When Dylan turned his head to look back, Faith elbowed him in the ribs and walked faster. Grace caught my eye and shrugged. I shook my head, then nodded at Logan. I'd have to see how Hal was doing later on my own.

"I hope he's back soon." Logan's voice sounded strained. "Hal's nice."

"Oh, me too." I shook my head, sighing. "You probably didn't notice what happened at breakfast."

"All I know is, I saw Charity headed your way, and then Elanor said we should get lost."

"Yeah, it's a good thing you did." I adjusted the strap on my bag. "So, what did you need help with?"

I let him take his time, even slowing down as he decreased our pace to almost a shamble. Whatever was eating Logan, it had to be embarrassing. Finally, he spoke up.

"It's my familiar, Aliyah." He held one of his hands in the other, picking at the cuticle around his thumbnail. Judging by the state it was in, this was a frequent nervous habit.

"Okay." I couldn't think of anything else to say that wouldn't scare Logan out of talking. I felt like I needed to walk on eggshells, but instead of letting it drive me crazy, I just rolled with the distractions.

"So, when I came up here with Elanor last week, we stayed at the Hawthorne Hotel with our folks." His voice was higher-pitched than usual—thready, like it'd snap any second. He picked faster at his thumb, and I worried he'd draw blood.

"Go on."

"Well, I had a familiar with me, the one my parents wanted me to bring to school, and while we were leaving the room one day—"

The bell rang, interrupting him before I could ask a stupid question, which was a good thing, considering I was about to go on a major tangent. How in the world could anyone possibly let their parents pick their familiar? Did all the Pierces think that was a good idea?

And then I remembered—Logan's family was in the business of flashy performing magical creatures. The roundabout explanation of his problem made a warped sort of sense. I should have known. He didn't get along with whatever critter his parents chose.

"Anyway, I was saying," Logan let out a nervous chuckle, "Little guy got out somehow, and I haven't seen him since. He's totally AWOL, and I've got no idea what to do."

"Maybe talking to Headmaster Hawkins would be a good idea."

"Well, that's the thing." He tugged at the skin around his thumb again. "Ow. Um, he'd tell my parents, and they don't know. Elanor doesn't even get how bad it is. She thinks I lost him here on campus. This is such a mess, and I don't know what to do, and your grandmother—"

"Say no more. I'm almost completely sure she can help." I nodded, looking up at him. His eyes were wide, rimmed with red like he'd been about to cry right here in the hall. I looked away. "But I don't get to talk to Bubbe until Friday. Do you think you can hold on until then?"

"I'll try, but yeah, I think so. It helps that Dylan doesn't have a familiar either, so he sort of tanks that aggro for me if you get what I mean." Logan tugged the collar of his expensive distressed t-shirt. "Ugh, my geek's showing."

"That's okay." I put on my best imitation of Captain America. "I get that reference."

Logan made a noise somewhere between a laugh and a sob. Something about Logan Pierce made me nervous, even though he was nowhere near perfect because looks aren't everything. It was like his own anxiety extended around him. All I wanted to do was help him get through it.

Helping someone was fine. I wasn't sure I wanted to date Logan, even though our siblings had tried to push us together before we'd even met, which didn't sit well with me. Neither did the knowledge that his family might be exploiting magical creatures instead of befriending them.

But befriending was what happened there between us, which was nice but not exactly productive. We both forgot a detail so important I couldn't help him without it. We were also almost at the door for Creatives and out of time for this chat.

"Logan?"

"Yeah?"

"What kind of creature is he?" I refused to speak about his runaway critter in the past tense. "Your missing familiar?"

"Oh, yeah." He smacked his hand against his forehead. "He's a dragonet, sort of like yours but different."

"Okay. Well, what does he look like?"

"I'm not completely sure."

I stopped in the middle of the hall because the idea was so shocking. I couldn't imagine forgetting what Ember looks like, or even Lotan, and that's my brother's familiar, for crying out loud.

"I mean, I can't describe him with words." He hung his head. "Not so good with that."

Logan got accommodations in class for a reason. What would Mom do?

"Maybe you can draw or paint him?"

"Okay, yeah." Logan's face actually lit up. "I love painting, but it does take a while when it's not on a computer."

"You're an artist?" I caught up with him again.

"I wouldn't say that, really." He pulled the classroom door open. "I'm not supposed to be one. But when we're all done with rehearsals and teaching the critters their tricks, it's what I do with my free time."

"Cool!" I smiled. "It's nice to have a hobby like that. I can barely draw a circle."

"It just takes practice." He shrugged. "And you seem smart. I bet you could learn anything. Anyway, thanks for helping me. Thanks for the idea about painting him, too. Never would have thought of that."

We headed inside the Creatives classroom. There were desks like in Homeroom, but also easels with stools. A handful of larger tables stood to one side, some coated in clay and others with precise lines for cutting paper or fabric.

The paneling was more wood, of course, in the light color that was used throughout the academic wing, but in here, the carvings were all rectangular. A girl from the other class had opened one of these panels and peered in, the Sphinx cat beside her looking on with his tail curled into a question mark. Supply closets, of course, built right into the walls.

"Wow." Logan clapped his hands. "This is the best place ever!"

I chuckled; I couldn't help it. His joy was infectious, and he might have been right about it being the best place at school so far. I found a cubby to stow my bag, then began walking toward a desk. But I stopped.

"Let's live a little, Ember." I held out one hand. "Pick a spot."

"Peep!"

She fluttered off my shoulder, doing a couple of circles around the massive room. She was so fast it only took a few breaths. Eventually, she landed on one of the clay tables, an odd choice, but I couldn't complain after leaving the decision up to her. Once I got there, I turned around to see that someone followed me.

"Hey." It was a boy from the other class. I remembered him from the mixer—Lee Young.

"Hi there." I sat on one of the stools by the table's side.

"Do you sculpt the clay or throw pottery?"

"Not sure. There's a first time for everything, I guess."

"Ah." Lee grinned. "Come on, Scratch." He patted the table.

A creature straight out of legend leaped up, sitting up as it peered at me, showing off a stretch of velvety white belly fur. It had floppy, folded ears that were pointed like a cat's, except larger. Those ears were as big as a dwarf lop rabbit's. This animal's haunches made it sit more like a squirrel or a rabbit than a cat.

"Wow." I blinked, watching as Scratch wiggled his nose at me. "Is your familiar a Sumxu?"

"That she is." Lee reached out, rubbing her chin. Scratch stretched out on the table, lying on her side. A bushy tail extended behind her, and I saw that the fur on her back had changed color to match the surface beneath her.

"I've never seen one before."

"Most people haven't." He laughed. "They're experts at hiding and native to my part of China."

"Hello, Aliyah." Hal approached the table. He still looked pale, but he wasn't shaky anymore.

"Hal, you okay?"

"Wouldn't be here if I wasn't." His smile was faint but there. "So, I see you met my roommate."

"Yeah. I guess we're all working with clay today." I grinned. "Totally new for me."

"It's fun." Hal's smile broadened. "Nin loves it. Lee's done some of this back home, too, so you can learn from both of us."

"That sounds awesome."

"Why'd you pick this, anyway?" He gestured around the room, where I saw Dylan carrying an armload of paints and Grace sorting through bolts of fabric like they were the most amazing things in the world. Faith had a sketchpad at one of the desks. "You could have gone anywhere."

"I let Ember decide."

"Peep." She'd folded her wings and was playing with Nin, some kind of game where they took turns jumping. Scratch bounced up to join them.

"By the way, when do we start?"

"Anytime." Hal waved at a man at the front of the classroom. He grinned, waving back. "Dad's busy, so he sent in Master Rosso. He's just here to answer questions and show us where stuff is. Otherwise, it's a free period."

"This is great." Lee smiled. "So, let's make something!"

We spent one hundred minutes working with clay, and ten on either side of that span gathering supplies and cleaning them up. All three of our familiars had a blast, and at the end, we each had something to set on the drying rack.

Hal's pot was pretty much perfect, Lee's was a little taller than he'd intended but still symmetrical, while I gave up on the wheel entirely. I figured my time was better spent making a pendant with Ember's paw print in it plus a handful of beads to match. It was fun to sculpt.

As I washed my hands at the sink, Logan headed over with a container of gray water and a set of watercolor pencils. We rinsed together.

"It's not done." He jerked his chin at the painting. "But it will be in a few more days."

At first, I was speechless. The sketch he'd made on the canvas was already impressively engaging. I almost sensed this dragonet's preening personality from what Logan had hashed out of his face. The artist stood there motionless, probably wondering what I thought because his considerable talent had been largely ignored by his family.

"Wow," I managed. "I mean, that is really amazing work, and it'll be done ahead of the weekend."

"Yeah." He set the empty cup on a rack, the pencils alongside it. "Hey, do you remember where we go next?"

"Gym."

He thanked me. Once we all gathered our things, it was time to head out.

Even though I hadn't been very interested in making art before, Creatives was something to look forward to. Being able to think in a different way and doing a hands-on activity helped refresh my mind.

But Gym was a totally different can of worms.

CHAPTER NINETEEN

"Hawkins, you're sitting this out."

"But, Coach!"

"Nurse Smith said there's no negotiation on this. You're sitting, end of story."

Coach Pickman stood in front of Hal, holding a magipsychic device out toward him. Her eyes and face were stern but a little ridiculous on her. She was five foot nothing, with a birdlike physique. Then again, physical appearance has nothing to do with magical power. For all anyone knew, she was the strongest magus on campus. That was Noah's theory, at least.

"Why are you giving me a chronogram?" Hal blinked at the device. Nin peered at it from over his shoulder, prompting the other familiars to have a look from their perches behind him on the bleachers.

"You're timing everyone today. And possibly tomorrow; I'm not sure yet." The coach tapped a sneakered foot, shaking the item she held. "Take it already, kid."

He finally did as she said. Hal might have been smaller and less advanced than the rest of us, but he was stubborn. That was an asset at Hawthorn Academy, from what I'd seen.

We'd need to be tough in this class. Noah had warned me about

Gym. Coach Pickman was a total taskmaster whose pep talks were angry at the corner of degrading—as if the boxy purple tees and yellow shorts we all had to wear weren't embarrassing enough.

"Stand up straight and pay attention, you maggots."

"I beg your pardon!" Faith glared daggers at the coach. Her nostrils flared. Something about being called maggot, in particular, set her off.

"There's no begging in this gym." The coach sneered. "I know your family well, Fairbanks. And if you don't want me to think you're a giant failure at this class just like Charity, you'll shut up, pay attention, and play your heart out."

"Woah, drama." Logan nudged me in the ribs.

"Pierce, shut your yap." She snorted. "I already know you're not a star like your sister."

I kept quiet. Noah had already warned me that I ought to keep my head down in here. Not that Coach Pickman ever made any sick burns about him. My brother got high marks in Gym just by following directions.

"If the peanut gallery is done, we'll finally get started. The name of the game we play here is Bishop's Row, and if you want to go anywhere with it this year, you'll do whatever I say and practice, understand?"

"Yes, Coach Pickman!" I didn't usually shout, but I was well aware that either this or "yes ma'am" was the correct response to one of her ersatz pep talks—or anything she said, for that matter.

"Morgenstern!"

"Yes, Coach Pickman!" I pressed my lips into a flat thin line to keep from laughing in her face as she approached. Remembering that if I wasn't so much taller than her this wouldn't be funny helped with that.

"If you can play half as well as you *comprendo*, you just might be the best student in this class. Everybody runs laps except Hawkins. You time them. When you've done three, report back here."

Running was something I was decent at, at least on flat surfaces like they had in the gym. There was nothing to trip over, no branches, statues, or passersby to tangle my arms or my feet. Just me, the track, and my long legs with their ground-eating strides.

It was tempting to bust out full speed at the beginning and impress everybody, but this gym was enormous—the size of a football field. Doing three laps at a flat sprint was beyond me and probably everyone else here, so I paced myself, which gave me a chance to watch the other runners.

Faith huffed and puffed, clearly annoyed at having to run laps. That was about what I imagined. But Bailey surprised me. She made the mistake I'd avoided, sprinting right out of the gate, but she was faster than I'd expected, possibly because she was an air magus.

I didn't know much about Alex Onassis, except that Professor Luciano had mentioned at attendance that he was a poison magus. He paced himself too, so either he had track experience, or this was all he had. He was tall, about my height, and wiry, so he had athletic potential but wasn't using it just then.

Logan might as well have been on the sloth running team. I couldn't even watch him because he was behind me. I wondered if worrying about his missing familiar was getting him down, or maybe he just had no motivation to excel at sports. Clearly, art was his thing, after all.

I lengthened my stride to picked up speed about a quarter of the way from the beginning of the second lap. I passed Faith with ease, slowly enough that I caught her eye roll. I just nodded and smiled, although I could have made a witty quip about having Faith that she'd finish before Logan if I weren't trying to save my breath.

About halfway through the second lap, I pulled ahead of Bailey. She winced as she ran, a clear sign she had overdone it already. I hadn't expected either twin to be a show-off. Until now, they'd struck me as almost extensions of each other, which was an unkind assessment. Clearly, Bailey cared about this extracurricular activity and being able to have her own thing, which made sense once I thought about it.

I was lucky Noah was a year older and had shared this information with me. The twins must have had trouble expressing their individuality, and I thought I had it rough, trying to figure out who I am. It didn't excuse either of them from backing Charity's cruelty, but at least I understood, kind of.

The only classmate left to beat was Alex. I measured my breathing, making sure I had enough oxygen to avoid cramps and the shakiness that plagued Bailey. After that, I gradually increased my speed.

There was something peaceful about running, even indoors. The feel of wind in my hair, hands and arms slicing through the air like a hot knife through butter, feet in a love-hate relationship with the ground.

It was just me and my body there, doing something simple. No mean girls or family secrets or dining hall disasters. I was in a zone, and it was the best I'd felt since getting here.

I stared down the track, the space ahead of Alex my ultimate goal. I was two-thirds of the way through the last lap, then three-fourths. That was when I knew I'd make it. I blew past my last classmate with feet to spare.

I was barely winded when Hal clicked the chronogram. Alex pulled up beside me, one sneaker dragging to squeak against the track. He leaned forward, placing his hands on his knees, then looked up at my face.

"Said you'd be the one to beat." He paused to take a few breaths. "Was right."

"It's all about pacing." I waved my hand vaguely in Bailey's direction. "She overdid it, but you're opposite. You never turned it up to eleven. The beginning isn't as important as the middle. Keep that in mind, and we'll be trading wins in the racing department."

"I'll remember that."

"Another thing is, we'll be a team most of the time." Hal scrawled some numbers next to names on a legal pad. "The laps are just to mark improvement. It's only this year, too. The next is another story. At least, that's what Dad said."

Before I could ask Hal what he meant by that, the coach came back.

"Hurry it up, Fairbanks!" Coach Pickman tapped her wrist even though she wasn't wearing a watch. "You're holding us all up."

Faith jogged slowly towards us, the last to finish her laps. Logan must've paced himself too, just at an overall slower speed. He came in almost neck and neck with Bailey, which meant he had stamina. Once we were all back, the coach motioned for us to sit on the bleachers next to Hal.

Coach Pickman picked up the legal pad and took the chronogram from him, eyes scanning the numbers before scratching her own notes under the list. She set them down next to a battered footlocker, which I immediately knew was full of equipment for Bishop's Row. I knew the rules too but decided that paying attention to the coach was overall less hazardous to my health than zoning out.

"Listen up because I'm only going to say this once." Coach Pickman glared in our general direction. "Bishop's Row isn't played with just any old sports equipment. It's not like your basketball, or your football, or your dodgeball, even though that one's the mundane version of the ancient Greek game this one came from. You gotta dodge the energy your opponent throws at you. Do this the right way as a team, you win. Do it wrong, you're out, and you screw your teammates over. Any questions?"

"Yeah." Faith said. She crossed her arms and looked sideways at Alex. "We have a poison magus here, which is unfair and unsafe. Does my father know about this?"

"That's why we've got this equipment." Coach Pickman slapped the top of the box. "It's protective and keeps the magic energy from hurting any of you cute little munchkins."

"Dude, rude." Logan looked at Faith like she came from Mars. "Nobody gets to pick their magic type."

"I'm used to it." Alex waved his hand. His eyes were half-lidded, a slight smirk on his lips. "Why aren't you?"

Faith's face turned an alarming shade of crimson. Her eyes narrowed, and her fists clenched. A gray haze emanated from them—undeath magic. Before I could stop her, Seth barked from across the gym, where he sat with the other familiars. She opened her hands, placing them flat against her legs. After a few deep breaths, she was back to her regular levels of surliness.

"Go and get those bands out of there. And call them ankyr from now on, except the one for your waist. That's the cestus. Directions for putting them on are in the trunk. After that, we get started." Coach Pickman turned her back on us, making more notes on the legal pad as she paced nearby.

Since I knew what to expect, I took the lead. Once the trunks were open, I started grouping the stretchy ankyr by size and setting them on the bench beside the trunk in heaps.

"Wow, you sure know this game." Logan pointed at the piles of ankyr. "I wouldn't be able to tell those apart. I mean, sure, I've seen them before since we host parties to watch the games at home, but that's it."

"It's pretty simple to play, just hard to master. The whole thing is an exercise in working together as a team, so we'll have to play to our strengths and cover each other's weaknesses if we want to win against the other class."

"I didn't think you'd be the jock." Faith snorted.

"Because she's a girl?" Hal raised his eyebrow. "How gauche." He made a gesture straight out of one of those teen movies, throwing in a selfie-style duckface.

"No, because she's a nerd." Faith rolled her eyes.

"What?" I blinked.

"Well, you got that perfect score in homeroom, didn't you?" Faith picked a set of ankyr up, pulling the smallest ones over her wrists.

"No, I didn't. Not from what I remember."

"See what I mean?" Faith shook her head. "She actually remembers the questions. She had to have gotten the perfect score. Definitely a nerd, and somehow a jock too."

"I'm serious. I didn't get ten out of ten. There's no way."

"Well, I didn't get it either." Bailey rolled her eyes. "Why don't you just admit it already—you're an evil nerd. Knowledge is power; everybody knows the bad guy is also smart. Every single time there's a story about a magus hurting people, the news always talks about their high grades or advanced degrees. Like her uncle."

"What a jerk thing to say." Logan gave Bailey a withering glare. "Well, I don't think you're evil, Aliyah. No way."

"If the idiot says it, it must be true." Bailey snorted.

"Whatever." Logan put on a good face, but clearly, she'd hurt him.

My temper and my temperature began rising, so I focused on getting everyone equipped. I'd be able to blow off steam when we practiced conjuring our orbs.

"So, Faith is right. The smallest ones go on your wrists. After that, the next size set of ankyr goes on your ankles. This medium-sized one is for your forehead, and the super-wide one with Velcro is that cestus the coach mentioned. You'll see it has a wide strap that leads to another band. Make sure you put it on with that on top and fasten the other part around your neck, like a choker. Oh, and one other thing— make sure the cestus covers your navel."

"What happens if it doesn't?" Hal asked.

"Projectile vomiting." I strapped mine on. "And that's the best-case scenario. Trust me, you want to avoid it."

"Noted."

Everybody got banded up. Hal even put a set on, practicing for next time. Once we were done, we stood in a line in front of the bench. Even with the goofy gym uniform on, I felt like a real athlete. Well, almost. The pros also wore wrist guards called ballistae to help with channeling and throwing accuracy, but that was a post-Reveal addition to the game.

"Good job banding up." The face the coach made gave me the impression she was almost unhappy we had done a decent job. "Hold your hands like this now."

She turned her right hand palm-up between her navel and her solar plexus, cupping it, then positioned her left hand on top with the same curve. It looked like she was holding an invisible basketball, which was the point.

"Now you're going to make your orbs. We'll go over how important speed and power are another day. For now, you just have to make the damn things, so conjure your magic into your hands and watch what happens."

I'd done it before, so I took the lead yet again. It looked like that would be par for the course in Gym so far, although I'd hoped it would be different. Keeping your head down is hard when nobody else steps up.

I felt heat before I saw the fire as I called on my magic. The energy from one hand pushed against the energy in the other, opposing forces that caved in on each other, making a ball. It's supposed to go clockwise, turning in the same direction as time.

Except mine didn't. Instead, it went in the opposite direction, and I knew from experience that was not normal for me.

"Are you a southpaw, Morgenstern?" Coach Pickman asked.

"No, ma'am." I shook my head but kept up the flow of energy in the backward ball it produced. After all, she hadn't told me to stop.

"Ambidextrous?" She followed up.

"I'm not sure." That was true. I never tried using my left hand instead of my right for writing, anyway.

"Well, your brother is a southpaw, and he's one of the best players in his year. Widdershins balls are easier to throw curves with but harder to control sometimes. Whatever works, you do it." The coach clapped her hands, pacing down the row of students. "Make it snappy, get those balls going."

"Oh! I feel something!" It was Alex. Sure enough, slick green energy whirled between his hands—clockwise, of course.

"Keep conjuring, kiddos." The smirk Coach Pickman made wasn't entirely unkind until her gaze fell on Bailey. "What's your holdup?"

"I got injured yesterday." She showed off her hand, the palm still covered with an extra-large Band-Aid.

"There's no note from Nurse Smith. Conjure already."

"I said, I can't." Bailey's lip trembled.

"Should I call him, then? Or maybe your mommy?"

Bailey shook her head. After that, she put her hands in the correct positions, and sure enough, almost right away, she held a whirlwind between her palms. It must have hurt since she grimaced the entire time.

"See? That wasn't so hard."

Logan made his water ball with no trouble. This was probably something he'd done on stage before because it was pretty and flashy. Faith's magic ball didn't appear even though her hands were in the right positions, her face placid.

"Good job, Fairbanks." Coach Pickman nodded. "You've outdone your sister on this one."

"Huh?" Hal blinked.

"Undeath magic is gray normally." The coach pointed slightly off to the side of Faith's hands. "It's off-kilter in an orb, and barely visible. You need to look left of center to see it. This magic is well suited to Bishop's Row. The opposite team will have trouble getting out of the way in time. Now all Fairbanks has to do is move faster than a turtle."

Her face reddened, eyes too shiny. I knew stifled tears of rage when I saw them, so I decided to use my jock privilege.

"I'll help her practice, Coach."

"Good."

"What?" Faith's eyes widened, the glimmer of impending tears vanishing in the wake of her feigned outrage. "You mean I have to spend time with this jock/nerd hybrid?"

"You'd better, or risk a failing grade in this Special." Coach Pickman held up the whistle she wore around her neck. "You'll learn to throw your orbs tomorrow. For now, class dismissed!" She let out a blast on her whistle, ending the session.

Logan and Alex good-naturedly punched each other's shoulders while I helped everyone put their ankyr sets and cestuses back in the footlocker. We all headed for the locker rooms, most in good spirits, except for Bailey. Even Hal looked excited in a tired sort of way.

"Totally unfair," Faith mumbled. But instead of rolling her eyes at me, she nodded.

Maybe our animosity was cooling.

CHAPTER TWENTY

I stood outside the cafeteria and took a deep breath. Going back in there after all the trouble I had at mealtimes felt like a bad idea, but I had no choice. This was part of our schedule. While I could opt not to eat, I couldn't skip it without the potential for trouble. I was already in this school's version of detention, so the last thing I needed was more disciplinary action and negative attention from the faculty.

I walked in alone and picked up a tray. Even though the panini sandwiches on order in the kitchen smelled heavenly, I avoided the prepared foods window. I didn't want to stand with my back to the door like an invitation, so I headed to the toaster and the bread.

I took out two slices of pumpernickel, then grabbed containers of sun butter and packets of jelly to make myself a sandwich at the table. I turned around to go back for the butter knife and napkins I'd forgotten and almost ran into Dylan and Grace.

"What's the rush?" Grace gestured at my tray. "Don't you want a hot lunch?"

"Maybe when it's pizza day." I shrugged. "Pizza is faster than panini."

"Well, you can always wait with us." Dylan gestured at the window where the food prepared on request come out. "But this lunch hour is only for our year. No upperclassmen allowed."

"Yeah, no need for sun butter and jelly sandwiches unless you actually like those." Grace wrinkled her nose.

"I'd rather have a panini." I nodded and went with them, keeping the food on my tray.

I couldn't put the bread back in the bag without it being gross for the next person and didn't want to throw it out, so I grabbed a brown paper bag from the stack by the breadbox. These ingredients would make a great snack later.

At the window, Grace ordered ham, Swiss, and mustard on rye. I ordered turkey and avocado on pumpernickel. It's my favorite bread. Dylan went totally overboard, ordering what I could only describe as a Frankensandwich.

"Hi there, Steve." He worked for the cafeteria, so of course, he knew this guy by name, or maybe he just cared about the other folks working here. "I want bacon, ham, chicken salad, turkey, roast beef, and one slice of every cheese you've got. Oh, and hot sauce too, if that's okay. Put it on a hoagie roll and bake it 'til the cheese melts. And don't go easy on that hot sauce, please."

Steve the sandwich professional started humming *You're Welcome* from *Moana*. You know, the song the demigod sings? Judging by the delicious scents wafting from the kitchen as he worked, he just might have had culinary magic. I'm kidding. No such thing exists.

"Are we secretly being recorded for that crazy reality show? What's it called again?" Grace snapped her fingers. "*The Biggest Eater*. Did I get that right?"

"You did, but nobody's filming. It's just that between work all morning, then class, plus having Gym before Creatives, I'm freaking starving. Like, my stomach's threatening vengeance on the Dylan Nation."

"Speaking of Gym, how did it go for you guys?" I only asked my friends a friendly question. I wasn't spying on their strategy and skills like Richard Hopewell might have. At least, I hoped I wasn't. Ugh.

"We don't have Coach Pickman, so we have it easier than you."

Grace feigned a shudder, then grinned. "Coach Chen is super chill. I heard he didn't even yell at Darren last year when he refused to run laps."

"Pickman's a taskmaster for sure. Judging by my class's experience, I think the twins might be the weakest link when we start playing." I told them about Bailey's overzealousness and then her reluctance to make her magic orb. "But I probably shouldn't be telling you all this since we'll compete against each other soon."

"It's almost like you're totally evil, fraternizing with the enemy and all." Faith elbowed her way between Grace and me, bellying up to the window. "BLT on wheat," she said to the worker behind the counter. She didn't say please or look them in the eye, and she called me evil?

"What's that supposed to mean?"

"Don't get all bent out of shape." Faith turned around, shaking her head. I'd have taken it as a gesture of superior defiance, but her shoulders drooped. "I've got resting- bitch everything and I hate breaking a sweat. Sarcasm's my only skill. It's not personal."

Somehow the BLT was done before the rest of our food order. Probably because of Dylan's famous Frankensandwich. In any case, Faith stalked off, taking a detour by the self-serve soup urns.

Our order came out so we all thanked Steve again and got our sandwiches, heading for the booth Hal already sat in, waving at us. He got up, so I took that as a sign that he wanted to sit on the outside. Eventually we're seated, Grace against the wall beside Hal and me next to Dylan on the outside.

All Hal had in front of him was a standard coffee mug filled with what looked like wonton soup. He lifted the cup wearily, almost as though it were too heavy, drinking down the last dregs of broth. After that he leaned back like he's exhausted from a hike through the desert and the soup in his cup was the first water he'd had in ages.

After that, the strangest thing in the world happened. Well strange for Hawthorn Academy anyway. Faith Fairbanks, self-styled resting bitch everything, marched up to our table. She looked Hal straight in the eye before setting an entire bowl of wonton soup down in front of him, along with chow Chow meinMein noodles and a big spoon.

"You need more than a lousy coffee mug if you're going to get better anytime soon. Eat your lunch and don't say I never did anything for you." She turned her back to us and flounced away, the flowing kneelength skirt she wore flipping with her legs as she walked.

Hal stared after her, almost mesmerized. Or maybe that's just how he looked every time he's a combination of surprised and under the weather. Someday I might know him well enough to say one way or the other but not yet. We all watched as Faith took a seat at the table with Alex, Lee, and lanky magus with glasses and curly hair who I didn't recognize. He must have been from the other class. Maybe he was Alex's roommate. Eventually I'd find out, I suppose.

Dylan tapped me on the shoulder and took a deep breath, about to speak. From my experience socializing with him this summer, I knew that look meant this was something important. But before he could say a word, we get interrupted.

"Hey guys, is there room for me?" Logan held a tray full of food.

Even though he obviously spoke to me directly, I didn't pick this table out. I looked to Hal for his decision.

"Yeah probably," he turned to Grace, "is it okay if we make room for Logan?"

Grace nodded, her mouth too full of food to speak. Just as they finished shuffling around enough to make space, the twins surrounded Logan. They were all smiles, the fake plastic kind.

"Oh no, Logan." Hailey said. "You've just got to come sit with us."

"But--"

"No really, there's someone who wants to meet you. Another fire magus." Bailey batted her eyes. "Please, she practically begged us to bring you over and introduce you."

"Go on." Hal nodded. "But there's always a place for you here if you need it."

Logan grinned back, then walked away with the twins. His shoulders remained high and tense. They headed for a table with the girl with the sphinx. She looked surprised to see Logan and I guessed the twins lied to get him over there. Of course, her cat wasn't with her. All our familiars were having their own lunches in the corner.

Something I failed to mention earlier about mealtimes was this. Our familiars got fed three times per day. In the morning, in our rooms. Their food appeared along with the wake-up bell. This was why they weren't hungry while we had breakfast. They got their third meal between class and our dinner hour. Folks stuck in Familiar Bonding fed their critters there.

Lunch was the only meal they needed to take while we ate. That's one reason the lunch periods were broken up so it was only served to one year at a time. Also, with customized hot lunches, it was easier on the cooking staff to serve fewer students each hour. I'd bet the hazing between upper and lowerclassmen might have been another reason.

Our familiars ate in a designated area of the cafeteria. Food appeared the same way as in our rooms every morning. Which is to say via mysterious teleportation. I couln't imagine Headmaster Hawkins was personally responsible for delivering every dish of magical critter food throughout the entire campus. He probably had a Magipsychic device on a timer or an assistant to help.

Or maybe not, judging by his apparent stress level. Maybe he wasn't prepared for this either. In any event, it was a good thing the upperclassmen weren't here with us. Because none of us had our familiars nearby to help defend against bullying.

As I sat, enjoying the simple pleasure of lunch with friends, I realized this was the most peaceful meal I'd had since coming here. I could have gotten used to it but shouldn't. Only one third of all my cafeteria experiences would be lunches.

Dylan didn't try talking to me again until after we cleared our trays and set our dishes at the window for the cleaning staff. When he did, he got right to the point without preamble or hesitation.

"Aliyah, I have to talk to you about Logan's familiar. The one he's painting."

"Okay."

"I've seen that dragonetdragonet before." He sighed.

"Where? At the Willows?" I figured since I met Ember there for the first time, maybe there was a dragonet-friendly hangout on the premises that would have attracted Logan's wayward little friend. "Was he okay?"

"This is going to sound really weird, and I want you to just listen. Don't say anything until I'm done, okay?"

I'd always had trouble managing my brain's internal/external features. Interjections just kind of happened when I was involved in a conversation, especially one that was weird. I was about to tell him I couldn't make any promises until I looked in his eyes.

Dylan Kahn, the nonchalant fun-loving king of tension breaking, was scared.

"I might put my hand over my mouth because you know what happens when I hear a crazy story."

"Yeah, I kind of figured, but I think you're the only person I can talk to about this who'd remotely understand, and I'm freaking out. So, will you hear me out?"

"Are you sure it's me you want? I bet Hal would listen."

"No. I mean, I'm sure he would. He's a great kid with a huge heart. But you know more about critters than anyone else here who isn't a professor."

"Well, Noah—"

"Stop putting yourself down, Aliyah. And listen, okay? We don't have a lot of time before the next Special starts."

"All right. And I promise to keep my mouth shut no matter what."

"Starting over. I've seen that dragonet before—the one Logan is sketching for a painting." Dylan took a deep breath and closed his eyes. "I've been dreaming about him since I was a kid."

I didn't say anything, because that was what he asked for. Promises matter, so I waited. Whatever came next must be difficult to say. Dylan lowered his voice enough so the clink and spray of the dishwasher shielded his words from prying ears.

"And I shouldn't have been because my parents had me tested practically the minute my magic started coming in. My level of aptitude is average. I'm not powerful enough to have a dragonet familiar, not like you."

I blinked. I knew dragonets were most frequently attracted to magi of above-average power level or higher, but I'd never been tested and wouldn't have classified myself as such. Dylan had just paid me a huge compliment, and I couldn't even say thank you because I'd promised not to talk until he was done.

"Logan's making that painting so you know what his dragonet looks like. I know he's missing, and I'm aware that he got your help."

Right then, I wanted so badly to ask how he knew. He only specified one piece that he got from Logan firsthand. Was Dylan spying on his classmates somehow, or was I paranoid?

"But what you don't know is that they never bonded. His parents picked the flashiest dragonet they could find and put a collar on the critter for appearances because that's all they care about. So, what you think of all this?" Dylan's eyes were wide and wild. "I can't figure any of it out, and it's driving me to distraction."

Fortunately, my brain spat out a course of action immediately. Unfortunately, I wasn't entirely sure I should help either of the boys. Even if they were both honest and had good intentions, the entire situation seemed too hinky. Was it a coincidence? And for good or ill?

While I tried to ask questions in my head now instead of later, my mouth shot first.

"I think we ought to prioritize finding this dragonet. And when we do, the three of us go in a room together and figure it all out. Logan says he doesn't want his parents knowing his familiar's lost. Spouting theories, questioning ourselves, and assuming will only make this worse." I took a deep breath before continuing, "I'm going home on Friday night after Familiar Bonding and talking to Bubbe. Izzy and Cadence said they wanted to see you this weekend. I think if I invite Logan along also, we might be able to settle this off-campus, away from—" I gestured at nothing. "Walls with ears."

"You know, that's a good idea. Dealing with this off-campus, I mean."

"Did it help? Talking about it?"

"Just saying it out loud was a big deal, but yes. Thank you, Aliyah. You have no idea much you helped just now."

"It's about time I did something right here." I smirked.

"You know, just because you make the right choice, it doesn't mean it turns out in your favor. You can be perfect and still fail. Intention is more important than outcome."

"Well, now it's my turn to thank you, Dylan. Thanks for being a friend. It means a lot, especially here."

The bell rang, cutting us off from any further discussion. Ember came flying across the cafeteria, fluttering to slow and make a soft landing on my shoulder. As Dylan and I went our separate ways to our next Specials, I knew at least one thing for sure.

My own problems might have been the most obvious, front and center for everyone to see, but everybody had their own struggles, visible or not.

It wasn't a comforting thought because distress is never like that. But knowing I was not alone had a value beyond expression.

There was safety in numbers.

CHAPTER TWENTY-ONE

I was in the library with the rest of my homeroom. It was enchanting, an open area in the middle with two levels. A set of wide stairs led from the lower level to the upper, which was bordered by wooden railings. The walls were darker here than in the rest of the academic wing, but not by much. They matched the inlay on the floors, a semi-spiral Greek Key pattern.

Somehow, the spacious area felt cozy, more so than our dormitory rooms. Even though the square footage was large, the stacks and the overhang from the upper level conspired to give it a warm and homey feel. There were no individual study cubbies, only tables, as though we were meant to work together instead of squirreling away on our own.

A long counter with wooden pushcarts behind it took up the far-right corner, positioned on the diagonal so the librarians could see most of the study area. One librarian, a person with ice-blue hair, sat in a wooden wheelchair reading a paperback, a hawk perched on the high back. Carved murals adorned the walls behind the librarian in the chair, depicting downtown Salem blanketed in snow. After a brief introduction and tour by the other librarian, a rail-thin man with silver hair and a kindly face, we were left to our own devices, allowed to study or work on whatever we liked.

I headed back to the circulation desk because I had a question. I kept my voice down, in part due to the sensitive topic of discussion, but also because it was a library. Libraries. Quiet. Duh.

"Yes, we do have books on that subject." Mr. Ashford nodded, smiling. His teeth were healthy but slightly crooked, which made his expression charming. "And you can use the student index to search."

He nodded at a large podium in the middle of the library, under the chandelier. It had the largest and thickest book I'd ever seen on it, bound in shimmering iridescent fabric colored like either dawn or dusk. The material either came straight out of the Under or was enchanted with every type of magical energy. As I watched, Faith approached it, bending at the waist, and addressed it.

"Bishop's Row tips and tricks." She enunciated clearly, and after a half a moment, the index's pages flipped on their own, glowing in prismatic color as the magic enchanting it activated.

"It seems the student index is already in use, so I will help you, Miss Morgenstern." Mr. Ashford pulled a smaller index out from under the counter, set it on the table, and began searching through it.

He did this with a level of respect and care that told me that books, even ones with long lists and nothing more, were extremely important to him. Mr. Ashford lifted his iridescent rainbow-framed glasses and pursed his lips, peering under them as he bent his head over the volume. His face was mostly unlined. From this angle, I realized his silver hair was an intentional choice and not due to aging.

"Here it is." Without looking up, Mr. Ashford reached out for a pencil and a blank index card. He jotted a series of numbers on its surface. "Scientific studies of dragonets and their ways, behavioral." He held the card toward me, straightening and smiling again.

"Thanks so much, Mr. Ashford." I smiled back. "I appreciate your help."

"May you find what you seek." His statement would have seemed ominously cryptic if it weren't for his friendly tone.

Because the tour was fresh in my mind, remembering where the section I was looking for was located was easy. Everything was done by numbers, familiar from my old school because the extrahuman community had adopted the Library of Congress system in the United States. I walked down the space between the stacks and found that there wasn't much in the way of research into dragonets. There were plenty of books on their anatomy and abilities, but little about their behavior and interactions with magi.

Being rare and special is awfully inconvenient sometimes.

There were only three books that fit my criteria. The bad news was, it limited the amount of information I could get. The good news was, I could carry all of them by myself in one trip. They were even on the middle shelf, which was a happy little accident.

I took my treasures to a table directly under one of the lower-hanging light fixtures, still wrought iron with solar globes but cozier. Two of those editions had been rebound and had old and yellowed pages. Without adequate lighting, they'd be difficult to read. I, of course, had my very own light source, portable and always literally at hand, but books were flammable, and I didn't want to risk damaging any of them.

Fire alarms were a thing here, too. Being suspected of arson was not something I wanted to go through again.

At first, I wasn't sure how to pull the chair away from the table. It was stuck to the floor. Well, that wasn't entirely accurate. The chair's legs were part of the floor, as though it was carved from or had grown out of the hardwood underfoot.

When I set my hand against its back, however, the chair came loose, or perhaps the floor released it. Either way, I could move the seat and use it, pulling it close enough to the table's edge to get some reading done.

I opened the first tome and began skimming the table of contents. It was a collection of academic papers, studies done on dragonet familiars and the magi who worked with them from various institutions of higher extrahuman learning. The titles of the papers were convoluted, which, according to Bubbe, was always the case when it came to this sort of publication, as though the wordier the title, the more likely it would be accepted into an academic journal.

This book contained twenty articles. After deciphering their titles, I realized only three had anything to do with dragonets as familiars. I flipped to the first, intending to mark it along with the others for later reading, but I got totally distracted. The author of this particular study was none other than Professor Luciano. No, wait—the given name was female, and the article was from the 1920s, so it had to be his mother or maybe an aunt.

I still marked it with a scrap of the index card but took a moment to read the abstract. I had a theory. Was this why my homeroom teacher had said he was excited to have me in his class?

Maybe he wanted to study me, and Ember too. What if he was trying to expand on this family member's research? Science was all about standing on the shoulders of giants, after all.

This idea might have disturbed some people, but I immediately began trying to figure out how to use it to my benefit. Maybe the mean girls were right, and I did have the makings of some sort of evil overlord.

I couldn't quit trying to get by here. People needed my help, and I'd promised it to some of them, so I couldn't abandon them just to salvage my failing reputation with faculty and the vocal minority of the students.

Did true kindness require total selflessness? After all, I was doing this research for two other people besides me. Bubbe always says you can't save a man from the ocean if you're drowning along with him. Until now, that had made little sense. I didn't mean any harm, so how could it go wrong?

But wasn't the road to hell paved with good intentions?

"Shut up." Oops.

"Shush!" It was Bailey. Because, of course, it was. "Logan's trying to study."

"No, you shush." Faith leaned a hip against my table. "Because she was already telling herself to be quiet. She doesn't need your help. If you don't like it, take the pretty boy over to the other side of the library already."

I sat there stunned, blinking up at Faith. She looked back down, first at my face, then past me to see what I was reading. I didn't know if it was nosiness or part of some information-gathering scheme. Maybe it was just a casual glance, totally normal.

But there was no question when she looked back at my face, meeting my gaze again. She'd seen what I was studying although she couldn't possibly know why, and I had no idea what she'd do with that information. She'd seen Logan's art project in Creatives. If she'd over-heard any of my conversations with Logan or Dylan, she'd suspect something was off. Logan could get into serious trouble with his family if she said anything. I wasn't having that, so I did the only thing I could.

I stood up to move myself and my research away from Bailey's and Logan's presence. Somehow, I managed this feat without closing the tome Faith had glanced at because nothing makes people think you want to hide something like slamming a book in their face.

As I walked past Faith, I leaned my head slightly in her direction and murmured my thanks. I wasn't snarking at her, I was grateful. Also, I figured it'd distract her from my readings on dragonets and why they bothered bonding with magi.

I'd apparently made the right call because she left me alone. I let Bailey and Logan stay where they were and schlepped to the other side of the library, to a table under the second level's floor. The library period was maddeningly short compared to Creatives and Gym. I had to get a move on.

On this side of the library, the light was dim. It was so low I couldn't read the old book without trouble, but the word "can't" hadn't stopped me so far. I toughed it out, leaning my nose so close to the page I might as well have asked it to start dating me exclusively.

I tried to take the information in, absorb it, but visions of Charity and the rest of the cruel and usual crew griefing me about book boyfriends danced in my head. I closed my eyes and leaned back in the chair, about to give up on deciphering it, but one more try couldn't hurt. After all, if it didn't work out, I'd just check it out and read it in my room.

But when I opened my eyes somehow, the page was lit. Not from within or anything creepy like that. As I said, the school couldn't be haunted because of its position between planes of existence. This was a no ghost zone, so I tried to figure out where the light was coming from. Before I managed the seemingly simple deduction, Mr. Ashford shook a little handbell on the counter. It jingled as charmingly as sleigh bells in the snow.

"If you'd like to check any materials out, you've only got a few minutes. Please make your way to the desk, and we will help you."

I brought my books up. As it turned out, Mr. Ashford didn't need assistance from the other librarian because I was the only one borrowing books. That totally reinforced my reputation as a nerd, and I wished I didn't care.

Because computers didn't work well here, the library used a system only accessible to magi. The librarian went through the motions, writing dates on cards and sticking them in the pockets on the books' back cover. The ink flowed, glowing with a gleaming white magic that originated in Mr. Ashford's hand. I was reminded of frost-laced windowpanes. So, he was an ice magus. Cool.

We exchanged pleasantries of farewell, and I headed out of the room with the rest of my class. Next was Lab, which seemed straight-forward enough. I doubted Professor Luciano would give us much more on the first day than a tour and a list of safety rules.

I couldn't have been more wrong.

CHAPTER TWENTY-TWO

The lab was brightly lit, open, and spacious, but its ceiling was not quite as high as the library's. It made sense because Hawthorn Academy had unlimited space to work with. Even with the severe deficiency of windows, which made me feel stifled at times, it was never claustrophobic on campus.

I was the first one in the room, so I took a seat at the front. There were two rows, with five benches in each of them. I needed to sit in the front because I didn't want to miss anything. Lab wasn't easy, and the only way through was to follow all the directions exactly. Front and nearly center was the best place for that.

Unlike the classroom, the library, and the gym, this room had space just for familiars. An entire section to the side of my lab bench contained perches, tunnels, and climbing trees for our critters. The intention was to keep them out of the way during experiments.

Ember flew directly to a T-shaped structure. On landing, she bent her head down and rubbed her cheek against it. The perch covered with carpet, like the kind of thing people with mundane cats had in their houses. Ember loved it. We didn't have any carpet at home in our apartment or in Bubbe's office downstairs either. It must have been a huge novelty.

The next familiar to check out the accommodations was Nin. She scuttled along the floor, her back sometimes humping as she hopped part of the way. I never would've guessed Pharaoh's Rats moved so much like ferrets, but you learn something new every day—which was the point of school, after all.

Hal slumped on the stool next to me, which fortunately had a back. He looked exhausted enough to need it. The seats were swankier than at my old school. Like the chairs in the library, they were fused to the floor until someone needed to sit in them. Hal either forgot or was tired enough for motor impairment to set in. He leaned back a bit too far.

"Whoa!" His stool came free, detaching itself from the floor.

I reached out, catching and righting it before it clattered down. Hal sighed, shaking his head. Then he concentrated, moving the errant furniture before getting back in his seat.

"Thanks, Aliyah."

"No problem."

Hal nodded, and I moved my own chair over. Clearly, he wanted to tell me something. One of the few things I seemed to do right at Hawthorn Academy was listen to people.

"What's up?" I lowered my voice in anticipation of whatever he had to say.

"I've got a problem."

"Oh?" I waited. Also wondered, since people in my year kept asking for help. I didn't know what I'd expected here, but it wasn't this.

"I don't think I have enough energy to get through this lab." As he finished speaking, Hal let out the rest of his breath. He didn't take another immediately. I'd seen this before at Bubbe's office with critters suffering a serious illness. He was in such a bad way I considered calling the nurse.

"How can I help?"

"I can't do any actual work in here." Hal glanced down at his notepad, where his folded letter from Nurse Smith was tucked under the back page. "Nurse Smith made me promise not to use any magic for the rest of the day. But you're a strong magus. Would you mind being my partner so I can stay and take notes? I'll help with setting up equipment mundanely, too."

"Professor Luciano can't have us doing experiments the first day!"

"Yes, he can. He's not as fair as you—"

"Welcome, class!" The professor stood at the front of the room behind the instructor's bench. He smiled, hands and arms out, palms up in a gesture to match his words.

I blinked, keeping my mouth shut for now. Not fair? How? He was pedantic, but he seemed decent enough.

The rest of the students shuffled in, choosing their spots and partners. Bailey practically pushed Faith out of the way when she tried sitting with Alex, leaving her to pair up with Logan instead. They sat behind Hal and me.

The lab portion of our education here at Hawthorn Academy was rumored to be its most intensive element. At least I didn't have to worry about being picked last or otherwise ostracized today. Even Faith looked like she'd keep her head down.

"Today, we'll do a quick rundown of the lab safety rules and then a brief but exciting exercise." Professor Luciano pulled a three-ring binder out from under his bench. "You'll find one of these in front of each of you. It contains the safety protocols and a summary of each experiment we will run during Lab for the entire semester."

I checked the table. Although it had been solid before, there was now a rectangular opening. The loose-leaf notebook inside was an old Trapper Keeper, the sort of thing students my age had carried back in the 1980s. Mine was emblazoned with an airbrushed unicorn.

Hal held his up, smirking. Its design depicted a round yellow figure with a pie-slice mouth, chasing a quartet of blue ghosts. Because we were in a magical school, the images moved, the unicorn tossing its head and the yellow man's mouth chomping. I couldn't help but giggle a little.

The professor glanced at his shoulder, where his familiar perched. He pointed at one of the wooden outcrops on the wall in the familiar-friendly space. The Strix swooped across the room, landing precisely where he'd indicated she should go.

"Please send your familiars to the designated area if you haven't already. That is always the first step upon entering the lab, and part of our safety rules. If our experiments include them, I will instruct you as to when they can be called over."

He opened his notebook, which was emblazoned with a neon-pink heart, flipping past a clear protective sheet and the title pages. After that, he turned his back, gesturing at the wall behind him, which was blank and white. A series of numbers with words beside them and a list appeared on the board.

"Take out your notebooks and turn to page eight, *Safety First*."

A rustle of paper filled the room as everyone did as instructed. The list was simple and straightforward, even for a magical textbook. The first part was about checking labels for ingredients and instruments. The second pertained to personal protective equipment. In the third, the one our professor had already referenced, familiars were to keep to the designated area. Finally, there was a note about not running experiments while impaired. No wonder Hal wanted help.

"Flip to the first experiment and gather the materials listed, along with your protective equipment. The supply closets are on the walls in the back of the room." The professor clapped his hands. "Go!"

"I can't imagine he'll have us do much besides search for supplies to learn where they're kept." I held out my hand and helped Hal down from the tall stool, which couldn't be comfortable for him. The poor guy's feet dangled, even with the footrest.

"Thanks." He took my arm, using it for balance until he got both feet on the floor. "But no. He's having us run something. I overheard at the end of the mixer. Didn't Noah warn you?"

"No." I blinked. "He hasn't talked to me since the orientation assembly."

"Wow." Hal shook his head. "It's lonely being an only child, but stuff like that makes me kind of relieved I am."

"It's just such a big change." I reached out toward the handle built into the wall and pulled a cabinet door open. "Coming here and staying overnight, nowhere near all my old friends or the rest of my family. And Noah acting this way."

"At least you're not alone." Hal peered in at the items on the shelf.

"The only good side to that whole equation."

"Yeah, at least I'm with my dad. Some people have nobody here." He grabbed a length of tubing. "This is on the list." Sure enough, the label matched the one in our notebooks.

"What about this?" I held up a wrought iron stand. "The engraving is worn, but it looks like number four there."

"Oh, yeah, that's right. Would you mind?" He handed me the tubing, swapping it for the notebook. "I'm feeling a little out of it, so if you carry stuff, I'll identify it, okay?"

"That's fine."

"Hey, Aliyah?" Logan asked. "Are there more of those tubes in that cabinet?" He pointed at the still-open door behind me.

"Yeah." I stepped aside. "The iron stand's also in there, so grab one, too. Hey, where's your list?"

"Faith has it, but she's over there." Logan jerked his thumb over his shoulder. "Her pup's being weird."

I saw Faith standing by the familiar area. She cooed at Seth the Sha, squatting beside what looked like a carpet-covered doghouse. I heard him in there, whining inconsolably and refusing to come out.

"Why don't you come with us? You need the same stuff Hal and I do, after all."

"Okay, thanks."

We continued looking through the different cabinets and occasionally passing other students. Alex and Bailey managed to collect everything and headed back to their bench first. It was almost like they were racing me in a non-athletic way.

I recognized the true purpose of this first lab. It was in part to help us get acquainted with the room, supplies, and where all the safety equipment was, including stuff like the sink and the eyewash and the fire blanket, typical parts of mundane laboratory classrooms as well.

Hal explained the eyewash to Logan after I excused myself. Carrying the armload of supplies back to the bench was easy. Once finished, I headed over to where Faith was still trying to coax Seth out of the weird doghouse.

"It's okay, I won't let you get hurt. Come on out, now." Her voice was thin, quavery, and anxious.

"Do you need any help?"

"Not from you." Faith had her back turned so I couldn't see her face, but it sounded to me like she was on the verge of tears.

Whatever had happened on the way from the library to the lab had upset Faith. Since bonds are a two-way street, maybe it was the other way around. She needed help, and I couldn't give it to her, but there was another option. I marched to the front of the room.

Luciano glanced swiftly down at his notebook, but I noticed. He'd been staring at me before I headed over there. I had no idea why, but clearly, he wasn't looking at Faith or any of the critters.

"Professor, we have a very frightened familiar. Can you help?"

"But of course." His brows drew down. "No one should do this experiment in such a volatile familiar-induced state. And you are helping other students follow the safety rules by bringing this to my attention." The wide grin returned. "Kudos."

While his words were benign enough, something in Professor Luciano's tone bothered me. It had since the first time I'd met him. Why? So far, I only had the vaguest suspicion that he might be studying me. That in and of itself shouldn't have been too upsetting, however.

I wasn't the only one who found him intimidating, so being cautiously formal wasn't unreasonable. Inconvenient, though. Having to question his motives while he provided my education was less than ideal, and maybe worse than that.

Was assuming he had ulterior motives cruel? And why? Because he watched us like teachers are supposed to?

That was what the mean girls did to me—make assumptions based on rumor and first impressions. I hadn't thought high school was this complicated or difficult back on the mundane campus I'd shared with Cadence and Izzy. The difference was how needlessly complex magus society is.

We held on to procedures and traditions that had served us when we had to keep magic secret, but things were different now. They had been for decades, so I wasn't sure why magi took so much time to adjust. Even vampires adapted faster, and they were the most legally restricted.

At the bench, I went through the motions and put on my personal protective equipment. Hal copied me. From the bench behind us, Logan did the same. At least I knew they'd be safe during the planned experiment, although I still doubted we'd do one at that point.

Faith's issue with Seth might prevent the professor from sticking to his plan. Even with his help, she was unable to convince her familiar to come out or calm down. She started hugging herself like she was outside in below-freezing weather.

"There's one way to soothe him and let him stay put." The professor headed to the front of the room, Faith following him like a tail on a kite.

Professor Luciano pulled open a drawer under the board on the wall. Inside the contents rustled, releasing an herbal scent. I recognized it instantly since Bubbe used supplies like these. Maybe she even ordered them for the school.

I'm talking about sachets used in extraveterinary medicine. Different varieties helped magical creatures in pain, shock, or distress. He pulled a pair of them from the drawer, then closed it and headed back toward where Seth was hiding.

"I'm sorry about this, Professor." Faith apologizing to anyone wasn't something I would have imagined, but there it was. She must have loved her little Sha.

"At times, the lab environment makes familiars nervous, some more than others. Sha do have the best sense of smell, after all. Certain ingredients can stress them, so I always keep my supply of sachets well-stocked."

He leaned down, dropping the little bundles of fabric at the entrance to the small enclosure. A few moments later, I saw a slightly curved muzzle with a wet nose emerge from the darkness. Seth opened his mouth, revealing a blue tongue. Almost everyone else in the class gasped at this detail, but I'd expected it.

"It's okay, boy," Faith cajoled. "You can take them in there with you."

He responded, snatching both sachets with an alacrity even I couldn't have anticipated. Seth was extremely swift for a Sha. They were mostly known for stamina. The whining ceased, replaced by a series of doggy snores as Seth's nervousness succumbed to exhaustion.

"I wish *I* could take a nap." Hal leaned his cheek on his hand, eyelids droopy.

He yawned. It was contagious. I added a stretch to mine, leaning back so I didn't knock any of our equipment over or bump Hal's head.

Out of the corner of my eye, I saw a flash of gold. I turned my head to see Ember fluttering down from the highest perch to the roof of the doghouse. She stretched out along the top, draping her wings on either side of the peaked roof in a protective gesture. My thwarted desire to help must have transferred to her.

Back at the front of the class, Professor Luciano instructed us to turn to the next page and read the experiment's instructions. He went on to explain them, which was nice because they weren't clear. The only obvious part was that the antler had to break down at the end. The description included archaic symbols straight out of an old English apothecary manual.

Calling it a difficult read was a gross understatement.

"What's wrong?" Hal peered at the text, jotting something down on his notepaper.

"I can't make heads or tails of this."

"Don't worry, I'm translating."

"How?"

"My mom taught me." He continued scribbling, glancing between the lab's instructions and his notes frequently enough for me to understand he welcomed the distraction.

He'd barely mentioned his mother, but he'd hinted he was only with his dad here. Probably Hal missed her, but I let it drop because I figured he wasn't ready to talk about it. I stayed on the subject of the lab.

"Am I the only one here who doesn't know how to read these symbols?"

"Probably not." Hal tapped his eraser on the paper for a moment as he mulled over a shape I could only describe as a fish hugging a hamburger.

"It's all surf and turf to me." Faith snorted, pointing at the symbol.

"You took the words right out of my brain."

"That's enough out of you, flame-broil." She flipped a lock of hair over her shoulder. "I was talking to Hal."

"It's the symbol for lime." Hal gestured with his pencil at the glass beaker with the antler inside. "Which makes sense if we want to dissolve that. That's going to be tricky because we need magic to combine it, but it says here that we can't use fire."

"'Can't use fire' is probably the best phrase in the universe." Faith turned her back on me, stalking toward Logan.

"I wish you were nicer." Logan bent his head over the instructions. "We'd have more help if you were."

"I wish you were smarter." Faith rolled her eyes. "We wouldn't need help if you were."

"I bet you think that's a real zinger, but I hear that line all the time, so whatever." Logan reached for the jars of ingredients he'd gathered on our journey around the room.

That silenced Faith. She was either stumped for a response or wouldn't bring something worse than what Logan had already heard. I hoped it was the latter.

Watching him, I realized Logan just had a different learning style. He lined up all the ingredients, matching the symbols on their labels to the ones on the paper. It wouldn't matter if he couldn't read them because he'd still get the combination right this way. Good sense, that.

"Now that you've all gathered the materials and equipment and have read through the instructions at least once, put on your protective devices. We're ready to begin the simple introductory experiment." Professor Luciano rubbed his hands together like he had applied lotion or contemplated taking over the world. "As you can see, we are dissolving a section of antler in a basic solution catalyzed by magical energy. We have twenty minutes to give it a try. I can't wait to see what you come up with."

The instructions told us how to set up the stand, tubing, and containers. Hal did all that without magic. I appreciated having a lab partner who actually helped. While he worked, I checked the ingredients and set them in order of use like Logan had, except using Hal's translations. That helped me learn the unfamiliar symbols and copy the notes at the same time. In fact, I did it twice, so Logan could have one later.

When Hal finished, it was time to make the formula, which was my job. I handed the beaker and antler to my lab partner, and he placed it on the stand with the tubing pointed down over it. It was easy to measure each powder and even easier to mix them with the yew spoon, but the rest, not so much.

All the ingredients had to be activated with magical energy after that. That was what Professor Luciano meant by a magical energy catalyst. It'd be a delicate process because my element is fire, and we couldn't use any in this experiment. I couldn't conjure it, but there was another way.

I thought back to the first night my magic declared itself. When I was almost fourteen, it came in a nightmare, one where I somehow got stuck in the Under, right in front of the Sidhe Queen. She dragged me away to her dungeon, a place of intense heat and constant solar glare.

Of course, I woke up from that screaming. I'd set my quilt on fire in my sleep. Mom came in and shut it down. Later, I'd asked her how because she's not a null magus, the sort who can drain the energy from any enchantment.

She'd done it by reversing her energy, the same way she'd have banished her own fire. One of the most important things she'd ever taught me was that a magus could banish their own element even if it came from another source, but only if it was weaker than whatever they could conjure.

So, the way forward for me in this experiment was to make a cute little mundane fire and banish it. Luckily, I had a plan.

I took out a box of matches, the wood kind, from the Hawthorne Hotel. I pulled one out, struck it, then placed it on a glass dish. I attached the round-bottom flask to the other end of the tubing, steadying it in the upper part of the iron stand. Afterward, I gathered magic energy into the hand still around the flask's neck.

The glass chilled in my grasp as I focused on the mundane fire. The lit match continued to burn, but how? My magic should have snuffed it. I looked at my hand on the flask.

I almost knocked the entire stand over and ruined the experiment. My magic had never been this color before.

Gold is a solar magic color, like Dad or Bubbe or Noah had. That was what glowed around the hand holding the flask—pure gold.

My eyes widened as I noticed my lab partner, my friend, and my frenemy watching. Maybe the lit match had attracted their attention, or perhaps they wanted to see how I'd get around not using my element.

"Queen's Glory, she *is* an extramagus," Hal breathed. The faerie oath stunned me, coming just after I'd recalled that awful nightmare.

"No shit, Sherlock." Faith rolled her eyes. "Told you."

Inside the flask, my impossible solar magic had turned the other ingredients to liquid, which reacted with the lime. The glass heated, contents rising up to the neck on its way to the tubing.

I was frozen in place. Who wouldn't have been?

"Miss Morgenstern," Professor Luciano's eyes widened. He noticed too. "Remove your hand. Quickly!"

The fact that he stared at the flask and not me helped me move, finally. He was concerned about my immediate safety, not that I was just like Uncle Richard after all. I managed to save myself from a third-degree burn.

The result was fast, though not immediate. Smoke, foam, and heat appeared in the beaker as the solution dripped down. We'd done it correctly and watched it dissolve, so at least I didn't flub things and give us a failing grade.

A shattering sound followed by a flashpoint of heat behind me signaled that someone else hadn't been so lucky. I turned on my heel, seeing Logan through a veil of rising smoke. His eyes rolled wildly as he tried to step away from the fiery disaster on the bench between him and the rest of the classroom. His arms extended in a posture that meant he was about to instinctively shoot water to extinguish the flames.

It's a chemical fire so that won't work. He's doomed.

DANGER: FIRE: LOCATION: LAB B

If the announce system cut on, emergency response would be too slow. So would Alex, running toward the closet with the fire blanket. I knew that after racing him that morning. The fire spread, raging toward the boy who had set it loose, and his back was against the door to a cabinet containing more flammable ingredients. I was Logan's only hope.

But only if my magic was stronger than this conflagration.

CHAPTER TWENTY-THREE

I said nothing, just held my palms out at the growing fire like a traffic cop ordering it to stop. The gesture didn't matter much; it was the thought that really counted. I imposed my will on the fire, not the flames at its edges, but at its heart. There was no point in trying to reduce the leading edge of something moving this fast. I needed focus to banish fire, and the situation worked against me.

Everything was too distracting, from the gasps and horrified cries of my classmates to footsteps pounding in from the hall, to smoke working its way toward my nose and mouth, threatening to choke me. And that wasn't all—the fire had grown from conflagration to inferno.

It was impossible. I couldn't possibly have been strong enough.

Ember landed on my shoulders, one hind foot on each side of my neck. She couldn't banish fire, but her wings wreathed the sides of my head like blinders on a spooked horse, damping all that noise, letting me be in the moment, letting me focus on the signal. That made all the difference.

I called for intervention from the heavens and was answered immediately.

My magic crushed the chemical fire. It guttered and sputtered, then caved in on itself and died. From under a layer of soot, Logan's expression eased out of primal terror and into an exhausted sort of awe.

My victory was sudden, total, and completely unexpected since I didn't know my own strength. Turned out, it was more than enough— and more than I should have used.

I dropped my hands and sagged sideways. There was nothing to hold on to or break my fall. I was going down and couldn't even swing.

"Gotcha." Dylan stood over me. I blinked up at him.

"You're not in my class." He got me halfway standing, supporting me under one arm. Someone else came in from the other side.

Grace snorted. "It's a fire. Everyone's in your class now."

"It wasn't my fault." I let them usher me away from the scene of all that glory and shame.

"It really wasn't." Logan came out from behind the lab bench, grimy but seemingly unscathed. "I did it. Used too much. Blew up the lab."

"Accidents happen, my dude." Dylan shrugged the whole thing off.

"Where's Hal?"

I tried looking over my shoulder but sneezed and didn't quite manage. A glance around told me everybody had evacuated, but I still didn't see Hal's short, stocky physique anywhere in the throng as we passed through the door.

In the hall, I caught sight of Faith and tried to flag her down because no matter how much we sniped at each other, she clearly cared about Hal. But she turned her back, ignoring me. I couldn't blame her, either. She'd been vindicated, right about me all along.

Tell your friends before she does.

"I'm an extramagus."

"What was that?" Grace tapped her earlobe. "Hard to hear in this din."

I waited until they brought me to a bench between classroom doors. Once seated, they fussed over me, doing a hack job of taking my pulse and peering at my eyes. Grace and Dylan talked over each other, arguing about whether to send me to the infirmary, but I cut them off.

"I said, I'm an extramagus."

They stopped and stared, not even blinking. Must have been totally shocked.

"Okay," said Grace.

"Yeah," said Dylan.

"You don't believe me?"

"We do." She nodded. "But I can't say we're surprised. Sorry."

"So why are you still here?"

Before they answered, a series of hissed and emphatic syllables from our right interrupted. Professor DeBeer and Professor Luciano argued while a tall dun-complected man with straight black hair and brown eyes stood by. He wore the awful Gym uniform and a whistle like Coach Pickman. I guessed he was Coach Chen.

"—can't believe you'd have them run one on the first day like that, Lucy." Professor DeBeer's nostrils flared.

Professor Luciano smirked. "They're quite advanced, Miss Susan."

"Don't call me that." Her lip curled in a sneer.

"Don't call me Lucy and I won't." His lips pressed into a thin, pale line.

"What were you thinking?" Her hands went on her hips, the motion nearly jostling her lightning bird from her shoulder.

"More than you, as always. And they handled it." He cut the air between them with the side of his hand in a chopping motion. His Strix flapped to keep her balance.

"You sound like a novice instructor, not a triple doctorate." Her hands curled into fists.

"And you sound like a hidebound old coot, not a dissertation failure," he snarled.

Coach Chen's expression was like a still pond, at least until Nurse Smith showed up. His eyes narrowed, lips pulling slightly down.

"Where are they?" Nurse Smith turned his head, eyes scanning the hallway. "The students who got stuck in there?"

"Here, Nurse." Logan raised one hand like he was answering for attendance. He sat on a bench, leaning against the wall, but still looked dizzy. "And Aliyah too, but she only stayed because I was stupid. She saved my life."

His eyes looked starstruck. Maybe they were just glassy from the smoke exposure. At least, I hoped. Or perhaps the light Nurse Smith flashed in them. He came at me with the mundane penlight, and I tried not to blink as he did his test. Sometimes the regular tools worked best.

"The two of you need to go to the infirmary." Nurse Smith planted his feet, ready to defy our objections.

"But Nurse, I should go back and help clean—" Logan tried to get up but couldn't manage it.

"You'll do no such thing." Nurse Smith tucked his penlight away in a pocket, then clapped his hands three times.

Finally, his familiar revealed himself. A crab crawled from the opposite pocket, somehow able to cling to the fabric. It scuttled down to the floor, then held its claws in the air, clacking three times with both.

We watched the critter grow. It remained close to the ground instead of growing taller, increasing its circumference and thickness of body and shell. I wondered how until I realized what Nurse Smith's familiar was.

A Karkinos, the same type of crab that had pinched Hercules as he fought the Hydra in the ancient Greek legends. I'd seen one at Bubbe's before, but not close up. Certainly never watched one change size like that.

"Mr. Pierce, do you need help?" The nurse tapped his foot.

Logan shook his head. In a moment, he pressed a hand to it, groaning, with his other hand over his mouth.

"I'll take that as a yes, but before we start, are the two of you going to help Miss Morgenstern, or should I call for more assistance?"

"Absolutely." Dylan nodded, his expression gravely serious. I wondered what had gotten him so concerned. It couldn't be me since I didn't feel that bad. "I'm game."

"Oh, yeah." Grace beamed. "Happy to help."

We watched Nurse Smith assist Logan to transfer from the bench to the crab's back. After that, we made a most curious line, heading down the hall past practically the whole school. They'd all come out of the classrooms to stare as we went by.

From behind us came voices of professors corralling their students and herding them back into the classrooms. There was no more argument from Professor Luciano and Professor DeBeer's direction, but I didn't think for one second that their issues were resolved. It sounded like a long-standing feud between the two of them.

I shuffled along between my friends, realizing how lucky I was. They'd stuck by me, even though I could have put them in serious danger at any time. I hoped they understood the risks, but maybe they'd never even heard of them.

An extramagus could tap more than one elemental school, unlike regular magi. Those powers came at a cost, however, and it was threefold.

First, there was always a catch, some hitch, limit, or restriction on where, when, or how an extramagus could use their power. I had no idea what mine was. Usually it took trial and error to figure it out. That brought us to the second point.

Extramagi had a harder time shutting their power off. I'd banished that lab fire easily, but a water magus had created it. When it came to flames I conjured myself, it'd always been harder to shut them off. Maybe it was not about focus after all.

Finally, the third and worst catch, the reason most other extrahumans didn't trust extramagi—they didn't have absolute power, but what they got corrupted them, and nobody was sure why. There was a general consensus on how.

All magi draw their element from the Under, through the barrier this very school occupies. The Under is a magical realm of pure truth. When shifters cross over, they're stuck in animal form unless one of the Faerie monarchs makes a talisman for them.

The going theory was that access to more than one element from the Under damaged their brain chemistry. I should have said, "we," because I was one and had better accept it.

We knew quite a bit about how the Under harmed brains because changelings took on their full faerie physiology by joining a court. After that, they spent a year and a day in the Under. It wasn't a political choice, but a matter of survival. If a changeling didn't tithe, they'd go mad.

Many went on to marry and have children with magi. Some of these had both a magic and a faerie destiny. When that happened, they could lean on their magic and supernatural bonds like joining a were-wolf's pack. That prevented the madness for a while, but any changeling who was also an extramagus carried double risk of insanity. That was what had happened to Richard Hopewell. My uncle had waited until he was in his forties to tithe.

Magi had a human psyche and a human brain. Magic stressed brain chemistry. The human mind wasn't made to handle an all-access pass to all its types long-term, so by calling multiple aspects of universal truth into and through their minds, extramagi eventually lose them. Nobody's come up with a therapy or medication to cure, counter, or even treat it.

In the future, I'd be a danger to myself and everyone around me. Guaranteed. I was destined to hurt people when all I'd wanted my whole life was to help. As my friends escorted me down the hall, I couldn't banish mental images of them recoiling in horror and pain at the distress I would cause them in some distant future.

I didn't realize I'd been crying until they sat me down in the infirmary, although not the room from the day before. This one had four beds. Once I was situated, Dylan and Grace helped Logan into the bed across from mine. Nurse Smith dismissed them, but they didn't leave right away. Everyone was defying the nurse this afternoon. No wonder his expression was so sour.

"I've got Familiar Bonding with you guys later." Dylan leaned in the doorway, blocking it. He refused to be brushed off. Good on him. Nobody should put Dylan Khan in a corner.

"Yes, and?"

"Will you be holding it? You know, considering the other two students are out of sorts?"

"That's a good point." The nurse nodded. "They should be up to it. Just come back when it's time. I'll run the course in this room."

"Smashing." Dylan dropped a wink. Grace giggled.

"Now get out of my way, or don't you want your friends to get treatment?"

"Thanks, Nurse Smith." Dylan turned his back and strutted out the door, Grace following closely.

Nurse Smith rolled his eyes, then clapped his hands three times. His familiar clacked those claws like an echo, shrinking again to scuttle back up into his pocket.

"Thanks, buddy." Logan waved at the pocket.

A series of clacks and chitters came from Nurse Smith's scrub top. I was almost annoyed at his complete lack of humor, but he surprised me with a chuckle as he headed out the door.

Maybe he was only stern because he cared.

"I can't believe I got to ride on the crab." Logan's grin was lopsided but genuine. It made him wince, though. He must have had one hell of a headache. "Cool story."

"Yeah, awfully nice of the decapod to give you a lift." I yawned, then wrinkled my nose. I was so tired it hurt pretty much everywhere.

"Aliyah, are you okay?" Logan stared at the sheet under his hands, picking at his thumb. "You didn't get burned, did you? I don't want you to get hurt. Ever."

I blinked, feeling for all the world like some day-blind owl. All this time, I had worried about hurting people in the future. Logan was upset because he actually did, and I totally ignored it.

"No, I didn't get burned, but I'm not okay." I grimaced. "Feels like that time I belly-flopped off the monkey bars in grade school."

"It wasn't all that magic you called to banish the fire, was it?" Logan's face got pale, all the color draining out of it. He must have been sick with worry.

"No. Let's just say I know how you feel, not wanting people to get hurt and screwing up anyway." I hung my head, partly exhausted but also ashamed. "I almost burned down the cafeteria, remember."

"But you did that on purpose." He slapped a hand over his mouth immediately.

"You understand, then. I'm a horrible person." The pit of my stomach went white-hot, roiling like a school of salamanders were playing water polo in there. I looked up, expecting to see him recoiling in fear.

Instead, Logan looked worn out, like he'd cast major magic and almost fainted. And he was crying. Not like ugly crying; nothing about Logan could ever be that. But a pair of cowboy tears made tracks through the soot on his face.

"You're not." He sniffled. "Because you did it to protect your friends. You're not horrible, I just always say and do the wrong thing. I screw up all the time. Can't do anything right, not even thank the girl who saved my life."

"Did you catch it back in the lab?" I raised my eyebrows, leaning back. I still couldn't say it out loud. "The truth about me?"

"Yeah, and I still say you're not horrible."

Logan wasn't the brightest bulb on the tree academically, but I knew he was canny enough. He also had a bigger heart than I'd expected beating in his showbiz-perfect chest. I could have dismissed his opinion. It would have been easy and probably right.

No. Nothing right was this easy, so in a convoluted sort of way, I had to believe him.

"Thanks, Logan." It was my turn to sniffle. "It means a lot."

Nurse Smith came back, followed by Zeke, who pushed a cart. The nurse handed Logan a small plastic cup with a foamy blue liquid inside and instructed him to drink. The vampire CNA tucked a box of tissues next to me, then poured me a glass of water and set it on the bedside table.

They switched places, repeating their tasks and gestures, except the cup Nurse Smith handed me contained a flat gray liquid. It smelled like nothing. Not like water, which has some vapor to it. This smelled like nothing at all. Like *nothingness*. Like you'd imagine the void of space might smell.

I hesitated.

"Drink that, please."

"What's in it?"

"It's a nullifying medicine."

"No way!" Logan sputtered, the water he'd just tried to drink flying back out. Zeke handed him a napkin.

"Relax, Mr. Pierce." Nurse Smith directed his next comment at me. "You overextended yourself. This will prevent you from casting any magic for the next hour because you need a rest. If you try conjuring or banishing in this state, you could become too ill to attend school at all, and you'll be stuck in my infirmary for a week at least. You can either take it like Hal did this morning, or you can have a sedative and sleep, but that carries a risk that you'll conjure as you slumber. Ultimately, however, your treatment is your choice."

"Okay." I drank the medicine, which was easier than I'd expected. It also tasted like nothing. "I've had worse than this."

"Yeah, that Augmentin they give for ear infections at mundane doctor offices is awful, so I'm told." Nurse Smith put on a weary grin. I realized he probably had one of the hardest jobs in here.

"Thanks." I couldn't muster more than that because the medicine had me feeling a little off.

The nurse left, Zeke following. The vampire CNA glanced back over his shoulder, giving me a small grin and a nod. As they closed the door, I yawned, suddenly tired enough to take a nap. I looked at Logan because I didn't want to leave him effectively alone in here with his thoughts, but he was already out.

I could safely close my eyes for a few minutes, so I did.

CHAPTER TWENTY-FOUR

I woke to the sound of the door opening, revealing Dylan and Grace. They'd both had a chance to clean up, which wasn't the case for Logan or me, but when I looked at him, I saw that Zeke had come back while we slept. He must have washed Logan's face, and probably mine too. I didn't feel grime when I raised my hand to my cheek.

"Hey, I brought some falafel sliders from the café." Dylan set two wrapped packages on Logan's bedside table and two more on mine. He sat on one of the other beds, pulled the table closer, and dropped six more on its surface. Grace sneaked in, snatched one, then sat in the chair at my bedside to unwrap it.

"Aren't you going to eat?" Grace jerked her chin at my untouched sandwiches.

"Just a sec. I only just woke up."

"Not stopping me." Logan's voice was muffled by a mouthful of food. He'd gotten his appetite back. I hadn't, but when in the infirmary, do as the less infirm do.

I unwrapped one small sandwich and took a bite. It was surprisingly good. I hadn't expected the café's fare to be anything special, but this was something else.

"When did the food in that little café get so awesome?" I dabbed the corner of my mouth with a tissue. "Not that I'd know firsthand, but Noah always told me to avoid it."

"They hired a new chef to work there this year." Dylan took another bite, chewing thoughtfully before answering. "He used to work down in Providence. Graduated from Roger Williams University in Culinary Studies."

"Bet he's expensive." Grace shook her head. "But the sandwich is so good, I can't believe he's not worth it."

"I hear they got him on the cheap." Dylan leaned toward us. "He got turned by a vampire, invalidating his restaurant's license. You need a totally different kind to run kitchens as a vamp, you know, and he was out of money. Couldn't afford the fees, so he needed work, and nobody else would hire him."

"That sucks." The paper wrapper around Logan's slider crackled as he clenched his hand. "So unfair."

"Well, stateside vampires certainly get the short end of the stick." Dylan sighed. "Not that they don't have restrictions in the UK, but it's worse here."

"I'd say the worst." Grace leaned back in her chair, rolling her empty wrapper into a ball. "In Canada, we don't have those laws. Not the ones prohibiting them from drinking out of bottles or cups in public or banning them from owning restaurants. Those are totally ridiculous."

"They're not, really." Faith stood in the doorway.

"What are you doing here?" Grace stared daggers at the other girl.

"Just setting the record straight," she said. "And because I just felt like taking Familiar Bonding."

"So, you think vampires shouldn't have rights?" Grace stood up.

"I didn't say that." She sauntered into the room and sat on my other side, which surprised me, all things considered. "But aren't we too young and uneducated to make that judgment? That's why we're here, right?"

"But you're an undeath magus." Logan scratched his head. "I don't understand. If vampires lose rights, they might take some from you."

"There's no use complaining about any of it until we can vote."

Faith smirked, but her eyes looked hollow. She was like a parrot, repeating things she'd heard without examination or thought.

"Anyway. I don't think I'll be able to eat two sandwiches." I changed the subject. "Does anyone want my extra?"

Grace snagged it before anyone else spoke up. As she ate, Nurse Smith walked into the room, accompanied by Professor DeBeer. They stopped to stare at Grace.

"Miss Dubois, you may go." Nurse Smith waved a hand at the door. "You're not required to be here."

"Can I stay, though?" She tilted her head. "All my friends are here. Well, except for Hal. Where is he, anyway?"

Professor DeBeer and Nurse Smith glanced at each other. I got the impression they didn't want to say, but we got an answer anyway.

"His father's taking care of him." The professor waved a hand dismissively. "At any rate, we need to get started if you want to be out of here at a decent hour to do your regular homework."

Nurse Smith clapped his hands, and his familiar strutted in with an enormous box on his back. From the noises, I correctly guessed that a variety of magical critters were inside. When the nurse opened the box, they emerged one by one.

Ember "peeped" from the headboard behind me and fluttered to the floor to join them, clearly excited. Lune hopped out from under Grace's chair, nose twitching as he raised his ears. I heard Seth stirring inside Faith's tote bag. She lifted him out and set him down. The Sha trotted over but sat a safe distance from the newcomers. Maybe she was here for his benefit.

A five-toed cat padded softly toward Logan's bed, bunching her haunches before leaping up to meet him. She sat at his knee, head craning forward as she sniffed in the general direction of his last bit of food.

A curly-haired poodle dog trotted toward Dylan, sitting at his feet and looking up. He cocked his head, lifted one ear, then shook it. He turned his back, although his tail wagged. Clearly, he wasn't impressed with the air magus. Poodles tended to favor earth.

"Come on out now, there's a love." Professor DeBeer spoke, coaxing the creature still in the box, but it stayed put.

"It's all right, Sue. Let's just get started." Nurse Smith carefully moved the box to the floor, then clapped three times. His crab did the clacking thing, then disappeared into the pocket.

The lecture Professor DeBeer gave was extremely basic. I'd heard it all before because she practically recited one of Bubbe's pamphlets on caring for a familiar and how it differed from a mundane pet. It would have been totally boring if Ember wasn't busy making friends. She already knew and liked Lune, but got along just fine with the poodle and the polydactyl cat. She even played with Seth.

I noticed that the Sha followed her, but the moment she turned his way, he pretended not to care. His behavior reminded me an awful lot of Faith's.

Professor DeBeer finished her portion of the lesson. Nurse Smith took over, asking us to give our familiars some basic commands. Dylan and Logan did this with the poodle and the cat. As they worked, the creature in the box finally decided to make its appearance.

The first thing we saw was a long snout and a bulbous pink nose, which I immediately recognized. Its wrinkly pink ears and gray fur were unmistakable, and before her shoulders emerged, everyone knew the little gray lady was a possum.

"Gross." Faith shook her head and rolled her eyes. "There's no way that is a magical creature."

"She definitely is," Grace corrected.

"You're correct, Grace." Nurse Smith nodded. "She knows precisely when discretion is the better part of valor, and is an excellent companion for anyone who hides their true self frequently. I hear they're a favorite amongst magi in intelligence fields."

"Interesting." Faith snorted. "Not. Still think it's gross."

The possum definitely wasn't ordinary. She had a red tail that glowed faintly. I wasn't a magical creature encyclopedia so her species name eluded me, but Grace was right. In moments, she headed straight for Logan, ears perked up and eyes bright.

"Oh." He turned away from the incoming creature, paying extra attention to the cat. "Um. You're looking for someone else, girl."

"Moving along."

I hadn't noticed Nurse Smith's note-taking during the earlier part of the lesson. The scratch of his pen against paper continued the entire time we practiced. He finished without having us demonstrate individually, which was a relief. Ember was usually well-behaved, but I couldn't handle any more attention.

After dismissal, Faith left. Logan and I were stuck until the nurse cleared us. Dylan and Grace didn't have to stick around but did anyway. After another check that took slightly longer than the one he'd given in the hall, we were allowed to head out for dinner.

I didn't want to go.

Don't get me wrong. I definitely wanted out of the infirmary. In fact, I was the first one through the door. But once we were in the lobby, I stopped, balking at the prospect of entering the cafeteria. I couldn't help it; I was afraid.

"What's up, Aliyah?" Logan stepped in front where I could see him before placing a hand on my shoulder.

"Isn't there any other way to get dinner?" I sighed. "Without going in there."

"I get it." Grace nodded. "Those sliders tasted amazing, Dyl, but they were tiny."

"Hmm." Dylan chewed the corner of his bottom lip, thinking. "You know what? I'm not sure."

"Are you guys talking about a to-go bag?" Lee stood at the bottom of the stairs, holding a paper shopping bag—the kind with handles. "Because I know how to get those. This one's for Hal."

"Oh, so you've seen him?" In the battle between hunger and concern, concern won. I'd better appreciate this trait of mine before it got swallowed by extramagus awfulness.

"Not yet, but the headmaster told me he's up in our room and can't make it down." He raised the bag, showing it off. "This is usually for second and third years cramming during exams, but they'll let anybody have one for dinner as long as you know where to ask."

"Wow, that's awesome." Logan grinned. "We sort of missed some stuff and have to study." He shrugged, lying easily about our reasons. That wasn't why we wanted to avoid the caff. "Where do we go for that?"

Lee gave us unexpected but somehow easy instructions. The four of us followed them, heading around the corner along the side of the staircase and then under it. We found ourselves in a tall yet narrow hallway. At least it wasn't a closet under the stairs. This hall was like something out of a dream, the confusing and only mildly disturbing kind.

The only door was at the end, which looked much farther away than it was. One little touch that had me instantly homesick was that it was a half door like the ones in Bubbe's office. My eyes stung, not from the smoke but threatening tears. I didn't want to cry anymore so I knocked, hoping whoever answered would shatter the impression of home and banish this feeling.

It worked. The door opened, revealing a matronly woman with a befloured floral apron. Her gray hair was tied into a low bun, over which she wore a hairnet.

"Hello, and welcome to Lunch Lady Land." She chuckled. "I'm Penelope, how can I help you?"

"Hi there, Penelope." Logan amped up his already high-watt smile. "We'd like some to-go bags, please. One kosher and the rest regular."

"Burning the mid-evening oil, huh?" She clapped four times. "Your food's on its way."

The woman pressed a switch embedded in the door frame. I knew from Bubbe's office that she'd activated an audio system. I shouldn't have been surprised that parts of Hawthorn Academy reminded me of the house I grew up in. They had been designed by the same magus, after all.

Unlike Bubbe's, the switch here didn't play music to soothe magic beasts. Instead, it was a lively polka with plenty of oom-pah. In moments, we heard hooves clopping on the floor behind Penelope the self-styled lunch lady, in perfect time with the polka beat.

A goat with curiously scaled horns appeared. He shook his head, then turned sideways. He was saddled with a set of panniers, which contained our to-go bags. One of them was marked with a K.

How'd they come out so fast?"

"Sandy's a Pricus." Penelope smiled, eyes gleaming with totally justified pride. Her familiar was extremely rare and very special.

"Oooh, a sea-goat!" I clapped my hands. "Cadence would just about die if she were here."

"What's a Pricus, if you don't mind my asking?" Logan treated Penelope like royalty, which for all I knew, she was. The headmaster's unorthodox hiring practices had taught me to stop assuming anything about his staff, including the ones in the background.

"They're amphibious creatures who have command of time for short spans, enough to get your meals out to you a full minute before they've been cooked." She beamed. "Thanks for asking. You might be surprised to hear this, but nobody's ever bothered in the seven years Sandy and I have worked here."

Penelope handed us our bags, and we thanked her. I took perhaps an unusual amount of time and effort on that since as far as I was concerned, Sandy and his magus were lifesavers. I could avoid Charity during two-thirds of my mealtimes now.

The rest of the week, meals would be on easy mode.

CHAPTER TWENTY-FIVE

For once, I was right that first night at Penelope's window. The following days went far more smoothly than the disastrous first two. At breakfast each morning, Faith and Logan rounded out our table, making our numbers high enough that Charity couldn't do more than stare, point, and whisper cruel nothings about us in her circle's ears.

Said circle included Noah, which stabbed like a knife in the back, but I said things went smoother, not perfectly. Our summertime high hopes had gone down in flames, and there would be no recovering them now. Life at Hawthorn Academy for the rest of the first week was like applying cream to a burn as far as my brother went.

The other issue was all the bickering between our professors. Luciano and DeBeer hated each other for reasons still unknown, a fact they tried keeping on the down-low. By the end of the week, I didn't know whether it was a professional or a personal rivalry, but it was like one of those magic eye pictures, unable to be unseen and distracting once known.

Their issues made it harder on the six of us because our class assignments weren't the same. Instead, each scrap of homework or required reading felt like a series of escalations in an epic academic arms race. We couldn't even be effective study buddies. What was worse, neither educator noticed it impacting us.

By the way, you heard me right. I said there were six of us. Faith and Logan officially joined Hal Hawkins' little out-group. Logan still followed me around like he owed me his life, which I periodically reminded him wasn't true. But did he listen? No.

I looked forward to the end of the week when I could find his lost dragonet already, because our dynamic was already pretty awkward, and this new element only made it worse. It also pissed Noah and Elanor off, judging by the dirty looks we got whenever they saw us together. And the first day they'd practically tried to arrange our marriage.

Faith was just there for Hal. Whether she'd glommed onto him because he was the headmaster's son and she was making an indirect power-play or there was some other reason, I didn't know. Either way, she lavished small and random acts of ingratiation on him multiple times per day. Little snacks were common, but on Thursday she gave him a friendship bracelet, the kind woven from embroidery floss.

She only tolerated the rest of us, reminding me of the cat Izzy's grandmother kept. Mittens loved Abuelita but had a withering stare for every other member of the household. The only other person she showed interest in was Bubbe, who had literally saved her tail the time she got frostbite.

Like Mittens with my grandma, Faith showed a grudging respect toward Logan, which was surprising because when it came to anything academic, his unorthodox learning style frustrated her no end. My best guess was she felt a sort of kinship with him. His sister Elanor was almost as bad as Charity when it came to mean behavior.

Grace and Faith still came to Familiar Studies with us, even though they didn't have to. Faith wanted Seth to have an easier time on campus, but for Grace, it was a different story. She and Lune had the kind of bond Dad used to tell us about in bedtime stories—like a fairytale. While Faith stuck around out of necessity, Grace was there because she cared. Maybe too much.

Grace had a crush on Dylan. I couldn't blame her. He was kind, funny, smart, and one handsome dude. He'd turned the heads of practically all the straight girls in school, including Grace. She was also a super-supportive roommate, giving me privacy when I needed it. Without that consideration, I wouldn't have been able to have my rule-breaking calls with Izzy and Cadence every night.

Grace was awesome. I didn't think I'd have made it past day one without her, so of course, I supported her crush on Dylan whenever possible even if I did feel a bit regretful about not letting Cadence push us into a date over the summer.

Lee hung around with us too sometimes, usually for dinner and homework in the lounge after Familiar Studies. He was quietly friendly and his Sumxu was playful. When Scratch was around, all the animals had a blast, even the nervous Sha. Sometimes it was distracting, but their antics outdid the best cute animal vids available on the mundane Internet, so we never minded.

Speaking of our familiars, the strangest thing happened. Ember flat-out befriended Seth. Somehow, the two of them put aside the instinctive animosity between their species to spend the entire Lab period and most of Gym curled up together, whuffing and peeping at each other softly. Nin often joined them, but she seemed fonder of Lune. These other unlikely friends had what I can only describe as dance-offs. If you've ever seen a rabbit dance and a ferret hop, you have some idea of what that looked like.

If Charity's group was our enemy, Alex's was like Switzerland. He hung around with his roommate Eston, and Lee bounced between them and us. The twins almost always added themselves in that group, largely because they idolized Kitty, who appeared to be dating Eston. Why a fire magus would want to date a water one was beyond me, mostly because when I tried wrapping my brain around that dynamic, my awkwardness with Logan got in the way.

Technically I was an extramagus, not straight-up fire, but the two elements were opposite, and my second magic wasn't much better. Solar plus water had no reaction or synergy. Then again, my long friendship with Cadence the mermaid seemed to fly in the face of that.

Alex didn't give us any trouble and kept the twins off our backs, which was nice because they still hung on every word Charity tossed in their general direction. He never came to our rescue either. Lee spent time with us because he was Hal's roommate. Probably, he acted on his own. I leaned on the side of assuming he fell outside the complex ecosystem of Hawthorn Academy's cliques.

That said, having both the first years' small groups go largely unmolested felt miraculous. Charity's circle included the entire third-year class and most of the second-years as well. Among those who didn't associate with her were Noah's ex-boyfriend Darren. He avoided everyone in our year, too.

He had his nose in a book almost all the time, like the three other second-years who hung around him. They worked hard on advanced placement courses. Darren and company were often in a corner of the library when we went in for our period. The Ashfords never kicked them out. Otherwise, they kept to the lounge. We always saw them there, eating out of Penelope's to-go bags just like us.

Logan, Dylan, Hal, and Grace accepted my invitations to visit and either meet or catch up with Cadence and Izzy that weekend. The days crawled, nights feeling truncated like sleep took no time at all. I didn't dream at Hawthorn Academy. Neither did any of my friends who talked about that sort of thing. And mine used to be so vivid. By Friday morning, I found myself wondering whether I'd have any during my weekend at home.

The morning went by uneventfully with one notable exception. At Gym, Hal was finally allowed to join Bishop's Row practice. He made mediocre projectiles but was excellent at dodging. I suspected he was using his space magic for something other than conjuring his orb. If so, it worked for him. He'd be the sleeper star player on our team if he could only increase his stamina, but his skills would be perfect for last-minute plays and scores against the timer.

At Familiar Studies, Nurse Smith brought out the possum again. She tried befriending Logan once more but eventually gave up. After spending four days with him, I understood why. He was under enormous pressure from his parents to have a familiar who'd look good on stage and in promotional photos.

I wondered what he'd do if my hunch was correct and the dragonet Logan's parents had picked out for him bonded with someone else. As awkward as the life-debt misunderstanding between us was, I'd do my best to help him.

Instead of going to Penelope's door for to-go bags with my friends, I bid them goodbye. What felt like the longest week of my life was over, and I got my reward—a weekend at home, surrounded by my family and oldest friends.

I hefted the knapsack with my library books, some laundry, and in the bottom, the forbidden communication orb. Walking across the lobby, I almost expected some incident, either an ambush by Charity and company or walking in on yet another argument between Luciano and DeBeer, but it was quiet and mostly deserted. In the hall leading to the school's exit, Headmaster Hawkins paced.

"Headmaster, thanks for an interesting week," I said.

"Oh?" Apparently, I startled him. His eyes were wide and his hands clasped under his chin. "And you came all the way over here to say that?"

"No." I grinned, hoping to put him at ease, but he didn't relax. If anything, he looked more anxious than before. "Just heading home for the weekend is all."

"I see." This revelation did what my smile couldn't. He dropped his hands, still folded but at his waist instead, and the wildness went out of his eyes. "Well, have a peaceful time, then. Remember, the doors are locked early on Monday morning, so it's best if you return Sunday night."

"Thanks, Headmaster."

Good thing he reminded me since I'd definitely have forgotten that detail. I waved before pushing through the door and out into the sunset light on Essex Street. It took a moment before I got my bearings. The door to Hawthorn Academy had migrated again, this time to the blank wall across the street from a touristy t-shirt shop.

It was almost two long blocks away from Hawthorne Street and my house.

But this was my town and my street, one I'd walked countless times through most of my life. The cobblestones beneath my feet welcomed me, the uneven surface lifting my spirits until the spring in my step was practically ineffable.

Ember let out a series of musical peeps, and I shared her good cheer. She was less elated and relieved than I was, but she was content, and that was what mattered. In two minutes, I walked up the driveway behind Izzy's house.

Just like that, I was home.

CHAPTER TWENTY-SIX

I didn't need to knock or ring the bell; I had my keys. The hallway was dark, usual for a Friday night. Upstairs, I kicked off my shoes on the landing, then entered the living room. Ignoring the tufted sofa with its fleecy throws and cushioned comfort was easier than I thought. I was here on a mission, after all, but the house was empty. Mom and Dad must've gone out.

Sure enough, there was a note on the kitchen counter.

Gone to dine at Bay Bridge. Pizza on counter. See you later! Love, Mom and Dad.

Of course. It was live music night, so they were on a date. I'd never let them know I planned to spend the weekend here or asked the school to do so on my behalf. They had no idea whether I'd come home, although last year they'd figured Noah wouldn't after the first week. My parents demonstrated their love by leaving food out anyway.

Last year, I was home alone while they went on their Friday night dates, but they always left more for dinner than I could eat, probably in case Noah felt the need to escape campus for even just one meal. Of course, they understood. Both of them had attended and graduated from the same school, after all.

I leaned against the counter, not bothering to sit at one of the stools, and ate lukewarm pizza over one of the plates they'd left with the box. Ember perched nearby, devouring the slice I'd set aside for her.

It was from Engine House, reminding me of slices grabbed all summer. I'd be sure to take my school friends there during the weekend, which meant plenty of pizza for everyone.

Once my stomach was no longer growling, I decided it was time to visit Bubbe. The light was on in her office, so she was there, but first, I needed to put the contents of my knapsack away. It wouldn't do for either of my parents to find the seaglass, and I wanted to do some laundry. I left Ember on the counter to finish her dinner.

I headed upstairs to my room, stowing the orb in my closet behind a bag of winter clothes. Once that was done, I set the library books on my bedside table. As I stood, I bumped my head, of course. I'd almost forgotten that low ceiling, which wasn't a problem at Hawthorn.

All the same, that was my room, my home. I belonged here, gabled roof and all. But it was time to leave it for the moment, at least. I carried the knapsack into the upstairs bathroom, opened the laundry hatch, and dumped the dirty clothes down the chute. After closing it, I returned the pack to my room and headed back downstairs.

The laundry machine was in the downstairs water closet, a stacked unit with the washer on the bottom and the dryer on top. I took my clothes out of the hamper under the chute and tossed them in the washer, then dumped some detergent in on top. I was supposed to do it the other way around. My generation wasn't killing household chores. I was just in a hurry, wanting to catch Bubbe before she turned in for the night.

I started the washer, knowing this cycle would give me an hour before I needed to put the clothes in the dryer. That would be enough time to chat with my grandmother downstairs.

"Come on, girl." I beckoned to Ember. She leaned against the paper towel holder, stomach distended, with an enormous grin on her scaly little face.

"Peep?" Of course, she wondered why we were leaving when we just got there.

"Were going to go see Bubbe. You'd like to see Bubbe too, right, girl?"

She stood up, fluttering her wings with excitement, but they didn't manage to lift her off the granite surface. After a few frustrated peeps, she made her way toward the edge of the counter and sat looking up at me expectantly.

"Okay, I get it. Pizza belly means you need a little help." I chuckled, stretching my hands out to lift her up to my shoulder, where she draped herself around the back of my neck.

I felt her rounded tummy against my left shoulder where I usually carried my knapsack. Ember weighed way less, even though she'd totally pigged out.

I headed down the back stairs and knocked on the service door for Bubbe's office. I heard voices inside, more than just my grandmother's. Maybe she had an emergency visit or a friend over. I waited patiently and listened to her footsteps coming down the hall toward the door.

"Aliyah, this is a surprise." Bubbe smiled.

"I'm sorry, Bubbe. I'll come back later if I'm interrupting anything."

"No, you're not. I do have some friends over, but you've met one of them before, and I've just been saying how I'd like to introduce you to the other." She pulled the door open wider and stepped aside to let me through.

We walked down the hall toward the kitchenette and break room, the place where she sat with clients to discuss issues with familiars beyond those of a physical nature—and where she brought them when there was nothing more she could do to help.

That was one reason it was fully equipped with a range, oven, sink, and refrigerator. The table had four chairs and enough room for the yellow and white earthenware tea set, which was in use that evening. Bubbe always said kitchens were the one room where anyone felt like they could sit down and talk.

Which was abundantly true that night. "Anyone" was a great way to define the diversity of Bubbe's guests. She'd mentioned before that I'd already met one, but only in a very vague way. Because, although I instantly recognized Dr. Elizabeth Rassmussen from photographs, I couldn't possibly remember her from the one time we met. I was still in diapers back then.

Of course, she looked exactly the same despite the passage of so many years. Round-faced, straight honey-brown hair, eyes that twinkled like the moon on frost. Dr. Liz was a vampire, the one I mentioned earlier from New Hampshire. Bubbe had pictures of her in her office, mostly ones with them at professional conferences. They were colleagues and friends.

I'd never seen the rotund older gentleman seated at the kitchen table before, but I instantly recognized the creature with him.

"Oh! It's the Grim." I couldn't help but smile and wave. "Hello again."

The shadowy canine thumped its tail on the floor, rapidly sitting up and cocking their head. Grims are pure faerie creatures, which meant this one was genderless and responded to they-them pronouns. It'd be rude to call them "it." But anyway, the man was no magus. Grims couldn't be familiars, but they did make contracts with psychic summoners.

"Dr. Brodsky, this is my granddaughter Aliyah."

"I've heard so much about you. It's lovely to finally make your acquaintance." His voice was heavily accented with the clipped and flipped vowel sounds that indicate a Slavic mother tongue. He extended his hand.

"Nice to meet you, too." We shook. "May I pet your Grim?"

"That's entirely up to them, but it's fine with me." He nodded and smiled.

I leaned toward the shadowy dog, my hand extended at a level with their eyes. I let them sniff and form their own opinion of me. At first, they leaned back, lifting their head to study my face. It was up in the air at that point whether they'd be okay with me.

Ember stirred on my shoulder, lifting her head and extending her long neck to get a good look at the Grim. They locked gazes, and something passed between them that my bond with Ember only let me sense to a small degree.

"Peep." She said this with certainty, for all the world like a person giving a definitive answer to a question I couldn't possibly guess. I mean, what kind of query would a Grim straight out of the Under have for a young dragonet? Apparently an important one.

The Grim looked at me, then stepped forward and did the last thing I expected at that point—they licked my hand. Smiling, I reached out to scratch behind their ears. The tail wag got more intense, to the point where Dr. Brodsky put his hands on his teacup and saucer to keep them from rattling.

"Well, she's certainly got your touch, Mildred." Dr. Liz smiled, showing fangs that were just slightly elongated. That meant she was well-fed, which made sense because the teacup in front of her was half-full of bagged blood.

Bubbe always kept some on hand. Vampirism happened. Any psychic or magus could get turned just like a regular human. She wouldn't turn away a critter in need just because the person with them happened to be undead. As an extraveterinarian, she even had a license to keep stuff like that here in her office. Some magical creatures also drank blood.

As I continued playing with the Grim, moving my scratches from behind the ears to under their chin, I tried to remember where I'd heard the name "Brodsky" before. I couldn't quite put my finger on it, but it seemed familiar, and recent, too. One thing for sure, nobody at school had mentioned him. Maybe on television? Could he have given a Ted Talk on summoning or something?

"Do you need anything, Bubbe?" I stood, stepping back toward the doorway. "I was thinking of heading down to Walgreen's."

I decided that our conversation could wait until her guests had gone. Some of it was sensitive, and critical of the Fairbanks family. They might have been more influential than I imagined. Coincidence was a thing, after all. After the week I had at school, the last thing I wanted to do was tempt it.

"Yes, if you don't mind." She nodded, bustling about with her teacup at the sink. "I'm running low on dish soap." She held up the bottle and shook it, sloshing green sudsy dregs from side to side.

"Okay, I'll be back in about fifteen minutes or so." I waved and smiled. "It was nice to meet you, Dr. Brodsky, and to see you again, Dr. Liz."

"Don't tell me you remember the last time, child." The vampire doctor grinned. "You could barely speak back then."

"All the same, *you* remember it."

Her grin grew into a smile. "Just so. And thank you."

This time, I headed out through the front of the office. There was a back door, but the small fenced yard behind the house was where we exercised the critters who needed it. We had quite the obstacle course back there, mostly for the benefit of four-legged earthbound creatures recovering from sprains or broken limbs.

At the end of the driveway, I glanced up at Izzy's house, which was dark. I should've expected that because she'd already told me it was Parents' Night at Messing Prep. "Parents" in the Mendez family always meant everyone, including Abuela and her grouchy old cat. I grinned as I turned right down Hawthorne Street, picturing Mittens ignoring a gymnasium full of psychics.

Ember hummed softly on my shoulder, contented with the bellyful of pizza and the cool night air. Salem's traffic picked up in September, even though all the big Halloween events were a month out. Folks interested in visiting during the busiest time of year sometimes came up early to familiarize themselves with the general area ahead of time. Others just wanted to see the history and didn't mind missing all the live events, costumes, and carnivals.

As I turned the corner onto Derby Street, I saw a trio of teenagers staring at the wax museum. They were not from Hawthorn Academy since I didn't recognize them. One tapped the others on their shoulders, jerking her chin at me. They whispered, smiled, and cooed, making it clear they'd noticed Ember. Back before the Reveal, kids like me had special amulets to prevent that kind of thing from happening.

It was a freer world now, something I tried not to take for granted.

"Go on, say hi," I murmured.

"Peep!" I felt Ember lift her head off my shoulder, and in my peripheral vision, saw her stretch out her neck as far as it would go as she greeted the mundane kids.

One of the teenagers, clearly my age or even older, clapped her hands. I smiled at them as I went by. It wasn't just me who appreciated this new, open world. Kids like these wouldn't even have believed in magic thirty years ago, or if they had, they would have feared it.

Overall, I thought the world had changed for the better, although vampires and some of the shifters still fought for their rights. That made me wonder again how the brother of someone like my mom, who raised me with this viewpoint, could take the opposite.

Because he's an extramagus like you.

"No." Stupid inside voice. And my protest didn't even work, because it continued.

Yes. Someday you'll be the one watching the world burn.

I shook my head, keeping my mouth shut because I didn't want to frighten my awestruck peers or anyone else on the street. And if that insistent little voice in my head was right, I'd better hold on to that feeling as long as I could—the one where I cared about other people even when they were total strangers.

Ember sensed something wrong. She curled her around my arm, twining it down my bicep, and rubbed her cheek against mine, humming softly. I recognized the tune, the one Bubbe always sang in her office.

"Thanks." This time I didn't keep my voice quiet. Instead, I reached up and scratched her under the chin to make it obvious to any passersby that I was talking to my familiar and not myself. Besides, who could possibly have taken a word of kindness as a threat?

Your magisupremacist uncle, for one.

I sighed, refusing to give in to that line of thinking. Besides, I was at Walgreen's already. Well, across the street from it, anyway. I stood on the sidewalk in front of the crosswalk, waiting for traffic to stop. When it did, I strode along, eyes up and waving at the drivers.

As I stepped inside the drugstore, I realized there wasn't anything I wanted from here. The errand was only a ploy, after all, so I headed down the aisle with household items and grabbed dish soap for Bubbe. I wanted to be convincing, I'd have to pick something for myself as well, so I wandered up and down the aisles, looking at nothing.

Finally, I knew what to do. I strode toward the registers, grabbed a pack of gum, and put it on the counter with the soap. I went through the motions of paying, exchanging common pleasantries with the changeling behind the counter. Yes, she was a changeling, and I knew because her glamour slipped as she helped me.

"Your dragonet's adorable." She smiled, flashing green teeth. In a moment, she covered her mouth with one hand. "Sorry."

"It's okay. I understand."

"You're at the prep school, aren't you?"

"Yeah, but I grew up here in town. Going to hang out with my family off-campus for the weekend." I smiled. "It's kinda nice to be home."

"Oh, that's true. I can't wait until Thanksgiving when I can go back to Fitchburg."

"Are you at Gallows Hill?"

"Yeah, just started. To be honest, I kind of prefer working here?" Her voice lifted at the end of her sentence as though asking me if it was okay to feel that way.

"Hey, my name's Aliyah. Me and my friends know this town, so if you ever have questions, you know, like cool places to visit or spots to escape the tourists, just message me here."

I flipped my receipt over and jotted down my chat handle, then tore the bottom off and pushed it toward her.

"Wow, thanks." She shook her head. "I'm Brianna. It's not easy to make friends around here, and most of the other changelings at school aren't cool with Goblins."

She scribbled her handle down on a section of blank receipt that she got off her register. I took it and smiled, tucking into my pocket.

"I'm not on much during the week because Hawthorn's a no-phone zone." I chuckled. "But I'll probably be here on weekends with friends from town and school."

"That's good to know. The only folks I know here are co-workers. I didn't know Hawthorn had rules against cell service."

"It's just impossible to get a signal on campus. Anyway, one of my friends goes to Gallows Hill and isn't even a changeling. Send me a message tomorrow, okay?"

"I will. Talk to you later!"

I headed out of the store, retracing the route I took there to get back home. The streets had quieted down a bit, and the walk back proceeded without incident. When I arrived at Bubbe's office again, I headed through the front door.

When I got to the kitchen, the guests were gone. My grandmother had tidied up—well, at least as much as she could without dish soap. I fixed that problem for her, taking it from the bag, opening the bottle, and squeezing a dollop onto the sponge she was holding.

"Thanks, Bissell."

I helped, drying the dishes and setting them on the rack. I wasn't sure where she kept the yellow tea set, and I didn't want to go rummaging through her cabinets. I studied the china, certain I'd never seen it used before and wondering why. Perhaps this was just for when Dr. Liz visited, to make the bagged blood more appealing.

When we finished the simple task, Bubbe gestured at the table. I took a seat and she sat in the chair opposite, leaning forward on her elbows. Instead of tea, a tall glass sat on the table between us, beside a spoon on a folded napkin, a can of plain seltzer water, and a bottle of chocolate syrup. She put the spoon in the glass, dumped in some of the syrup, then popped the can and poured the seltzer over it all.

The mixture foamed up, reminding me of the disastrous lab experiment. I closed my eyes and sighed. Would my experiences at Hawthorn Academy ruin even the simple pleasure of sharing an old childhood treat with my grandmother? I hoped not.

"Sha got your smile?"

"I wish it were that simple, Bubbe."

"Everybody says high school's supposed to be the best time of your life. Well, almost everybody. I won't say it, and you won't hear your mother repeat that platitude either. So, what's wrong?"

I explained to her. Not everything, though. Absolutely not about being an extramagus, and I didn't tell her that Noah had turned on me or bring up the rivalry between DeBeer and Luciano. But I mentioned that I was being teased about Richard Hopewell.

Bubbe didn't interrupt. It wasn't her way. She liked to hear the entire story before asking more questions, let alone commenting. I wasn't sure where her patience came from, but it wasn't a trait I inherited, at least not for anyone but magical critters.

That was how I avoided naming names or getting into details about the incidents. She'd heard about the fires in the cafeteria and the lab, and I left the formation of Hal's clique for the end. That way, at least she'd know I'd be okay. After that, I moved right along, changing the subject to Logan's problem.

"So, remember the dragonet you had here in your office? The blue one? Logan painted a picture, and I think that's the critter his parents sent from Vegas with him."

"But Bissell," Bubbe shook her head. "That little fellow's not bonded to anyone."

"Are you sure?" I blinked. "He's supposed to be my friend's familiar."

"I've been in this business for a decade longer than your father has been alive and studied with your great-grandfather in this field for half as long as that to boot. Are you really asking if I'm sure?" The twinkle in her eye and her smirk told me she wasn't angry, just engaging in a little banter.

"Okay. There's more." I took a deep breath before continuing because this was a whammy. "I also think I know the magus who belongs with that dragonet, and it's not the friend I just mentioned."

"It's your fellow, isn't it?"

"Excuse me?" I blinked.

"You know the one. He was around half the summer with Izzy and Cadence."

"Dylan? He's just a friend."

"Well, then your friend fellow." She nodded.

"How did you know I meant him?"

"He's at least as powerful as you are with magic, and dragonets are particular about that sort of thing."

"That can't be right."

"Why?"

"Because he said his parents had him tested and he's average."

"That's nothing. Your tests were average too."

"What? Nobody tested me."

"Your parents didn't, but your grandfather did."

"I didn't know that." I stirred my egg cream absently.

"It was a secret between him and me."

"I thought he was mundane."

"Yes, that he was." She sighed, her eyes focused inward on something buried deep. "But his work was not."

"What did he do?" I knew already, but I thought Bubbe would feel better saying it out loud.

"He was a military doctor who cared for the early extrahuman enlistees." She smiled kindly. "This, of course, was why you were so inspired by that mundane student down at Providence Paranormal."

"He never had the sort of opportunity Lynn Frampton did, and I think it's pretty amazing how times have changed for the better." I closed my eyes, tears threatening a critical breach. "So, how could my own uncle try to murder her?"

"Your grandfather and your uncle never met, but they'd have been enemies if they had. Some see change as a miracle—people like your mother, your father, and I. But others? Well, they see it as a threat."

"I don't understand." I opened my eyes, sniffling. The tears hadn't come yet.

"That's a blessing and a curse, Aliyah. May it prove to be more the former than the latter."

"Speaking of blessings and curses, Bubbe, what we do about the dragonet? No matter what happens, at least one of the guys is going to suffer."

"Any sentient being knows suffering is inevitable, but any healer knows one thing more—suffering ends. I'm proud of you for offering them help. Bring them by sometime this weekend, and we'll see what we can do."

"Thanks, Bubbe. I love you." And there went the waterworks. Tears rolled down my face, dropping to the table, onto my arm, into my egg cream, even on Ember.

"Peep." She rubbed her cheek against mine, not caring that she got all wet.

"I love you too, Bissell."

She said no more that night, but it was more than enough.

CHAPTER TWENTY-SEVEN

I made my way up the back stairs in the dark. I didn't need light to see. I had used that staircase for sixteen years, practically learned to walk on it. But as I ascended, a pale golden light banished some darkness in front of me. I glowed.

"Go away." I tried shutting off the solar magic, but it was no use. No matter how much I wanted to wish away being an extramagus, the powers I didn't want wouldn't leave me alone.

I stood on the top step, my hand on the doorknob, unable to open the door and enter the apartment. It wasn't that I didn't want to be in there. All I wanted was to go home, and it was right there for me on the other side of the door. All I had to do was turn and push.

But did I have the right? I wasn't the person I had been when I left for Hawthorn Academy. Was this why Noah spent so much time there and seemed so reluctant to leave school? Had he changed too?

No. He was just like Dad, except for being a gay teenager. He even looked like our father when he didn't have time to straighten his hair. My brother was a Morgenstern through and through, down to the serpent familiar, even if he wasn't happy about it.

But I was different. I resembled evil Uncle Richard more than my mother, despite what my family had said my whole life. Were they lying? Did Mom see the brother she'd never mentioned in my face every day? Was I the reason she seemed so tired all the time?

The glow persisted, even growing stronger. I wished I'd never have to see it again, so I closed my eyes and focused, telling it to get lost, scram, beat it, make like a tree and leave. When I opened my eyes, it was still there, like a rotten smell under the sink even after you took the garbage out.

"Just go already!" I didn't know if I spoke to the solar magic or myself at this point, but that time, it worked. The glow vanished.

I almost fell into the apartment as the door was pulled open. Ember stretched her wings out behind me, steadying me.

"Go where?" My father stood blinking into the darkness. "We just got home. Did you want to get some ice cream?"

"Nowhere, Dad. Sorry." I shrugged, stepping through the door and into the space between the kitchen and the dining room. "Sorry."

"Did you get in a fight with your friends?" Dad lifted his glasses, peering closely at me. "Are you okay?"

"No, but school was a whole week of stress."

"Do you need a hug?"

I couldn't say another word or I'd burst into tears, so I flung my arms around my father instead. He hugged back, lifting me off the ground even though I was almost exactly his height. Or maybe a tiny bit taller. This was exactly what I needed.

I couldn't possibly think him even secretly disappointed in me, let alone afraid I'd turn out like his criminal brother-in-law, not after a hug like that.

"Don't forget me."

Mom stood behind Dad, her arms outstretched. He pulled her in for a group hug. I got exactly the same feeling from Mom—that she loved me. Both my parents did, and while I wasn't wrong to question it, I probably wouldn't be making that mistake again anytime soon.

While I moved the laundry from the washer to the dryer, I thanked them for the pizza and told them I'd been to visit Bubbe and that I was tired. I didn't have to feign a yawn as I said good night and headed up the back stairs.

I lucked out in the parental department.

It wasn't until I washed my face, brushed my teeth, and got my pajamafied self into bed that I realized almost none of my school friends shared that luck. But that was a concern for tomorrow. For now, I needed sleep.

I woke to Ember peeping in my face. It wasn't loud, more chirpy and social. She was probably lonely after being at Hawthorn Academy for a whole week, playing with other familiars.

"Don't worry, girl, we'll see another dragonet today."

She flapped her wings, letting out a trilling sound I'd never heard her make before.

"I'll have to ask Bubbe what that means." I sat up, stretching before cautiously making my way out of the bed. The last thing I wanted was a goose egg from the low ceiling to start my day.

Once I'd showered, brushed my teeth, and gotten dressed, I headed downstairs. My laundry was in a basket at the foot of it, so I picked that up and turned back around, putting it on my bed to be folded later. No, I didn't expect my parents to do laundry chores for me, especially not while I slept in. I was just glad they paid the bills.

Down in the kitchen, Dad made pancakes. With blueberries. Ember fluttered down to the counter and started prancing around, peeping and making an epic fuss until Dad reached out and tossed a blueberry in her direction.

Ember had to swoop off the counter and dive in order to catch the fruit before it hit the floor. When she came up, she held the little blueberry in her mouth, facing the shiny glass front of the stove. She must have liked how she looked holding it or something.

I headed to the dining room and set the table except for the plates, which I kept stacked where Dad could reach them. Mom came out of her office to carry each plate to the table once he'd laden it with cakes. I got syrup, cinnamon, butter, and cream out of the kitchen. Once we were seated and half the pancakes were gone, Mom asked about my plans for the day.

"My friends Dylan and Logan are coming from Hawthorn. Logan's coming first, before lunch. Dylan can't make it until later because he works in the café."

"Oh." Mom's smile was unexpected. "I used to work there."

"Really?" I tried not to blink or otherwise seem more than casually curious. I'd have never thought she'd been a work-study student, not with the kind of money the Hopewells came from. I wouldn't have been surprised if she'd said that last week.

"Yes. It's how I met your father. I served him coffee."

"You mean, you spilled on me." He chuckled.

"Well, at least it was iced."

"Doesn't matter. You were still hot."

"Mom! Dad!" I had grown out of thinking boys were icky, but somehow the idea of sex put me off, especially when it involved my parents. "Eww!"

"Aliyah." My mother tilted her head, arching an eyebrow with an expression I recognized as faux-serious. "You and Noah didn't spring fully formed from your father's brow and calf like Athena and Dionysus."

"Still." I shook my head, my expression sobering. I couldn't help it at the mention of my brother, but the rest of the family had no clue about the issues between Noah and me yet.

My parents finished their breakfast with faint grins on their faces. The two of them were still very much in love, although it was a mystery to me how anyone ended up together. Every remotely romantic interaction I'd had was more awkward than a turtle on its back. Maybe someday I'd figure it out. Or maybe not. Izzy didn't seem concerned about it. I wished it didn't bother me.

The doorbell rang as we were rinsing dishes. Mom and Dad finished up, letting me answer it. I opened the door to find Izzy and Cadence. They came in, and we sat on the living room sofa. I sank against the cushions, relieved to be with my most familiar and best friends.

"We're going out." My father poked his head in through from the kitchen. "Bubbe has some critters that need exercise, the kind you walk on a leash, so we're taking a stroll around town. See you girls later!"

We all said goodbye. Cadence grabbed the remote, flipping through channels on the television absently. She usually had to occupy part of her attention with something while trying to focus. I was used to that, although it drove other people up the wall. By other people, I meant all of Izzy's siblings. They didn't have much patience.

"So, what's this big thing that came up?" Cadence didn't look at me, but I knew she was asking because she cared. "The one you wouldn't even talk about over the you-know-what?"

"Remember the explosion in lab I told you about?" They nodded. "Well, it's worse than just property damage because I realized I can do this."

I held out my hand and called up that awful solar magic. Cadence dropped the remote. She leaned over and picked it up again but stared the entire time at the globe of light in my hand. Izzy smacked her face with her palm.

"No way." The mermaid's lips were dry, her voice a parched whisper. She cleared her throat. "No freaking way."

"Yes, way." Izzy held a card in her hand, plucked from the bag slung across her body. "Yes, freaking way."

It was the sun reversed. In case you don't know what that means, just wait. Izzy laid it on me.

"This is some unclear, fake, sad, oppressive shit right here." She slapped the card down on the coffee table, then looked me straight in the eye. "Who's griefing you about being an extramagus?"

"I already told you. Some upperclassman named Charity Fairbanks, even though she doesn't know for sure." I swallowed past the lump in my throat. "And someone else who's even worse."

"Stop acting like this cryptic-ass card, Aliyah, and tell us the whole story."

I didn't have to hide this from my friends like with my family. They weren't related to Noah, and they didn't even like him that much, so I told them all of it, down to how he ignored me. I even mentioned the unspoken detail that had disturbed me for the entire week.

"I was in the infirmary twice, and he didn't even visit."

"Wow, what a jerk." Cadence shook her head. "I can't believe I almost set him up with my neighbor. Shelby dodged a bullet right there."

"Mean people suck." Izzy frowned.

"You guys want coffee?" I stood up, rubbing my hands against my legs where my elbows had pressed too hard on my thighs. "My folks will be back any minute, and I don't want them to know all of this."

"Coffee sounds great." Izzy nodded, swiping her card off the table and tucking it back in her bag. "Should we go now?"

"Okay, but we might go back again after Logan gets here."

"Is that your non-Dylan classmate?" Cadence stood up, fluffing her hair. "Is he cute?"

"You'll figure it out, Cadence." I stepped toward the door, grabbing my knapsack off the hook. "Oh, wait."

My friends waited by the door as I left a brief note for my parents, telling them I'd be out. They did the same for me, and I didn't want them to worry. I also grabbed my phone off the charger, checking it first to see if Brianna from Walgreens had sent me a message. There was nothing, so I just brought it along.

We headed down the stairs and out into the sunlit day. It was the best kind you could get in early autumn, where the light fell through just enough cloud cover to look dreamy and the breeze only just barely nipped. We headed around the corner and down Essex Street, taking our time. We all knew where we were going and how to get there since there was only one place extrahumans our age went for coffee.

The Witch's Brew wasn't technically on Essex Street, or any other for that matter. Instead, the front door was in an alcove. We pushed through the door with its weathered wood and cauldron-shaped stained glass, stepping into a space steeped in the warm aroma of freshly ground coffee.

This place didn't heal all the sore spots inflicted by my week at Hawthorn Academy, but it came close.

We waited in the short line, then ordered beverages. The enormous ornate mural clock on the wall had the broomstick halfway between eleven and twelve, with the wand just a hair off noon. The hour and the nice weather were two reasons we took our drinks outside. The third, of course, was that we had to search for the door to my school to meet Logan on his way out.

Essex Street was about as busy as it got on a day outside October. Most of the tourists walked with food or drinks instead of sitting inside, for one thing. That was probably why the tricycle-powered Polaroid cart almost ran us over, but it swerved out of the way just in time before screeching to a halt.

"Not again." Izzy rolled her eyes.

"Uh-oh." Cadence put one hand to her cheek.

"Hi." I stepped in the way as the camera dude hopped off and jogged over. "We're okay but running a little late, so no time to talk, Azrael."

"Are you sure?" He peered past me at Izzy with stars in his eyes. He didn't even notice Ember peeping curiously at him. She'd never met this fixture of Essex Street atmosphere yet.

I mentioned before that Isabella Mendez isn't interested in boys, and probably not girls either. Azrael Ambersmith was the main reason I was sure this is true. He was a Goblin changeling, the youngest member of a family otherwise made up of magi and psychics, and he'd been crushing on Izzy since second grade. He was also almost as pretty as Logan, but in a shabbier steampunk sort of way.

His name sounded like it came from the pages of an old pulp fantasy novel from the 1960s. Maybe it did, for all I knew. The Ambersmiths were the local magipsychic crafters, tinkers, and second-hand item dealers. Certainly, they'd read some of the books lining the walls of their storefront farther down the block.

Plenty of people's trash got turned into treasures in their workshops and sold from one of their storefronts or this cart. Azrael's aunt had married the cobbler, too. Ambersmiths were all over the wi-fi-negating zone around Hawthorn Academy, and by all appearances, they made a decent living because of it. The Polaroid cart had plenty of customers once folks realized they couldn't reliably use their phones to take pictures here.

"I'm meeting a friend from Hawthorn, Az." Out of the three of us, I had remained on the best terms with Azrael since the end of elementary school. That was why, whenever he came around, they left deflecting him to me. At least this time, I didn't feel like I had to lie.

"Oooh, I know where the door is today! Just saw someone come out of it, in fact."

"Thanks, Az." I grinned.

"I'll just hop on the trike and lead the way." He jogged back to his ride, and I followed.

"Whatever." Izzy followed too, staring at the cobblestones.

"At least he's nice to look at, Iz."

"I don't care about that stuff, Cadence." Izzy shook her head. "Flowers are pretty, too."

"Well, think of him like a painting or statue or something, then."

"Not helping."

"Sorry." Cadence twirled a lock of her hair between her fingers. Suddenly, she stopped cold. "He didn't ever do...anything? Like, improper?"

"No. I just don't want to date people." Izzy shrugged.

"Okay. Because I was gonna say, if he did do anything—"

"Thanks, Cadence." Izzy finally looked up. "You're a good friend."

"Hey, what's with the cat?" I pointed.

They looked in the direction I indicated and saw it too-a scruffy stray cat. Well, she was only scruffy because her long hair was all matted. Also, she seemed awfully underfed. I was about to call out to her, thinking maybe Bubbe could help. Even if she was mundane, food was food. But Azrael rang the bell on his handlebars and stopped his cart. He jerked his thumb at what was usually an old boarded up door. I knew better, of course.

Az took one last long look at Izzy before ringing his bell again and taking off down the street. I looked around for the cat again but didn't see her.

Just then, the door opened and Logan walked out. He noticed us right away. We were super-hard to miss, standing right in his way like that. It only took him three steps to cross the distance. That was when I realized why I felt so awkward around him.

Logan Pierce looked at me the same way Azrael Ambersmith looked at Izzy.

And I'd thought I was so slick, noticing Grace's crush on Dylan. Of course, Cadence saw it right away. I was surprised she didn't whip out a wedding planner instead of just elbowing me in the ribs.

Before my merfriend could say anything, I introduced Logan to everybody, then invited him down to visit Bubbe. It was a short enough walk to pass the time in conversation with basics about Logan's life outside of school. He had ready answers for questions like that, although I wondered how many were well-rehearsed and designed to please his parents.

By the time we turned on Hawthorne Street, I realized the cat had come back. She trotted to keep up, but only because she was so worn out. I saw her stop before Izzy's house, dropping to the sidewalk too suddenly.

"Just a sec, guys. Animal in trouble here."

I turned back for the poor kitty. She was on her side, panting heavily, almost like a dog. Logan hovered, peering over my shoulder.

"Peep?" Ember fluttered down, landing on the sidewalk. Once there, she sat back on her haunches, lifting her head straight up in the air and letting out a long, keening wail.

"Easy, girl," I said to both critters. "I'm gonna help. See?"

Bending down was easy, scooping the cat up too much so. She was very light, like the wind could have carried her away with ease. I got the impression of a dried-out husk, but she was cool to the touch, not hot like an animal fighting an illness.

"Just around the corner and into a building, okay? Then you'll have a chance to get well."

Izzy and Cadence knew better than to get in my way in situations like these. Logan, not so much, or maybe he was just as concerned about the unfortunate stray. At any rate, he followed closely. And for once, he didn't stare at me. He only had eyes for the cat.

I thought back to Familiar Studies and how he always played with the polydactyl. And then that the possum tried bonding with him twice. At that moment, I understood the shortcomings of that entire series of lessons. They don't do what they were designed for—helping magi without familiars meet suitable companions.

For some people, only crisis could create enough vulnerability to bond with a magical creature. I should know since it happened that way for me. Why not Logan? But I had to hope this kitty was more than she seemed to be because if not, Logan's need to appease his family might lead to rejection. In this state, that could kill her.

The moment we got inside, Bubbe came out from behind the counter. She took charge immediately, rushing the cat back into a room—the one right across from the blue dragonet's, in fact. Logan glanced over his shoulder, directly at the half-open door where the blue-scaled beauty strutted.

He turned his back on the dragonet without hesitation, following Bubbe and the cat into the empty treatment room. His shoulders were square, his jaw set, but both trembled.

We all watched, silent and barely breathing as my grandmother worked. She managed to revive the cat, or at least her paws stirred, and she opened her eyes.

"Peep?" Ember perched on top of the lamp in the corner, casting a winged shadow. She blinked, tilting her head one way and then the other, but she didn't keen again. Considering that dragonets only do that while mourning death, that was a good sign.

"Cadence, fetch me some water, please."

"I'll do it, Bubbe."

"No. You shouldn't touch any of the things we'll use for her at this point. She can't handle any more fire energy in this state, Bissel."

"I'm water." Logan stepped forward. "I mean, I'm a magus, and it's my element."

"Well then, no need to fetch a basin." Bubbe gave him a faint smile.

"Please conjure an orb for me. They've taught you that much at Hawthorn by now, yes?"

"Yes, ma'am." He held his hands at his middle, one over the other like in Gym for Bishop's Row. The space between his hands filled rapidly, and without needing to be told, he walked up to the table like he'd been doing this all his life.

"Now drop it all right on her."

"What?"

"Won't she drown?"

"Who does that to a cat?"

All those questions came from us, not Logan. He followed orders, drenching the poor critter on the table.

The next thing I knew, Ember swooped in arcs overhead, singing happily. The cat sat up, her fur clinging to her sides. It was still matted and bedraggled, but her eyes were brighter. The warm, soothing sound of her purr filled the room. She curled up in a cozy ball, gazing up at the boy who'd saved her until he glanced down and their eyes met.

Logan's entire face lit up. I'd seen that exactly once before, when Noah bonded with Lotan, and that moment had been fleeting. This one was sustained, so grounds for doubt remained, but mostly I recognized the truth because I'd had the feeling behind his expression myself.

The day I met Ember.

Logan's familiar troubles were far from over because of his parents, but at least he could stay on the Familiars track at Hawthorn. I watched him approach the table to stroke the cat's flank. When he pulled his hand up, a matted clump of fur came with it. He blinked for a moment, then grinned.

"A mercat." Logan shook the shed fur off his hand, tossing it in the trash. "I can't believe it."

"Yes, and it's a miracle you found her in time. I've never seen one this dehydrated in all my years as an extraveterinarian." Bubbe handed him a brush with rounded bristles.

"Well, she doesn't have to worry about that anymore." He went to work, pulling the bristles gently along her sides. She turned so he could reach more of the matts.

He brushed them out, and not the same way as with a regular cat, either. Mercats only got like this if they spent too much time without a bath. Like Cadence, they could walk on land, but in saltwater, they had fins and a tail from the midsection down. Unlike merfolk, who could go years without setting foot in the ocean, the cats needed a good drenching every few days. She must have been out on the street for a week with no rain. Bubbe was right—we did find her just in time.

It wasn't a miracle, though. Finding the cat at the same time Logan came out of the school smacked of coincidence. That was just fate for extrahumans.

CHAPTER TWENTY-EIGHT

We all sat in Bubbe's kitchen, chatting as the mercat rested in the other room. Bubbe set out a basin of salted water for her to climb into as needed, but the best thing to help her recover was rest.

"What's her name, Logan?"

"Uh, I'm not sure."

"Oh?" Bubbe raised an eyebrow.

"Yeah. It's not like I bonded with her or anything." He sat up straighter as though remembering something. "I almost forgot to mention, Doctor Morgenstern. I came to find my—"

Just then, Bubbe tapped her earring. I knew what that meant.

"Someone's in the lobby. Hang on a moment." She rose and headed out.

We all heard the murmur of voices out there. And of course, everyone recognized the new one. Dylan arrived early. He followed Bubbe in and leaned against the wall because we'd run out of chairs.

"They let me out of work because I got deliveries done so fast." He grinned at Cadence and Izzy. "Good to see you two ladies again."

Everybody said hello, the girls getting up to give Dylan hugs. Of course, I'd just seen him the day before, so I didn't bother. Logan didn't either, but he did stand up to share a handshake.

"You were saying, Logan?"

"Yeah, I'm here for my dragonet. Well, technically he's my parent's, but they sent him here with me, so he's my responsibility." He pulled his painting from the tube slung over his shoulder. "That's him."

"That's a handsome little fellow, and yes, he's here, although I'm not sure he'll be happy to see you, Logan." Bubbe raised her eyebrow. She'd seen him turn away from the dragonet then, just like I had.

Dylan's mouth dropped open. He closed it before Logan, Izzy, or Cadence noticed, but I did. Ember too. She fluttered off my shoulder and over to Dylan's, rubbing her head against the side of his head, tousling his hair.

"What's up with that?" Izzy pointed, blinking at my dragonet's disloyal behavior.

"I don't know?" I slumped against the back of my chair. "She's never done that before. Bubbe?"

"Hmmm." My grandmother sighs. "I think it's time you all met our scaly runaway. Come along, everyone."

She led us down the hall toward the back of the office. The last room on the left was unoccupied and clean. Bubbe asked us to wait there, then left, heading back toward the blue dragonet's room. She returned in moments with the creature in her arms.

"So, here's the little man of the hour."

Logan was about to speak, but the dragonet cut him off. Instead of peeping like Ember he had a chirping voice. He clearly had no regard for the magus he'd come to Salem with, either. In fact, he squirmed madly, trying to get out of Bubbe's arms so frantically I was worried he'd scratch her.

Before anything like that happened, my grandmother let go. She was a good doctor and has developed a way with just about every type of magical creature over years of practice. It might not even be mysterious to her why Logan's parents would try to pair him with a dragonet that wasn't even representative of his water element. But then again, it was her business to understand magical creatures, not the minds of magi in showbiz.

The dragonet flew up and down the hall a few times, flitting past the doorway as we watched him. He shimmered in the lights of the hallway, clearly frustrated that this wasn't open sky. Air creatures were like that. Coop them up for too long, and they got downright hyperactive.

After three laps, he divebombed Dylan.

Ember leaped off his shoulder, getting out of the way but leaving Dylan off balance. That was why he tumbled to the floor, nearly as tangled with the dragonet as I had been with my own the day she'd found me.

Moments later, their eyes met. It was just like what happened between the mercat and Logan in the other room, but of course, Dylan had no reservations about this occasion, unlike his roommate. Or at least he was free of them at the moment.

"His name is Gale."

"Oh, no." Logan crossed his arms on the examination table and leaned forward, burying his face in his arms. "My parents—"

"Sorry, Logan." Dylan looked up from the floor, eyes wide and face slack. "Didn't mean it."

"Yeah, it just happened." His voice was muffled, hard to hear the tone in it, but I caught the hitch between words—trying not to cry. "I get it."

Bubbe was like someone watching a ping-pong match. Her eyes moved from the boy by the table to the boy on the floor, her face as still as stone. She grew up at a time where all magic, including bonding with familiars, was totally secret. From her perspective, an unbonded familiar could choose any magus. Maybe she didn't automatically understand what was wrong here, so I decided to explain, but not with everybody just sitting here. This was Logan's business, though clearly, he shared it with Dylan too. But not Izzy and Cadence. He'd just met them.

"Hey, girls?" I stood up. "I was thinking we ought to go for pizza, but considering everything that just happened here, we need takeout."

"Sure, we'll pick it up." Izzy grabbed Cadence by the shoulder, shaking her. "I'm short on cash, though."

"Here you go." I dug in my knapsack, took out my wallet, and got the money Mom and Dad had left for me this morning. I handed that to Izzy. "I think we'll need more than one pie."

"Yeah, I remember how much Dylan the bottomless pit eats." She chuckled. "Come on, Cadence. You have to help me carry pizzas because I'm not gonna be able to bring that many myself."

"Thanks, Izzy."

Having a psychic friend insured that she always got it when you couldn't say what you meant. I missed her so much at school. My friends from town headed out, leaving me alone with Bubbe and the boys. Once I heard the door between the clinic and the waiting room close, I explained.

"Logan's parents wanted him to bond with a dragonet, and Dylan's parents left it up to him to find a familiar on his own." I sighed. "I know this is super-complicated and not what you're used to dealing with. Honestly, I didn't think it would go this way myself, or at least, I'd hoped it would be better. I'm sorry, you guys."

"It's not your fault." Logan looked up, his eyes rimmed with red and his face tear-stained. "It's mine."

"You bet your bottom dollar it's not." Bubbe crossed her arms over her chest, her expression sterner than I'd ever seen it. "This is on your parents. I've never heard of such a thing, trying to force a bond. Who do they think they are?"

"You haven't heard of the Magical Menagerie? I mean, it's on TV and everything." Logan shook his head. "That's my parents. Or it might as well be, because as far as they're concerned, the show is their life. It's supposed to be mine and my sister's too."

"Noah never said anything about Elanor going through anything like this."

"That's because my sister bonded immediately with the firebird they picked for her. The creatures they keep around never want anything to do with me, and they never let me near more understated critters. They say those won't look good on the show. It's all my fault. There must be something wrong with me."

"I may have just met you today, young man, but that's absolutely incorrect." Bubbe stepped across the room, placing her hand on

Logan's shoulder. "The empathy and concern you showed earlier indicates you're a good lad with his priorities straight. You saved that mercat just in time."

"Mercat? Did you seriously rescue one? That's awesome!" Dylan tried to coax Gale out of his shirt. "Come on, dude, get out of there."

"Yeah, her name is Doris." He scratched his thumb again, mangling the cuticle and the nail this time.

"So, you did bond with her." I sighed, trying to muster some form of consolation for my friend. It was what Bubbe would do, after all. "Logan—"

"My parents are gonna kill me for this. Me and Doris will never look right."

"If they so much as try to harm a hair on your head, Logan Pierce, you come straight to me." Bubbe's color heightened, her eyes bright with righteous anger, her hands aglow.

I never thought I'd see my grandmother like this—fierce and protective. My whole life, she'd been solid and caring like a rock, and here she was, acting like...well, like me in the cafeteria.

"Wow." Dylan gazed at her, then at me. Even Gale stopped to stare.

"Do you really mean that, ma'am?" Logan put his hands flat on the table.

"I protected other students from your school years ago, and I told your headmaster I'd do it again if it ever came to that."

I didn't dare ask what she meant by that or bother clarifying that there was a new Hawkins in charge at Hawthorn Academy this year. She'd given my friend a choice, same as she'd do with a critter in need.

"Thanks, Doctor Morgenstern." Logan straightened up, pulling down the hem of his shirt. "If you don't mind, I'd like to go check on Doris now."

"Come along, then."

Bubbe led the way out the door and down the hall. As I followed, my phone beeped. It was Brianna from Walgreens. I showed Bubbe the message and explained. Once I had permission, I invited her over to have pizza with the rest of us.

As we walked toward Doris' room, Dylan grabbed my hand. I

stopped and turned, blinking at him since that was the last thing in the world I would have expected. We stood there staring at each other until Bubbe's and Logan's voices started up again, crooning at Doris and chatting about her care.

"What's up, Dylan?"

"I didn't want to say this in front of your grandma or act like my problems are worse than Logan's, because they're not. But—"

"Look, your problems are valid, and I already said you could talk to me."

"Okay." He nodded. "Remember when I said they had me tested? For magic ability?"

"Yeah. You said it was average, right?"

"Yeah, but well." He pointed at his midsection, where Gale had wrapped himself, clinging to Dylan's belt with his claws. "How?"

"I mean, he's an air dragonet, and you're an air magus?"

"That part makes sense, but don't they need to bond before they reach a certain age or something?" He scratched his head. "And aren't I going to have trouble? He's not exactly docile. I'm worried I'm not strong enough to work with him."

"You were there the day I met Ember." I arched an eyebrow. "Did I control her then?"

"She got caught in your hair." He smirked. "And no, you didn't."

"Opposite of docile." I grinned. "And then she got hurt, which sort of forced her to chill out. But I think that would have happened eventually anyway, so maybe give it time?"

"I don't have much of that. Gotta go back to work. Most of my hours are on the weekends. What if he flies off into a no familiars area and I'm not strong enough to stop him? Or something? I need the work-study, or I'll have to drop out and go home."

"I can't say I know what it's like, working through school, but you're not alone. You'll meet someone in a little while who's in the same boat. Anyway, as far as training your dragonet, it's got nothing to do with magic."

"Really?"

"It's all about caring, which you're good at. The whole magic power thing is just what gets their attention in the first place, and Bubbe says those early tests aren't too accurate."

"So, all I have to do is care?"

"Help Gale. Play with him, give him affection. Let him pretend to be a wardrobe accessory." I pointed at Ember, who was dozing on my shoulders. "Half the time she thinks she's a scarf. Let him be a belt or whatever."

"Okay, I'll try it." Dylan let go of my hand, then used it to pat Gale on the head. "We're gonna be friends, okay?"

"Cheep," said Gale. Or at least, that was the closest approximation to the sound he made.

"Do you wanna meet a mercat? We can watch her get a bath."

"Okay."

We made it down the hall finally, peering over the half-closed door. Logan was in there with Doris on his lap. Bubbe put the collar that used to be around Gale's neck on Doris', their magic mingling as she helped the pair with that last formality to make their bond official.

As she straightened, we saw the mercat fall asleep. Logan stroked her back with the brush. Most of the matted fur had come away, revealing her actual coat. Instead of dull gray, Doris's flanks looked something like a cross between a tabby and a seal. Her markings were silver with shimmering blue stripes that almost looked like scales.

"Woah, Logan." Dylan whistled. "She's adorable."

"Yeah, she's awesome. But I'm totally biased, and my parents aren't gonna agree." Logan sighed. "Cute's not enough for them."

"Hey, but at least we get to stay in the Familiar program at Hawthorn."

"Good point."

"Do you want help with Gale's collar, Dylan?" Bubbe asked. "Even if we don't get to that today, I can still write all the familiar license paperwork up before you two go back to campus later."

"Um, I don't—"

Bubbe's earring went off again. The aroma of pizza wafted under the door to the back of the office.

"We'll have to wait for now." She opened the door to let Izzy, Cadence, and Brianna in.

Cadence chattered at Brianna in a run-on sentence about the new changeling Bishop's Row team and how she ought to go out for it. Brianna smiled, at ease enough that her glamour totally covered her faerie traits. That was a big difference in demeanor from the stressed-out girl I'd met at Walgreens the night before.

So, I guessed I had met my good deed quota for the day. I smiled as we all headed back to the kitchen to pig out on pizza. Bubbe made her rounds, leaving us to our social time. Logan was quiet, but my friends from town probably thought that was because he held the sleeping Doris in his lap. Only Dylan and I knew better. Logan Pierce just wasn't a social creature.

Dylan was another story. He spun a yarn about some interaction he'd had, working in the café. Somehow, he effortlessly made it sound larger than life. He was in his element here, interacting with a group of people his own age. Most anyone would think all his problems were solved.

The boys went back to campus after finishing their pizza, when Bubbe's signatures on their familiar licenses were dry. Trouble still loomed on the horizon for those two, but it was distant for now.

CHAPTER TWENTY-NINE

I spent the rest of Saturday at Izzy's with Cadence, binging last year's *Ultimate Shifter League* on StreamFlix. We always had a blast doing that because there was something for each of us in it. Cadence, of course, drooled over all the shiny abs on the men. Izzy loved flipping a card or two, trying to predict heel turns and rivalries, and I appreciated the athleticism in all the moves, even if, in reality, they were more acrobatic and choreographed than other sports like Bishop's Row.

We stayed there until well after midnight, not realizing how late it was. Izzy's mom called Cadence a Swyft ride back to her house. Even though Salem wasn't a rough neighborhood, Mrs. Mendez was a divination psychic just like Izzy, so we never questioned her caution. If she'd thought it was safe, she wouldn't have bothered with the car.

On Sunday morning, I slept in. Hal wasn't due to come over until noon, so why was Ember peeping in my ear like the world's scaliest alarm clock? And why was it always so hard to wake up as a bona fide teenager? Ugh.

I sat up, feeling the indent on my cheek where my face had pressed against the seam on my pillowcase. The sheets and blanket were twisted. My pajamas, too. And my hair—some of it stood on end like I'd slept with a small critter trying to burrow into it.

"Ember?" I turned my head, blinking at the dragonet perched on the headboard. She looked awfully disheveled. "Did you do this?"

"Peep." She hung her head.

"Well, there's nothing to do but go in the bathroom and fix it, right?"

"Aliyah!" Dad's voice called up from the bottom of the stairs. "Your friends are here!"

"Crap!" I bolted out of bed, smacking my forehead on the low ceiling. But I had to keep moving.

In the bathroom, I splashed water on my face, rubbing that indented cheek. It was no use, so I moved on to my hair. A bottle of spray conditioner and the old detangling brush Mom had used on me in elementary school made quick work of the bird's nest. After that, I put it up and hopped in the shower. Thank goodness Noah always took forever to get cleaned up. Otherwise, I wouldn't have had this much practice at the sixty-second wash-down.

After tossing my pajamas down the laundry chute, I wrapped the towel around myself. There was a basket of clean laundry in the hall, with some t-shirts on top. I snagged a black one and dashed into my room, where I paired it with some hounds-tooth leggings, maybe too hastily. I didn't realize that until making it down to the first floor, skidding to a stop in front of the dining room table, where Hal sat with Lee and Grace.

"Interesting," Lee tilted his head, peering at the shirt. The left side of his mouth tilted up.

"Woah." Hal blinked. "Probably not a good idea to wear that one back to school."

"I don't know." Grace shrugged. "I totally agree with the sentiment, but you're probably right. It's pretty controversial there."

"Huh?" I tugged the hem of the mysterious shirt, reading upside-down.

Vamp Rights Are Extrahuman Rights

"Oh." Well, at least they hadn't seen the state of my hair or the seam line on my face. "Yeah, this isn't my shirt."

"No?"

"No." I shook my head. "It's...well it *was* Noah's. I thought he tossed it in the donations bag over the summer, though."

"He did, but I took it out and washed it." Dad came in from the kitchen carrying a pitcher of lemonade, his other arm laden with a tray of hamantaschen. "Here are some snacks for you."

"Wow, thanks, Mr. Morgenstern!" Grace popped out of her seat, pacing toward him. "Do you want help carrying those?"

"Thanks, Grace. And you can call me Aaron."

"Those cookies look amazing." Lee smiled. "Did you make them yourself?"

"No. My mother did."

"Oh, Dad never told me Dr. Mildred was a baker." Hal shook his head. "You learn something new every day."

"Your father wouldn't have known, but your grandfather certainly did." Dad chuckled. "Do you know she almost burned down the cafeteria kitchen, trying to bake kosher treats in the middle of the night?"

My classmates responded with gleeful awe. I tried to join in with their mirth, but it felt fake. Bubbe had done all kinds of wild and crazy things and never told me about them.

I noticed Grace stealing a few of the cookies, taking extra and tucking them into the satchel still on her shoulder. Lune sat on his haunches near her, ears up, on alert.

Seeing my roommate outside of school and in my house drove something home. I still thought of her the same way as before—sort of a rebel. But maybe there was a reason, something I couldn't imagine, let alone understand.

Before I could make an excuse to take Grace aside and offer cookies to go, the doorbell rang. I got up and ran to let Izzy and Cadence in.

As they joined the fun, I headed into the kitchen, where I still heard all of them gabbing away. Bubbe must have been baking all week, practically. This made sense because business slowed once Hawthorn started each year. Almost nobody needed educational familiar licenses after that. It didn't pick up again until the middle of

October, when the Halloween tourist season increased the number of extraveterinary emergencies.

I filled a tin with hamantaschen to bring back to school. As I stacked the cookies, Hal came around the counter. Nin dashed down his arm, skidding slightly on the granite as she swiped at a crumb.

"Here, have this." Hal placed his half-eaten treat in front of her and the Pharaoh's Rat picked it up, munching contentedly. "But don't say I didn't warn you about getting a tummy ache later, Nin."

"She's been awfully peckish lately." I grinned at the little critter.

"Yeah, but it's typical for her species. They get a little ravenous in the fall and spring." He reached out to give her a pat on the back.

"A little?" I blinked. "If you don't keep them well-fed, even properly socialized and domesticated Pharaoh's Rats can go feral."

"Yeah, okay. I made a pretty big understatement there." Hal stared at the counter. This topic was not a good look on him.

"So, where's Faith?" I changed the subject.

"Oh, I looked everywhere for her this morning." He sighed. "Told her last night I was going into town and everything, asked if she wanted to come along, and she said maybe. But then, this morning I couldn't find her before we had to leave."

"I'm sure you'll see her later."

"By the way, thanks for inviting us." He grinned. "Everybody's having fun."

"Yeah. Like most of yesterday."

"I heard there were a few hiccups, though?"

"I'd tell you more, but I think that's for Dylan and Logan to do."

"Understood." He nodded. "I saw them come in yesterday after dinner, though. With a mercat and a dragonet."

"You're sort of a gossip, Hal. You know that, right?"

"Yeah. Nobody's perfect."

"Peep!" Ember swooped down from the top of the fridge, holding another empty tin.

"Clearly, she wants me to pack more treats."

"Well, I'll leave you to it, then." Nin dashed across the counter and then up his arm.

As he headed back to the dining room, I considered his familiar. She was friendly and cute, but all the same, Nin belonged to the same species of critter that had murdered an immortal air dragon down in Newport, Rhode Island. Hal would be responsible with her, but people could get scared. The critters were all over the news because of Richard Hopewell's criminal trial. Pharaoh's Rats were rare on this continent. Pretty much the only people who had access to them were Hal's relatives.

Was that why Hal's father was headmaster now instead of his grandpa?

"Ember, can you get my phone, please?"

"Peep." She took off from the counter, speeding toward the stairs on golden wings. In moments, she returned with the device.

I tapped the news app and searched Rhode Island—and there it was. An article about a subpoena over the summer for one Head-master Hiram Hawkins, which he'd defied. The next article I read said he was detained by state law enforcement and awaiting his trial for contempt. There was nothing else about the connection, but it was obvious why they went after him. The simplest explanation was usually correct.

The critter that had somehow ended up in the Harcourt hoard had come from here. From the Hawkins family.

The one thing I couldn't glean from any of these articles was how, although there were opinion pieces that speculated magical lamp involvement. Until the trial progressed next year, I wouldn't know, so there was no use worrying about it. All the bad guys were locked up, right?

I came around the corner toward the dining room again, and we prepared to head into town. I watched Hal, thinking about how someone from his family was in trouble because my uncle had gone on a rampage a couple of years back.

Or maybe there's actual guilt and corruption in that family.

Yesterday, I'd have told that little voice to shut up. Today, it made a sick sort of sense.

I'd have gone downstairs and asked Bubbe to get real with me about the Morgenstern connection with the Hawkins family because it's there. They'd built the school and this house, while we'd brought in all the magipsychic light and sound.

But there was no time. My friends were waiting for me, and I was sixteen. At that age, people like me were supposed to be out doing fun teenage things, not following some obscure theory about crime and magical families.

I took a moment to dash upstairs and change my shirt, though, because knowing me, I'd only forget to do it later and end up wearing it to school, where I needed to keep my head down.

But I kept the tee. In fact, I wrapped it around the communication orb so it'd be with me at school, even if I didn't wear it there. I wanted it as a reminder, so I didn't forget who I was—a girl who believed in equal rights for all beings. Maybe it'd do my brother some good, too, because he was the one who'd bought this shirt in the first place.

Once upon a time, this sentiment had been Noah's, too. He'd decided to set it aside, leave it at home, forget about it. He wasn't talking about whether he'd lost faith or just felt safer hiding, but he wasn't an extramagus.

The stronger my magics got, the more I'd need reminders like this one.

Out in town, we ambled, letting Lee and Grace take the lead in exploring. Neither of them had spent much time here, and part of the fun in downtown Salem was wandering around to see everything.

Grace noticed The Witch's Brew, and for the only time that day, Lee disagreed about going in with a wrinkle of his nose. He waited outside, and I stayed with him. Cadence and Izzy knew what I liked from there, so I handed them a couple of dollars.

"Thanks, Aliyah."

"No problem. I've been in there about a million times, anyway."

"Scratch doesn't much like the smell of coffee. I'm not sure why."

"I get it. Ember can't stand peanut butter."

"They sure are finicky sometimes, huh?"

"Yeah."

We chattered on, trying to anticipate what we'd learn over the rest of the semester. Impossible, of course. If we already knew that, there'd be no point in going to school.

After a few hours during which we wandered up to the Willows and then all the way down to Salem Pioneer Village in Forest Park, the sunlight went amber and gold. It was late afternoon and time to head back. Grace, Hal, Lee, and I collected our familiars, each of us sorry they couldn't play outside together for a while longer.

We walked up Lafayette Street, cutting through Lafayette Park to get to Washington Street. That led us directly back to Essex, with little on the way besides chain stores and sit-down restaurants we'd see another time.

The door to Hawthorn Academy was next to a dental office. I waved goodbye to my friends, telling them I'd see them later. I wasn't going back without my knapsack and communication orb. More importantly, I wanted to talk to Cadence and Izzy in person one more time before leaving them in Salem for another week.

"I like your friend Lee."

I stopped in the middle of Essex Street, staring at Izzy. Cadence actually squeed, jumping up and down. My psychic friend's reaction to all this fuss was an eye roll and a forehead smack.

"Not like that. Seriously."

Izzy didn't even blush. Cadence pouted. I nodded my head.

"Okay," I said because somebody had to break that silence.

"I'm just saying I think, out of the lot of the Hawthornites, he's got his head on straight. So, if you're looking for some truth in that place, go to him."

"Not Hal?"

"I mean, he's okay, but that kid is definitely hiding something." Izzy shrugged.

"Yeah, Aliyah." Cadence agreed. "I don't think he looks old enough to be there. Is his birthday this week or something, or did he spend like a year in the Under?"

"You know what, I don't know." I chewed my bottom lip and started walking again. "But Hal does. Always seems to have unexpected information, and be in the right place at the right time. I'd think he had a psychic power if I didn't know any better."

That was because an extrahuman could either be psychic or magical but not both. Getting turned into a vampire, becoming a changeling, or picking up a magical shifter item could happen to anyone, but magi and psychics were born without overlap.

"Maybe he's got a device." Izzy shrugged. "But if it's not that, I'm not sure he can be trusted."

"Have you guys been watching the news out of Providence?"

They both nodded, so I let them in on my conspiracy theory about Hal's grandpa being in jail and the Pharaoh's Rats. I was surprised when Cadence added to it.

"Did you hear about his mother?"

"Wait, what?"

"She's from Rhode Island, I heard. There's a rumor that the reason she and his dad split up was because he caught her checking out some man from there. A vampire."

"Where are you getting this?" Izzy blinked.

"The social papers." Cadence chuckled. "You know my mom loves that gossip-column stuff. Whenever I'm bored at home, I pick it up to have a laugh. Apparently, Hal's dad is considered one of the North Shore's most eligible extrahuman bachelors."

"Huh." I snorted. "I had no idea."

I made a mental note to keep an eye on the Hawkins family. Rhode Island was where my uncle had done most of his dirty deeds, and if one or more of them had helped him, I ought to know. But I had less than an hour left with my best friends, so I set all that aside to make the most of that time, having fun together in one of the most magical towns on Earth.

CHAPTER THIRTY

Back in school on Monday, things started feeling normal, finally. Breakfast was uneventful, continuing with the trend late last week of Charity just rolling her eyes, pointing, and occasionally glaring in my general direction.

Despite the fact that I'd been gone for a couple of days, it almost felt like I'd never left. The main difference this week had more to do with Dylan and Logan having familiars, and that they'd gotten them while visiting me.

Doris and Gale fit in nicely with the rest of our group's critters. Gale spent a good deal of his time strutting whenever Ember was nearby. He had a habit of perching on anything high up, fortunately not items or surfaces where familiars weren't allowed. Dylan didn't have much trouble handling him, either, so his worry about controlling his critter got set aside.

Gale was just as much of a ham as his human companion. Whenever Dylan asked him to do something, no matter how nicely, the dragonet made a big show of completing the task like it was a performance. For whatever reason, he put on the appearance of defiance, although he never quite crossed the line into disobedience.

Curious about that, I went out of my way to visit the library and renew my books on dragonets for another week. The Ashfords helped with this. I even asked if they'd seen behavior like that from dragonets before. They told me no, but said they would look into it. It made me wonder what resources the librarians had that students didn't. Perhaps there was an entire second library just for faculty and staff. I wouldn't know unless I decided to teach here someday.

Speaking of teaching, our lessons went fairly well in Professor Luciano's class. He gave us few assignments, although they required a good deal of focus and attention to complete. In the lab, he had us doing safer experiments with stabler substances than on the first day. Anything we needed to infuse with magic was done for visual effect only. I wasn't brave enough to ask why, but Faith didn't have that problem. I overheard her talking at him one day before Lab.

"I don't want us to get behind, is all," she explained. "And I know people in the other class. They're doing real experiments, making solutions with magical precipitates, and infusing materials for use in magicpsychic devices. When will we do that kind of stuff? I'm losing patience."

"Patience or not, science is important, and you will learn everything the other class does eventually." The professor sighed. "It's nobody's fault but mine. You see, it was my decision to run an experiment that should have commenced during the latter half of the semester, so if you want to blame anybody, blame me."

Faith couldn't argue with that, but she did take it up with Grace, asking her to speak to Professor DeBeer about the experiments in her lab. She flat-out refused, at least the first time, but a couple of weeks later, she came to me and said that Professor DeBeer had moved some of the more complex labs up in the syllabus.

"But why, Grace?"

"She wouldn't tell me. Just dodged around it, sort of." Grace shrugged. "I think she's trying to show Luciano up. She went to all community and state schools, yet still somehow managed to get a tenured position here. That's one reason I think they fight all the time. Luciano went to all the best schools everywhere and had tenure overseas, then came to Hawthorn after getting turned down at Providence Paranormal."

"That's interesting, but not really our business, I guess." I shook my head. "As long as we all end up learning the same stuff and don't have trouble in our second year because of it."

"Do we get new professors next year or what?" Grace rolled her eyes. "It's just that their feud is so annoying. Distracting, too. Where I'm from, when teachers don't get along, they don't fight about it in front of the students."

"I hear you." I nodded. "Maybe it's cultural, but neither of them is from the States, so I don't know what's up. Anyway, we don't get new professors. We're stuck with them for three years."

"Wow. Here's hoping we don't get screwed academically."

The day after that conversation, I found Grace sitting outside the headmaster's office. He invited her in as I walked by, and although I didn't hear their conversation, I was pretty sure it was about the professorial feud. I was glad she'd brought it up. The last thing I wanted was to draw attention to myself while hiding the fact that I was an extramagus. Only the folks right in front had seen me use solar, and if Professor Luciano had said anything, I'd have been summoned to Headmaster Hawkins by now. I still couldn't fathom why he'd stayed mum.

Halfway through September, I started seeing the fliers on the wall. Noah had talked about it before, and it happened at all the specialized schools, so I should've expected it. But it'd be problematic for most of my friends.

I was talking about Parents' Night.

That morning at breakfast, I sat with Hal at our usual booth. A few minutes after I sat down, Dylan and Logan practically bumped into each other, each grasping one of the fliers. They sat down, noticed that they were both upset about the same thing, and began complaining together.

"I don't know what to do, man." Dylan shook his head. "They're just gonna tell me they can't afford to come, and if they do show up, it'll be an endless guiltfest. If they don't come, it'll be Mum writing seventeen letters about how sorry she is they couldn't make it, and how they're bad parents for having no money. If they do show, they'll go gaga over Gale, and draw all sorts of attention to the fact that he doesn't match up with my test scores."

"I wish my parents could just give yours plane tickets and stay home." Logan sighed. "If your folks come on someone else's dime, they can't complain, and I could avoid mom and dad finding out what's been going on around here. You know."

"I've had an idea about that, actually." Hal scribbled a few last-minute sentences on his homework. "Why don't you just swap familiars for the night and pretend things went the other way around?"

"You know, that might actually work." Logan leaned his cheek on one hand. "We're roommates and everything, and my folks know we hang out together, so if we just tell Doris and Gale it's a game, maybe my parental units will chill. It's just for one day."

"My parents wouldn't know how to chill if they got locked in a walk-in freezer." Dylan snorted. "It's probably for the best if mine don't show. But yeah, we can do a switcheroo if it'll make things easier on you, Logan."

"What about Elanor?" I jerked my chin at her table, where she sat with her back to us. "Won't she rat you out?"

"No." Logan shook his head. "Everything's all about her when it comes to Mom and Dad. It's like having a walking photobomb for a sister. She jumps in and does her thing loudly between our parents and me. She won't go out of her way to get me in trouble because it takes attention away from her. That's how it's always been."

"Wow, that sucks." Dylan elbowed Hal good-naturedly in the ribs. "Kinda makes you relieved to be an only child, huh?"

"Maybe." Hal bent his head over his paper, putting the finishing touches on his answer. "But anyway, if this works out, I'll be glad for you guys."

Setting up the critter swap was only the beginning. It ended up taking loads of extra work for Dylan and Logan. So, of course, I made it a point to help. I pulled Grace in on it, too.

Faith tagged along. I wasn't sure why, unless Hal put her up to it somehow. Mostly all she did was hang around and watch. On occasion, Seth and Ember teamed up to try to curb Gale's ego, and maybe that was the answer. Seth wanted to help, and Faith was indulging him. The bonds between familiars and their magi work both ways, after all, and Seth was probably the friendliest Sha in the known universe.

Faith's help turned out to be serendipitous since she got the bright idea to ask Nurse Smith if we could switch familiars as part of our Familiar Studies exercises. That was perfectly valid, but not an activity Nurse Smith or Professor DeBeer had planned for our remedial course, which was about to end. Familiar Studies only went for the first month of school.

In a way, I'd miss going to the extra class. It only felt like a burden when we got a lot of homework assignments. However, having extra time to practice Bishop's Row from October onward would be nice. Our team was coming along well. Okay, that was an understatement.

We'd competed against the other class during the last week of September. I got a chance to see how my friends had managed in their version of Gym with Coach Chen, and we'd won the first game.

Chen wasn't remotely like Pickman. He was not a taskmaster, but his teaching style was effective for some of the students in the other section. Dylan was an absolute terror on the court, someone even I had to watch out for. I had a hard time keeping up with him, and the only player on our team who ever got the jump on him was Hal. The reason we won that game was because his unexpected distraction allowed me to take one last player out along with me. Space magic was super useful in Bishop's Row. Who knew?

The second game had ended in a stalemate, but our times and outs were up there with the second-year teams. Because of that, they decided to include us in Intramurals in spring, a Bishop's Row tournament that was usually for second and third years only.

I guess we all performed well enough for them to add another bracket. That meant we'd make a single team, with tryouts the week before Thanksgiving. Also, I might have to face my brother on the court, which was nerve-wracking, but it was something to worry about later.

The thing on everyone's mind that last week of September was Parents' Night. It'd be a big deal for everyone, and possibly trauma-inducing for half my friends. Of course, they freaked out. Parents' Night wasn't just some tour around campus for the adults; it was also a full social function for us students, including a semi-formal dance.

I had gone stag to all the dances at my old school with Izzy and Cadence, so that didn't bother me, but I worried for my friends, and that made it harder to hide my solar magic. The last thing I wanted was to glow like a firefly in front of everyone. The worst-case scenario was full-on panic with a crowd clamoring for my expulsion. At best, parents would take their kids home, leaving Hawthorn Academy at a low enough attendance to justify closing the school.

Nobody knows for now. Keep it that way.

The only other person who might have noticed was Coach Pick-man. In the middle of a game, it was hard to tell whether I combined solar and fire energy, but since she hadn't demanded I flash sunlight in my opponent's eyes, I assumed the inside voice was right.

Still, avoiding detection and worrying about passing as a plain old fire magus was both anxiety-inducing and distracting to such a degree that I neglected an awful lot of items on my to-do list. That was why it wasn't until Thursday, the day before Parents' Night, when I realized something was bothering Grace.

"Are you sure you're going to wear that? To the dance, I mean?"

"I know there's a whole lot of fancy clothes in my closet, Grace, but Noah packed them. Honestly, I prefer just dressing like it's a normal day. You can't trip over skirts if you're not wearing them, right?"

"Well, it's just that, I mean, your parents are coming here to see you look all grown up and stuff. Isn't that a special occasion or something? Or do your parents really not care what you wear?"

"Huh?" The way she'd phrased the questions had me on edge. Not because of her, but for her.

"I know, I know, it's none of my business." She had her back to me, but the hitches in her voice showed despite her efforts to hide them.

246

"Just, my aunt, well, she can't afford the trek out here." She waved a hand at her ubiquitous jeans and flannel. "Or anything but this for my wardrobe."

"Grace?" My brain couldn't come up with any way to solve her problem, which was similar to Dylan's but worse. She'd only ever mentioned her aunt, wondering aloud about things parents might care about, like she was being hypothetical. My brain finally made the leap.

Grace had no parents, and she didn't want to talk about it, or she wouldn't have hidden it. Nothing I could have offered would help. The only thing in my head was a story told at my bedside in early childhood. One about another orphaned girl and a dance she had no means to attend. I wasn't a changeling and nobody's godmother, but maybe there *was* some small comfort to offer my friend.

"Do you want to borrow something from my closet?"

She turned, eyes wide as she stared at me. Her mouth opened, and her color got high. Had my question embarrassed her?

"I think I'm just going to stay in this room on Parents' Night."

"Why?"

"I just shouldn't go. Nobody will care whether I'm there anyway, even though I like dancing."

"I'd care. I'd miss you if you stayed in here." I watched her shoulders. The trembling in them had slowed. "Besides, Dylan's parents probably won't be there either. I bet he'd love some company."

The moment the words came out of my mouth, I realized I didn't want Grace to go to Parents' Night with Dylan like some sort of date. Because that was what I wanted to do. Ember landed on my shoulder, rubbing cheeks with me. But I had Mom and Dad. Grace and Dylan were in the same boat, alone in a foreign country. Leaning on each other to get through this could help them. What I wanted was less important than what two close friends needed.

"I guess I could ask him." She looked away. "If he says yes, is your offer still good for borrowing something?"

"Yeah, Grace. Always."

She nodded, then grabbed her pajamas and bathroom bag and

headed into the hall. She returned maybe an hour later, much longer than her showers usually took. Her face practically glowed, and her smile was wide as she walked through the door.

"He said, yes!"

We spent the rest of our time before lights out trying things on. It was more fun to pick outfits for a party together than alone.

CHAPTER THIRTY-ONE

It was the first Saturday I didn't spend at Hawthorne Street. In a way, home came to me because even Bubbe would be here tonight. I was relieved about but extra worried about controlling myself. If she found out what I really was, my relationship with my grandmother might never be the same.

I couldn't talk about it to Grace or Dylan. The two of them had their own problems. I'd have talked to Hal, but he was totally preoccupied with Faith. She was in a near-panicked state, which I should have expected. Seth was so nervous that even Ember's crooning couldn't relax him. If her parents were even remotely like her sister, it was no wonder. I even found myself fearing their arrival.

The only other person I trusted enough was Logan, so I followed him into the library after breakfast. He'd taken to doing all of his class reading in there. It was the most distraction-free place on campus besides the dorm, and at the library, the Ashfords were there to help with questions.

Doris blinked as I strode over. Her surprise must have carried because Logan sat up straight, posture tense. When he recognized me, my friend nodded and waved me over.

"Hey, Aliyah." He was stiff and formal, and I didn't know why.

"What's up?"

"I should be asking you." He cleared his throat. "About what's up, I mean. Besides us this morning. And Ember on the chandelier." A nervous little laugh erupted from his throat.

"Oh, right." I nodded. "Hey, I just came over to ask if we could chat, but now I've got to ask, are you okay?"

"Um, maybe." He folded his hands together, placing them on top of the notepad sitting beside his textbook. His thumbnails were such a wreck I wanted to put antiseptic and bandages on them.

"How can I help?"

"Well, gimme a sec." He took a deep breath. "Will you go to the dance with me?"

"Wait, what?" I stepped back so unconsciously, I tripped over the chair rooted to the floor behind me—and ended up on my backside, of course.

"Oh, no!" Logan jumped out of his seat in a flash, leaning down to give me a hand up.

I took it. When our hands touched, I felt a flash of heat, but no flames appeared. My solar magic acted up, and only the bright light in the library stopped anyone from noticing. If this was my response to a surprise in this comforting environment, I barely stood a chance of escaping detection tonight.

"Thanks, Logan." I got up, a feat made much easier with his help.

He didn't reply, just stood as still as a pond, waiting. Of course, because he'd asked me a question and I'd replied by falling over.

"Yes, I'll go with you." I nodded, grinning. It was a relief, knowing one of my friends would be by my side for most of the evening.

"You mean it?" He got the floor to release the chair, then held it out for me.

"Absolutely." I sat, and he helped me push it in.

"Thank goodness." He settled back into his own seat, posture relaxing. "So, you wanted to chat? It's important, right?"

"Yeah." I told him my problem, how I'd have to work extra hard at hiding my magic. Asked if he had any idea how to go about that.

It wasn't easy. I was ashamed about lying to my parents. My biggest fear was that Logan would judge me.

He totally surprised me.

"You came to the right guy." He nodded. "I mean, my family's all about how to make magic look certain ways. They raised Elanor and me to make it seem larger than life, but reversing some of what they taught me will work."

"We don't have much time. They get in for the assembly before dinner."

"Oh, I know, but don't worry." He grinned. "We're lucky. Most of it is stuff I can do with my water magic. Watch this."

Logan showed me a few tricks around the solar light fixtures. After watching him for less than a minute, I suspected this might work out after all. As long as I could stick with Logan Pierce for the entire event, maybe we'd make it through unscathed.

The four of us waited upstairs until the last minute. None of us really wanted to go down to where the rest of the school happily greeted their families. For a few minutes, I almost thought we'd stay there, in some sort of social limbo between bailing and attending. Then Hal showed up wearing a three-piece suit in jet with a silver vest.

Faith Fairbanks was on his arm, and I mean on. As in, she was dressed to the nines in a black cocktail dress with silver accents. I'd seen runway models while Noah watched Fashion Week who couldn't have held a candle to her.

Seth trotted behind them, his behavior befitting an AKC champion. He glanced at Ember, who dropped the Sha a wink as though she understood it wasn't playtime.

As Hal began escorting Faith down the stairs, walking instead of activating the magical conveyance, he beckoned to the rest of us. Even with his encouragement, we still stood immobile. The real catalyst was his date.

"I refuse to go out there without an entourage." Faith tossed her head, hair cascading over one bare shoulder in chestnut waves. "So, move your butts already."

"Come on, then." Dylan offered his elbow to Grace. "Let's not awaken her inner mean-girl."

"Oh, yeah, don't want that." Grace stepped up beside her date.

"How about it, Logan?" It was up to me to get us moving.

He'd been silent the whole time, except he had one hand clenching hard enough to break the skin on his palms. I recognized that from class, when he made huge efforts to focus and get everything right.

"Are you sure?" He shook his head. "What if it's not perfect? Because I mess things up?"

"We don't have to be perfect, Logan, just present. We can do this."

"Okay." He took a deep breath.

And just like that, we made an entrance so cinematic, our class-mates literally talked about it for years. Gale and Doris even managed to remember it was "opposite day," too.

Hal and Faith brought all the glitz, but Dylan and Grace were just as head-turning. I decided to let her keep the purple dress she'd borrowed. The plum flattered her complexion, and the hemline that was too short on me was a perfectly classy knee-length for her stature. Not to mention, the dress's hue represented umbral magic. It was perfect on her, and complimentary to the ice-blue tie Dylan wore.

I noticed my mother watching our descent. Her hand went to her breastbone, and she gazed at me like I'd stepped out of an old photo-graph. She had good reason. That mint green dress Noah had tossed into my suitcase a month ago had originally belonged to Mom. She'd worn it at this very school on her own Parents' Night years ago. She'd told me this when she hung it in my closet last spring, which Noah encouraged because that style had come back in again this year.

She and Dad must have been on a trip down memory lane, but not Bubbe. Her gaze appraised, as though she analyzed the lot of us and how we had paired off for this event—like she was aware we had a strategy, although she couldn't suspect why when it came to anyone besides the boys.

Logan's parents also studied us. Their eyes narrowed at first until they caught themselves making unflattering faces. After that, they both put on figurative masks, but in that short span of time, I understood their confusion. They expected to see us together but perhaps not clinging so tightly. I mean, we were, but not in an inappropriate way.

The worst were the Fairbanks. They took one look at the lot of us on the stairs and turned their backs like they didn't even care that their middle daughter was dating the headmaster's son.

Yeah, they actually were dating. Hal looked practically giddy, and while Faith's face wore its usual expression of deliberate ennui, she went farther than just putting one hand on his arm. Instead, their hands were twined together like a litter of sleepy Sha pups. There was a comfort and solidarity in that gesture, one I'd seen before.

Between my parents.

The mean girl and the nice guy. Who knew?

At the bottom of the stairs, it was easy enough to navigate to our seats for the assembly. We took up an entire row, so no worries about sitting next to any enemies. Kitty's group went in behind us like they were playing rear guard, or maybe they were also avoiding Charity and her minions. Not that they could get up to much with this many parents plus all the faculty and staff in attendance. Even Zeke was there, standing in the back with Penelope.

Our parents sat on the other side of the aisle. Seats were marked out for them, so the ones who hadn't been here before weren't confused. I counted heads and looked for familiar faces. As we expected, Dylan's folks hadn't come.

Headmaster Hawkins appeared literally out of nowhere, silencing the din of cross-chatter. He clapped his large hands until the chatter died down, then cleared his throat to begin his speech.

"Welcome, families! Some of you for the first time, and others for the second or third. Tonight, you will tour the campus and see some of the projects our students have been working on. After a divine dinner prepared by our newest chef, we'll have a mixer with dancing. I'm an educator, not a public speaker, so I'll keep this brief. Thank you, students. Without your dedicated and excellent work, we'd have nothing to show your families this evening. Now, go and enjoy the evening together!"

He clapped his hands once again, not in dismissal of the crowd, but for himself. The headmaster vanished immediately after, while the echo still lingered at the corners of the room. More than a few parental-aged women, here without a date, sighed in dismay.

There was something to Cadence's gossip columns after all.

The group of us stuck together during the tour. Logan's parents chattered away at my folks but didn't say a word to Bubbe. Logan leaned in, whispering that this was typical for them. They didn't bother with anyone my grandmother's age. Their loss.

The Fairbanks took a moment to say hello to the Pierces as we sauntered through the academic hallway, but they totally ignored Faith. Her mom, who looked almost exactly like Charity, gave me one withering glare, and that was it. They ignored my parents.

The entire time we were on the tour, Gale stayed perched obediently on Logan's shoulder. It helped that Ember peeped at him the whole time. He chirped back, too, which made me wonder what they were talking about.

Because Logan and I brought up the rear, we noticed that Lune and Doris had a modified game of tag going. Each time the mercat reached out with a paw, the moon hare hopped out of the way. On occasion, it was Lune moving sideways toward Doris, who dodged just in time.

I hadn't seen Nin and Seth in a while, so I looked around for them. They were in the last place I expected—in Faith's tote, cuddling, which would have been cute if familiars usually got that friendly with each other. I'd seen it exactly once before, in the one photo Bubbe keeps of her parents on their wedding day.

Were my friends in love?

I spent the rest of the tour studying them, looking for clues, but either Faith and Hal were both better actors than Logan's slick entertainment family or were still unaware of their potential.

The idea that something positive could come from our defensive social maneuvers had me walking on air. That was why I spent most of the dinner hour smiling at everyone, even Noah when he sat with Elanor at our table. This was the first time in a month he'd even looked at me. He rolled his eyes immediately and started whispering in his bestie's ear, but even that couldn't get me down.

After dinner, we almost had a collective heart attack. All of the familiars went to their corner for their meal, as usual. But when they returned, Gale and Doris forgot about opposite day.

Logan froze. Doris leaping up into his lap wasn't at all what he expected. My date couldn't roll with those punches, so I did.

"Aww, look!" I pointed at the mercat, doing my best impression of Cadence. "Dylan and Logan are such good friends, they even get along with each other's familiars. So cute!"

Ember played along, stopping on the back of Grace's chair to ruffle her hair before returning to me. She peeped at Gale for good measure, who got the message and only chirped at Dylan before landing on Logan's shoulder.

Doris put her paws on Logan's chest, stretching up to rub cheeks with Gale. Once they made their greeting, she jumped off Logan's lap and padded back to Dylan, who scooped her up for a cuddle and a scratch behind the ears.

Once dinner was over, we headed back out of the cafeteria and into the lobby. Streamers hung from the walls, and the solar lights flashed and pulsed under globes of various spell effects. From the looks of concentration on faculty faces, they'd worked hard to make the occasion literally magical. Earthbound familiars scooted to the sides, while winged ones made way for their magi by fluttering toward perches or the rafters.

Logan stepped lightly across the space between the seats at the sidelines and the dance floor. He must have been looking forward to this all night because we were the first ones there, arriving a breath before the music started—a waltz, but popular. *With a Little Help from My Friends*, the Joe Cocker version. His easy smile meant he was in his element here.

"I can't dance," I managed.

"That's okay, nobody will know." He leaned closer, voice low beside my ear. "Even if you get nervous, they won't see anything they shouldn't."

"How?" My hands were already warmer.

"Pretend I'm a mirror and copy me." He put one of my hands on his shoulder and held the other, pressing our palms together.

Our arms made a frame. I clung to that, and he was right. The soft glow of his water magic hid everything. When solar light gleamed between our hands, he narrowed his eyes and magical focus until it flickered like my good old flames instead.

My tension eased, loosening its grip until I could forget about being an extramagus. Almost.

As we moved together, traveling across the dance floor, a series of startled gasps followed us. When we passed our friends, clapping and low whistles took over. If Hal and Faith had made the biggest entrance, we made up for it now with sheer entertainment value.

For once, my legs didn't feel coltish and clumsy, and being at eye level with my dance partner made all the difference in my ability to focus and do more than let him lead. We circled past our siblings and parents. Logan's mother was still stone-faced, but his dad's lips wore a small smile. Noah stood, slack-jawed and wide-eyed, only snapping out of it when Elanor elbowed him in the ribs and dragged him off to dance too. My father had his arm around my mom. They swayed together, grinning.

Bubbe studied us like critters under her care, which made sense because she knew more than Mom or Dad about the trouble Logan and I had at school. She didn't take this at face value like everybody else in the room because she knew better. She paid more attention to Logan than me, though.

I made it through the entire song, but even better, we danced to three more before I was out of breath. We regrouped at a table with a cascading fountain of punch. I didn't dare leave Logan's side, even though it sort of ruined the attempted chivalry in his act of fetching me a drink. Judging by his smile, he either didn't mind or understood.

Dylan and Grace trotted over, huffing and puffing after their turn around the dance floor. They didn't do anything nearly as structured or formal as waltzing, though.

"How 'bout that chicken dance, hey?" Grace chuckled.

"More fun than a barrel of monkeys." Dylan smirked. "But we're talentless hacks, of course."

"Here's to Team Hack!" Logan raised his glass.

Faith sauntered out of the shadows, Hal in tow. She was still cool as a cucumber, but he shuffled his feet with a furrowed brow. Just as I wondered what the two of them were up to, hiding out together in the corner, she told me.

"Watch your back, Aliyah." Faith reached out, putting a hand on my shoulder. "Charity's going to try something."

"Why?"

"She's jealous, of course. Does she need another reason?"

"But I didn't do anything."

"You don't have to." She shook her head. "I'm going to try to deflect her, but this is your warning. Avoid the twins, okay?"

"Thanks, Faith."

"Don't thank me. Just do as I say."

I nodded. Logan stood beside me as Faith stalked off. Hal followed her at a distance like a satellite. They circled the dance floor like gulls over the beach at low tide.

As the last song ended, Charity detached from her dance partner and strolled toward us, eyes on the punch bowl.

"Let's make like eggs and beat it," said Grace.

The lot of us hustled away from the refreshment table, heading toward some of the seats at the other end of this side of the dance floor. On the way, we passed the twins. One of them stuck a foot out, trying to trip me. I got tangled and almost toppled over despite my sensibly flat shoes.

Logan grabbed me around the waist, literally sweeping me off my feet. At his touch, I was buoyant, as though immersed in water. He spun us in a circle in the direction of the dance floor, and then we were out there, stopping the show again.

As we navigated around the other couples, which included my parents, I noticed Faith and Charity facing off beside the punch bowl. My friend trembled until Hal stepped behind her, placing his hand on the table. As the sisters argued, I watched Charity grasp the tablecloth and pull, toppling the entire fountain toward Faith.

It vanished for a moment, during which Hal pulled Faith into a hug. When the fruit-punch fountain reappeared, it was directly over Charity's head, spilling its contents all over her. Faith and Hal faded into the shadows. I spotted Grace in the corner, eyes narrowed, with one finger directed at their vanishing point.

Charity Fairbanks stood with the tablecloth in her hand, soaked from head to toe in fruit punch. It looked like she'd had an embarrassing accident.

The room went silent, the lights low-watt incandescent. My hands felt like blacktop in the middle of July. Everyone's focus sat squarely on Queen Mean, but once my hands lit up, it'd be all over for me.

"Oh, shit."

"Shh, I've got you."

And Logan did. He led me to the bottom stair, then named our floor to start it moving. As it rose, light poured from my hands, and my date had that covered too. Literally.

Globes of water surrounded the fists I made, turning the solar flares inside them into what looked like fire underwater. It was dim enough for me to escape with Logan up the stairs. A few heads turned, one of them Professor Luciano's. Our teacher was the only one who didn't mistake it for a deliberate farewell display.

At the top of the stairs, we almost tripped over Hal and Faith. They were on the floor, leaning against the wall together. Both smiled, although Hal looked pretty beat.

"Let's get out of here."

"That's the only time you've talked sense, Pierce." Faith snorted. "Come on." She didn't exactly help Hal up as much as scoop him off the floor, but the end result was the same.

We all headed down the hall, where Faith helped an unsteady and exhausted Hal negotiate the route to his room. Logan paused.

"I've got to say goodnight to my parents." He almost ran right into our roommates.

"They're already gone." Dylan shook his head. "Sorry, man." Gale swooped down and landed on his shoulder.

"That's okay." Doris trotted up and rubbed against Logan's legs. He reached down to scratch her ears. "All in all, I think we did all right."

"Yeah." I held out my arm to give Ember a place to land.

"Did you see Charity's face?" Grace leaned against the wall, holding her sides. Lune was beside her, kicking his feet up. "She looked like a B-movie vampire from back before the Reveal!"

We all had a laugh at that because the last thing Charity Fairbanks would ever want was to look remotely like a vampire. It felt like fitting payback for all the abuse she'd dished out to the undead staff and her own sister.

The boys walked Grace and me to our room. I thanked them both and opened the door, stopping so Logan and I could wave to each other. Dylan lingered, Grace remaining outside with him.

When she came back in, her face was even more flushed than when she'd laughed. Her lip gloss was smudged, too. That meant my roommate and her crush had hit it off, on top of all the other stuff we'd managed with our hard work and preparation. Something different had happened with Logan and me. We understood each other, anyway, and I could trust him.

If this were an exam, we would have passed with flying colors. My ultimate goal was hiding what I really was. I'd met that and then some. Our entire group might have just leveled up socially, too.

So why did I feel sad?

CHAPTER THIRTY-TWO

It was midweek, and I went home right after Lab. No, I didn't get expelled. It was *Erev Yom Kippur*, the eve of Yom Kippur and the most important holiday my family observed. Hawthorn Academy had always let students keep their individual faiths, which was why I was walking down Essex Street a half-hour before sunset with Noah, who still wasn't talking to me.

The biggest indirect lesson I'd learned at Hawthorn Academy: doing good was Punk AF.

I'd secretly hoped my brother and I would settle things after the punchbowl incident. That somehow, he'd see how ridiculous it was, marching to the beat of an unusually cruel bigot's drum. I even wore his discarded Vamp Lives Matter shirt that day, but it was no use. He wasn't interested in joining my kindness rebellion.

That was what I'd been doing all week since Parents' Night—my friends too—going out of our way to thank the vampires on staff in front of other people. Making it a point to hold doors, even for people we didn't like. Helping folks when they dropped something. Inviting the rest of our year to study groups.

And it was catching on, slowly but noticeably. Even Hailey stopped snickering when Logan got called on and stuttered an answer. I caught Coach Pickman helping Coach Chen with Bishop's Row trunks. And Noah's ex, Darren, had more of his classmates at his study group, kids who weren't doing so well academically.

The biggest change was in Faith. She smiled more, laughed longer, and with people more often than at them. That was more likely because of Hal, though. They lit each other up, reminding me for all the world of Mom and Dad. At first, I thought they made me homesick, but that wasn't right. Maybe during my break, I'd figure it out. Yom Kippur was the day to reflect on the previous year, after all.

I glanced at Noah as we approached the corner of Hawthorne Street. He looked away, down at the wheeled suitcase he'd overpacked instead of meeting my gaze. I adjusted my knapsack and waited through his luggage hiccup before walking along. His attitude didn't justify me leaving him behind, no matter how satisfying it might have been to walk away and leave him in distress. He was my brother, and I'd help him if he needed it.

Doing the right thing was harder than giving up, but that was how I knew this was the right track. Well, one way. Lotan peeked out from under Noah's collar, bobbing his head at me. The serpent appreciated my gesture, at least.

My brother tossed away the stone jamming his suitcase's wheel, then continued on. We walked past Izzy's house and down the driveway toward 10-1/2, and just like that, we were home.

Lunch wasn't that long ago. All the same, Bubbe had set out a loaf of challah bread in a braided circle as she always makes it for Yom Kippur. Sliced apples, honey, and dried apricots accompanied it, with iced lemon tea to wash it down. Noah and I sat in silence at the counter, having the last food we'd eat over the next twenty-four hours. After that, I washed my face and wrapped a white pashmina shawl around my shoulders to get ready for the services. Ember burrowed under it, draping herself across my shoulders in the process.

Dad and Bubbe each lit a yahrzeit, the memorial candle, for Grandpa and Bubbe's parents. Five minutes later, we headed to our temple across the bridge in Beverly.

The synagogue was full, like it had been every year for as long as I can remember. We were secular Jews, not Orthodox or even Conservative. Surely, you've heard of Easter-and-Christmas Christians? Well, we were the Jewish equivalent, but it wouldn't have felt like the High Holy Days if we weren't there. Bubbe reminded us that the freedom we had to celebrate publicly was a privilege our ancestors didn't always have.

I refused to take it for granted, not after I was old enough to hear the stories about our great-grandpa's escape from Poland.

We took seats together. Don't be surprised by this. Our synagogue was egalitarian, which meant men and women sat together instead of in different sections. Noah sat so our parents were between us, but this had happened in previous years inadvertently, so they didn't think it was strange.

I knew better.

As Cantor David sang the Kol Nidre prayer, we listened. It was all about how we came to temple on the holiest day of our year to be absolved of obligations, bonds, and other pressures put upon us under duress. Historically, this came from ages past, when Jews living in those times were forced to convert or die. The Spanish Inquisition was a prime example, though certainly not the first.

We were freed from burdens like this by singing this prayer.

This year, the words had a striking impact. Renouncing vows made under duress meant giving up Ember. We'd bonded after a moment of extreme agony for her and stress for me, after all, but I also realized that release was important exactly because of this.

So I focused my thoughts on her, making it clear that she was free to go if I wasn't the right magus for her.

At that moment, with my familiar's tail curled around my arm, I was acutely aware that she'd agreed to renew our bond, without the baggage this time, and that reinforced its strength.

My mind took me back to a sunlit day more than a decade ago, before my grandfather passed. Ember made the trip back through my memory by my side.

"Scars are tougher than unblemished skin." Grandpa finished wrapping the gauze over the sterile pad.

"But it hurts." I sniffled, but it was no use. The trickle under my nose wouldn't budge.

"It's got to hurt if it's to heal." My grandfather tore paper tape. *"And once it does, that sidewalk will have a devil of a time trying to skin that knee again."*

"Really, Grampy?" I blinked, tears drying sticky on my cheeks.

"And how." His eyes twinkled.

Before I remembered my response, the present dragged back me back again.

My mouth moved, reciting three times the prayers of forgiveness I knew by heart.

When the services were over, we headed home. Usually, we'd be quiet and contemplative like this each year. We all had tons to reflect on, although that was the first time I was fully aware of how hard it must have been for Mom. She never once complained about not getting to see her relatives.

Clearly, her brother Richard was a seriously bad egg, but what about her parents? She must have missed them, even if she was estranged from them, like Dylan missed his. Maybe she felt more like Grace—a stranger to typical family dynamics.

This time of year, we did an awful lot of reflecting, especially when it came to stuff like my horrible extramagus secret. I was torn because the right thing to do wasn't clear here. If my life were a video game, both of my choices were Nightmare Mode.

Don't tell Mom my secret. She was still stuck without half her family, wondering whether they were well or even alive, except for Richard, whose fate was being decided on national news. And she got to wonder whether either of her children would grow up to be like her brother.

Tell Mom my secret. She'd still be stuck like now, but in that scenario, she'd know it was me she had to worry about. I'd turn evil someday and end up in prison or worse.

Both of those sucked.

"What was that, Bissel?" Bubbe sat in the middle of the back seat between Noah and me.

"Just my inside voice escaping again." I sighed.

"Well, at least this is the day for it." She reached out, taking my hand.

"I'll do all that when we get home."

But it took longer than that. Hours, in fact.

Later that night, despite being ready for bed, I couldn't sleep. So I got up, leaving Ember asleep at the foot of the bed. Last year I would have paced my room, but that was impossible now unless I wanted to give myself a concussion and spend the rest of the holiday at Salem Hospital, so I headed downstairs.

The television was on, so I walked into the living room where Mom sat up alone. She wasn't really looking at the screen, just staring out the window, so I took a seat beside her and tucked my feet up under my legs.

"I hope you're getting enough sleep at school," she said.

"Yeah. The day usually wipes me out."

There was a pause, not just between us but from the TV, too. We both decided that was a good time to talk.

"I'm sorry—"

"Mom, I—"

I blinked, but she chuckled.

"Who should go first?" she asked.

"You, I guess, Mom."

"Aliyah, I'm sorry." She sighed. "I should have mentioned Richard sooner. Well, maybe not just him, but also where I came from. The family who raised me and why I left them behind when I made my own family here. Half of you is me, and half of me is them. Raising you and Noah halfway like that wasn't the right thing to do."

"Why, then?"

"I thought it would protect you. Not physically, but your hearts. I saw how afraid of everything your brother was, and how you have such a hard time loving yourself, and I didn't want to make it worse. You're both so strong when you forget all that and just act, and now I

265

bet nobody on that campus is letting you forget that you're both Hopewells."

The silence struck like a Tallin Serpent guarding a nest. It hadn't hit me until just now that Noah got his own share of grief over Richard, even though I was the one who resembled him. Maybe he wasn't ignoring me because he hated me now. Maybe he was scared, even if I'd never thought of my big brother that way before.

Older siblings had a sort of armor. Izzy's one, plus she has one, and she'd told me this before. The younger kids think the older ones are like Superman, impervious to almost everything, and with extra abilities to boot.

After all this time, it turned out he wasn't. I should have listened to my best friend. I'd have to go apologize to her tomorrow…but I'd left my mother hanging.

"Mom, I forgive you." I opened my arms, and the hug she gave me was warm and welcoming if a little tear-stained. "I love you."

"I love you, too." After we let go, she pulled a tissue from her sleeve and dabbed her eyes. "Okay. It's your turn, Aliyah."

I still didn't know what to say. The choices in front of me were the Lady and the Tiger, but for me, there was a door number three.

"I made a ton of assumptions about all this for the whole month." I waved my hand at nothing, but her face told me she understood. "The why and the how about the Hopewells, and I know you must have worried all that time. Wondering whether I was mad, whether I was really busy every weekend or just avoiding you. But Mom, I'm sorry. I did avoid talking to you about it, how some of the kids at school pick on me because of my uncle. And I'm sorry."

"I forgive you. But you've talked to someone about it? It's important to take care of your health in all ways."

"Yeah, I talked to my friends. And Bubbe, a little."

"Aliyah, I'm proud of you."

I sat back, not daring to speak. Right now, all the words wanted to come out—the ones I shouldn't say until I was sure she was ready to hear them. The truth.

All my focus was on keeping my hands from glowing, and it was a miracle because it worked.

We thanked each other and then Mom said goodnight, heading upstairs to bed.

It was empty down there, so I sat for a while, not really looking at the *Buffy* reruns Mom had been watching. I thought I was all alone because Bubbe couldn't possibly have been down in her office at this time of night, so I scooted over, cozying up to the box of tissues and just let the tears come.

It was a knock-down-drag-out ugly cry.

That was what I got for holding back tears for a month and change. A deluge. A flood. The microbes living on my face should have gotten into an ark, two by two. Biblical floods of tears felt extra, even on this high holy day.

"Bissel?"

It was Bubbe. Of course, she was downstairs in her office instead of up in her bedroom. She crossed the living room like a ship on storm-tossed waters pulling into the shore. Her hand rubbed my back, a comfort sorely missed.

"Oh, Bubbe. I'm so tired of it all."

She said nothing, just pulled me into a hug. It never mattered to my grandmother why or how I got in a state like this. She just didn't want me going through it alone. She treated my brother the same way, which was why her next words didn't surprise me.

"Noah's tired of it too." She kept rubbing my back. "That was why I told him to talk to you already."

"You noticed?" I pulled back to see her face.

"That you two weren't speaking? Yes. And he wants to apologize if you give him the chance, although he knows that's not guaranteed."

"I'll listen, Bubbe."

"Good. I'll have water for the two of you downstairs tomorrow morning. Seven-thirty." She studied my face. "Now, go have a wash and get some sleep. You need rest while fasting, after all."

"So do you." I made use of some tissues. "But you were down there all this time, helping the animals."

"Right, because it's our responsibility to care for them. And each other. Remember, a meaningful life is within our reach, if only we—"

"Choose to care," I finished the sentence with her. It wasn't just a thing she said, but a core belief we have as faithful Jews, even if we were pretty secular. Trying to make the world better by caring was our duty.

We hugged once more before saying goodnight. As I headed upstairs, my steps were lighter.

Maybe I wasn't as far off course as I thought.

At the table downstairs, we sat together over water. Bubbe bustled in the hall nearby, feeding and watering the handful of critters in her care. For once, Noah, the king of extra, kept it simple.

"Truce?" he asked.

"I want to be your friend again, Noah. I can't stop caring."

"We can't act friendly at school." He sighed. "Not beyond nods and waves. Too dangerous. You've seen what Charity does to her enemies, and if she thinks I switched sides, she'll torment us both worse than she does to you now."

"Yeah, I know. And you gave danger a hard pass before I was born."

"Mood. Anyway, do you accept?"

"For now, but I'm going to try repairing our relationship as well if it's all the same to you."

"Whatever. But I can't afford to play in your little Mean People Suck sandbox, Aliyah."

"I understand. But who knows? Maybe things will change, and so will your mind. At any rate, I didn't mean to scare you. Fire bad, girl sorry."

"And I'm sorry for pretending you don't exist."

"See? That wasn't so hard."

"Peep."

"Ssss."

"Two out of two familiars agree." I dropped him a wink. The grin he gave back was barely there, but I'd take it.

Back at temple that afternoon, we attended more services. After last night, I felt like I should stay for Yizkor, the memorial part of Yom

Kippur services. Noah and I used to stay out with the other kids our age and younger. There was a superstition that attending while your parents were alive was inviting trouble, but I wanted to remember my grandfather. There had to be a reason he had come so strongly to mind during the opening service yesterday, and honoring that felt right.

The Cantor sang some prayers and the Rabbi read, but the heft of the service came during silent prayer, read to ourselves from books. Standing, we recited Ancestor of Mercies, and Yizkor was almost over. Just one part remained.

Tzedakah, which is an act of charity. I must have somehow known I'd do this part of the service, because I actually had a few dollars to put in the box.

After that, the final sprint toward the end of the holiday began. Neilah, the closing of the gates. Noah and the other young folks came back in as the ending started. This was our last chance to atone for the previous year.

The ark, where the Torah scrolls stayed most of the time, was closed as everyone recited.

"Seal us in the Book of Life."

Now we literally had minutes to affirm our faith, praise God's name, and deny idolatry of any over Him. We did it together as a family within the congregation.

When the Rabbi blew the Shofar horn, it was over.

But it was also the beginning of a new year, one in which I'd vowed to do better. And as we left the temple to break our fast at home, I silently prayed that I was up to the challenge.

CHAPTER THIRTY-THREE

Overall, my prayers were answered. Or maybe I answered them myself. Either way, it wasn't easy. Serious effort was involved, energy spent on hiding my solar magic and keeping my temper at bay. Choosing kindness over retribution didn't come easily for me anyplace but inside my head.

I wasn't doing it alone, and all through the rest of October, I was grateful for my friends and for Ember. The campus would have been a pile of ashes if it weren't for them, so I made it a point to thank them, even for the small stuff.

Halfway through the month, Headmaster Hawkins announced that we'd have an all-day outing into Salem on Halloween. That meant my friends and all the other students got to see and participate in the parades, concerts, and general festive atmosphere I had experienced every year in town.

Everyone was excited, even the teachers. They decorated their classrooms, including the gym and the library. Grace came running into our room one night, saying that Professor DeBeer gave her permission to work in Creatives for extra time to make her costume. Her excitement was almost palpable and I joined her, kicking off over a week of early mornings and late nights spent working with textiles and sewing machines.

Dylan was there too, even though he said his wardrobe idea was easy. Mostly, I thought he liked the excuse to spend extra time with Grace. We also worked on the costumes during Creatives period each day, drawing no small amount of attention from our classmates. Even though Hal and Faith had ordered their outfits, they looked on with us. Alex and his clique checked on our progress at least twice a day.

Sewing was a pretty obscure skill here at good old Hawthorn Academy. I learned loads about it from Grace, who was a master. She could have been a cosplayer, while I walked into it with the basic skill of how to reattach a button. Good thing my idea was relatively simple.

I wasn't sure why I was so excited about wearing another mask. Maybe because the holiday was all about disguise, or because I wouldn't be the only person wearing one for the day. Pick whichever you'd like and run with it, I guess.

Once again, I caught Luciano and DeBeer arguing heatedly, except this time, it wasn't about lab safety or course materials. It was far more festive than that.

"I don't care what you say, *Lucy*. They're talented for sure, but I just can't stand the way they conduct themselves in interviews."

"They've got heart, and one of the most important causes in the post-Reveal world, *Miss Susie*. And don't call me Lucy, it's Luciano. Professor, if you're being horrible."

"Are you sure we're talking about the same band?" She snorted. "And I'll call you what I like. What are you gonna do about it anyway, cry?"

I trotted off, increasing my speed to catch up with Logan. I wasn't sure I wanted to hear more. Disagreements about music were all fine and well, but our teachers were getting too personal, and I didn't want to witness any weird fallout. I was still curious whether there was some deeper reason why they were constantly at odds, though.

In the last four days leading up to Halloween, Penelope put treats in our dinner bags. On Monday, we sat in the lounge, grinning at the jack o' lantern-shaped cookies adorned with orange and black frosting.

"Oh, ho ho, I'm Santa Pumpkin, coming to bring candy corns down your chimney on Halloween Night!" Hal held his cookie in front of his mouth and nose.

"Eeeek!" Faith leaned back with her hands on her cheeks. "No! Anything but the worst candy ever!"

Everybody laughed, even Darren, who had come by to chat for once.

"I hear you have quite the craft project going on," he said.

"Me? No, I'm just making a mask." I jerked my thumb at the corner, where my roommate sat with headphones on, hunched over some stubborn homework. "It's Grace who's doing big things with fabric."

"Well, regardless, we're all waiting to see how it all looks in a few nights." He smiled, waving as he left. "Happy studying!"

On Tuesday, Penelope gave us cups of chocolate pudding with gummy worms inside. I knew from peeking into the cafeteria while passing that these weren't the usual fare, so I decided to ask Dylan what he knew about the special treats.

"Oh, those are from the café." He grinned. "They're test batches, really. The rest of the school won't get to try these until lunchtime on Thursday."

"Wow."

"Do you know there's a rumor that Penelope is dating the new vampire chef?" Faith studied her nails as she perched on the arm of the cushy chair her boyfriend sat in. "Scandalous, they say."

"No." Hal shook his head, but he reached out, and Faith took his hand. "Well, it shouldn't be, not in a perfect world."

"World's flawed. Sucks to be Gaia." Grace shrugged. "But what else is new?"

"Hey, but aren't we trying to do our best here?" Logan waved his hand at the lot of us, but he looked right at me. "Make it even just a little better?"

"Yeah." I nodded. "And this whole campus plus the entire town outside it has an enormous party coming up. More chances to shake all the haters off."

"Please don't tell me you're planning some sort of Taylor Swift flash mob, Aliyah." Faith closed her eyes, leaning against the back of Hal's comfy chair-and-a-half.

"Definitely not." I chuckled, glancing at Logan. "I can't dance that way."

Wednesday, the dessert in the bag was a cupcake. You might guess the decoration because Logan's reaction was to yeet it across the room.

Yup. It looked like a tarantula.

It was inside a clear plastic clamshell case, though, so it was still good. Doris trotted over to retrieve it, the package crackling in her teeth as she carried it back. When she dropped it at Logan's feet, she curled her tail around her haunches and purred.

"Yeah, okay, Doris. You're a good girl, but I still think someone else should pick that up?" Logan shuddered. "I've got a bad case of arachnophobia."

"Here, let me help with that." I took the cupcake from Doris, then opened the package. Using the knife that came with our dinner bags, I cut the legs off the sides and the mandibles off the front. After that, I grabbed a handful of trick-or-treat-sized Twizzlers from my bag, the kind you peel. Once I arranged them on the spider's legless body, the dessert had a completely different look.

"Ta-da!" I held it out for Logan's inspection, but he still had one hand over his eyes. "It's harmless, I promise."

"A ladybug?"

"Uh-huh." I grinned. "Definitely not a spider pretending to be something else."

"Aliyah Morgenstern, I could kiss you."

Our friends went so silent you could have heard a pin drop. As far as I knew, everyone else had gone there except us, but I think for Logan and me, things were different, even though we'd had plenty of perfect moments for that since Parents' Night.

I liked Logan. He might have been frighteningly pretty and somewhat awkward, but he was also sweet and kind. I had no idea what his motives were. Maybe that was the problem.

I wasn't sure if he was serious. It was impossible to tell whether he was into me or not lately. The dynamic that reminded me of Azreal Ambersmith had vanished since the dance. I should be as certain as possible before I said or did anything definitive.

My concerns weren't entirely emotional. They were practical, too. Heightened emotions plus new situations might equal solar magic surprise. Also, Logan's discomfort was plain to see on his face.

"Uh, we gotta talk about this later," I managed.

Conversation picked up again, the usual banter that almost had its own personality in our group. But it was a little too loud and slightly strained, as though it were a clock somebody had wound too tight.

After dinner, we went our separate ways, and Logan didn't follow me. I couldn't blame him, but maybe we'd get a moment the next day. We all got a half-day and left campus after lunch. I knew Salem proper like the back of my hand. If anyone could find a secluded corner, even on the busiest night in town, it was me.

Lunch was more spectacular than we'd imagined. I know we were all used to spellwork as an everyday part of our lives. All the same, the meal made every student at Hawthorn Academy realize we shouldn't take magic for granted.

Sandwiches were cut into shapes and stacked to look like spooky faces gazing up from plates. Stews swirled in bowls, shimmering with effects that made them look like glitter bath bombs. Everything was totally delicious. We didn't stand in line for our food; instead, it got delivered right to our tables by amazing magical animals.

Not all of the kitchen staff had familiars—it wasn't a requirement for working here, after all—but enough of them did to make even the delivery of the food a stunning presentation. Sandy led a line of other four-legged familiars, equipped with trays on their backs.

"The waitstaff is totally amazing!" Grace clapped her hands, eyes wide with wonder.

"I never would have thought of anything like this." I shook my head. "Say what you will about my brother, but at least he's good at keeping spoilers a secret."

The desserts weren't a surprise, which was a good thing for Logan. He escaped the cafeteria with two pudding cups and a quartet of cookies wrapped in a napkin before the spider cupcakes came out. The rest of us made shorter work of our desserts than the rest of the students in our year, which was good since we needed the extra time.

Upstairs, I helped Grace put on the costume she'd worked so hard on, and it was amazing. I felt almost bad that mine was only a mask with a couple of other accessories, but at least we went together.

"Ready?" I stood at the door, waiting to open it.

"Okay." Grace nodded.

Students lined the hall, waiting to see the big costume reveal, and they weren't disappointed. Ember and Lune peeped and stamped their approval as well. Of course, they were elated.

We had dressed as each other's familiars.

My half-mask gave me a pink nose, whiskers, and connected to the ears on top of my head. The rest of my outfit was a soft silvery-gray cardigan over gray leggings. Of course, it was Grace who took the cake.

She was dressed from head to toe in gilt fabric. A set of golden spikes and whiskers sat on the top of her head, connected at the bottom to her own half-mask in the shape of a dragonet's muzzle. On her body was a golden jumpsuit she had sewed, but the main attraction was the set of fully articulated wings stretching between her back and arms.

In the hall, Grace raised her hands, revealing the wings. I bet she could have glided down the staircase on them if she wanted to, but she didn't. Instead, my roommate activated the stairs and headed down like it was any other day.

It was only a short walk through the lobby and out the door, but what a difference a handful of steps made. Outside on Essex Street danced a scene of particolored celebratory chaos. Mundanes and extrahumans alike flooded the streets, and we walked with the current of folks headed toward Salem Commons.

That was the park enclosed by yards of French Gothic picket fencing in the middle of town, complete with walking paths, a playground at one corner, and a bandstand. Vendors had set up tables, carts, and food trucks along the fence. Some of them were from out of town, but most were staffed and stocked by town shops and restaurants.

I led my friends immediately to one of them, where I saw a familiar face.

"Izzy!" My smile was so big it hurt my face.

"Aliyah? Is that you under there?"

"Yeah."

"Holy guacamole!" Izzy pointed at Grace. "That's the most amazing costume I've ever seen, and I've lived in Halloween Central my whole life."

Her opinion was far from unique. Loads of passersby stopped to ask Grace for pictures and ask if she'd entered one of the many costume contests. She hadn't, in part because many of those are in the 21+ bars, but it gave me an idea—one that'd get my roomie some recognition, and possibly a little money, too.

I strode off, leaving my friends at Izzy's booth, where they waited to get card or palm readings from Izzy's parents. I overheard Dylan trying to turn it down due to the cost, but Hal offered to pay for everyone, even Lee, Eston, and Kitty, who showed up as I walked away.

My goal was the bandstand, where the emcee for the evening's festivities stood directing the road crew. I knew him, of course, because it was Michael Ambersmith, Azrael's dad.

"Well, if it isn't young Miss Morgenstern. Novel costume. Moon hare, is it?" He raised one ruddy eyebrow. "Are you entering the town costume contest?"

"No, I'm here to enter my roommate. Grace DuBois." I pointed her out.

"Wow." He stroked his mustache, appraising her work from a distance. "That's something else. She ordered that online?"

"No, she made it herself in Creatives."

"Your roommate has some serious talent, then." He nodded. "Consider her entered. Wait here, and I'll note her down on the list and bring her number back to you."

I leaned against the nearest column instead of sitting on the bandstand's steps like I'd usually do. The last thing I wanted was to get in the way of the roadies as they set things up for this year's musical guests. Because I'd been on campus so much, I hadn't had a chance to find out who was playing, so I glanced at the poster near my head.

"Night Creatures!?" I almost toppled over.

"Yeah." The voice behind me was deep and mirthful but totally unfamiliar. I turned around to see who was talking to me. I recognized him instantly from the news.

"Fred Redford?" I blinked. "From Tinfoil Hat?"

"Sort of." He shrugged. "Just helping some friends."

"Wow!" I tried to recover and maintain some semblance of calm and decorum. "I mean, that's cool."

In case you were wondering why I was so flustered, it was because they were one of my role models. Fred was part of the Tinfoil Hat Pack, the group of students who'd played a major part in putting the extrahuman world back together a few years ago.

More specifically, they'd thwarted Uncle Richard's attempt to subjugate humans and take over both faerie courts, and now he and a bunch of his friends were here in Salem.

I was so glad I had decided to wear a mask.

Fred threw his head back and laughed so hard tears formed at the corners of his eyes. It was the last thing I expected from a Redcap, even a Seelie one. His laughter attracted the attention of another hero, a woman with long dark hair who set a violin down in a case before sauntering over. It was Irina Kazynski, also famous for being an awesome musician.

"What's so funny, Lunk?" She elbowed him in the ribs, smirking.

"It's just, we've got a fan." His smile could have cut diamonds. "Which rocks."

"What else is new?"

"Not you. We. Plural. As in, Tinfoil Hat."

"Really?" she asked me.

"Yeah." My giggle came out with a snort at the end, like Izzy's. "I mean, you all saved the worlds."

"Huh. You're right, it does rock." She reached into a pocket on her brown leather jacket, producing a handful of badges on lanyards. "Here. These will let you and some friends come right up front when the show starts."

"Wow, thanks!"

I headed back to Izzy's booth, where we hung around through the readings. I knew it'd be a while before Night Creatures went on because they were all vampires, so once Logan's reading was done, I grabbed his hand and snuck off with him.

CHAPTER THIRTY-FOUR

"I think we're alone now."

"What's going on, Aliyah?" Logan's voice was flatter than usual. He dropped my hand.

"Look, I wanted to apologize." I shook my head. "I mean, we got off to sort of an awkward start, and I felt like last night, you got embarrassed because of me."

"Awkward is kind of my default, though." He sighed. "I'm never gonna be chill like Hal or have game like Dylan. Or be good at faking it like Elanor. My parents hate it, but there's nothing I can do. And believe me, they've spent years plus tons of money trying to change practically everything about me. It's not you, it's me, and it always will be."

"Woah." I reached out to him again, taking him by the shoulder this time. "Hey. You're Logan, okay? You shouldn't try to be someone else, and I don't want you to be."

"Really?" He froze, his tension on hold but not gone yet.

"I mean it."

"But you don't like me? I mean, like-like, the way Grace likes Dylan."

"I never liked anyone before, not that way," I lied. Because now that the words were out of my mouth, I knew it wasn't true, but I couldn't come clean without hurting a lot of people's feelings. There was only one thing I could admit to, so I did. "It's nothing personal."

"It's not because I'm, you know." He closed his eyes and tapped his temple. "Slow."

"No, absolutely not." That was true. "I had no idea you were, actually, and it doesn't matter."

"Oh." He blinked. "Really?"

"I mean, you learn differently, but that's no big deal. And if your family gives you grief about that, remember, we're friends. We help each other, end of story."

"Peep!" Ember fluttered down from wherever she'd been flying and perched on my shoulder, snaking her neck out toward Logan. "Peep, peep."

"Okay." He looked Ember in the eyes. "I get it."

"Wait, you understand her?"

"Yeah." He nodded. "Most of the others, too."

"What did she say?"

"You don't know?" He blinked. "I thought every magus could understand their own familiar."

"Absolutely not. Logan, almost nobody has that talent." I grinned. "How long have you been able to understand critters like that?"

"Since my magic showed up a couple of years ago." He shook his head. "But my folks don't believe I can really do it."

So, Logan's parents hadn't just put him down and tried to squash him into the mold of their expectations, they'd totally dismissed his abilities. I swallowed the sudden flare of anger. Showing it would be futile right now, but if I ever got the chance, I'd give them a piece of my mind.

"I can't believe you don't know how rare your abilities are." I shook my head, picturing all my frustration rising up into the sky. I had to channel it somehow.

"Well, Ember asked me not to tell you what she said." Logan grinned sheepishly. "Which confused me, so thanks for the explanation, Aliyah."

"Hey, do you want to go and get some cotton candy or something?"

"Come to think of it, yeah, I do." His chuckle was higher-pitched than usual. "I didn't eat so much at lunch. Nervous, you know."

"Sorry about that. I should've talked to you last night." I sighed. "I was worried I'd hurt you because most of the time I care too much."

"It's okay, and I totally want us to be friends." He shook his head. "It's just, I felt weird because our whole group was pairing off, you know? I thought maybe we sort of had to get together because otherwise, we'd be the odd folks out."

"So, what are you saying here?" I blinked.

"I'm saying I like you. Aliyah, but not like-like." He nodded like he'd just made up his mind about it. "It's a good thing that you care too much, and I'm really glad we're friends. Honestly, it felt like I never had any until I came here. Not really."

"I'm glad we're friends, too. Come on, Salem's finest food trucks are waiting." I beckoned and he followed, Doris walking between us.

We held hands and it was totally platonic, almost exactly like walking around Salem with Izzy and Cadence practically my whole life. Logan should've had that growing up too, but it was okay to come late to friendship. True friends didn't care how long that took.

We spent about an hour sampling different foods and selecting the best treats to bring back to our friends. By the time we returned to Izzy's tent, Cadence had arrived. She had Brianna with her, plus a couple of guys who looked vaguely familiar.

Before I could ask for any introductions, Noah showed up. He was with Elanor, who stared at Logan and me. At first, I didn't know why until I remembered we were still holding hands. He let go before I did. I tried to hold on, but he wasn't having it. Maybe he was making the right call because once we stopped touching, she looked away.

"Aliyah." Noah's voice was low, almost reverent. "Night Creatures is playing, and we get to see them. Live! Can you believe it?"

"I know, this is awesome." I smiled because we were having a conversation that wasn't about our strained relationship or how choppy the social waters were at Hawthorn Academy. "But it gets better, Noah."

I rummaged in my bag, then dangled the lanyards. Noah's eyes went wide and his jaw dropped. If he weren't holding on to Elanor's arm, he might have fallen down.

"Are you serious?"

"Totally." I held out two of the passes.

"Thanks!" Noah couldn't move so Elanor took them, putting one around my brother's neck.

I made the rounds through my friends, handing out passes to each of them. Izzy declined; she had to man the booth. Cadence took one, but when I asked if I should go request a few more for her companions, she declined.

"I actually took this one for Brianna. Check it out." She pulled a press pass out of her jacket. "I'm covering this concert for the Gallows Hill school paper."

"Wow, awesome!" I directed my next question to the two guys. "Are you on the paper too?"

"Not exactly," the bigger of them said. He had a ring through his septum and a broad, stony face. "Let's just say we're in entertainment also."

"And you are?" Noah finally got his wits about him and raised his eyebrows at the two characters.

"Just a couple of lunks," the smaller one said with a shrug. His jet-black hair hung past his shoulders, softening the sharpness of his nose and jaw. There was something almost birdlike about him.

When I said larger and smaller, I meant that one was beanpole-thin, while the other was built like a Panzer tank. Both of them stood over six feet tall and were unsettling in a feral sort of way. I figured they were either shifters or changelings.

"All right." I shrugged. There was no point in asking more questions with this much evasion. Besides, they were with one of my best friends. How bad could they be?

"Aliyah? Don't you want to know who they are?" Noah blinked.

"Any friends of Cadence's are friends of mine."

"Thanks." Cadence grinned.

"Whatever." Noah shook his head. "The show's about to start, so finish your snacks on the way to the bandstand, okay?"

My brother's default was bossiness, but those were sensible enough instructions and we had no reason to protest them, so for once, my friends and I did what Noah said. It helped that Charity was nowhere to be seen. Surely, she had every reason to avoid a vampire concert.

Before the show went on, Michael Ambersmith got up in front of the mic stand. He didn't touch the band's equipment, though, because the Ambersmiths had all sorts of magipsychic devices, and right now, he used one to amplify his voice over the roar of the crowd.

"I'm here to call up our finalists in the costume contest."

Folks in the crowd milled about, making small talk. When he announced the five names, I wasn't surprised. Grace was. She jumped up and down, screeching in a way I'd never heard as she dashed toward the stage, up the steps, and all the way down the line of runners-up, which only made her costume seem more amazing. The rest of the contestants didn't have anything like that amount of mobility in their getups.

That was because Grace had used her magic while making it. I wasn't sure how she did it—maybe some technique learned in Quebec —but it paid off, judging by the awed gasps from the crowd.

This final round always got settled by a call for applause. Michael held his hand over each of the costumed heads, listening to and gauging the crowd's response.

When it was Grace's turn, practically the entire group from Hawthorn screamed at the tops of their lungs. So did everyone in Izzy's booth, and another huge section also cheered for her. At the front of this stood the two self-styled "lunks" with Cadence and Brianna.

Grace won. Michael handed her an envelope, which I knew contained several gift certificates from local shops and eateries, plus a bank check from the city for two hundred dollars. That was first prize every year for as long as I could remember.

She tucked that into her costume almost like an afterthought. I could tell that the real prize for her was acknowledgment. She had done something brilliant, and now everybody knew it. As she came back down to join us, her high color and springy steps told me Grace was totally elated.

Finally, it was time for the concert.

Up toward the front of the bandstand, there was a roped-off area that our passes let us access. It was as close as you could get to the wooden stage built on one side of the stone and metal structure. A bus with sunproof windows was parked across the common. That was where we first saw them.

Night Creatures was a punk band whose members were all vampires. They'd started back in the '90s when they were all still mortal and played regularly in Providence later that decade, but during the ten years after the Big Reveal, old vampires afraid of losing their powers went on a turning spree.

Lane Meyer and his friends got caught up in that disaster, ending up as second-class citizens like all the other vamps in this country. To this day, nobody was sure who'd arranged to have them turned or why. So, they changed the subject matter of their songs from dissatisfaction with a world that hid for so long to biting back against the flaws in this brave new society.

Noah had listened to them practically his whole life, which meant I had too. A handful of years ago, they'd gotten super popular after winning the Newport Battle of the Bands. Since then, they'd been in demand for appearances but didn't often play outside Rhode Island before graduating from Providence Paranormal. Now they had their degrees, and the Halloween gig in Salem was part of a short New England tour this winter. Next year, they'd go nationwide, so this might be the only time we'd see them in town.

There was an opening act, of course, but I didn't expect it to be one called Fred Redford and the Pixies. I'd had no idea he could even sing, let alone get up in front of a whole crowd of people like that. Everything I knew about him was from the news, mostly about how his intervention in the Under had helped foil my uncle's plans there.

Fred was actually pretty talented, although most of the crowd paid more attention to his dropped glamour. That's right, he went full Redcap for his performance. He was tithed to the Queen and Seelie but still totally scary. Redcaps were absolutely the sort of thing people wanted to see on Halloween in Salem. They had sharp sharkish teeth, gray skin, blazing red eyes, and of course, bloody red hats on their heads. Totally spooky and awesome in this town.

He sang a set of classic covers, the Halloween-type novelty music people played at parties. You know what I'm talking about—the *Monster Mash*, *Werewolves of London*, that sort of thing—but it was different from those old recordings. Sort of like a Postmodern Jukebox version, with a big band sound and bluesy vocals. At first, I didn't know where the instrumentals came from.

Turned out, he had a full complement of Pixies backing him up. Their tiny instruments were the real deal, and they used magic for amplification. Pixies were pure faerie creatures like Grims, but water-based and Seelie—perfect for Salem with its coastal charm.

Once Fred and company finished their set, he knelt, letting the Pixies climb up on his shoulders and arms so they could bow where everyone could see them. The gesture went along with everything I'd heard about the Tinfoil Hat folks—that they were determined and powerful, but also kind.

He got a good response from the audience, plenty of cheering and whistling, along with applause. I was glad for him; he deserved no less. But of course, everyone was really there for Night Creatures, and that was exactly what we got, plus a little something extra.

They had Irina Kaczynski join them on electric violin for three covers in their set. She was an internet-famous psychic fiddler. These were the songs they'd played the second night of their competition when she'd subbed in. This time, however, the guitarist and electric violinist performed together.

Everyone went nuts behind us—in a good way, of course. The covers went over well, exactly the sort of performance people loved here on Halloween. Usually, bands stuck to covers or their most popular songs. And for Night Creatures, that meant the ones that weren't blatantly about vampire rights.

Lane Meyer pushed the boundaries of the formula. This band was punk, which meant all their songs were political somehow. Even with their more understated tracks, they made a statement that was hard to argue with, but someone in the crowd had a different idea.

I didn't see the person in the horrifying costume earlier. They hadn't gotten passes like we had, but that didn't stop them. Earth magic quaked the ground, jostling everyone on it and knocking down the ropes. After that, the magus using it strode forward, mask covering their entire face. I noticed they had a familiar, something on the ground. I couldn't see it clearly in the dim light and commotion.

Riding the wave of the quake, a mound of earth lifted them above the rest of the crowd. This was some seriously powerful earth magic, stronger than I'd ever seen. Maybe it was because the autumn grass was thin in the Common, with more earth exposed. It let the magus manage something I'd never thought possible.

The quake rattled the bandstand.

Vampires had excellent reflexes, which was the only reason Lane and company were still standing. All the same, the drum set had toppled, and the bass drum had escaped its stand to roll around the stage. Irina fell backward, nearly cracking her head open on the marble. She would have been seriously injured if Fred hadn't gotten between her and the floor.

The magus on the mound didn't say a word. They didn't have to. Because they held an enormous sign. That and the costume made a blatant and ugly statement.

It was a vampire slayer's garb, as terrifying to folks with fangs as an SS uniform would be to anyone in my family. For five years after the Reveal, a group most people called terrorists but some considered vigilantes had gone around dressed in hoods and masks, stakes strapped to their chests. Any vampire they met got staked and decapitated.

That still happened on occasion.

That was one reason this magus was downright terrifying, but there was another. The sign they staked into the earthen mound was painted with fake blood, the kind you get in a costume store. It said this:

Burn All Leeches

In the other hand, they held a Molotov cocktail. And lit it.

They chucked it at the stage, aiming directly for Lane Meyer, the frontman of Night Creatures. He didn't duck, but faced the threat head-on, a matched set of birds taking flight from his fists. There was nothing else he could have done to fend off the fire arcing toward his flammable undead body.

"Hit it!"

It was Fred's voice, so the band didn't start playing, but he was one of the queen's knights, able to command her creatures. The Pixies jumped up from the railing they'd been sitting on during the Night Creatures set. All ten waved their hands in unison, and a matching gout of salty water flew toward the projectile.

The seawater slapped the bottle, crashing it into the wooden stage on top of the bandstand. It must have been filled with a mixture of oil and alcohol because it didn't go out right away.

Lane tried to stand his ground, hissing, fangs protruding as his vampiric instincts responded to the threat of an open flame. I recognized it. It was a magical fire, but not one cast by any magus. It was made from infused chemicals like we'd used that day in the lab.

Was the magus in the costume from my school?

The idea stole my breath. The next one was worse. What if it was a professor? Fear paralyzed me, but someone with more experience at working through that emotion snapped me out of it.

Logan grabbed my hand again. He directed his own jet of water at the blaze on the stage, and I knew his unspoken request. He wanted my help to banish the fire in case even more water couldn't extinguish it. I narrowed my eyes, glaring at the flames, and in moments, we'd put them out together.

"Security!" Fred Redford's voice roared from where he'd managed to sit up.

A group of burly figures clad in red ran out from the sides of the bandstand, dashing toward the costumed magus. As they turned, the back of their hood flipped up to reveal a ponytail. Before I could be sure of the hair's color, the attacker dove into the crowd.

"One, two, three!" Lane growled into the mic.

Matt the guitarist picked up his instrument and shredded out a sick riff. I recognized it; they were playing *Points*, their most defiant song. The drummer and the bassist joined forces, building a scaffold for the rest of the music. When Lane added his voice, the entire performance was a clear and present act of resistance in the face of terror.

> *"Without a doubt, I knew it sucked that night*
> *We'll never win, 'cause no one thinks we're right*
> *We had to walk away, and give up all our plans*
> *Why do I stop and turn around?*
> *And every time I smile they walk away from me*
> *A loser just because I'm fanged, you see*
> *And I'm seen as a guy with blood-lust rage*
> *Why am I stuck on this page?*
> *Eternity spent in a cage.*
> *What's the point again?"*

Salem's extrahuman community had a long memory because this town was steeped in a history of persecution. The immigration of the last surviving Morgensterns back in the 20th century only reinforced the attitude that we couldn't afford to tolerate intolerance.

So of course, the crowd sided with the vamps that night. Deafening applause marked the end of the song. My ears rang, and Ember hid her head in my hair. As it finally died down, my friends huddled together, hearts racing with fading adrenaline.

"We'd better get back to the school right away." Faith's voice was flat and hollow. "I'd bet dollars to donuts that was my megabitch sister. The headmaster will hear about this from me first."

She startled every one of us except Hal, who squeezed her hand and smiled at her. The crowd mostly dispersed, many disappearing as we stood there trying to catch our breath. Noah even stayed, although Elanor vanished into the crowd. It was almost an apologetic gesture.

I wasn't sure whether Faith was right. Charity was definitely a bullying bigot, but in the cafeteria, she'd waited until I turned on the magic. So far, she hadn't seemed like the sort who'd get her hands that dirty.

All the same, I hoped my brother would drop Charity like a hot potato the next day, but I didn't expect much. Courage didn't spring up fully formed overnight.

I'd hoped to meet more of my role models in person that night, but under the circumstances, I was relieved they left uninjured and safe, at least physically. They made their way to their bus under the park's municipal lighting. I watched them go, hoping that someday I'd have half their bravery.

CHAPTER THIRTY-FIVE

After Halloween, everyone on campus talked about the incident at the Night Creatures concert. Almost every student had been on the Common that night, but nobody publicly speculated about who the magus behind the mask was. In private, things were different.

"I can't believe nobody agrees with me, that Charity must have done the attack." Faith crossed her arms over her chest, sticking her nose in the air. "Everyone knows my sister's the wicked bitch of Park Avenue."

"Whoa, take it easy there." Dylan stepped back. He didn't like confrontation much, I'd come to realize. "I mean, we believe you. We're your friends, and you know her better than anyone here. But if nobody saw anything, what can they do?"

"Well, they must think somebody here did it." Grace shrugged. "Nobody whispers this much all over campus if they don't suspect someone here."

"I'm totally sure it was Charity." Faith stomped her foot. "I have no proof, but I'm not alone. All her lackeys are walking on eggshells. They must think she did it but can't figure out why they're not in the headmaster's office right now."

"Maybe they're too scared. Or they agree with her." Hal sighed. "But I don't want to believe that."

"What if she's saying it's someone else?" I couldn't stand it anymore, so I walked up to the elephant in the room and punched it right in its lousy trunk. "What if they suspect it's me?"

"Why would anyone think that?" Logan blinked. "You're not popular, but everyone knows you're a good person."

"Everyone does not." Faith sighed. "I know how public opinion works, and people in the upper classes are not cool with Aliyah. No offense, but most students still judge you for the cafeteria and think you set the fire in the lab. Charity's made a scapegoat out of you."

"I think Faith's right." Hal nodded. "The blame game jives with what I read in Charity's file. That masked magus attacked with a fire weapon, one that was hard to put out, like the lab. The attacker wore a mask and made that hill so people couldn't judge their height, and the hill cut us off from the crowd, so nobody saw our friends put the fire out except the band. So yeah, maybe she's blaming Aliyah."

"We're doing something about it, then." Grace set her jaw. "She can't go around spreading rumors about one of the people who stopped the fire. That's just wrong."

"You're right." Faith nodded. "But when I went to Headmaster Hawkins on Halloween, he just took a statement. It wasn't enough, my word alone against whatever she might have said."

"Maybe more of us need to go to him and make our own statements." Logan stood up. "It can't hurt."

Logan totally made sense, so that was what we did. All five of my friends from school went in separately to see the headmaster, even though they all had less proof than Faith. We had extra time now that nobody did Familiar Bonding anymore.

Tuesday went by, and Wednesday. Charity didn't get in trouble, but neither did I. My friends all saw me putting out the fire, which meant Charity's blame game couldn't go any farther than the rumor mill.

That night at dinner, there was a series of posters on the walls, announcing an informal party in the lounge for Saturday. It was even fire-themed, something about a hearthside gathering. Charity was throwing it.

She's trying another way to get you on probation. Or worse, expelled.

The evil inside voice had a point, so I decided to make myself scarce over the weekend. I told my roommate about it as I packed a knapsack before bed, but Grace didn't like that idea at all.

"Aliyah, you shouldn't leave. You're letting her win if you do." Grace paced the room, swinging her bathroom bag in one hand. "You should just go to her party and say it's stupid, then go to the library or something."

"But who knows what she'll try to pin on me if I stick around?" I leaned against the wall on the side of my bed. "If I'm not even on campus, all that happens is she threw a party I missed." I dropped my roommate a wink. "So, I'm going home."

"I guess you have a point." Grace sighed. "If that's your plan, don't stay too late."

"I guess I can go early in the morning before breakfast." I patted Ember, who was asleep in my lap. "That ought to do it."

"Well, you'd better inform the headmaster then, so the doors will be open. They're locked after lights out until breakfast time." She turned her back, finally heading to the restroom for her bedtime routine.

"Hey, Grace." She stopped. "Thanks for believing in me."

"You'd do the same." She waved and headed out the door.

I took my roommate's advice, sending a message to the head-master before setting an alarm so I could leave at the crack of dawn on Saturday, but I had to make it through Thursday and Friday first—and Friday was sort of a big deal. It was a Bishop's Row game but also a tryout.

"Listen up because I'm only telling you maggots once." Coach Pickman paced in front of the bleachers, where we all sat during Thursday's Gym period. "This game is important because this is how we pick your year's team. You know, the one that's going up against all the upperclassmen this spring?"

"That's not fair." Bailey snorted. "Second and third years have always gotten two teams each, and we only get one."

"If you want to talk to me about always, don't complain." Coach Pickman laughed *at* us, not *with* us. "If we keep things the way they've always been, you won't compete at all. Shut your yaps and be thankful. And play your hearts out."

Our time in Gym that day was spent on drills: conjuring, throwing, and ducking each other's balls. Hal didn't use any of his special moves, and I didn't blame him. He'd want to save his stamina for the game. He'd told us all about a million times how he much wanted to be on the team.

In the library, I even found him looking over books of game strategies with Faith. She gave him advice instead of taking notes, which made me think she'd given up on making the team to help her boyfriend. She had changed an awful lot in a good way.

At dinner, none of us could eat. Our to-go bags sat half full. When we went upstairs for the night, we all brought leftovers. I fed mine to Ember.

On the way downstairs in the morning, we wished each other luck. Soon enough, Logan, Faith, Hal, and I were in the gym, waiting to get started.

We'd figured out our formation earlier in the week. Since Hal was so good at dodging, he was up front, on first. Unlike in many other sports, it was a defensive position. I was fast, so I was on second defense. Logan was right behind me—second mid was what they called that. He was slow and his water magic matched, but that was a good thing.

If I ducked, Logan might still be holding his ball. One way to avoid getting tagged out was bumping the incoming ball with yours, but that only worked if you hadn't launched it yet. The lag in Logan's magic meant he'd most likely manage that tactic.

Bailey was beside him on first mid. That was mostly because we weren't concerned if she got tagged out. Her air magic wasn't much use against the other side, in large part because both her sister and Dylan were air and more likely to make the first-year team. The other drawback to her magic was that it couldn't move most of the other elements. It only affected fire, and Kitty wasn't likely to be much of a threat.

Alex was in the back, playing reverse point. That was what we called the position between the columns. Reverse point was the most balanced player, the one whose magic and athleticism were about even. Normally, that would have been me, but I couldn't risk revealing myself as an extramagus to get on an intramural team, hence Alex's promotion. I shouldn't have minded, but I did.

I'd had a long conversation on Monday with Logan about how I should be reverse point, because technically I was the strongest player. But without the ability to fully unleash my magic, I couldn't play to my potential. I had to minimize just about every move I made on the court, and that stung. The very fact that he understood had softened that blow

Our familiars acted sort of like a cheering squad. They hung around on the sidelines, watching us. Most of them were openly excited, except for Alex's basilisk Aceso, who curled up in a scaly ball with her head on her tail. I was exhausted too, so I didn't blame her.

Coach Chen watched over the coin toss. Eston called heads, leaving us with tails, but we won, so Hal returned victorious. That meant we got the first throw. I conjured my fire, forming it into a ball between my hands. It was practically second nature at that point, but the flames crackled in response to the nervous excitement singing through my veins.

Coach Pickman blew the whistle and I threw, aiming directly for Dylan. It was a long shot because he played reverse point, but if I tagged him out, we'd win the game immediately.

Everyone said he was the strongest player in our year, but I had at least as good a throwing arm as he did. Also, somewhere deep down, I wanted to impress him.

But he was prepared, or at least his team was. My throw would hit him since I'd aimed properly and he had no time to dodge, but Kitty leaped out from her position behind Grace, taking a hit that immediately removed her from play. Her ankyr and cestus absorbed the magic, flashing red to indicate she was out. She jogged back to the bleachers while everybody else had their orbs halfway conjured or more. I noticed Lee was especially fast at this. I'd have to watch out for him as well as Dylan.

I had got another fireball ready before Lee's wooden orb reached me. I hung onto my ball, incinerating his because fire almost always beat wood. After that, I dodged left as Eston's water projectile buzzed past me. It was always better to go toward the middle of the court than risk eliminating yourself by stepping over the line on the right.

Logan was there, his orb absorbing Eston's. When two types of magic hit each other, the outcome varied depending on the elements. Water added to water, so Logan had no choice. He needed to throw his too-heavy orb or banish it and conjure another.

He tossed underhand, aiming at Grace, who played first defense opposite me. She dropped to the floor, flat on her face, the orb of umbral magic held over her head. It was an amazing dodge, brilliant even, because she skipped up off the floor almost right away afterward. That move right there would probably get her on the first-year team.

I was on one knee, but if I didn't launch my fireball soon, it'd be too hot to handle. I aimed for Hailey, knowing that air fed fire. She'd dodged in front of Dylan to avoid her own sister's airball, so it was possible I might get a two-in-one throw.

The fireball hit Hailey straight on. Since she had her ball over her head, preparing to throw it, my magic hit her ankyr, which flashed red. She stomped off toward the bleachers, glaring over her shoulder at Bailey, who'd somehow managed to last longer than her despite being less powerful.

"We're getting killed out here. Come on, guys!" Dylan clapped his hands. It was only then that I realized he'd launched his ball.

"Asshole!" Bailey jumped in front of Alex, taking the hit in a move similar to Kitty's.

"Language." Coach Pickman blew her whistle." If you weren't out, you would be now."

Hal sidestepped, avoiding Grace's umbral magic. In the space he'd previously occupied, Alex made his throw. The poison magic headed directly toward Dylan, who hadn't finished conjuring his next water ball yet. Grace couldn't defend him either, but Lee came to his rescue.

The wood Magus threw a brown spiky ball in an atypical play. Instead of jumping up to block the poison while holding his projectile, he tried to bump it out in midair.

Lee had amazing aim, but his throwing power left something to be desired. He didn't manage to deflect the poison all the way out of bounds. Instead of vanishing after crossing the line, the poison ball hit Eston. Lee did too, but in Bishop's Row, the ankyr and cestus are programmed to account for friendly fire without penalty.

His ankyr flashed red, and he left the court to sit next to Kitty. Faith took some initiative at that point. She'd been holding her undeath magic back all this time, in no small part because it was more dangerous than most other elements in Bishop's Row. Practically nothing but fire could beat it. And, like with poison, any player whose ankyr weren't on exactly right could end up in the infirmary if it hit them.

Faith threw at Grace. Dylan was too far away to protect her. Then again, that wasn't his job. She was the one playing defense, and you couldn't fault Faith for trying to make what was probably her only throw count.

Grace only just managed to conjure a ball of umbral magic to block the incoming orb, which dissipated on impact. Normally this would just mean that Grace had to keep conjuring, but because Faith had held back for so long, her projectile was twice the strength of my roommate's.

Not only did that undeath orb destroy Grace's next one, it bled through and hit her ankyr. They flashed red, and she was out—in more ways than one.

She hit the court, falling on her side, thank goodness. Lee followed up by tossing a wood orb at Faith in retaliation, striking her out, but I could see it was worth the risk.

Faith's play had totally intended consequences. She'd used strategy from the library books, which included getting in the other players' heads. With his girlfriend down, Dylan froze, a big mistake while playing this sport.

Alex struck. He wasn't quite as fast as me with creating his orbs. That meant his projectile wasn't as strong as mine. Dylan's air orb would block Alex's poison, but there was no way he could dodge two at the same time while he stared slack-jawed at Grace on the floor.

I left myself open to Lee's next attack, pitching on a curve. It was a long shot, but either I'd hit Dylan or Hal would. He was still in play somewhere on the court.

My fireball blazed by, narrowly missing Dylan's head as he tilted his neck to one side. Maybe it was even accidental, but that was okay.

Hal's space magic came in like a wrecking ball. He'd been conjuring since Grace's last throw, so the orb he tossed was too big to dodge. Dylan gave it a try, tensing his legs to jump over it, but he didn't leap in time.

His ankyr flashed red, and he was out. Game over.

Coach Pickman blew her whistle while Coach Chen took more notes. We were all a bit out of sorts, but otherwise okay. Even Grace sat up, not any the worse for wear after getting hit by that undeath orb.

But Hal was breathless and pale, like the day he'd ended up in the infirmary. Faith rushed away from the bleachers and to his side. Dylan crossed the court's midline. Between the two of them, they got Hal to a seat. Nin immediately bounced into his lap. Seth tried to pull the cooler over, but he was too small. Ember, Doris, and Gale helped him by pushing from the back.

"Overtaxed, huh?" Coach Pickman strode over to Hal. "Nice strategy out there, Hawkins, but you'd better build some stamina before next semester if you want us to win anything."

"What?" Hal held an ice-cold bottle against his forehead.

"You're on the first-year team."

"How?"

"The other years don't even have a space magus. They can't counter any of the plays we can do with you on defense. As long as you didn't choke out there today, including you was always our plan."

"What about the rest?"

"Chen's on that now. You'll find out after your Turkey Day break. Take a rest. Dubois, you too. Full-force undeath orbs are no joke." She turned her back to walk away but added, "Not bad, Fairbanks. Not bad."

"Who, me?" Faith blinked.

Coach Pickman either didn't hear her or pretended not to. It didn't much matter. Faith went totally silent, face pale, eyes wide, until Hal took her hand, and she blushed. She pulled him closer, tilting his head so it rested on her shoulder.

Watching them, you'd never have thought she was the second meanest girl on campus just ten weeks ago. I'd almost fought her, which would have begun a cycle of harm and retaliation that might never have ended. Hal stopped that, just by caring. It was no surprise to me. Love was important; I'd had ample demonstration of that in my family. But I'd never understood how much of a difference it could make for people who'd gone through life with the bare minimum.

Some of what you learned in school had nothing to do with class-rooms and everything to do with the people you met there.

I woke and dressed in darkness the next morning, escorted through the doors by the headmaster because avoiding an attack isn't just a strategy for Bishop's Row. Refusing to attend one party was no big deal if it'd keep my friends and me out of trouble. On the way down Essex Street, I thought that lesson about caring from yesterday was over.

But it had only just begun.

Thanksgiving was just another weekend at home for me, but for Dylan, Grace, and Lee, it'd be time spent on campus alone. Because my roommate was Canadian, her version of the holiday was already past. The bus back to her aunt's wasn't too expensive, but she'd told me there was little point. Nobody in the UK or mainland China observed the day, either.

Hal and his family usually had dinner in the cafeteria on campus together, but this year, they'd be missing Hal's grandpa and mom.

Even with the three students from abroad in attendance with them, it would be lonely.

The last thing I wanted on my mind all weekend was my friends and the headmaster rattling around on campus like the last handful of peas in a can, which was why I asked my parents if we had room for five more.

My folks said yes, so I invited everybody. Grace and Dylan accepted just about right away. Lee hesitated but decided to go once he found out Izzy and Cadence always came over to hang out after dinner. They all asked about spending time around town, but everything was closed on Thanksgiving day besides the hospital and gas stations.

Hal knew all this, of course. Technically, he was a Salem local too. He definitely wanted to come but had to ask his father. He talked to me about it the next day in the library.

"I'll attend, Aliyah. Dad won't, though."

"What's up?"

"He's not saying." Hal shook his head. "But this is pretty typical for him. My dad doesn't much like going into Salem. Not since last year, anyway."

"Well, okay. As long as he knows he's welcome."

"Oh, yeah, he definitely does. It's nothing personal."

"I'm kinda surprised you're coming, Hal." Logan shrugged. "I mean, I'd have figured you'd take the train down to New York with Faith."

"Oh, I wasn't invited." Hal sighed.

"Are you okay?" Logan blinked.

"Yeah. It's her parents. They never invite guests on Thanksgiving, only family."

"Should have figured. Sorry." Logan winced. "Guess they're a bit like my folks that way. I'm dreading going home."

"By the way, what are you going to do about Doris?"

"I already asked to board her with your grandma, Aliyah." Logan grinned. "My parents had a devil of a time trying to get Gale on the plane when they sent him here with me, so they just think I'm doing things the easy way. They paid the fees, too."

"They're going to find out eventually." Faith paused on her way past our table with a book. "You can't hide something as personal as a familiar from anyone for long."

"Good thing they live in Vegas, then." Logan leaned back, letting Doris leap into his lap. "It'll take them way longer to figure it out."

"Still." She sighed. "They'll pitch a major fit, and it's gonna hurt. Are you sure you want that at some unknown point in the future instead of at a time you've picked?"

"Faith's got a good point." I nodded. "We should plan it out." Doris purred. "See? She likes that idea."

But Logan either didn't agree, or he was just not ready to think about it. At least there was time, but not before this holiday.

CHAPTER THIRTY-SIX

We had no classes on Wednesday, although the cafeteria was open so students could still have meals before heading for the airport or train stations. Logan had departed the night before on a red-eye flight, leaving Doris with Ember and me. I'd bring her to Bubbe's tonight when I went home.

In the early morning, the campus felt almost normal, but the rest of the day was an exercise in reduction. Dylan, Grace, Lee, and I waited through the day together, watching our classmates leave campus.

Hal spent every moment he could with Faith, who was pale and fidgety. Seth was nervous, too, despite Nin's and Ember's best efforts to cheer him up. He had that same snippy energy as the day I'd met him in Bubbe's office, which finally made sense.

Faith's abrasive attitude must have been defensive, designed to protect her from a toxic and apparently large family. Izzy had mentioned to me last weekend that there was a psychic Fairbanks boy at Messing who was a year ahead of her, with another to follow in the next. Apparently, the younger one was the twin of Faith's little sister, Temperance. The boy at Izzy's school acted like the dudebro version of Charity. A bully. Ugh.

After dinner, we left campus together. It was time for Faith to catch her train, which she had booked separately from her sister. I'd asked if she felt safe traveling alone. She'd said Charity was the most dangerous person she could think of. We all insisted on seeing her off.

It was cold enough that we could see our breath. Ember and Gale got a kick out of that happening to people. Their amusement reminded me of being a kid and the games I'd play with Noah outside in winter, pretending to be dragon shifters. I held Doris part of the way, but eventually she got down. Mercats can tolerate lower temperatures with ease.

Nin rode with Seth in his tote. Hal and Faith held hands the entire way down Essex and then Washington Street. Scratch stayed tucked under Lee's overcoat instead of walking on the ice-rimed cobblestones, peeking out at times to chirp at Doris and Lune. The moon hare must have been used to colder weather than this because he hopped along like it was no big deal.

At the train station, we said goodbye, the rest of us turning to give Hal and Faith some privacy. Dylan took Grace's hand, squeezing. She squeezed back. Gale swooped overhead, chasing Ember in circles around the parking lot's streetlamps. Lune just leaned his head against Grace's foot, a common display of affection between them.

We waited until the train pulled away, waving at Faith. She'd have to switch to an Amtrak in Boston, but the Commuter Rail out of Salem only took half an hour. She could go right to bed when she got home, avoiding her siblings for that much longer. She warned us that she might be extra cranky when she returned on Sunday.

After that, we all walked back to campus. The rest of my friends would stay in the dorms until dinner tomorrow, but I went home, thank goodness. Noah had already left at lunchtime, so he'd probably been baking and helping set up tables for hours.

We waved goodbye at the school door, which was next to one of the bank's barred windows that night. After that, I walked down Essex Street with Ember on my shoulder and Doris by my side. The street was almost deserted. The only person out was Azreal. He didn't have his cart at that hour so he trotted to catch up with me, chatting good-naturedly about how Gallows Hill was having its first Bishop's Row tournament this year.

"But how?" I blinked. "You sort of need to conjure magic to play it."

"Plenty of changelings have magic, and even the ones who don't can always conjure glamour away from their appearance." Az chuckled. "It's going to make us look extra scary on the court, too. Want to see?"

"Some other time, Az." I grinned. "Probably not a good idea out here in the street. But that's cool. We find out who's on our team this year after we get back from break."

"Wait." He gasped. "They're letting first years play?"

"Yeah." I shrugged, jostling a peep from Ember. "I'm not sure why. They've never done it that way before, but I'm glad since I like playing."

"To me, it feels like at Gallows Hill, we're practicing for something." He scratched his head. "We've got as many teams as you guys do at Hawthorn, but I don't know what they're planning, so keep your eyes and ears open on campus after break. I'll do the same, and we can compare notes another time."

"Sounds like a plan." We were at the corner of Hawthorne Street, so we said goodbye and I turned toward my house. "Thanks for walking with me."

"Hey, what are friends for?" He waved and turned back down Essex Street.

I'd never considered Azreal a close friend, but he'd looked out for the other townie kids for years. Goblin changelings can scare pretty much anyone when they drop their glamour, and he'd always used that power to chase off bullies and the crueler sorts of tourists.

I know Izzy wasn't interested in romance, but someday, I hoped he'd find a partner in crime. He always seemed lonely, despite his many siblings. I suppose being the only changeling in the family was similar to being an only child.

I stopped at Bubbe's office, where she was expecting me. Doris padded across the threshold and down the hall. I followed, watching as she curled up on a cushion near the kitchen sink. Bubbe left a basin of water in there in case she had to take a dip at some point. I gave my grandma a hug before heading up the back stairs.

At home, there wasn't much for me to do except clean. Everything we cooked the night before was already done, cooling on racks or stowed in the fridge, so I washed dishes, pots, pans, and utensils. I also rinsed the serving platters and bowls we only used for big meals.

When I was done, my arms were tired, my eyelids heavy, and my hands pruned and itchy from all the soap and water. Ember peeped from her perch on top of the refrigerator, where she'd surely been sneaking biscuits, judging by the roundness of her belly.

"Yeah, girl, okay. It's time for bed." I headed toward the stairs, and when I got there, I practically crawled up them. I was just that tired. I managed to put my pajamas on, though. I didn't want to sleep in my leggings and tunic, even though they were pretty comfortable. Nothing beat flannel for bedtime during Salem's brisk autumn weather.

I hadn't brought any clothes home from school, so there was no laundry to do. I'd just wear what I had at home all weekend. We didn't do much besides hang out around the house and go for walks around town as a family the day after Thanksgiving. I could include my friends from school in all that stuff if they wanted.

As I brushed my teeth, I found myself wondering why Noah had never invited anybody home, not last year or this one either. There were plenty of other students who lived halfway around the world from Hawthorn Academy. Maybe not as far away as Lee from China, but at least one of the kids in Noah's year came from Costa Rica, and there was a third-year from Poland.

It crossed my mind, what Bubbe said about the difference between my brother and me. How he was always afraid, and how I didn't stop and think. It was almost like we were opposites. Noah had been at the Parents' Night dance alone, which meant he didn't have a date. I wonder if he got turned down, or if he just didn't bother asking anyone from fear of rejection.

Was Darren the one who'd asked him out, or was it the other way around?

I practically leaped out of my skin because somebody spoke. I managed to spit into the sink and not on the mirror, thank goodness.

"Oh, he asked me out." Noah stood in the doorway, which meant Ember hadn't spontaneously started speaking English and imitating my brother's voice. "And we're never, ever getting back together. Not ever."

"Okay, Noah. Back away from the protestations." I rinsed my toothbrush, watching the water carry foamy toothpaste down the drain. "Sorry about my wayward inside voice, but it was about due for an outburst."

"It happens." He shrugged.

"So, what's up?" I was relieved we were having a relatively normal conversation.

"Just here to brush my teeth, much like my sister, who's hogging the bathroom."

"I'll be out of your way in a sec." I tapped the toothbrush against the sink to get the water off, put it away, then wash my hands and got out of his way. "Good night, Noah."

"Good night, Aliyah."

I headed into my room, closing the door behind me and treading carefully to avoid bumping my head on the ceiling. I hoped I remembered it was low in the morning so I didn't have to spend all of Thanksgiving Day with a bump on the head. I fell asleep almost as soon as my head hit the pillow.

I didn't get a goose egg. I got dressed and helped my parents. Bubbe came up with the baked goods she'd finished in the downstairs oven. She also let Doris come upstairs to share the holiday with the rest of us, which was good because I didn't want to think of her all alone for the day. After that, it was time for the walk down to Essex Street to meet my friends, but they were already at the intersection with Hawthorne Street. Dylan, Hal, and Grace knew the way. They'd all been here before.

It was time for dinner.

In Salem and most of the rest of New England, that meant it was one in the afternoon. Some people around here had it as early as noon. Why did we have Thanksgiving dinner that early? Because why shouldn't we eat all day instead of having a tiny lunch and then feasting? This was just the way it was done here.

I was well aware that in other parts of the country, folks didn't bring out the turkey until actual dinner time, like five, six, or seven o'clock. An internet friend from Florida had told me they did it even later, like eight, which boggled my mind. Who wanted to wait that long for the main event? I certainly didn't. Even if I moved away from New England, I'd still be cooking turkey on the last Thursday of November so it was done in time for lunch, even though it's dinner. And it'd still be kosher.

"What's up with all the separate plates?" Grace asked.

"It's kosher, right, Aliyah?" Hal tilted his head.

"Right." I nodded.

"Thought that was all about not eating pork and shrimp." She shrugged.

"No, they also don't mix the meat with the milk." Dylan pointed at a cream pie on the dessert table, which was on the other side of the room from the one we had dinner at. "We don't want that on the same plate with turkey, or with the same forks and stuff."

"How did you know?" I blinked.

"Dad's chummy with the guy who runs the kosher deli down the street from our apartment." Dylan chuckled. "I paid attention."

The best way to know whether a dish was successful was by how quiet your guests were during the meal. It was dead silent in there. Nobody talked until they got second helpings. Even our familiars were quiet. They had their own meals of scraps selected by Bubbe.

"What's that?" Asked Lee.

"Cranberry sauce, the jellied kind," I answered.

"It's a travesty." Noah snorted. "Try the homestyle stuff. I made it. And have some sweet potato pancakes with it. Bubbe makes those."

"The turkey is amazing." Hal grinned. "Who made it?"

"My husband, the gourmet chef." Mom smiled. "He grew all the herbs he rubbed on it himself."

"I'm not a gourmet." Dad chuckled, dropping her a wink. "You are. Whose idea was it to make cinnamon corn? That's what I call fancy."

"I like the potatoes best." Grace spooned another helping of them onto her plate. "How do you get them creamy like this without butter or milk?"

"Coconut milk." I got myself a helping of beets and sweet potatoes. "Non-dairy milk is super versatile."

It was hard to believe it, but after getting the dinner plates and utensils in the dishwasher, we all had room for dessert. I helped Noah move the sweet stuff to the table, along with the dairy plates and utensils.

"What's this one?" Lee pointed at the casserole Noah cut into. "Almost looks like a dinner dish."

"Noodle kugel." I laughed. "And of course, he's already attacking it. Noah ate almost an entire pan of that after school let out last spring."

"It's the best comfort food ever. It's got raisins in it." He hefted his full plate. "Who doesn't like raisins?"

"Me." Dylan wrinkled his nose. "What's that bread? Does it have chocolate in it?"

"That's my babka." Bubbe nodded. "Yes, it does. Try some! And the rugelach. It's raspberry." She put some of each on a plate and handed it to him.

I got myself some too, plus small slices of apple and pumpkin pie. Grace got rugelach and apple pie. Lee tried a little of everything, although he went back for more babka.

Every year, I was amazed at how much baking Bubbe managed to do. My grandma made all the cookies, the challah, and that decadent babka in the kitchen downstairs. She made more this year than on any other because we'd never had this many guests.

After everyone rested, we sat watching a rerun of the Macy's Day parade in the living room. Halfway through that, Izzy and Cadence came by to join us. We chatted about the floats, wondering how they used to make them without magic back before the Reveal.

It was almost too cold this year to take a walk outside. We had to, though. My friends from Hawthorn needed to head back eventually.

We needed the exercise too after all that food, so we sat, planning our route to include a pass by the wharf.

Bubbe had care packages for our foray outside, baggies of rugelach and babka slices, with a thermos each full of hot cocoa. For Lee, Dylan, and Grace, she'd also packed up a second dinner and dessert, so they'd have more for later if they wanted it. We headed down the stairs and out of the building together. Noah even came along.

The streets were quiet, nearly deserted, the polar opposite of Halloween the month before. It'd be a bleak and lonely scene without company, so that was one reason to be thankful for my friends and family this year. The world was a magically beautiful place, and company only enhanced it.

CHAPTER THIRTY-SEVEN

"I can't believe this." Faith blinked, her hand at her chest in a gesture I'd come to recognize as her expression of shock.

"I honestly think nobody can." Bailey turned her nose up in the air, snorting at Faith. "You're just going to make us lose games. I have no idea why they put you on the team, even though you're in reserves."

"How dare you." I planted my feet, placing my hands on my hips and looking Bailey right in the eye. "After the first day of Gym, you barely made any effort. Faith busted her ass, and now you're criticizing her. And you used to call yourself her friend! Don't try to deny it, just shut up and go away."

Bailey stood there, her mouth opening and closing like a goldfish that had accidentally jumped out of the bowl in the face of my anger, which made sense. I practically spontaneously combusted my first day here. I'd since managed to lengthen my fuse, but it was shorter when someone else got attacked.

"Whoa, Aliyah." Logan put his hand on my shoulder, reminding me of the way Noah used to help me chill out. "Tone it back a little, okay?" He gave it one more pat, then broke contact.

I guessed what he was thinking; I might have conjured solar magic in front of everybody, but the verbal outburst had helped me blow off steam and avoid an extramagus accident. It was nice to know my friends cared, though. Logan wasn't the only one supporting Faith or my defense of her.

Grace and Hal flanked me, both staring daggers at Bailey. Behind us, I heard Faith gasp like she'd taken her first breath after swimming several laps underwater. She couldn't possibly be surprised we took her side, so there must have been something else going on.

Sure enough, Coach Pickman strode past Bailey, stepping between us, her presence cutting through the tension like a hot knife through butter. Our anger didn't break as much as dissipate, which was a good thing because even though I had my solar magic under control, fire was another story. It was harder to curb in general.

"Enough." Coach Pickman brandished her whistle in my general direction. "Supporting your teammates is fine." She glanced at Bailey. "Giving your classmates grief is not. Fighting in here is unacceptable. No more of this in my gym, or you're all doing laps for the rest of the year."

Bailey spun on her heel, flouncing away from us. Good thing she did, because Faith couldn't take any more high emotion, not even the positive kind. She dashed toward the girl's locker room, her breath hitching. Seth jumped up from the cozy pile of familiars on the bleachers and followed her, his little paws tapping on the floor.

I turned to go after her, but Grace stopped me.

"Let me. You need to calm down." She turned around and took off across the court, following Faith. "I'll send Lune if we need you." The moon hare hopped after her.

Coach Pickman barked orders at Logan and Bailey, directing them to go get our equipment. Alex sauntered away from the team list, grinning. He had good reason because he was on it, although Dylan was playing Reverse Point. He headed our way and I was about to wave, but there was a tug at my sleeve.

"Shouldn't I go after her too?" Hal asked me. But someone else answered.

"Are you kidding?" Alex put a hand on his shoulder. "You're the headmaster's son, but you're still a boy, and that's the girl's locker room. Besides, you look like you need to sit down."

That was how I ended up sitting on the bleachers with Hal Hawkins, trying to banish this sense of unease instead of celebrating the fact that almost all of our friends had made it onto the team. The only one who didn't was Logan, and he told me before tryouts that he'd prefer cheering us on anyway.

"Are you guys okay?" Alex Onassis sat down between us. Maybe he meant well, but it'd be hard answering when he wasn't in on my secret, so I let Hal speak first.

"I'll be all right." He leaned forward, propping his elbows on his thighs. "I knew I'd make the list because Coach said so at tryouts, but none of us had any idea Faith would get into the reserves. I guess that included Bailey."

"Yeah, I was surprised too." Alex grinned at me. "I didn't think I'd make it on the team either."

"How come?" One of the best ways to avoid talking about yourself was to ask your conversational partner a question. And boy howdy, did I want to avoid talking about magic.

"Lee is just so fast. His wood magic may not let him conjure very powerful orbs at this point, but I figured that would be more valuable on the team than my garden-variety average-speed poison."

"Average is exactly what Bishop's Row needs, though, right?" I shrugged.

"No, you're confusing average with balance." Alex's eyes lit up as he talked about the sport. I guess he was the closest thing we had to a jock. "Which I guess I have, but you've got more power. The best Bishop's Row players have mundane reflexes, balance, and conjuring swiftness, plus magical power, control, and speed in equal measure. By those standards, you're all that and a bag of chips. I always wondered why you didn't volunteer to play reverse point during tryouts in the first place."

"Um." I wasn't sure what to say, but Hal came to my rescue.

"She lacks control sometimes." Hal winced. "Sorry, Aliyah, but surely you remember the first day of school?"

"Oh, yeah, right." Alex directed another question at me. "Is that why it always feels like you're holding back in here? At Gym I mean? The only thing you go all out with athletically is plain old mundane running."

"You could be reserved just like me, Alex." I let snark be my guide. "All you have to do is nearly burn down a cafeteria. Once." I snorted. "And have people blame you for lab fires you didn't set. After that, you're too nervous to cut loose with much of anything, magically speaking."

"I've always wondered about that." He scratched his head. "Did you really get into it with Charity Fairbanks? Weren't you afraid?"

"Definitely." I nodded. "She's a scary person, and Noah told me all about her last year. But it would've been worse to just let her have her way."

I was about to launch into an explanation of how I wasn't the only person who'd ever stood up to Charity—after all, Alex was sitting right next to Hal, who'd done more than his fair share of confronting the mean girl—but Coach Pickman blew her whistle.

Grace went off to her next class, Faith returned from the locker room, and it was time to do all our Gym exercises. Bailey grumbled about practically everything, probably because she was still sour about not making the team. Logan kept on keeping on. He smiled, laughed with Hal, and helped us improve. The easy set of his shoulders told me he wasn't stressed about this, that making the team might have been harder for him in a way. He hated being the center of attention, after all.

I didn't much like it either, but it was nearly impossible to avoid at that point my academic career at Hawthorn Academy. I hoped I could handle myself both on and off the court since it felt like everyone's eyes were on me, even though they'd had two entire months for that before our team assignments.

Alex, in particular, watched me like a hawk. When he wasn't looking, his basilisk was. I wondered why. Maybe he had some strategy in mind for Bishop's Row, but exams took up all of my time, so I didn't get the chance to find out about it until much later.

The exams were all on paper. There were no lab practicals on midterms for the first years. I breathed a sigh of relief as Professor Luciano explained this in homeroom. Exam anxiety was something I went through, and the last thing I wanted was to get involved in another lab incident. I felt like I wasn't ready to be tested on what we'd learned in there anyway. From the looks on my classmates' faces, almost everyone agreed.

Hal was the exception. He'd become quite good at labs because he approached them like a recipe using magical ingredients. All semester, he'd chatted about the things he'd learned to cook before starting here.

Making food had been a huge part of my upbringing, too. I just couldn't get my brain around the magic part because so much of my experience was mundanely based. Maybe if my family had used magical recipes, I'd have been more comfortable in there.

During the tests, our familiars were in the gym, hanging out and playing games with the coaches. That kept them from distracting us and had the added benefit of letting them blow off steam during an extremely stressful time for all of us. I raised my hand.

"Professor, will we be able to see how they're doing in there? I mean, if we finish early or something?"

"You will, in fact." His smile was kinder than I'd ever seen it. If Luciano had a soft spot, it was for critters. "But it won't matter whether you finish early. Coach Chen has agreed to record your familiars as they play. That way, you all get to see what they were up to once your exams are finished. You can even bring the recording home to show your parents if you'd like."

Logan swallowed audibly. I probably only heard it because he sat right behind me, but I knew who wouldn't bring a video home. I wondered how he'd get away with leaving Doris here for almost a month. Mercats needed their magi when they lived on land. When I'd asked him that morning whether he'd board Doris with Bubbe again, he'd said he wasn't sure.

We spent every library session between Thanksgiving and winter break studying for exams. The Ashfords were super helpful with this, having set aside all of the first-year material and putting it in a temporary section just for us. The one drawback was, we couldn't check any books out, but that was understandable. I could only imagine what it might have been like for folks in Charity's year if she'd been able to deprive people she didn't like of the means to study.

At dinnertime, we continued our practice of ordering to-go bags from Penelope and Sandy. Even with the differences in our coursework, it was beneficial for both Luciano's and DeBeer's students to study together. Because of this, Eston and Kitty joined in, along with Lee. Kitty was practically a genius, but Eston needed help with Extrahuman History, and she wanted to get him as many study buddies as possible.

Hal quizzed him on specific stuff, but the rest of us tried giving him a few general study tips. The person who helped most was Logan. He had tons of alternative study hacks. It seemed like water magi had more trouble focusing than most. This was a problem for fire magi, too, but not in the same way. When Logan suggested wearing noise-canceling headphones without any music in them, Eston was amazed to find it a useful strategy.

In the first week of December, Alex started hanging around at dinner without studying, or at least he didn't seem to be. I don't know every learning style, though. Maybe just sitting nearby and listening to us discuss all the material helped him wrap his brain around it. Maybe learning by osmosis wasn't a joke.

Dylan and Logan both sat closer to me while Alex was around. Gale and Doris even came over to hang with Ember during those times. I wasn't sure why, and I didn't bother asking. It might make Logan feel awkward, and as far as Dylan went, I already had a big brother. I really didn't want to start feeling like he was a de facto sibling. The idea just bothered me.

Halfway through the last week of school, I was in the bathroom, brushing my teeth and otherwise getting ready for bed. Faith walked in for what I'd come to recognize as her weekly dip in the baths. She did laps and everything. This time she hung around at the counter, as though waiting for me to finish making my dentist happy with my mad toothbrushing skills.

"Do you like Alex?" She looked me in the eye indirectly, using the mirror as a buffer. I didn't blame her. This was an odd sort of conversation for me to have with anyone, let alone Faith.

"He's okay, I guess. A good athlete." I still couldn't put my finger on what it was about Alex that bothered me, so I repeated what I'd heard from other people. "But he's sort of like Switzerland. Totally neutral about everything, isn't he? Why do you ask?"

"I think he's into you."

"I had no idea." I blinked. "Thought he was just being friendly."

"You seem to notice just about every other social dynamic, Aliyah." She shook her head. "It's not a good idea to ignore stuff like this."

"It's not likely I'll end up with anyone anytime soon." Why was I thinking about Dylan and Grace all of a sudden? "I'm too busy for dating, anyway."

"Well, dating isn't too busy for you, it seems." She snorted. "It's dangerous to just ignore stuff like people having unrequited crushes on you."

"What?" I blinked because this didn't make any sense to me. Dangerous?

"Peep?" Ember swooped down off the counter and peered up at Faith, Seth mimicking her expression almost perfectly. They both looked almost as baffled as I felt. I guess attraction in the critter world was way less complicated.

"I don't know much about Alex. Maybe he's okay. But some people get downright nasty if they feel rejected." Her small smile was surprisingly gentle. "I'm not gonna stand here and tell you I'm worried about you getting hurt. You can take care of yourself in a fight. But subtlety isn't your thing, and there are other ways people harm each other. I'm not trying to be a bitch here, just give you a heads up."

"Thanks, Faith." I nodded. "I'll try talking to Alex alone."

"Maybe find out more about him first. Ask around before you decide." She looked down at the sink. "I did that before making things official with Hal."

"If there's time." I shook my head. "It might be hard finding any."

"Our friends keep watching you. They're worried for you over your thing." She looked up at one of the solar lights and then at my hands. "Exam stress. If you want to talk to Alex and need me to head them off, let me know."

"Thanks." I packed up my bathroom stuff. "Have a good swim, Faith. Thanks for straightening my crown instead of knocking it off."

"You've done that much for me already." She waved. "See you tomorrow."

That conversation had gone better than I ever would've dreamed. Taking advice from Faith Fairbanks was something I would have flat-out laughed at in the first week of school even if Izzy had predicted it, but now she was looking out for me. Who'd have thought?

CHAPTER THIRTY-EIGHT

Just when I thought my night would end on a high note, I walked into my room to find Grace on her bed sobbing. Ember swooped down, landing on her headboard. I brought a box of tissues and sat at the foot of her bed, reaching out to take her hand. She let me, only just barely squeezing back. Lune lay beside her, lifting his head briefly to acknowledge my presence. He pressed his chin against her shoulder, keeping it there even as it shook with sobs.

I didn't say anything, just sat there. It had to be rough on her, the prospect of holiday break. The postcard on the bed beside her spoke volumes with only a sentence. Her aunt had written *Stay at school*. Grace didn't have much to celebrate from the little she'd mentioned of life back in Quebec, and she couldn't even go there. In situations like that, when the people around you seemed to have everything you didn't, words didn't always help.

I sat with her for maybe half an hour before she finally calmed down enough to sit up. Her pillowcase was totally soaked. Probably the pillow under it was too, and she only had one of those, school-issued. Everyone else had brought extras, their favorite and most comforting pillows, throws, and blankets from home. Even Logan, whose parents were neglectful at best. And Faith, who dealt with daily abuse back in New York.

Grace had brought nothing but her familiar and a wardrobe of threadbare clothes. Did her life lack that much comfort, or had she brought so little because she worried it was too shabby for prep school? She never said a word about it or did anything to direct attention to the things she lacked.

I'd noticed it, and had done almost nothing all semester besides lending her a dress. Had I stopped caring? Why? How?

You're an extramagus, that's why. Destined to stop caring about everyone else.

I decided to subvert the inside voice with kindness.

As Grace reached for the box of tissues to blow her nose and dry her eyes, I went to my bed and picked up an extra pillow, then opened the dresser to get a spare pillowcase. I changed the one I'd been using for the clean one, then swapped it with the tear-stained pillow, which I set at the foot of Grace's bed. A small gesture, but better that than nothing.

Grace didn't glance behind her, oblivious to my actions. She wasn't thanking me. That didn't matter. Given the state she was in, manners weren't important. Not everyone who needed help was in a position to be polite, but that didn't somehow make them unworthy.

She picked up her bathroom bag and a change of pajamas. If it weren't for the fact that Faith was having her weekly swim, I'd have worried about leaving her alone in there. She looked out for me, and she'd do the same for Grace. We'd all become friends somehow, despite our extremely different backgrounds.

Lune went after her, turning his head to look up at me before hopping out the door. His ears were up, nose twitching. He cared, too.

Since Grace typically showered at night, I had time, so I got out my contraband communication orb for the first time in two weeks. We hadn't planned on communicating tonight, so I hoped that at least one of my friends from town answered.

After a moment, Cadence's voice greeted me.

"Aliyah, what's up? I thought you'd be studying for exams."

"I was, but there's a problem." I closed my eyes, feeling the sting of threatening tears.

"Not another fire? Or—oh, no." She leaned in, whispering. "You didn't go solar, did you?"

"No, nothing like that." I shook my head. "It's not me. It's Grace, my roommate."

"Oh, no!" Cadence gasped. "Is she okay? Did she get hurt playing Bishop's Row or something?"

"I wish." I told Cadence that Grace's aunt wasn't letting her come home, then I described the scene I'd found in my room tonight.

"Why not invite her to stay with you over the break?" Cadence asked. Her solution to practically everything was adding more people. "I mean, I know your parents would probably have room for her to stay for that amount of time."

"That's a good idea, but I wonder whether she'll take me up on it? Grace has a lot of pride, which is great for some stuff but not so much in this situation."

"Do you think it will hurt to ask?" She chuckled. "Something like that happened at Gallows Hill and asking made all the difference, even though the offer got turned down. Sometimes people just want to feel welcome."

"Yeah, you're right." I nodded. "Thanks, Cadence. I have to go. Somebody's coming."

"Okay, talk to you later."

The orb went dark, which was a good thing because I heard voices in the hall. It wasn't the door opening yet, thank goodness. I wasn't sure who was out there.

Regardless of the mysterious talker's identity, it was time to stow the orb back in my suitcase, zip it up, and tuck it under my bed. Once that was done, I trotted to the door and put my ear against it.

"Mark this one. One of these girls is staying." It wasn't a voice I recognized, but low pitched and probably male.

"Okay. Anybody else on this floor?" The second voice was raspy and slightly higher pitched.

"The kid from the UK. We're already keeping the Hawkins brat's

323

room open, so it doesn't matter whether his roommate is staying here or in China. We'll keep the lights on in there at any rate."

I blinked, wondering who at the school would dare refer to Hal Hawkins as a brat. He was the furthest thing from that, first of all. Second of all, talking like that about a space magus' son in a pocket realm he maintained was sort of a bad idea.

"I know the boss wouldn't be happy if he heard that, so why did you say it?" The second voice asked my unspoken question.

"He knows how some of us feel. Kid takes too much after his mother, and nobody trusts that bitch except the people in her school of misfits. Be glad you don't have to work there. Place gives me the creeps. Named after executions and all."

He was talking about Gallows Hill. So, Hal's mother worked there in some capacity or other, since she was definitely too old to attend as a student. I knew next to nothing about her, just that she and Headmaster Hawkins were divorced, and what Cadence had said about a vampire from Rhode Island. The only one who knew more was Hal, and he didn't talk about her.

Hal Hawkins seemed stressed and tired. He'd been peaky and listless lately, and hadn't been to the infirmary. It worried me, but he wasn't alone. Logan was just as stressed. He'd ripped his cuticles more times than I could count in the last week, so we'd been trying to take it easy as a group. I hoped we'd all get some relief after exams, but my gut told me that was unlikely. The same part of my intuition that said Grace was in serious trouble emotionally.

I wished we could figure all this out. Just sit down and talk, be teenagers. But when you were magical, the world expected more from you. More restrictions, more requirements. Our powers weren't even all that big yet, but our responsibilities were enormous. It was impossible to just live life as an extrahuman unless you planned to try going without powers. Or maybe lived on an island in the middle of the ocean.

When Grace returned, I took Cadence's advice and invited her to stay with us. She said she was too tired, she'd think about it later, and we'd talk sometime this week.

But Thursday and Friday went by. I stayed in school all weekend studying, and still Grace kept silent on the matter. She practically clung to Dylan, who was there for her. But she was silent every time I saw her, no matter what company she kept.

I cornered Faith in the bathroom on Sunday morning and point-blank asked her if Grace had talked to her.

"Just a bit, on Wednesday after my swim." She sighed. "It was pretty obvious she'd been crying that night, but she wouldn't say a word about what was wrong. Didn't she tell you?"

"No. I don't even think she's talked to Dylan." I took a deep breath. "This is bad, Faith. I don't know what to do."

"I'll get Hal on it. He's got a way with this sort of thing."

I saw Hal manage to approach Grace exactly once. She avoided him for the rest of the day unless she already had someone with her. That wasn't normal for her, and it wasn't even within the realm of academic stress. That initial hunch about her family might have had merit, then.

I tried putting myself in her shoes. Tried to imagine what it would be like if my parents were dead and gone was nearly impossible, not because I had no imagination at all, and not because I lacked empathy. Maybe it was too enormous to contemplate. I tried thinking about what it would be like to lose Noah instead.

Tears sprang to my eyes. Even though we weren't on the best terms this year, I couldn't handle that. I wasn't sure when Grace became an orphan, only that it must have happened before she came to school. My intuition told me it was years ago, but recently enough that she remembered her parents and how different her life was with them in it.

See where kindness gets you? Closer to your inevitable insanity.

This time, I silenced the voice with action. Doing nothing wasn't an option anymore.

Grace was in crisis, in a medical emergency. Emotional states weren't considered medical by some, but they called it mental health for a reason. So, I went to Nurse Smith on Sunday night before exams.

"So, you're telling me your roommate has been crying, avoiding people she normally hangs out with, and won't talk about it? And it's been going on for how long?"

Nurse Smith had his notepad and vial of magical water out again. Of course. As annoying as it was, I couldn't blame him. He was probably used to students lying about all kinds of things to do with their health that would interfere with their medical care, and it was his job to make sure we were healthy enough to be in school.

"Since Wednesday."

"I see." He jotted something down. "Why are you coming to me now?"

"I went to the rest of our friends, trying to help her together. She just kept brushing us off, though. You're her last hope."

"Students are always under extra stress during exam time, and when that coincides with holidays, it only gets worse. I've seen stuff like this before. I think I can help her, but let's lay off until after the exams. I'll be keeping an eye on her from a distance, but if you see anything you think I need to know, find me immediately."

"What are you going to do?"

"She's staying on campus over the break, so I'll help her then. We'll have privacy and time with no class or sports obligations. As far as what we'll do, that's confidential. But Miss Morgenstern, thank you for coming to me. You don't know how much I appreciate this."

I wasn't sure what to say to that, so I nodded and left. I couldn't find it in myself to smile, not with the situation as grave as it was. But I was somewhat relieved.

The day of exams came. Like so many other rites of passage, the reality of taking the test felt like a tipping point. Let me explain this better.

Gallows Hill was the name of Cadence's school, but also an actual hill in Salem. Back when we were kids in pigtails, all the children in town would sled down it. There was a drop-off at the top, where the sled hung for a heart-stopping moment before tilting to hurtle down. Sitting in the room with the pencil, the blue book, and the Scantron sheet was like that suspended moment.

The rest was a wild ride, full of graphite stains on my hands, paper cuts, and gasping in disbelief as I realized I knew more than I thought I did. When I walked out of the room and down the hall toward the gym to reunite with Ember, I thought maybe I had done better than the C- I expected.

I sat in the gym, cuddling my dragonet and waiting for my classmates to come through the door as they finished. Alex was the first to enter after me, his basilisk Aceso rearing her head up and flicking her tongue out as she glided across the polished wood toward him.

He sauntered over once she had twined up his arm and took a seat beside me. I tried to remember what Faith had said that night in the bathroom and realized I hadn't asked around about Alex. So much had been on my mind since then, beyond the brain fry that came with cramming and spilling all that information back out onto the page afterward.

As it turned out, I needn't have worried. Alex just stayed nearby, letting Ember and Aceso play. I got the impression that he was okay with just being there and not saying a word. Whether that came from being bonded to a reptilian familiar was beyond me. Dragonets were warm-blooded like birds.

I hadn't paid attention to him all semester, not outside of Gym, anyway, so maybe that was typical for Alex. He might be one of those folks who liked quiet companionship or simple things. It seemed odd for a jock, but then again, I was odd for a magus. Who was I to judge?

When the rest of the first years entered the gym, they did it as a group. I caught Faith looking in my direction, her eyes narrowing. Maybe she was trying to figure out if I'd had my chat with Alex. She didn't approach to ask. Hal wasn't looking great, so Faith stayed with him.

Logan made a beeline toward his familiar, oblivious to everything and everyone else. That was how he was after any test, and this exam had been three times as long as any other. It looked like Logan was going into extreme introvert mode, only comfortable interacting with Doris. He didn't ask about boarding her, even when I moved down the bleachers. He noticed me there but only waved without smiling. It seemed he was bringing her to Las Vegas after all.

Once we were released from the academic wing, it was time to go home. My bags were already packed and downstairs in the lobby, waiting. The semester was over, finally. Grace had never told me she wasn't staying with me, but that conversation with Nurse Smith meant she'd be well taken care of on campus. I'd have a little peace at home with my family until January.

Maybe I'd earned that much.

CHAPTER THIRTY-NINE

INTERLUDE

A Christmas Misery
Grace

Oh, yeah, I was miserable. Don't worry, that was only a little south of normal for me. My life in Québec wasn't the greatest, hadn't been since my parents passed away from carbon monoxide poisoning. Even magical folk get done in by the most mundane and stupid accidents, so replace the batteries in your alarms yearly, kids. And don't run kerosene heat without good ventilation. The more you know...

Anyway, I figured I was tired of being my internally melancholy self in the claustrophobic yet hallowed halls of Hawthorn Academy. It always felt weird in there, like there was too much room and not enough all at the same time. Too much light, also.

Since I'd moved in with my aunt on her farm, I'd anticipated and dreaded wide-open spaces at the same time. That might have had something to do with Lune, my moon hare, finding me that same year, after I turned eleven. He didn't much like being out in the open, so the prospect of going to Hawthorn Academy with its wooden campus between worlds had appealed to both of us.

It had lived up to its expectations and then some. The first few weeks were pretty good, despite the fact that my roommate Aliyah Morgenstern nearly burned down the cafeteria and the lab on the first day of class. It felt exciting, though. And it was such a relief, having a friend who wasn't totally normal. It helped that she was uncommonly honest and kind, even though it turned out she was an extramagus. Normal people kind of freaked me out, so Aliyah being weird helped me relax.

I keep getting off the topic, don't I? Which was that dreaded holiday nobody can escape.

Christmas.

I hated it. If you guessed that the reason for this had something to do with my parents' untimely demise, here's some good news. You win. The bad news is you get nothing because everything about me had something to do with being an orphan. How could it not?

There was this idea, especially in extrahuman circles, that losing your parents made you special somehow, but all I wanted was to be just like everyone else. What I wouldn't have given to have my mom back, even if it meant she'd tell me to put on a little makeup and smile more. Or my dad, even if he'd give my boyfriend seven levels of grief just to be sure he treated me decently. But all I had was this hole in my life.

Anyway, Hawthorn Academy went big at Christmas, and I couldn't go home or otherwise escape the halls decked with holly, the faculty and staff getting jolly, or any of that other crap. My aunt's farm wasn't really my home, and I never counted on it feeling that way. Yeah, I know. I sounded awfully grouchy for a Canadian, but we weren't all sunshine and roses, and if you thought so, you're the one with unrealistic expectations.

The only way for me to get out of this mess of red and green and silver and gold and those little blinking lights that annoyed me so much was to get out on the streets of Salem, which was exactly what I did on Christmas Eve about an hour after the sun went down.

Everybody said it'd be dangerous to walk around in the dark alone. It was true, I'd give them that. We all knew what kinds of things went bump in the night because that was part of Hawthorn's curriculum, but everything in this world was dangerous. Even sleeping in your bed on a night like any other, cozy in winter but lacking oxygen-rich air. Life was a terminal disease.

So, I figured I'd take my chances on the street, searching for something beautiful that didn't tear my heart out while looking at it. Don't get me wrong. This little city was decorated for wintry celebration too, but there was something charmingly pagan about it. That made sense since this was the witch city, after all. Yule decorations were like the more reserved cousin of the garish Christmas kind, and that difference helped my state of mind more than I'd expected.

I was on Washington Street, having walked almost all the way to the end where it intersected with Bridge Street. For a moment, I considered getting on the commuter rail and heading down into Boston, but I'd have been stuck in that large, unfamiliar city unless I turned around immediately and came back because no trains would run the next day. There went Christmas, ruining my mood again.

I turned and continued down the other side of Washington Street. This was one of the main drags in the walkable part of Salem, so it had lots of shops and restaurants and other places where it was fun to window shop. That was the only kind of shopping I did because I was poor as dirt. It was good, though, because I got inspirations to make my own things, and there was no shortage of materials in Creatives class.

I flipped the bird at the fake wooden Indian outside the smoke shop. I'm real, and preferred the term "indigenous," thank you very much. Canada was awfully enlightened when it came to things like health care and good citizenship, but it had a long way to go before it did right by us. The United States wasn't much different. I got better treatment here due to being a magus than I would have if I were mundane, though.

On the next block over there was a dress shop. I stopped and stared, mesmerized by the display in the window. The quality of the work was astounding. I knew for sure it had been magically enhanced, much like I did with my own creations, but I'd never seen anything quite like those dresses before. They were clearly holiday attire, the sort of thing one might wear to a party. I told myself they were intended for New Year's so I didn't get maudlin and walk away.

"Bet I could make one like that. Better, even." I smirked at my translucent reflection in the glass, imagining myself wearing the shimmering copper garment on display. "And I'll make it for a different holiday, one I actually like."

"I bet you can't."

The sudden voice made me spin on my heel. Salem after dark— dangerous, remember? But it was only a guy I'd met before. Someone Aliyah knew. A townie, changeling if I remembered correctly. He was my age, attending Gallows Hill instead of Hawthorn because he wasn't a magus.

We stood gazing at each other. I remembered his face but not his name yet. His eyes were wider than I'd ever seen them, partly obscured by the ruddy hair hanging over his brow. Dude needed a haircut. His clothes were worn, too. Not shabby; I could tell they'd had quality once. They must be for working in at something distract- ingly physical.

I realized he was startled and probably recognized me, maybe in the same boat trying to remember my name. And just like that, his glamour slipped, and I recalled it. He had the pointy ears and dusky skin of a Goblin, and he was part of a big family here, the Ambersmiths.

"Azrael?" I got ready to ask him loads of questions, which was my default. That way I didn't have to talk about myself or my misery, which was present in abundance that evening.

"In the flesh. Mostly." He held up a bandaged hand.

"What happened?" I blinked. "You didn't cut anything off, did you?"

"Almost. I'm just nearly Fingerless Az." He chuckled. "I got into a fight with a pair of pinking shears in the shop. Not that one, though." He jerked his chin at the window I'd been looking at.

"You know what pinking shears are?" I smiled. Nobody at Hawthorn had the same passion for crafting that I did.

"Yep." He smiled back, revealing front teeth that reminded me of Lune's. The tension in my shoulders faded.

"How?"

"I'm making the rounds as an apprentice to my various family members. It's totally an Ambersmith tradition. Also, I'm pretty sure Aunt Marjorie is going to tell me to look elsewhere when our agreement ends."

"What does she do?" There I went with the questions again.

"Marjorie does home decor. Curtains, tapestries, lampshades—you get the picture."

"Have you worked here yet?" I jerked my thumb at the shop behind me.

"No, not yet." He shook his head. "But it's on the docket for the summer. That's when they make most of this stuff, you know."

"Yeah, I know." I nodded. "The fashion industry has to work two seasons ahead in order to get everything done in time."

"You know an awful lot about that. Are you a dressmaker back in Canada?"

"You remembered." I wiped that smile right off my face because this dude was dangerous with a capital D. I was cautious around people who paid too much attention. Distraction was my jam. "But no, not professionally. I just made stuff for my cousins and me."

"Would you like to see the workshop in there?"

I stopped, staring at Azreal Ambersmith. He'd offered me the equivalent of a day trip to Eden without even realizing it, but I couldn't take him up on it, because then I'd owe him. Don't get it into your head that I assumed he'd want some weird sexual favor either. What he'd expect was conversation, sincerity, and details I wasn't ready to be honest about outside a therapist's office at this point.

"That would rock, but I kinda have to go back to school now."

"Okay, some other time, then." He met my gaze, which I admit, must have been pretty intense just then. Dylan, who favored distraction almost as much as I did, would have looked away, but somehow, this townie didn't.

His eyes were clear and untroubled despite sustaining an injury that could have lost him an appendage—and facing down a magus bold enough to be out alone after dark. Changelings our age weren't much different from humans, besides the glamour. This was a guy who knew the risk and somehow didn't fear it. I was speechless over this. Nearly breathless, too.

Because I didn't want to go back to campus.

"Oh, yeah, another time." I started walking because I had no other choice.

"I'll walk with you. It's dangerous to go alone."

He had no idea that the opposite was also true. That the heart sustains the cruelest wounds, and it was just as dangerous going together.

Especially on Christmas Eve

CHAPTER FORTY

ALIYAH

I woke up in January on Sunday morning before the first day of my second semester at Hawthorn Academy. When I packed, I included outfits for social engagements. We'd have another one this semester, though Parents' Night wasn't a thing in the springtime.

Since I was on the Bishop's Row team, I also had a uniform, which was shipped to my house the week of Hanukkah. I took it out of the drawer and ran my fingers over the shiny purple fabric. It had my last name in white on the back, plus my number, fifteen. I laid it flat on the bed and stood staring at it, still awed about making the team. Ember peered down from her perch on the headboard.

"Peep." She opened and closed her mouth a few times, a new gesture for her. Usually, it meant she was curious about an object. I'm pretty sure she'd picked that up from Gale.

"Go on ahead and check it out, girl." I figured the worst she could do was chew on it a little. There was plenty of time to throw it in the wash if that happened.

I folded up the white shorts and purple knee-high socks that went with the top, stowing them in the larger suitcase. I didn't bring the mint green dress this time, and the plum was still at school, hanging in the closet on Grace's side of the room.

Speaking of my roommate, I'd managed to make it into the school to visit her during the break, bringing along a gift for Winter Solstice, which was what she celebrated. Grace was doing okay, although she was sick of hanging around with Nurse Smith, who she called "that Nosy Parker." But her eyes had been brighter, her smile easier, and her shoulders more relaxed. Grace thanked me for the gift—a matching set of throw and neck pillows, and cozy socks. She also had Lee and Dylan for company most of the time, which they split between the gym and the library.

Dylan worked over the break, of course. Mostly in the kitchens, although the Ashfords had him bring Gale to help them with cleaning the library for a few days. I didn't see him or Grace until New Year's Eve when I met them at the Witch's Brew. We made caffeinated toasts to the secular turn of the year, during which I prayed silently for Grace to have a smoother time this semester.

Lee came by our house a number of times, mostly with Izzy. Apparently, they'd spent some time together on their own, according to Cadence, although they had an extremely platonic vibe going on. The mermaid had her own things to do, though, and didn't talk about them. Maybe over the summer, she'd let us all in on what had been happening at Gallows Hill. I'd have asked Brianna, but she got stuck working doubles at Walgreens all the way through break. Retail at that time of year is intense. Azreal was in the same boat with his cart and the Ambersmith's storefronts.

I wasn't entirely sure where Hal went while school was out. He wasn't on campus much, though. Lee tried to find out but had little success. His father was around, popping by while I visited in the lounge. It was a relief that he'd stuck around, making his presence known to my friends and the kids in other years who'd stayed for the break. The headmaster had a benevolent presence, even if he came across as mildly intimidating. We'd all much rather have seen Hal, of course, but every time we asked where he was, Headmaster Hawkins answered vaguely.

I wondered if he'd gone to see his mother. Most custodial arrangements allowed for visitation on holidays, and it made sense for a kid who hadn't been feeling well to want his mother. All the same, each of us worried about him in our own way during his absence.

My mind moved its focus back to the present, where I tried to decide between three dresses for the two semiformal events at school this semester. As I stood there waffling between a turquoise maxi dress, a black and orange floral A-line, and a yellow Empire waist with a hi-low hem, there was a knock at the door.

"Noah, go away." He hadn't bothered with me much over the break, but he freaked out about clothes any time we went someplace.

"I'm not Noah."

"Mom. Come in."

She stepped inside and closed the door behind her. I turned to see that she held a garment bag, one with no small amount of dust on it. It must've come from the utility closet in the basement because there was no way anything in her closet would get into that state.

"I thought I'd come in while you were packing and show this to you. See if maybe you'd like to bring it."

I shrugged. "I can't decide, so yeah, why not? I'll have a look."

Mom hung the garment bag on a hook by my desk. It was over the trashcan, which was good because when she opened the bag, dust fell off it. Mostly in the trash, thank goodness. I stopped worrying about any of that moments later when she unveiled the item inside.

"Wow." I gasped. "Where did you get that?"

"Actually, from Bubbe." She removed the dress from the hanger inside the bag, carefully easing the bottom of it out to avoid getting dust on it.

She held the garment up to the light, and I saw why she'd brought it up here. I stood with my mouth wide open in awe and wonder. It was almost impossible to imagine a time when my grandmother would've worn a dress like this.

"It's gorgeous."

That was an understatement. The pale-pink satin fabric on the bodice was embroidered with golden thread and accented with amber beads. The bottom of the dress must've been dipped in red dye and allowed to hang, giving the fabric an ombre effect. The deep red faded to rust, then russet and salmon as it moved up the skirt. A wide metallic copper ribbon graced the waist. The entire thing reminded me of a sunrise, all the rosy colors of dawn.

"Do you want to bring it to school?"

"I'm not sure." I was instantly worried about how things tended to go sideways for me at school but didn't feel like discussing it now. "I mean, should I even wear something like this? It's too nice. Does Headmaster Hawkins really intend for us to get this dressed up?"

"Do you know your grandmother wore it in her first year there?" Mom grinned. "And she lent it to me."

"No. I wouldn't have imagined." Her statement was nearly impossible to fathom. "How did that happen?"

"It's a long story." She sighed, but in a good way, like she reminisced about something good. "Suffice it to say, your father wasn't going to wear it, and Bubbe doesn't like waste."

"That makes sense."

I thought about how my grandmother treated the friends I brought home, always welcoming them. Even sticking up for Logan in a big way. Considering that, it wasn't so hard to imagine, although I had no idea what things were like for my mother back then. Were the Hopewells like the Pierces, or more like the Fairbanks?

I had a closer look at the dress, noting that there was a tag sewn into the back by hand. It was yellowed with age but easy to read since the lettering was embroidered in the same thread as the designs on the dress. "Ambersmith Fashions?"

"Yes. Michael's grandmother was a dressmaker, and she made this specifically for Bubbe."

"Wow. It must've cost a fortune." I shook my head. Maybe I shouldn't bring it after all.

"Not really. Back in those days, the extrahuman community was extremely tightly knit. They did an awful lot of barter, and your great-grandfather took excellent care of all the Ambersmiths' familiars. All it cost was kindness."

"Do you think it will fit?" I wanted nothing more than to wear this dress and come walking down the stairs at school, maybe even dance in it awkwardly with my friends. But it seemed too good to be true.

"Why not try it on and find out?"

My mother's smile reminded me of all the times she'd helped me with my homework in elementary school, like she knew something I didn't. This dress had been made by extrahumans for extrahumans. For all I knew, it was downright magical, aside from its appearance.

I nodded. Mom turned her back, giving me privacy as I changed into the dress. When I slid the sleeves up my arms, at first I thought they'd be too big, but once I reached behind me to pull the zipper up, I realized that wasn't the case.

This garment fit like it had been made for me. I'd never worn anything quite like it, something that felt so precisely tailored to my particular shape. My eyes stung slightly, and my vision misted over. Mom turned around at that moment.

"Aliyah? Are you okay?"

I had the best mom in the world. There I was wearing this work of art, and the first thing she thought about was my feelings. Which weren't the greatest, I guess, at the moment. And because she cared and always had, I could speak freely about them.

"Maybe not. I mean, I love this dress. Who wouldn't? It's the most amazing thing I've ever tried on in my life." I sniffled, trying not to actually cry. "But the fact of the matter is, I don't have a boyfriend. I'd only be going with friends to probably both of the dances this semester, so it seems like a waste."

"Oh, Aliyah." She held out her arms, and a moment later, I was in them. "There's no such thing as 'only' when it comes to true friendship. Platonic love is still love, and it makes more of a difference in life than society gives it credit for."

"Really?" I sniffled again. "Two of my friends are practically engaged to each other already. I don't want to miss out on dating because everyone makes such a big deal about romance."

"It's a big deal at your age because it's new." Mom stroked my hair. "Dressing up is something you can do for yourself at any age. That's the way it was for Bubbe. Back when she was a first year at Hawthorn, she didn't have a boyfriend either, and she wore that dress."

I blinked, surprised. It was practically a legend in our family, how much my grandmother loved her husband, the man she'd cared for unconditionally for so much of her life. It had never occurred to me there was a time in her life before she met him.

But then I stopped and considered this further. Bubbe was independent, strong, and lived her life the way she felt was right. If she'd been that way since she was sixteen, then it made complete and total sense. Hawthorn Academy was a fancy school. Why wouldn't she wear a fancy dress? I can't imagine my grandmother limiting herself over something as incidental as having a date. Maybe I should do the same.

"Do you think you'll bring it, then?"

I couldn't answer my mom. It wasn't that I didn't want to. She deserved an answer because after this winter, I was aware how lucky I was to have a mother like her. But if I started talking, I'd say too much. I might have started wondering out loud what was wrong with me, why I didn't seem able to have romantic feelings about any of the unattached boys.

I might even have said I was jealous of my friends, and I didn't want to say that out loud. It'd be almost as bad as setting the cafeteria on fire, just in an emotional way. And it could get worse than that. My inside voice might even push me farther down the road toward becoming an out-of-control extramagus.

I stood up straight again, easing out of the hug, partly because I needed to see her face in case I did speak my secret aloud by accident. It was also really not fair to take up her whole day with this. She was Noah's mother, too, and what if he had his own problems?

So I nodded. Mom seemed mollified, or maybe she recognized inner turmoil when she saw it and understood. Either way, she asked me to put my regular clothes back on while she got a fresh garment bag.

After changing, I went about the business of packing all the essentials in my suitcase: Regular clothes, some extra pillowcases and sheets, and of course, the contraband communication orb. I wouldn't go back without that, because it had been a lifesaver last semester. Hal's dad had changed an awful lot at Hawthorn Academy already. Maybe I should ask him to reconsider the no-communication policy. I still took pains to hide it in the small suitcase underneath stuff like underwear that no one would look through.

I decided to bring the turquoise maxi dress, along with Bubbe's. It didn't hold a candle aesthetically, of course, but it was comfortable, I liked it, and the color was soothing, like my tankini. I decided to toss that in too because maybe this semester, I'd join Faith in her weekly swims. Increasing my physical activity would only help prepare for the tournament.

Since we were allowed to arrive on campus anytime on Sunday or even early Monday, I didn't rush through my day. I spent some time downstairs in Bubbe's office, playing with the critters who felt up to it. None of them were strays or otherwise unattached, although a few were in for medical care. Over the holidays, some extrahumans boarded their pets and familiars while traveling overseas.

I thanked Bubbe for lending me her dress, and she seemed glad that I had taken her up on the offer. She asked for pictures if I decided to wear it.

Upstairs, I had breakfast and lunch with my parents. Noah was there too but didn't participate in the conversation. Either he was nervous about going back to school or tired. He had been out an awful lot over the break, making me wonder if he'd started seeing a boy in town. It didn't seem like there were many romantic prospects for him at Hawthorn. I think Darren was the only other gay man on campus.

I'd have to remember to ask him how the old dating life was. Maybe my brother even had some advice. Noah knew more about romance than anyone in my year. Then again, he was guilty of attempted matchmaking in the case of Logan and me, so maybe not.

Talking to Cadence might have been a better idea, although her advice on most things was usually just do it. I wasn't talking about sex; I mean like speed-dating. That was just not my style. I felt like I had to know someone before I could decide if I wanted romance. It had been difficult enough going with Logan to Parents' Night because I'd only known him for a month at that point.

My thoughts were cut off when my parents said it was time for us to go. They asked one more time if either of us wanted to stay the extra night and go to school at breakfast time, but my brother and I both said no. So, we all headed out, walking down the snow-lined streets. There wasn't much coating the ground, just enough to be a slippery nuisance for the suitcases.

The cobblestones on Essex Street were even harder to navigate now than in the fall. I was glad we all went this time. Mom and Dad stayed outside.

The lobby was mostly deserted when we arrived. I looked across it at the stairway, knowing I should go up to my room first and drop off my luggage, but I missed my friends. I had seen most of them over break, but it felt like longer.

They weren't in the lounge or the cafeteria, so I figured they must be upstairs. I should have just gone. Noah already had since the stairs were still moving. I got on, stating my floor. Once they stopped, I walked down the hall toward my room, whistling. When I put my hand on the flat space next to the door, the latch clicked. Inside, I heard frantic rustling and low voices. I stepped back from the door and waited before opening it.

I stood in the hall, counting seconds. One Mississippi, two Mississippi, three Mississippi. Once I got to ten, I opened the door and rolled my suitcases ahead of me. Ember swooped in over my head, flying directly to her preferred perch on my footboard.

Dylan and Grace sat on her bed. They were both rigid, perfectly still, barely even breathing—and their cheeks were flushed. I didn't bother looking at their clothes, because I'd heard plenty from out in the hall. Some adjustments must have happened, since my whistling had signaled someone approaching.

"I'm going down to the lounge for coffee. Once I put these suitcases down, anyway." My back was turned as I tried to compose my face. I don't know what I looked like, but if the heat I felt from the neck up was any indication, I didn't want them to see.

Everything swam: light, sound, the cool air around my flushed face. There was a rush too, the kind I got the year I had walking pneumonia and collapsed on the stoop outside my house. It was nearly impossible to swallow past the lump in my throat, so I cleared it instead, trying to breathe. I managed enough respiration to blurt a question.

"Did you guys have dinner yet?"

Talking about food seemed like the safest topic. My stomach felt like someone clenched it in their fists and squeezed, and Ember's silence spoke volumes. Usually she'd peep at Grace and Lune and Gale and Dylan, but mum was the word for my dragonet.

"Um, no." Grace managed an answer. "I'll meet you down there in a few minutes."

"Sure, no problem." But it was. It shouldn't have been.

I called for Ember and waited until she perched on my shoulder before leaving the room. Then I closed the door behind me, letting it latch. I probably wouldn't see either of them in a few minutes. Maybe not even for a few hours. I wasn't sure what I interrupted, but I had the general idea.

It felt totally wrong to want something Grace had, especially when she had no home and family. I had to stop it now, even if it meant distancing myself from Dylan.

You're powerful. You deserve whatever you can take, even from other people.

"Might does not make right," I muttered to the empty hallway. "Sit down, shut up, and let your friends have what little happiness they can get."

Downstairs, I settled down in the lounge with coffee and biscotti. Lee joined me, and his mild yet comforting presence helped me calm down. Eventually, Logan arrived, hurrying out of the hallway with a backpack and rolling suitcase. Doris paced behind him, and it was clear neither of them was in a good mood.

I stood and sprinted to catch up with him, Ember swooping along behind me. He headed straight for the stairs, and I recognized this tunnel vision from Lab. He was hyper-focused on getting himself and his luggage upstairs and out of sight, but after Grace's near-collapse at the end of last semester, I wasn't about to let Logan deal with whatever this was alone.

"Hey, do you want some help with that suitcase?" I didn't want to make this about his mood unless he wanted it to be.

"No, but company's cool." I got on the stairs with him, and we rode up in silence. At the top, he spoke again. "Aliyah it's terrible. Mom and Dad almost turned me around at the airport and put me on a plane back the second they saw Doris. They were horrible every day. They keep saying I broke our family, ruined their plans for our future. Even Elanor acts like she hates me now, and I don't know what to do."

Logan's voice was strained, cracked, under pressure. His eyes were rimmed with red too, in lines so perfect they could have been drawn by a makeup artist. His hands shook so much he ended up grasping the straps on his backpack until his knuckles went white. My friend needed a lifeline.

"Listen, if anything like that happens again, let them turn you around. Call me. I'll tell Bubbe. She said you're always welcome, right?"

"Thank you." His back was toward me, his head down as he opened his door. I already knew Dylan wasn't in the room, so I followed Logan inside.

We spent some time putting his clothes in the dresser and the wardrobe. This wasn't due to any immediate need to unpack, but it gave him some time to realize he wasn't at home. Instead, he was at school, surrounded by friends.

We all were. Now all we needed to do was navigate the rest of the semester without making any more mistakes.

CHAPTER FORTY-ONE

"Mind if I sit here?"

I looked up, blinking at Alex. It was Lab, and usually Hal was my partner. It'd been that way for all of last semester and all of January. But Hal was late. He had been through the entire first week of February.

"Sure, I guess." I wasn't sure why, except I was tired of rushing through all of our experiments. It wasn't like Alex had gone out of his way to hang out with me since last semester. Maybe Faith had been wrong about him liking me, or maybe he'd found somebody else over the break.

Alex set down his bag and started rummaging through it. Bailey took one look at where he sat, then pouted and stomped off to team up for the lesson with Logan.

I doodled in my notebook, letting my mind wander. Hal Hawkins hadn't been well. He had low energy, shortness of breath, his skin was ashy and dull, and he'd barely done any magic except at Gym during drills. Professor Luciano even infused his materials in Lab.

If he were a critter, I'd have brought him to Bubbe right away. Nurse Smith knew what he was doing, but Hal didn't seem to get any better no matter how much time he spent in the infirmary, and that was a considerable amount this semester.

For the last two weeks, he'd brought his to-go bag down to the infirmary instead of the lounge. Faith had joined him every single night, diminishing our group by two. We missed having them around. Of course, the best solution was for all of us to go down there. Don't think we hadn't tried it.

Nurse Smith had turned all of us away, even Lee, who claimed he needed to talk to him about roommate stuff. Only Faith was allowed to remain, something about how school was stressful, and our friend needed his rest. But nobody said why.

The medicine I studied with Bubbe wasn't specifically for extrahumans, but bodies with magic had plenty in common. The rest of us were stressed and weren't stuck in bed for extra hours each day. Hal Hawkins should have been on the mend by then. He shouldn't have been adding trips to the infirmary to the break between class periods.

Unless there was something seriously wrong with him.

One of the drawbacks of being in our group was that we didn't hear much gossip. Sometimes I wished Cadence went here because she'd tell us everything, even stuff we'd want to unhear later. But hadn't I called the guy sitting right next to me Switzerland? He visited just about every circle of friends in this place. Maybe he knew more about this than we did.

"Alex, what you think is up with Hal?"

"What you mean?" He locked eyes with me, which was a little unnerving, maybe because he had a basilisk for a familiar. I had no reason to think he was hostile or otherwise someone to fear.

"He's been sick all semester." I tapped my pen on the paper. "And I'm worried about him because he's my friend."

"Oh." He shook his head. "I don't know for sure. All I've got are rumors, stuff overheard from upperclassmen. Repeating that isn't always the best idea."

"I think I'm smart enough to take gossip with a grain of salt." I wasn't totally honest, but nobody ever solved a mystery by refusing to ask questions.

"Fair enough." Alex glanced at the door, probably to make sure Hal hadn't just walked in. He was pretty sharp when it came to people, apparently. "Last year, Hal collapsed on his campus tour. Before that, everyone thought he was just a regular space magus like his dad, who taught second year here before the old headmaster left. But the third years had a theory about the other side of his family."

"Go on."

"Students here now never met Mrs. Hawkins. Hal's parents got divorced, and she hasn't set foot on this campus since, but Darren told me his sister, who graduated two years ago, heard she was a Dampyr." He shrugged. "I know next to nothing about them, so that's about all I can tell you."

Maybe Alex didn't know much about Dampyr, but I did. They were the offspring of two vampires, and extremely rare. Back before the Reveal and its early days, they'd often get abducted by extrahuman traffickers. From infants to elders, it didn't matter.

They had high value as blood dolls because their entire biology was different from the humans they resembled so closely. Their blood was the most potent nourishment for vamps, so of course, a woman married into such a high-profile family like the Hawkins wouldn't go around advertising her heritage.

She might even have kept her status a secret from her husband, but that had risks. Dampyr genetics were wonky, making it risky for them to have kids with anyone besides another Dampyr. Their offspring were born with magical maladies that had no cure and only experimental treatments.

Since Hal had a mysterious health condition that wasn't getting better, maybe there was some truth to the rumor.

And if it was correct, he might have qualified for experimental treatment in one of the many medical trials down in Boston. None of them were cures, but according to the medical journals in Bubbe's office, they improved quality of life.

Hal might want to try something like that, but he'd need proof he had Dampyr blood.

There was a fairly simple blood testing substance, one also used in extraveterinary medicine for identifying blood-borne illnesses in magical critters. I'd been helping Bubbe with those for the last few years, and she knew how to run the test and read the results. It wouldn't be official coming from her or even Nurse Smith—you needed a medical doctor for that—but with an unofficial test, he'd know where to go from there.

Bubbe had loads of them in her office. If Hal's problem came from his mom's biology, I might be able to help him find out, but I'd need to smuggle a testing kit on campus and also Hal's permission.

Permission? He's sick. Help him out and just do it anyway. You've got the power. Use it.

It felt like my heart stopped. The voice, the one trying to convince me to do the wrong thing, actually made sense. But it couldn't be the right thing, not coming from this part of my brain. Was this how Uncle Richard had felt? Did he have a devil on his shoulder, too?

"Thanks, Alex." I nodded. "I'm not sure it helps. I feel pretty powerless about now." Take that, evil inside voice.

"It'd be pretty easy to check on without anyone knowing." Alex's tone was casual, light, nonchalant.

See? This boy speaks sense. Why not hear him out?

"What do you mean?" I blinked. He had no idea I waged war with a voice in my head, and that he was unintentionally on its side.

If we're only trying to help, are we wrong?

I tried thinking one of Bubbe's sayings at it, about how intention's only ever part of the bigger picture. Fortunately, my inside voice stayed where it belonged.

"My mom's a genealogist." Alex leaned his head on his hand. "Most of her work is trying to get people back with their families. You know, folks who got separated during the messes during the Reveal. The Boston Internment, that kind of thing. All I have to do is ask her to check the Hawkins family. It's all public information, just compiled."

I waited for the evil inside voice to chime in, but it was silent. I should have been glad about that. It'd been a thorn in my side since I started hearing it. But I had trouble getting my brain around the ethics of the whole situation. It might have been a moot point, though.

If Alex's relationship with his family was like any of my other friends', I couldn't imagine her helping, but we could team up to do our own research.

"What research, now?" Alex's mouth wore a faint grin.

"Sorry, rampaging inside voice coming outside once again." I sighed. "Story of my awkward life."

"It's cute." The grin asserted itself. "Let me know if I can help, aside from talking to mom. Hal's a good guy, and I don't like seeing him sick either."

"Thanks."

After that, we spent the next twenty minutes of lab time working on our experiment. It wasn't too bad, just obnoxiously slow. We had to do something called titration. It was supposed to identify how much acid was in the magically infused solution we were preparing for use next week. Only one drip at a time could go into the flask, and it was super tedious.

Hal didn't make it to class until half an hour in. Faith was with him, so they started the experiment together. Professor Luciano went over to help them, setting up the burette and the stopcock in its stand. Because Hal's hands were too shaky to do fine motor tasks, which made me feel like a goose walked over my grave—or maybe his—Faith helped him with everything else, including taking notes.

Even though they were behind on the experiment, they managed to finish right before the bell rang. Alex and I were with them right down to that wire. We went over to help because we finished early. As we went about our business, watching one solution drip into the other, Faith gave me major side-eye.

I could tell she wanted to talk, so I jerked my chin toward the hall, letting her know we could chat out there. But Alex headed me off as she walked through the door. I was stuck between the last bench and the exit, caught by the strangely paralyzing weight of his hand on my shoulder.

"It might be a little early for me to ask this, but I figure there's no time like the present." He took a deep breath. "Do you want to go to the Valentine's dance with me?"

"I kind of plan to just go by myself." I shrugged. Not with the shoulder he touched, though. I wasn't entirely sure how I felt about it. "Didn't consider a date."

Why are you lying? Tell him how you feel.

I shook my head. Alex took this as emphasis of my spoken point because nobody would have suspected I was hearing a voice. At least, not anybody as sane as he seemed to be.

"Sorry. I sort of assumed since you went to the Parents' Night dance with Logan, that you might want company. And you guys are obviously not dating, so I figured maybe you were ready to move on?"

He seemed surprised. My reaction hadn't been what he expected, and probably wasn't normal. I couldn't for the life of me imagine what that normal was, anyway. All I could do was stand there, blinking. He let go of my shoulder, too, and I wasn't sure how to tell him he didn't need to, that I didn't mind.

Don't mind. That's interesting.

For the second time that day, the evil voice had a point. Wasn't it supposed to be earth-shattering? When someone who was interested touched you, I mean? The world was supposed to go away. At least, that was what it looked like on TV, and how Noah had described getting together with Darren. They'd held hands, and he just knew everything. That he was definitely gay, and that his as-yet future boyfriend was a total hottie. But apparently, I was different.

You're perfectly normal for an extramagus. Yours is a high and lonely destiny.

"I don't know," I answered both Alex and the voice in my head. Ember alighted on my shoulder. She didn't take up a protective posture. Instead, it seemed like she sought comfort. Or maybe tried to give me some.

"But then again, you're not obviously dating anyone." Alex cleared his throat. "Oh. Are you like my cousin? He's asexual; doesn't go out with anyone, ever."

"I don't know?" I shrugged. Ember craned her neck out so I could see her face, tilting her head so far to the right it almost turned completely around like an owl's.

"This whole conversation got weird, sorry." Somehow, Alex managed to smile. His teeth were the tiniest bit crooked, the angle of his grin canted to the right. Maybe he was just as confused as me. "But would you go with me anyway? As friends?"

"Peep!" Ember broke the tension as usual, and we both laughed. Actually, all four of us, because his basilisk was basically a magical snake, like Noah's Lotan but venomous. Despite that small difference, I knew a serpent's mood when I saw it, so I knew she also expressed mirth.

"So, yes," I finally managed, staring at the floor. "I'll go with you to the dance."

Look up. You owe him at least that much after all your waffling.

I did, by reflex, and almost looked away on principle. Why did I listen to a feature of my mental landscape that was probably the opposite of healthy? But what was done was done.

"Wow." Alex's new smile was practically effervescent. "I expected a no after all that. Thank you."

A throat cleared nearby.

"Yes, yes. You're clearly comporting yourself in a manner befitting a gentleman for once, Mr. Onassis. And I've never doubted you're a well-mannered lady, Miss Morgenstern." Professor Luciano tapped his foot. "Now that the matter of your impending date is concluded, I'd appreciate you vacating my lab if it's all the same to you. Unless you'd like to help me sweep and mop the floors in here?"

There was nothing quite like an impatient professor to motivate a couple of pokey students.

We headed out into the hall, where Faith didn't bother pulling me aside for a chat. She nodded, though without a smile. I couldn't blame her. Hal was a mess and so was she, so I wasn't surprised to see them heading to the infirmary.

Alex sauntered toward the cafeteria, raising an eyebrow at me, but I was definitely not ready to take dinner in there and anyway, I had something other than food on my mind. I headed back down the hall to order from Penelope and Sandy anyway, because it was routine and familiar.

"Where's the rest of the crowd, Aliyah?" Penelope glanced past me down the hall.

"They had plenty on their minds today." I shook my head. "Would you mind giving me a couple of extra soup and sandwich meals? I want to make sure some of them don't forget to eat."

"But of course."

Once the order was filled, I thanked Penelope. I brought the bags to the infirmary, hoping they'd provide a reasonable excuse for visiting. Nurse Smith agreed to let me in on the condition I only stayed for ten minutes.

"Hey, you guys." I sat in the chair at the foot of Hal's bed because Faith was in the one beside it. It reminded me of the time they came to see me while I was in here with Logan.

"What's up, Aliyah?" Faith held Hal's hand in both of hers.

Oh, he's not well at all. Look at the wall behind Fairbanks.

I blinked because I was already gazing in that general direction. The last thing I wanted was for either of my friends to think I was staring at the circles under Faith's eyes or the drawn and dried-out look of Hal's face, but once again, the voice was right. There was a tube, an opaque one, leading from a bleached pine panel on the wall to Hal's right sleeve. It disappeared under his shirt, likely ending somewhere on his chest.

I took a deep breath before speaking, focusing on the words I wanted to let out instead of questions better left unspoken. All of them were things I could ask Bubbe this weekend.

"I'm just checking to see what's going on." I set the dinner bags on the bedside table, not bothering to roll it over the bed. "You've been sick for so long, Hal. My grandma knows a lot of folks in the medical community. Is there's anything I can do to help? Like maybe see if she can get you a referral?"

"No." Hal shook his head. "After all this, Dad wants to bring me to Boston, see some specialists, but Mom won't sign off on the forms. With the custody arrangement, she gets to decide. She only lets Nurse Smith treat me."

"What?" My hands curled into fists, just about the only thing I could do to contain my magic. I was suddenly furious, almost as much as at Charity the first day of school. Even with the effort, my hands warmed up. I lifted them off my lap.

"Don't go nuclear, Morgenstern." Faith's tone was droll, but her back straightened, and she dropped Hal's hand. I felt the energy in the room change, some coalescing around her. And I understood. She was prepared to protect him, even if it meant putting me in the next bed over.

A romance for the ages. If only it weren't doomed to end in tragedy.

"Half a minute." I closed my eyes and counted to five as I took long slow breaths in and out, partly to shut the voice up, but also so I didn't go full solar. By then, my hands felt normal again. "I'm sorry, but that was a total shock and definitely not a pleasant one. Are you serious? Doesn't your mom know how sick you are?"

"I'm not sure. It's a moot point anyway." He closed his eyes. "Because without her consent, I can't see any doctors."

Bet your soul the mother knows. Doomed, as I said, unless you do what's needed, even without permission.

"What about an extraveterinarian?" Take that, evil voice. "Do you need permission for Nin to see one of those?"

"No." He opened his eyes. "But how's that going to do any good?"

"Because Bubbe has her friends around all the time. Lots of doctors at Salem General, some who do rotations in Boston, have familiars in her care. Sometimes, they leave stuff there, screening tests in case Bubbe notices a critter's magus is also not well. So, if you brought Nin in for a checkup—" I tapped my temple. "Do you get what I'm saying?"

"Ha." Faith smirked. "Clever."

"Yeah, I think Nin should definitely get a checkup." Hal's smile was faint and wan but still there. "I'm sure me being so sick has got her stressed out, and you know how Pharaoh's Rats are. Prone to illness when under too much pressure."

"I absolutely do." I nodded and smiled. "Oh, there's one more thing.

Just to try getting extra information. Alex offered to ask his mom for a family tree analysis. For you, both sides."

"Don't tell me you agreed to go on a date with him in exchange for that kind of favor." Faith snorted. "I know you're not scared of playing with fire, but poison should give anyone pause. Even you, Aliyah."

"No, it's got nothing to do with that," I admitted before the evil inside voice got a word in edgewise.

"I hope he doesn't think so." Hal sighed. "Quid pro quo is no fun."

"I'll remember that." I tried on a grin that didn't quite fit, partly because I couldn't imagine what else Alex Onassis would want from a mixed-up girl like me. "Do you want me to tell him to go ahead?"

"Yeah, why not?" Hal locked gazes with me. "My mom never talks about her family. I figure you of all people understand what that's like."

"Yeah, I do." Now I wanted to help him even more.

What you really want is leverage over the headmaster through his son. That isn't empathy, and you know it.

I was about to protest by telling my friends I loved them, but the knock on the door meant it was time to go. Nurse Smith was a stickler about the ten-minute limit, so I said goodbye and headed back to join the others in the lounge. Alex was there, and I told him to go ahead with the genealogy. Dylan overheard that but said nothing. At the time, I believed he thought it was for me about Uncle Richard.

Later on, my way up the stairs, he caught up with me and turned all my ideas upside-down.

"What are you doing with Alex Onassis?"

"Why is everyone asking me that?" I stepped to the side, trying to get past Dylan, but he didn't play reverse point for nothing.

"He just doesn't seem like your type." He blocked me. "Because you're, well—"

"I'm what?" I planted my feet and put my hands on my hips. This jostled Ember from her power nap on my neck.

"You wear your heart on your sleeve, Aliyah." He stood in the middle of the hall, taking up more space than I'd ever expected he could, like he expanded to fit it somehow. "You care too much. You commit your whole heart in just about everything you do, and I don't want to see you get hurt."

"I don't want to sound like a bitch, but it's none of your business what I do with Alex." My voice lowered because I wished it were his business. But it wasn't, so the only thing I could do was call him out on it.

"Guess what, you don't sound like a saint." Gale reared up on his shoulder, turning his head to blink at me. "I'm just trying to warn you. He's not into commitment. Not even having it around, generally speaking."

"Get specific then." I tossed my head. "If I wanted vague advice, I'd go see Izzy."

"I can't." He pressed his lips together. They're full, so they didn't make a thin line like Noah's do when he got confrontational.

"Why not?" I raised my eyebrow, feeling totally ridiculous. Of course, good-natured, confrontation-avoiding Dylan Khan could only get into a fight with a Hopewell.

"You know, for someone who's trying to save the world all the time, you're oblivious to personal danger." For the first time, I noticed his hands clenched in tight fists, a mirror of my own, like he was holding something in himself back. "Everybody else sees right through him."

"For someone trying to help, you're awfully insulting." My eyes widened, nostrils flaring. "Last time I checked, you were the world's biggest advocate of neutrality. So, if that's all you've got to say about Alex, stop talking." I palmed the panel next to my door, opening it.

"Ask Noah about your new boyfriend sometime."

I walked inside without saying another word, but that last bit Dylan had said made me curious. Not the boyfriend thing since it wasn't true, but dropping my brother's name. I could definitely talk to Noah and ask what he thought of Alex. Maybe Dylan knew a secret that wasn't his to tell, but Noah might not have that sort of restriction.

"Of course, you've got nothing to say now."

My empty room didn't answer, of course. Neither did the evil inside voice—another sign it wanted to corrupt me, not help. Did all extramagi go through this? I'd have to check in the unlikely event there are books in the library on the subject when I got the chance. *If.*

I brought Ember with me to the bathroom, letting her splash around in the baths while I got ready for bed. Over the week, I tried to find time to talk to my brother, but the opportunity didn't present itself before Friday's dance.

CHAPTER FORTY-TWO

On the day of the dance, I was with Grace, carrying our dinner bags upstairs because both of us were sort of nervous. I wasn't sure what had my roommate in such a bundle of nerves because she and Dylan had been a thing for six months now, but there you go. I guess like stage fright, official and formal date anxiety was something that never totally went away.

Just as we stepped off at the top, I saw something waving at us from the bottom of the stairs. No, someone. I stopped and turned around.

It was Faith. She had Kitty with her, and they alternated between looking over their shoulders and up at us. I got the impression Grace and I were a train they wanted to catch.

"Hang on, Grace." My roommate turned and saw what I did. She nodded and leaned against the banister to wait.

They got to the top and trotted past us, tugging at our sleeves before turning the corner. We followed them, and I noticed they also had their dinners. Hurrying down the hall, we headed toward their room. Grace kept going, but I paused.

"How are we going to get ready without our clothes?" Everyone knew what I meant, so I didn't bother elaborating.

"Aliyah, you can't be out here." Faith's whisper was so loud she shouldn't have bothered with it.

"I'll drop my dinner bag and grab our stuff." Grace patted me on the shoulder. "Don't worry, I'll remember the shoes." She glanced at Faith. "Unless you think I can't be out here either."

"No, you'll be okay." Kitty palmed the plate beside her door, and it unlatched. She pulled it open and gestured inside. "Go get it, and when you come back, do this knock."

Kitty demonstrated a series of raps and taps complicated enough to be Morse code. For all I know, it was. I never learned any. My roommate handed me her dinner and I walked inside with Faith, looking over my shoulder at Grace as she went back down the hall.

The lights came up and I blinked. This dorm room was the same shape and size as my own, but all the furniture had been moved around. Grace and I had decided to keep things simple and leave the beds, desks, and such as we'd found them on arrival.

Faith and Kitty totally redecorated. They'd opted to stack their beds to make bunks. This gave them way more room, and one of them had brought in a long rectangular table from somewhere. It'd been set up like a vanity, with one of the standard-issue mirrors propped against the wall lengthwise along its top.

Their desks sat back to back as a unit with one end against the same wall as their beds. The dressers and wardrobes flanked the vanity table. The whole set up left space in the middle for yet another purloined table, this one round. It had four stools around it that looked suspiciously like the ones we used in Lab.

I scratched my head at first, wondering how in the world they'd gotten all the extra stuff up here or managed to move the heavy wardrobes and dressers around. Then I realized it must have been Hal. He was a space magus and could easily have moved all sorts of stuff just by expending a little energy. He'd have had enough at the beginning of the school year, but it must've taken him a few weeks, even back then.

Looks like love put your old pal Hal on his deathbed. Are you sure all this empathy for your friends and family is good for your health?

I stood in the middle of the room, wishing the evil inside voice away. It had been silent since Monday, and I'd hoped it was away on a long vacation. Or maybe a permanent one. But no, it was back—with a major beef against the Hal/Faith ship staying afloat, apparently.

I closed my eyes, imagining myself setting it on fire, but all that came to mind was solar magic. Opening my eyes, I shook it off, and I had that maddeningly catchy Taylor Swift song stuck in my head. Thanks, evil inside voice.

You're welcome.

Sighing, I set the dinner bags on the table. Following Kitty's lead was probably for the best. She clearly used this table for something other than food most of the time, because there were a few notebooks on top of some hardbacks that looked vaguely familiar. I lifted one to check out the covers.

"Truncheons and Flagons?" I smiled. "I used to play this with some of the kids in town a few years ago."

Yes, until Azrael tried telling Izzy he loved her. More of your life ruined by romance.

"Get out of town?" Kitty laughed. "No wait, don't. Faith, why didn't you tell me Aliyah played?"

"I didn't know." Faith's deadpan delivery exploded into sarcasm the moment she dropped me a wink. "You're pretty mysterious, you know."

I blinked because I never would've thought of myself that way. I felt like my life was an open book, and had totally agreed with Dylan when he said I wore my heart on my sleeve. But transparency like that wasn't specific on stuff like hobbies, especially the ones I'd had before coming here.

We heard the series of knocks at the door, and Faith let Grace in. My roommate carried both of our garment bags and our dressier shoes, which she hung on the wardrobe doors and set by the door respectively. She also brought my makeup case, but nothing like that for herself. Grace never seemed to wear or even own any makeup. I didn't think she needed it anyway.

She disagreed, especially after the Parents' Night dance when she saw a photo of herself and declared she looked washed-out, which was why I'd brought the entire eye and lip sampler pack I got on Hanukkah, which included the inevitable shades that didn't remotely go with my complexion. Surely Grace could find something that worked for her in there.

Apparently, she liked Truncheons and Flagons too because she stared at the books like they were unicorns. Which are definitely mythical, by the way. Bubbe's told me millions of times not to bother looking for one.

"With this many erased notes, there's no way you're in the planning stage." Grace snorted. "So I guess you guys have a game running."

"You'd guess right." Kitty giggled. "What do you think we do when you guys are in the lounge half the night?"

"I had no idea it was something this fun." Grace smiled. "But isn't studying important too?"

"Oh, we study, all right." She picked up a stack of homework, moving it from the table to her desk. "Usually in the library right after Lab."

"So, are you full?" Grace set dinner boxes out. "Not like this," she said, patting her stomach. "I mean the game."

"Most of the time." She nodded. "But Eston wants to run a side campaign. He gets bored with just playing, but I don't have fun that way. He might need an extra player or two."

Now I understood their outwardly odd-couple relationship. Kitty looked like she could be on a magazine cover, and Eston's whole vibe was beanpole Mensa member. Most magi wouldn't consider them compatible because she was fire and he was water, opposite elements, but they'd bonded over a mundane hobby, so connecting on a magical level wasn't essential for them.

"If we don't want to be late to the dance, we should start dinner." Faith grabbed some bamboo cutlery from the pile she and Grace had made on the table. Then she pulled out a stool and sat down.

"Right." I sat next to her and ate my own dinner, even though I wasn't very hungry. The last thing I wanted was my stomach growling all night long, although it was a fine line between that and anxiety-induced nausea.

"So, what was the whole thing back in the hallway?" I gestured at the door with my fork. "What did you mean? Why can't I be out there?"

Faith swallowed her last mouthful of coleslaw. "Elanor's looking for you."

"What?" I blinked, almost leaning back. It was a good thing I didn't, considering the stool had no back.

"You heard me." Faith pushed BBQ pulled pork around the box it came in. "And she doesn't look happy." She took a tiny bite. Apparently, she didn't have much of an appetite, either.

"Does anyone know why?" I picked up one triangle of my tuna salad on pumpernickel but just stared at it. Even one of my favorites, prepared especially for me because the main offering had no Kosher hacks, didn't improve my appetite.

"Maybe it's got something to do with the fact that Logan has no date." Kitty shook her head. "He's totally fine with going stag, or at least that was what he said on Monday."

"Well, considering she and Noah practically tried to arrange our marriage on the first day of school, I can understand that." The sense this made alleviated some of my gut agitation, so I took a bite of my sandwich, finally.

"I think you might be assuming wrong." Grace talked around a bite of her pork, which she shoveled onto a roll. She realized her breach of etiquette and swallowed before continuing, "Because Logan does have a date. He's going with Hailey."

"I had no idea." Kitty blinked. "I can't believe I didn't hear about that."

"Everyone makes mistakes." Faith grinned, and I nodded in return. I got with her double meaning. "I'm glad he's going with her instead of Bailey, at any rate. Hailey's all but stopped hanging around with Charity. I'd figure both of them would have come around by now. I mean, my sister's only here for a few more months."

I dropped my sandwich because I was still in the dark. "I still don't know why Elanor's on the warpath, guys. Do you think I should avoid her during the dance too?"

Everybody nodded. Uh-oh.

"I'll try to help." Grace wiped her hands on her napkin. Her sandwich vanished. "I'm not sure what I can do, though."

"The last thing any of us needs to deal with is a bunch of inter-year drama." I stared wistfully down at my sandwich because it'd probably go to waste now. "Why do half the upperclassmen give me grief?"

"I don't know." Kitty sighed. "I guess we'll find out if she ever tells us what her problem is. Maybe you won't have to wait too long, but I hope she decides to tell you calmly and in private."

"Right. Because I definitely don't want cafeteria part two, Bonfire Boogaloo."

Everybody laughed, and it was good because they laughed with me. If I couldn't solve a problem, the least I could do was make the best of it. Laughing helped with that, most times.

We finished our dinner, then made use of some cool beauty products Kitty had stashed in her dresser. Her two moms ran a magicpsychic cosmetic company. She got to test all sorts of new gadgets and stuff before anyone else even heard about them.

She gave each of us breath-freshening tablets to put in our mouths. They cleaned teeth as well as a toothbrush, flossing, and mouthwash, but without effort. We just popped one in our mouths and went about other business for two minutes. After chasing them with water, we were all set on the fresh breath front.

I brought out my makeup sampler, and Kitty clapped her hands as she jumped up and down. This kit was part of her family's collection. Lucky for me since I wouldn't have known how to use some of those applicators. They were very different from the mundane cosmetics I'd always gotten in the drugstore.

Kitty also gave us magical cloths for washing our faces before applying makeup. Once we used them, we tucked them into a special container, which used magic and psychic energy to disinfect and infuse them with new cleansing solution.

"How did they ever come up with this stuff?" Grace smiled. "This is amazing. I've never seen anything like them. It must be awesome for the environment too."

"Both my moms graduated from Ellicot City Magitechnic." Which made sense. It was definitely something to be proud of.

ECM was every bit as prestigious as Hawthorn Academy, just for magipsychic technology instead of familiar studies. Noah had looked at applying there before he bonded with Lotan. It was similar to Providence Paranormal in that it had been founded as an alternative to a mundane school. In ECM's case, Baltimore Polytechnic Institute.

Kitty continued, "One majored in botanical sciences and the other in magipsychic chemistry out at Cal Magitech. They learned way more advanced stuff than we do in Lab here. Anyway, extrahumans have been improving skincare with their powers forever, but after the Reveal, they realized there'd be a market for magic cosmetics anyone could use."

"You mean this doesn't take any energy to run?" I picked up the package we'd put the used cloths into. "It's already charged and everything?"

"They keep working for about six months, but then you can send them back to get recharged. My moms have psychics, magi, and faeries staffing an entire department for this sort of thing since even the most powerful magi can't replenish the glamour or psychic energy in these."

"That's so cool." And it totally was. What an amazing world we lived in.

We sat in front of the makeshift vanity, which was long enough to accommodate all four of us, and got glamorized. It was cool spending time with Kitty. I never would've thought she was this interesting just by looking at her. It made me wonder how many other people I'd misjudged or otherwise made incorrect assumptions about every day. The reverse was also true.

The entrance we made for the Valentine's Day dance was nothing like Parents' Night. For one thing, we weren't on the arms of our dates—just a gaggle of girls, friends heading out for a good time. There were two reasons for this.

Without phones or other means of sending instant messages, there was no way to inform the guys when we'd head down to the lobby. That was simple and general and applied to all four of us. But the other reason was just for Grace and me.

The two of us balked, lagging behind Kitty and Faith because we were both more than a little self-conscious about formal socializing. Even though my dress was a literal work of art, and Grace's handmade one came close, we were still nervous. That was why we held hands on our way down the stairs.

I couldn't look at the crowd or the lights or even think about meeting up with Alex at that point. I was too busy being amazed by my roommate's handwork. Once again, she'd made something to wear during Creatives. It was practically miraculous and made her look like she belonged on the red carpet.

Grace had chosen two types of fabric, one opaque and the other sheer, and combined them into two layers for her dress. The lower was a rich earth-tone orange. I was no expert on textiles, but whatever fabric it was made from moved with her athletic frame, accentuating her natural lithe strength. But the fabric she'd layered over that took the cake. It was bright as a new penny, mesh and lace with a geometric pattern of zigzag lines. The way the long bars caught the light reminded me of strands of beads.

"Your dress is awesome." I grinned at my roommate.

"Said the pot to the kettle." She dropped me a wink. "You know where mine came from. Where'd you get that?"

"It's a hand-me-down from Bubbe." I chuckled. "Would you believe Azreal Ambersmith's great-grandmother made this?"

"I've seen the shop downtown. Do they still make stuff like that, though?"

"I don't know, but I can ask Az next time I see him. Any particular reason?" I immediately thought of one—that Grace might try seeking an apprenticeship with the Ambersmiths in summer. They'd probably accept her based on the Halloween costume alone.

"Not really, just curious. It's interesting how even though we get Creatives, there's no emphasis on actual teaching when it comes to the process of crafting here at Hawthorn."

"Don't look now," I toned my nervous titter back in hopes it'd become a vague sort of chuckle. "But we're sort of being watched."

And we were. By pretty much everyone. While we were talking, the stairs had stopped, depositing us on the main floor. Faith and Kitty had already stepped away toward Hal and Eston, leaving us in prime viewing location for the rest of the folks waiting around for the dance to start.

The first thing I noticed was Noah's dropped jaw. He stared in what looked like abject horror. Maybe he'd seen this dress before, maybe he hadn't, but either way, he freaked out over me wearing it. He stood next to Darren, holding a cup of punch toward him like a peace offering. He didn't move, only stared, so I considered myself safe from whatever level of wrath he had going for now.

The next thing I saw was Dylan. He stood in front of a chair, thank goodness, because his knees collapsed out from under him as he stared. At Grace, I think. He'd literally been swept off his feet, but that was okay. Once she saw him, she was in motion as sure and swift as any she made on the court.

I didn't know what happened next between the pair because Alex was too smooth for the shenanigans plaguing Dylan. He sauntered toward me, all half-smile and twinkling green eyes. His tie was pink because I'd told him that was the main color of my dress. I noticed that as he gave me a flourishing bow, one that might have flattered a marquis at a faerie court gathering.

Until that moment, I had not quite realized how handsome Alex Onassis was. He wasn't pretty like Logan, whose looks were delicate and chiseled. And he wasn't solid and present like Hal, or even quietly charming like Lee. Alex brought to mind those painted pottery shards from ancient Greece, the ones depicting men at the peak of their athletic prime.

While his skin wasn't bronze like the ancient Greeks', its unblemished paleness reflected light like the moon when at apex. He'd done something with his hair, which was normally dark brown with a natural loose curl. Tonight, he'd used some sort of wax to give it highlights with a silver sheen. And there was one more thing I noticed, just as I took the hand he offered me.

"Is that eyeliner?"

"I wanted to look my best." He kissed my hand. "For you."

There was no response I could think of that didn't feel awkward or sarcastic in a way only my friends would understand, so I said nothing, only nodded and gave him the best smile I could muster. That was hard, because Alex went beyond cleaning up well. He was pretty much gorgeous, and it hit me harder than I would've expected. He seemed so plain on a daily basis that this was a huge surprise.

You might think from the way I described Dylan and Logan, and now Alex, that all the guys at my school are hunky, or at the very least endearingly cute. Sometimes, it's more about the moment than anything aesthetic.

We walked along the sides, avoiding the same thing everybody else did—stepping on the dance floor. I mean, really, who wanted to be the first couple to kick off an evening that was supposed to be all about romance? Who wanted everyone's eyes on them that way, so that the person they were with was indelibly linked to them for the rest of their time at Hawthorne Academy?

Faith and Hal, of course.

I won't get flowery and tell you that they stepped lightly out onto the parquet floor, letting their emotions carry them to all sorts of ballroom dancing heights. That would be a lie. Hal was a wreck, after all, and Faith's concern for him, while touching, was the farthest thing from light.

But together they had courage, and that bond let them tread where no one else dared. At the Parents' Night dance, Hal had led our whole group through the event. Although his presence hadn't diminished, he lacked the energy he'd had at the beginning of the year. But they were true partners, probably destined. I knew that when I saw it because of my parents.

Faith rose to this occasion more so than anyone expected, judging by the faces of the upperclassmen and especially her sister. Faith didn't smile to light up a room or even to shame the devil. Instead, it was gentle, kind, and slow, and I realized she was totally brilliant in more ways than one.

There was no way Hal Hawkins could have hoped to keep up with anyone on the dance floor, not without Faith setting the pace on it before anyone else could. Again, like on Parents' Night, this was a waltz, measured steps in a particular and recognizable pattern. It should have worn Hal out, but somehow Faith worked pauses for him where she flourished into the three-quarter time. That put the focus on her so he had space to breathe.

It was heartrendingly touching. My mind kept going back to that tube in the infirmary, the one sticking out of the wall. I didn't know what that tube was, but I knew what was on the other side of it.

The Under. The unending source of magic that we each had access to, depending on our body's ability to absorb it through the barrier between worlds. While an extramagus like me could access more than my fair share, Hal had the opposite problem. His illness must limit his magic.

Clever girl. He's dying, you know.

I almost did something supremely stupid and shouted at the voice to shut up and go away forever, but in the space between the breath I took and the sound I'd have made, Alex spoke.

"Shall we?"

"Yes." The word came out louder and more strident than it might have at a different point in time, but that couldn't be helped. At the very least, Alex knew I was ready to dance. He had no idea about my reasoning, that I needed distraction from a voice in my head. That I couldn't face the likelihood that my friend was dying.

That was how I ended up as part of the second couple on the dance floor at a Hawthorne Academy function. The dress caught everyone's attention, and there I was, the girl who'd always said she couldn't dance.

CHAPTER FORTY-THREE

This time, the song was *Blackout* by Muse.

It wasn't as easy, managing to waltz. Logan had been good at leading because the Pierces had insisted he learn every dance known to man. He did that with Hailey, who seemed to be enjoying herself. Dylan just goofed his way through it, with Grace playing along. Alex Onassis was neither of those things, not a reluctant performance artist or a class clown. He was a showman.

My date wasn't concerned with taking precise, measured steps or teaching me to waltz properly. What Alex wanted was to show me off, or maybe the dress, or both. Instead of sticking to one corner or even one side, he paraded me around the dance floor like he needed us to be seen from all angles.

I felt like he was on a date with the dress, not me. Anyone could have worn that garment and looked amazing, twirled around in his arms. He was handsome and impeccably well-mannered, but I barely knew Alex and wouldn't know if I had feelings for him until much later. Being considered an ornament didn't bother me. I was okay with that. But also, wrong.

"Everyone's staring in a good way," he murmured.

"No, they're not."

"If that's what you need to tell yourself. But you look stunning, so I'm not surprised."

"It's the dress."

"Do you have any idea who you look like?"

"Do I want to know?" I shrugged one shoulder. "That sort of stuff isn't a big deal to me. This dress was my grandmother's."

"It really isn't the dress, though." He leaned closer, enough so I felt his breath in my ear. "You look like the Sidhe queen."

"No, sir." He was so close I didn't dare shake my head for fear of bumping his with mine. "You can't mean that. Besides, if a changeling ever heard you—"

"Well, you could be related to her." He twirled me, putting some distance between our faces for a moment. "Are you sure you haven't got any Sidhe blood?"

"You know I do." I sighed. "My uncle's a Hopewell, remember?" I refused to refer to my mother as one, but I didn't say that aloud.

"Yes, that's right. I'd forgotten."

No, he hasn't, and you know it. He appreciates these things about you, the ones others would shame you for. Unlike that fool you secretly pine for. And it's something you ought to take pride in.

I continued moving, dancing along and trying not to pay any heed to the evil inside voice. It was awfully flattering all of a sudden, which wasn't typical. I didn't like it.

"Would you like to rest, then? Have some punch, perhaps?"

"No. Just something in my shoe." The quick save wasn't genuine, but at least it was realistic. Thank goodness, because I wasn't sure I could handle all the comparisons in my brain right now.

In case you weren't current with the news, my uncle Richard wasn't just in jail for attacking students at Providence Paranormal College. He was also on trial for crimes against extrahumanity, including a coup in which he'd tried to murder both faerie monarchs. Alex telling me I resembled said royalty right now was more than a little unnerving.

"Are you sure it's a shoe and not that every song is a waltz?" He chuckled, raising an eyebrow. He almost looked like one of the pointy-eared aliens from that series on TV. You know the one.

"Maybe." I managed a smile. If only the evil inside voice would shut up and let me have anything to myself. I didn't want to feel like this. "I'm pretty sure they played most of the same songs on Parents' Night."

"Yeah, but at least it's not *Hide Your Love Away* by the Beatles again." He shook his head. "Yet. The upperclassman say that gets played at every dance in this place."

"Isn't that a little inappropriate for a Valentine's Day dance?"

"Yes and no." His eyes were half-lidded, an expression I'd come to recognize as noncommittal from him. "Perspective rules all."

"Hey, I've got an idea." His comment about perspective helped me realize there was a nearly universal one, and I knew just the song to express it. "Does the DJ take requests?"

"Yes, but only waltzes. That's all they do here."

I shook my head as I led Alex off the dance floor. It felt strange, taking the initiative and changing something even if it was only a school dance playlist, but it was good to actually have an opinion and be proactive with it for once.

Nobody else was over by the DJ's table. I felt downright rebellious.

"I'm guessing most of the students here don't bother with this sort of thing."

"Does that matter to you?" His half-grin lit his whole face somehow.

"No, not at all. In fact, I kind of like this." I smiled.

"It looks good on you. Almost as good as when you get competitive on the court."

I didn't know what to say to that, so I turned away. My face heated up. Alex was mostly a mystery to me, but the one defining feature of our interactions was flattery. Big time. I was out of my depth and wondering whether he knew that.

"Aliyah Morgenstern, what a surprise."

"Zeke?" I blinked. The last person I'd expected to see manning the DJ booth was a vampire CNA straight out of the infirmary.

"The very same." He gave me a half-bow, which was weird coming from a guy wearing scrubs. "How may I help you?"

"If it's not too much bother, I'd like to request a song. I've heard that's not the way things are done here, but there's something I'd like to try dancing to."

"It's been decades since anyone's made a request, but it's not unheard of." Zeke nodded. "However, there's a rule here we both must follow regarding the music."

"Let me guess: I have to select something in three-quarter time."

"Correct." He nodded. "Although six-eight is also acceptable."

"Could you please play *Somebody to Love* by Queen, then?" I wanted to hear this so badly I clasped my hands in front of my chest.

"But of course." He put on a glove to tap the screen in front of him. Vampire fingers didn't register on touch screens, and apparently, his rig was digital. "I'll need to set it up, so you'll hear it two songs after this one that's currently playing."

"Thank you so much."

"You're quite welcome." He gave us the sort of wave most often seen on parade floats. "Have a lovely evening."

I turned, heading toward the punch bowl. First, I glanced around, making sure Charity Fairbanks wasn't watching. The last thing I wanted was for her to try to get revenge for the stunt Hal had pulled on Parents' Night. But she was nowhere to be seen.

"Let me get that for you. You've got to fix your shoe. Right?"

"Oh, yeah." I'd almost forgotten about the quick save. Of course, it came back to haunt me since Alex paid more attention to things than he appeared to. I took a seat nearby, turn my back, and took my shoe off. I went through the motions of pretending to knock something out of it.

You wouldn't have had to lie if your uncle had pulled his gambit off. That pathetic Fairbanks girl wouldn't dare look at you sideways. You'd be related to royalty for real.

I slipped my shoe back on and stomped it on the floor a couple of times, not because it didn't fit. It was pure defiance of the evil inside voice since I couldn't just come out and say what I was thinking where people could hear. I didn't care one bit about what it said anyway, except the part about lying. Did the voice come from all the deceit I'd practiced? I leaned back in the chair, trying to recall the first time I'd heard it, but came up with nothing.

I didn't like lying, but unfortunately, it had become part and parcel of my social landscape here at Hawthorn Academy. And at home. No one in my family had any idea I was an extramagus. How did I go from being a girl who loved the truth to somebody living a lie?

"Here's your punch." Alex sat beside me, handing over a cup. "Drink up before your song comes on."

"Thanks." I leaned back in the chair and took a sip.

The beverage wasn't what I expected. It was tangier than any other juice I'd had before, but maybe that was just the punch flavor at Hawthorn. I wouldn't know from experience since I'd left the welcome ceremony early, and the punch had ended up on Charity's head at Parents' Night.

Go on and laugh. I know you want to.

I listened to the music instead of the voice. Alex had a point. We had maybe half a song left before my request played. I didn't hold my nose, but it was a near thing. I needed to chug this punch or risk missing my dance. I held the cup to my lips and tilted, guzzling it down.

"Whoa, go easy there." Alex glanced at something behind me. His eyes were little wider than usual.

"Too late." I shrugged and handed him the empty cup.

"Okay." He'd gotten stiff and awkward all of a sudden, something I never expected to see on him.

Even on a regular day, Alex was the opposite of a stuffed shirt. He had a rolling gait and a near-constant ease of existence about him in class and at Gym. Practically low-strung. So, I couldn't help but wonder what was going on with him.

Something moved out of the corner my eyes. I turned my head to see Elanor and Noah standing in the doorway from the hall that led to the bathrooms. She held him by the arm as he struggled to pull away. I hoped they weren't fighting since she was his best friend, and he'd been extra moody this semester. He needed her. Finally, she shook her head, speaking words that calmed him somehow.

When Alex returned from disposing of the cups, he immediately took my hand, leading me to the dance floor again. This time he went the long way around, putting distance between Noah and Elanor and us like he was trying to avoid them.

I was about to open my mouth, ask him what was up. He still looked awfully stiff. My vague and frustrating argument with Dylan sprang back to my mind, and I realized the other person who could answer questions about Noah's and Elanor's beef with Alex was the boy himself. But it was too late. I heard the clink of a piano as the song began.

We stepped onto the parquet along with several other couples and even some folks by themselves or in larger groups. Apparently, I had made a popular choice, or maybe it was just that the song felt more upbeat than the others Zeke had played this evening.

As we danced, the floor got more crowded. It seemed like every-one, even the faculty, joined in. I spotted Professor DeBeer dancing with Coach Chen—not a pair I'd have predicted, but it looked like they had fun. Even Professor Luciano was out there with us, doing something that reminded me for all the world of videos Noah had showed me on the internet of a now-shuttered Goth club down in Boston.

By the time the bridge played, the part where the incomparable Freddie Mercury sang about how he was going crazy, I felt practically weightless. If it weren't for all the other people on the dance floor, I'd have felt like I was flying. Ember soared overhead, swooping and dipping in the air along with the music, which enhanced that sense. It was dizzying, almost maddening.

Perhaps you are, in fact, mad. Already. That would be a record, even for an extramagus.

"No." Oops.

"What?" Alex blinked, but his feet didn't miss a step.

"Nothing." All of a sudden, I wanted to get away from him. In my mind's eye, I pushed him away to run off the dance floor and up the stairs toward the sanctuary of my room, but I couldn't. There were too many people there. Familiars, too.

"You can tell me." He spun us, letting centrifugal force pull us closer together.

"I can't." The entire situation, this proximity of our bodies, was untenable.

At least that's true. But you ought to tell him. He might even like it.

"Stop! Stop already. I can't take this anymore!"

I didn't scream, but it was certainly loud to Alex, whose ear was next to my cheek. At that point, I didn't think things could get any worse. Glancing up, I saw Dylan staring at me. Grace, too. And Logan looked away from Hailey, furrowing his brow at me. So, I wasn't exactly quiet either.

Oh, dear, it looks as though I've gone and made a mess. Or rather, you have.

I looked down, expecting to see the floor on fire or something extremely horrific like that. It wasn't quite so bad but still qualified as terrible because my hands glowed. With solar energy.

Not noticeably yet, partly because of the strobing lights but also Alex swinging me out with both of my hands in his. It was about to get worse fast, and if I didn't get out of there soon, the entire school would know my secret.

"Hold on, Aliyah. You can snap out of this. Come on." He gripped my hands, and I felt energy between us. Not just my solar magic but his poison.

I wasn't sure what he expected to accomplish. Solar and poison weren't opposites but not reactive either. So, mingling his energy with mine didn't seem like it'd do much good, but I was wrong.

I felt lightheaded all of a sudden; my feet got stumbly and my breath shallow. I found myself leaning on Alex instead of dancing with him, like the song was a power ballad instead of pleading gospel.

I still wanted out of there. I'd have run, but it was all I could do to keep my balance.

I had less control, less agency, here with Alex. I was worse than vulnerable, and even though I'd seen it in movies, it just felt wrong. He diminished me somehow.

The glow started fading from my hands, but the heat remained. Now I wouldn't reveal my secret as an extramagus, but I did have to worry about setting the dance floor on fire. The poison had gone beyond sapping me of strength to conjure solar. It had lost me control of my fire.

"Sorry." Alex's jaw dropped. I'd never seen him this emotional before. "I overdid it."

"It's not your fault. I am what I am." I whimpered, ashamed of the new disaster. "Can't I go a semester without setting stuff on fire?"

"At least you didn't let the sunshine in."

I couldn't move my head without feeling dizzier, so I rolled my eyes to look up at him.

"I figured it out." He gazed down into my eyes. "I think you're incredible."

"You won't feel incredible when you catch fire. I should go." I tried to walk away, but I stumbled.

"Don't." He caught me. He hadn't looked away from my eyes the entire time.

"Why not?" I'd almost have preferred falling on my face at that point. At least I'd have made the effort to leave.

"I can fix this, but it's gonna cost you."

"Anything." All I could think about were my friends and classmates who would get hurt if I couldn't hold back my fire.

"Okay, then." Alex Onassis tipped my chin up, then bent over me, placing his lips on mine.

It was my first kiss, which was disappointing. Like I said, I'd only been interested in one guy so far, and it was not Alex.

As far as kisses went it was fairly tame, at least compared to what I saw on TV and Noah's descriptions. The main purpose in those instances was getting romantic, after all.

What Alex did was all about banishing his element. I suppose I had that going for me, at least. I can honestly say my first kiss was truly magical, even if not in a fairytale way.

Some of the fog in my mind and weakness in my limbs eased. Not all of it, but enough of my faculties returned that I could hold back the fire on my own. But that wasn't the best way to explain it.

Firsts are important because they shake you out of complacency and make you question the way things are. When the shield of the way things have always been slips, you see truth. Because that kiss wasn't romantic, its effect was entirely unexpected.

It gave me a major epiphany about my whole magical situation.

Every time something was unjust or someone got hurt, my fire turned up to eleven. In the cafeteria, I couldn't abide Charity abusing Faith and bullying Noah.

Every time I tried to hide myself, I let the sunshine in. That night on the stairs between Bubbe's office and home, I'd had to conceal that obnoxiously persistent solar magic from my whole family.

Which is exactly why you ought to realize your entire situation is untenable.

"I'm a ticking time bomb."

"You just need an outlet." He patted my back. "Some way to use what you're hiding, where only the people who know can see. Otherwise, it'll only get harder."

"How could you possibly know anything about this?"

"I'm not like you, but my cousin is."

"Oh." I sighed, shaking my head. "All the same, I think it's probably for the best if I leave this dance early."

"Would you like some company?"

"I don't think so. I'm sorry."

"I'm not."

Alex escorted me to the stairs, then waved as I ascended. While nowhere near as triumphant as my exit from Parents' Night with the rest of my friends, at least this social outing wasn't a total failure. I'd managed to escape with everybody unscathed. Well, almost everybody. Because the last thing I saw as I stepped off the top of the moving staircase was Noah shaking his finger angrily at Alex. I couldn't imagine why, but I was exhausted and not going back down there.

It was time for a bath and sleep. The last thing I wanted to do in a state like that was to forget self-care. When you're an extramagus, the worst-case scenario is usually total disaster.

CHAPTER FORTY-FOUR

Alex was right; I needed to use my solar magic to understand it better, so I practiced in small ways, starting the day after the dance. After that, I could contain it a little more reliably. I still ran the risk of accidentally using it at the wrong time, but it was a more conscious kind of mistake, like grabbing grapefruit juice when you wanted orange.

How did I practice something this secret?

I'd taken to turning the lights on and off with my solar magic in the privacy of my own room. I had done it in the bathroom once before too, but Kitty walked in shortly after. That was the end of that.

So far, I hadn't busted out with it in Lab or anything, and as long as I ran laps before all of our Bishop's Row practices, I didn't seem to have a problem in Gym or practice. All the same, it was on my mind all day, every day.

Mundane teenagers worried about acne, bad hair days, and not knowing any of the answers to what's on a pop quiz. I got all that and more, and to top it off, Noah was breathing down my neck. Apparently, he had a problem with Alex and me.

I ended up sort of going out with Alex Onassis. By default, maybe. At the beginning of the year, I couldn't even have told you his last name, and here I was, engaging in an understated sort of couplehood with the last person I expected. Mostly it was no big deal. We walked together in the halls, sat together at lunch. While he didn't have dinner in the lounge with us because of Kitty's Truncheons and Flagons campaign, he visited our booth at the end of breakfast.

We'd held hands maybe twice since the dance, briefly and awkwardly. And we hadn't kissed since then either, which was a relief for me. Kissing was scary, which meant I wasn't ready for more. If that bothered Alex, he didn't show it. The whole thing felt like still needing training wheels on a bike.

Maybe I was being too harsh about it. My parents were my relationship benchmark, and they had serious big love energy. The same was true for Faith and Hal. It'd be unfair to expect something that epic for myself because clearly nobody else had anything like that going on. Not even Grace and Dylan.

Those two spent a good amount of time together, but their familiars practically ignored each other, which hinted at some sort of tension. And I hadn't seen them show any affection since the night I'd walked in on whatever it was they were doing after winter break. They seemed more connected on the Bishop's Row court than at any other time, but that made sense since they shared athleticism.

Their new vibe reminded me of how I was with Logan, which was to say, they partnered in Lab, laughed together over Professor Luciano's far-fetched mnemonic study suggestions, and clowned around. Dylan seemed comfortable with it. Grace didn't. She blasted him with longing stares almost every time his back was turned.

I wanted to talk to my roommate and ask if she was okay. Every time I did, she avoided the subject of Dylan altogether. If I mentioned his name, she made sure the rest of our conversation was all about the tournament, or a quiz, or something cute that Lune did. It wasn't healthy for her to be silent about what bothered her, so I confronted her in the café one Saturday morning.

"Look, Grace. I wanted to sit down and touch base." I reached across the table and grabbed her hand. "You're my friend, and I care. How are you doing?"

"Oh." She blinked, her hand tensing under mine. I couldn't imagine why. "No, I'm hanging in there. I've been talking to the headmaster. He's a licensed counselor."

"Okay." I nodded, my exhale heavier than usual but not enough to qualify as a sigh. I'd gotten sickeningly good at hiding things. "That's good, then. Do you need anything?"

"Well, spring break is coming up in a week." Grace stared at the table. "And I'm not going to my aunt's."

Sometimes, the people who needed help most couldn't take that extra step and ask for it, so I offered.

"Do you want to hang around with me in town? I can ask my mom if you can stay over for some of the break. And Passover is next week. Do you want to come to Seder? There's a full dinner but served with only matzo, no bread. It's traditional but fun."

"That'd be awesome, Aliyah. Thank you."

She asked about the holiday, and I explained that Passover was about remembering times of oppression and celebrating liberation from them. She asked if there was anything she could bring and I gave her the standard answer: an item that symbolized liberation for her. Our conversation continued on, mostly about class.

Once again, she avoided the subject of Dylan, who I happen to know was also staying for break. He'd mentioned it before. He'd also told me that over winter break, he and Grace had spent most of their time on campus together. Grace apparently wanted to avoid him this time.

Maybe it was just being shut up here in the school. The spring weather was much nicer than the frigid temperatures we had at the end of December and beginning of January, and there was more going on in town to boot.

I guess the whole confrontation/intervention thing was going around like the plague because that same afternoon, Noah knocked on my door. I let him in even though it was an enormous surprise for him approach me in the middle of a weekend day. Either Charity was in New York, or he didn't care what she thought anymore. I hoped it was the latter.

No such luck.

"You have to stop seeing Alex." Noah crossed his arms, leaning against the door he'd just closed behind him.

"You don't tell me what to do." I snorted. "You've barely spoken to me all year at school over practically nothing, and now you're trying to dictate my dating life?"

"You don't understand, Aliyah." He closed his eyes.

"Then explain it to me because you coming in here and saying something like that is super rude." And it was, even if I was mostly indifferent about my so-called boyfriend anyway.

"He's poison." Noah opened his eyes but stared at the floor. Lotan slithered out of his collar and rubbed cheeks with him, a sign his familiar knew there was something wrong.

"Tell me something I don't know. Duh, poison magus. That fact's right there in front of me in Lab every day. And in Gym, to boot. You know we're on the team together, right?"

"That's not what I'm talking about." My brother's voice sounded like it came from the bottom of a well. "I'm trying to tell you he's no good."

"You said the same thing about me at the beginning of the semester, and I'm your sister." Ember got between Noah and me, perching on my desk and thrusting her neck out.

"I'm sorry." Noah opened his eyes, and I saw the tears in them. "I thought you'd want all the same things I did out of school. I didn't realize you'd always be different from the crowd I hang around with now, and I let myself think that was more important than you. But nothing is. You're my little sister, and all our lives, I promised to take care of you. I seriously dropped the ball, and it was the biggest mistake I've ever made in my life. Well, almost."

"What you mean by 'almost?'" I froze. "What could be worse? You're not a bad person, so there's no way you could have done something so terrible you're this afraid to talk about it."

He'd been hiding something enormous. I couldn't assume it was the same as mine, though. As much as I'd love to not be alone with my secret, he wouldn't be going on about who I dated if the problem he'd hinted at was being an extramagus.

"It'd be worse if I let you keep dating Alex after what he's done." He took a deep breath and closed his eyes again, as though he couldn't bear to see my face when he told me the truth. "Aliyah, he—"

The door hit him in the back, and he stumbled forward into the room. Noah righted himself, but the moment was lost. There was no way he could finish the sentence now, not with who'd just walked into my room.

Grace wore gym clothes. She had a chest of ankyr and cestus under one arm and wasn't alone. Dylan, Alex, Lee, and Faith all followed her in. My roommate chattered away, totally oblivious to anything besides what she was focused on, Bishop's Row.

"The gym's clear, so I talked to Coach, and she says we can use it. Lee and Faith need more practice in case Coach Pickman takes them off the bench and they're not getting it during the week. So, I figured, since you were just studying up here anyway, we could— Oh."

She saw Noah. Well, she noticed his presence almost right after she walked in, but she really *saw* him now, shrouded in all that misery. Grace blinked, standing still like she was in the woods and had just noticed a bear. Or maybe something more delicate, like a fawn or even a flight of monarch butterflies drying their wings after escaping their cocoons.

"You go practice, Aliyah. We'll talk later." Noah's voice was choked, which made sense. He was on the verge of tears, after all. He and Alex didn't look at each other, both sets of eyes finding something else to fix on as they passed each other in the doorway.

I was about to stop Noah or go after him, I wasn't sure which, but my indecision cost me my choice because Grace rummaged in her dresser, grabbing some compression socks. I shook my head, turned to my own dresser, and got my gym clothes. Our reserve players needed extra practice.

Our tournament was the week after Passover.

———

Noah and I didn't find time to talk that week. The second-years had standardized tests in the middle of the semester, so he was super busy hitting the books with Elanor. They were in the library, which made it hard to discuss anything emotional. And even though I approached him once, he only told me to be careful and that we'd discuss everything over break.

But that didn't work out so well because Noah wanted to talk to me alone, not with my roommate around. I refused to stop being kind to people who needed it, but sometimes it was damned inconvenient to have a houseguest when your sibling's trying to have a deep and confidential conversation with you.

Grace came home with me on Friday night after class and didn't leave until Tuesday. In the kitchen over breakfast with my family, she said she had to stay in shape and needed time in the gym on campus. But I knew better, because she told me the night before, whispering up from the trundle bed in my room.

She had an appointment with Headmaster Hawkins, the therapy kind. So of course, Izzy and Cadence decided to bring me down to Engine House for pizza. Noah tried to stop me and I almost let him, but I needed a little time out of the house too. At the counter, we grabbed some slices and sodas and hustled into a booth beside the window so we could people watch.

"So, tell me about this boy." Cadence smiled. "The one who took you to the dance."

"Is that what you brought me here for? To go boy crazy?" I raised my eyebrow. I didn't really want to discuss Alex.

"Not exactly. It's just a topic." She shrugged. "Why? What would you rather talk about?"

"How about that Bishop's Row team at Gallows Hill? Let's talk about that instead." I rattled off a string of questions about whether the teams are just limited to changelings or if they'd somehow figured out a way for shifters to channel energy.

"There's not much to tell. I'm not on it." She chuckled. "But we've got a cheer squad. That's what I'm doing."

"So, tell me about cheer squad, then."

"It's not too exciting." She shrugged, then took a bite of her pizza and talked around it. "Mostly, we jump up and down making a lot of noise. The outfits are cute though."

"Don't tell me you're wearing miniskirts with lollipops under them?" Izzy rolled her eyes. One of the things she never liked about the mundane schools we attended earlier in our lives was cheer-leading uniforms. She thought them boring and stereotypical, even if the girls wearing them found miniskirts empowering.

"No way." Cadence pulled out her phone, tapping it to fetch a picture. I was totally envious of the fact that cell phones worked at Gallows Hill, but that was beside the point.

The outfit she showed us was something like a jogging suit but covered with sequins. No wonder she loved it. I saw that the squad wasn't just for girls, either.

"That's actually kind of cool." Izzy looked up from the phone. "We've got nothing like that at Messing." She chuckled. "People applaud there by snapping their fingers like a bunch of beatniks."

"But you've got a team, right?" Cadence's eyes widened. "Because your school's going to need it for—"

"Ixnay!" Izzy made a cutting gesture across her throat, reminding me for all the world of a pirate. "Yeah, we do. Nobody who's not on the team admits liking it, though." She snorted. I was getting the impression folks at Izzy's school annoyed her immensely.

"Are you on it?" I realized I sounded like Grace, all questions and no answers, and I got annoyed with her and Dylan for avoiding confrontation. Not a good look, Aliyah.

"I guess." Izzy shrugged. "Shocked everybody I know there, but it's no big deal." Clearly, sports weren't that important to her. But she'd been pretty flat over the whole break. Should I be worried?

Worrying over a psychic? That's a bit beneath you, isn't it? People like them exist for people like us to use as we see fit.

I rolled my eyes at the evil inside voice, but my friends didn't need to know anything about that. Or maybe they did. Could I tell them? I knew I could trust them to keep secrets, but I wasn't sure I should divulge that in a public place like Engine House. Or at all.

Because once again, the voice had a point. Extramagi have a long history of chewing psychics up and spitting them out. And mermaids had gone into hiding ages ago because of them. What if I scared them away and they didn't want to hang out anymore? I wasn't sure I could handle losing the friends I'd known since kindergarten.

"Well, you and Aliyah have something in common, then." Cadence's smile was like sunlight on water.

"Yeah, I know. She's Jane Football, in a manner of speaking." Izzy chuckled at me. "Who knew you'd be a jock?"

"And dating one, too! So, tell us about your boyfriend." Cadence had finished her pizza so she folded her hands, making them flat like a table, then set her chin on them and batted her eyes. That pretty much meant she wouldn't drop the subject of Alex Onassis.

"It sort of happened by accident." I stared at the crumbs on the paper plate in front of me. "Us dating, I mean."

"Like in a rom-com? You spilled coffee on him or something?"

"Not really." I shrugged. "It just sort of happened. I think I'm dating him by default or something because ever since the dance he's just been hanging around with me all the time practically."

"Well, uh. So, what's he like?" Cadence's hand flopped like a fish out of water. Her accompanying laugh was more of a gasp. The conversation was awkward with a side order of cringe sauce.

"Hang on a minute there, Cadence." Izzy shook her head, dropping her pizza crust and placing her hands flat on the table. She meant business. "He's just following you around so you're dating. That sounds majorly unhealthy."

"I don't know from healthy." I sighed, shaking my head like my body couldn't decide which emotion to show. "I've never had a boyfriend before, so I don't know what normal is."

"Let me ask you something." Izzy narrowed her eyes. "It's extra personal, so I hope you don't mind."

"Personal's what I expect from my best friends. Right?" I was worried that the worst was happening. Were we growing apart? "Go ahead."

"Okay, so Logan Pierce took you to the Parents' Night dance." She tilted her head, brown hair cascading over one shoulder. "And you didn't end up dating *him* by default, right? Why not?"

"Because Logan and I talked about it." My breath caught in my throat because, like any psychic worth her salt, she'd led me to a conclusion. "We agreed both of us feel totally platonic about each other. Like good friends, and we're happy like that."

"So how come you're default-dating this Alex guy when I assume he didn't bother discussing your feelings on the matter?" Her nostrils flared.

"Wow." I struggled to swallow past the lump in my throat. "Time's just kind of gotten away from me. There's some pretty serious stuff going on with friends at school, like potentially life-threatening."

"Oh, my God, Aliyah, I'm sorry." Cadence leaned back, blinking. "If I'd known, I never would've kept bugging you about this whole Alex thing."

"No, it's a good thing you brought it up, Cadence." Izzy nodded. "Because Aliyah definitely needs to stop and think about whether she even wants to date this dude."

"Yeah, you're right." Cadence sighed. "So, tell us about your other friends, then."

"Okay." I took a deep breath and leaned forward so I could lower my voice and keep name-dropping to a minimum. Medical information was private. "You remember Hal Hawkins?"

They nodded. After that, I launched into a brief timeline of his health's deterioration, what Hal had told me, and my theories. Cadence chewed the inside of her cheek, a common habit when she was deeply worried. But Izzy went pale, which did not bode well. Not at all.

I told you he was dying, but did you listen?

"He's felt too sick to leave campus. Class takes a lot out of him even when he takes it easy." I sighed. "But when Grace went to campus this morning, I asked her to track him down and see if he'll come over tomorrow. And bring him to Bubbe's office."

"Why?" Cadence blinked. "What's an extraveterinarian going to do for a magus?"

"A blood test on a separate record from the ones his family controls, for one thing."

"Is that legal?" Cadence pursed her lips. "He's a minor, right?"

Izzy turned her head, staring in shock at Cadence. Thinking of the law was not usually her wheelhouse.

"I don't know, but at this point, I hardly care." My hands curled into fists. I was prepared to fight for my friend's life, legalities be damned.

Izzy stood so suddenly she knocked her chair over. The entire staff and all the customers stared. Everyone saw her pointing at me with one hand while rummaging in her bag of cards with the other. And when she slapped the omen down on the table between us, I had nothing at all to say about it.

For once, an intelligent choice.

It was the nine of swords. Izzy has been reading cards around me since before she could read words, so I was fully aware of what this one meant. Guilt, plain and simple. Secrets that kept you up at night, weights on your mind and heart that you couldn't shake.

But it got worse. Not because of the card, but because Izzy sometimes channeled coincidence. It was all part of being a precognitive psychic who saw the future with the aid of items instead of in dreams or through scrying. She was about to unleash a major truth on me right here in the middle of my favorite restaurant.

No pressure. Who am I kidding? It was like being at the bottom of the sea.

"You must cast off your burdens or sink with them. The time is sooner than you imagine, and You. Are. Not. Prepared."

Izzy collapsed backward, which meant she'd fall. Her chair was on the floor, legs stretching and threatening like the swords on that card. She could seriously injure herself on it.

"Ember, go!"

My dragonet launched herself off my shoulder, swooping down toward Izzy to grab her by the shoulders of her cardigan. Golden talons punched holes through knit fabric, which held, thank goodness.

But a critter no bigger than a small cat couldn't hope to keep a swooning psychic upright for long.

Cadence and I stood, but we were on the other side of the table. We were too late. Fortunately, the person at the table behind her turned and rose to the occasion. More like he raised the chair.

With magic.

It was Lee Young, from Hawthorn. I knew he'd be staying in Salem this week, but I had no idea he loved this pizza place as much as we did. His wood magic easily affected the fallen seat, since aside from the screws, it was entirely made from his element.

The chair slid into place behind Izzy just in time to catch her as Ember lost her grip. Lee stood and moved to the empty seat beside Izzy. He reached for her soda cup and placed it in front of her, then opened his coat and let Scratch out.

"Make sure she's okay, then we'll try reviving her."

Cadence nodded. This looked like familiar territory for both of them, which had me totally stumped. Clearly, Lee had become well acquainted with both of my friends from town. Which was good, all things considered. Nobody else I know could've pulled off that rescue stunt.

Ember returned to my shoulder as Scratch climbed into Izzy's lap. The Sumxu stood on her hind legs, peering at Izzy's face and tilting her head from one side to the other. Her voice was squeaky with a lilt at the end like she asked a series of questions. Scratch sounded for all the world like an inquisitive guinea pig, even though she was a magical lop-eared cat.

Now that things were relatively calm, the other bystanders turned away and went about the business of enjoying their pizza. I stuck around, watching Lee do his thing. It was clear he was planning to go into some sort of extrahuman medicine in the future. Wood magi often did.

I wondered if maybe I should let him in on Hal's problem, but that wasn't for me to decide. Izzy came out of it in half a minute, immediately thirsty. I wondered how Lee had expected that. Maybe she'd done readings for him before or something, but if she'd channeled coincidence while doing it, it must've been a heavy topic.

She sucked down soda, grabbing the nine of swords off the table and putting it away in her bag. She looked up at me, saying nothing. I nodded, understanding. This was just part of her being psychic.

Cadence and I decided to cut things short, packing up Izzy's pizza and helping her out the door. Lee came along and walked all the way to Izzy's house with us. Once we handed her off to Abuela, Lee nodded and waved, heading back toward campus.

Cadence lingered for moment, so I asked if she was all right.

"I've been better, honestly. Sorry for acting so weird. But there's a lot going on I can't talk about. You probably don't understand."

"No, I get it." I reached out, patted her shoulder. "Hey, I'm the one who got the nine of swords, remember?"

"I thought I did." Cadence blinked.

I stood there musing. Izzy pointed across the table, where Cadence and I both sat. It could have been either of us. "Or maybe both."

"Both what?" Cadence chuckled softly. "Your inside voice is out of control again, huh?"

"I guess. I never could quite get a handle on that." I sighed. "It's gotten me into all sorts of trouble lately."

"I'm sorry about Alex. All the pushing I did, the assumptions I made." She held out her arms. "Can you forgive me?"

"Always." I hugged my friend, realizing that we were going to have loads to catch up on over the summer. But right now, standing out in the rapidly chilling air of late afternoon, wasn't the time. "Listen, Cadence. I'll definitely see you again this week. Hang in there. I've got to talk to Noah; it's overdue and important, and there's something I need to do before I can really figure the whole Alex thing out."

"Okay." She nodded. "Don't be a stranger. It feels like ages since you used the orb. Don't forget about us while you're in school. We all need each other, always have."

"I won't. I promise."

I walked up the driveway, glancing up at the living room window.

Noah sat in it, watching me approach the house. My parent's car was not there, so we'd finally have time.

CHAPTER FORTY-FIVE

Upstairs in Noah's room, we sat at the foot of his bed, our hands curled around mugs of hot chocolate. His had whipped cream with sprinkles and mine, marshmallows. But otherwise, we were practically mirror images of each other.

"This chocolate is forbidden." I smirked. "In your room."

"I can't risk Mom and Dad walking in. Or anyone else, for that matter." Noah shook his head as though he wore a ten-ton crown.

"You can't even talk about this in front of Bubbe?" Our grandmother was always more accepting than Mom and Dad. She could afford it, because our discipline wasn't in her hands.

"No. Well, I mean, I could." Noah stared at the ceiling, searching for words. "I'd trust her with that, I mean. But this is all just too painful."

"I understand."

"You can't possibly." He gazed down at his nearly melted whipped cream. "You've never been in love." Lotan slithered down the bed toward Noah, twining around his forearm, a gesture of support.

"Is that what this is about?" I was totally confused, and not just because I'd never been in romantic love with anyone. "Were you in love with Alex?"

"No, never." Noah's nose wrinkled like that time a skunk got into the backyard. "I caught him and Darren. You know, in the act? It was the day we got back to campus. Alex said some pretty awful stuff when I walked in there, like how he knew Darren had a boyfriend and didn't care. That was why we broke up."

"Holy shit, Noah." I spoke the oath so softly, it was barely there.

"Did he even tell you he was bi?" Noah's lips pressed together, paling. "Risky stuff, not talking about that sort of thing after dating for this long."

"I should have figured." I shook my head. "I mean, he asked if I was asexual. I totally don't know, and now I'm all confused."

"Maybe he's right." Noah shrugged. "But you know what they say about broken clocks twice a day, so that's why he's no good. Why you should dump him."

"I get it. Alex hurt you and Darren, and you don't want him to hurt me too."

"Pretty much." Noah closed his eyes, holding the hot chocolate under his nose. I did the same.

There's just something about chocolate. Even if you don't have a major sweet tooth and prefer it salted or spicy like Izzy, it helps. If there was anything on this Earth totally comforting and benign, it was chocolate in any way, shape, or form.

"I'm not even sure how we started going out. I went over it today with Izzy and Cadence."

"What did they have to say?"

Only last year, Noah would've snorted, skeptical that my friends could possibly give me any useful input on romance. But he understood that seven months at a specialized high school changed a person.

"That it sounds pretty toxic, actually. I'm only with him because he won't leave me alone. It's like default mode, you know?"

"No, I don't know. Because I've never been with someone just for the heck of it." He tilted his head, dark hair falling over one side of his face. "I won't date a guy unless I'm totally into him, whether that's because he's hot or fun or smart. Or even all three, like Darren."

"I'm not sure I've ever felt like that about anybody." I shook my head, immediately rescinding my lie before the evil inside voice butted in. "No. There's exactly one person."

"But he's taken, isn't he?" He raised an eyebrow. "You don't have to say his name."

"That's the size and shape of it, Noah." I leaned against his bedpost. Ember hopped off the dresser, gliding down to settle in my lap. "I'm doomed."

"No, you're not. One of the things Elanor kept telling me since the breakup was that they call it first love for a reason. It's the exact opposite of last love, right?"

"That's awfully deep stuff coming from her." I shrugged. "Logan always talks about how shallow she is."

"It's an act because that's what their parents want." Noah sipped his chocolate. "Logan never got with that program and he suffers for it every day."

"I know. I'm his friend remember?" I sighed. "Why do they make it so hard? His parents, I mean. And Faith's are even worse, encouraging their kids to terrorize each other. Why are they so horrible to their kids?" I drank some chocolate because it was the only thing I thought might ease my anguish.

"I don't think there's any particular reason, Aliyah." Noah leaned against his bedpost, taking a long sip of his now-temperate beverage. "Maybe we're just extremely lucky in the parental unit department."

"I love them so much. How do you deal with missing them at school? You don't come home very often, and I never understand why."

"That's exactly why I don't. If I did, it'd be like ripping off a band-aid every single time and I'd never heal."

Even growing up under the same roof and only a year apart, we were practically opposite—another mystery in the familial department. I was unsure of what to say about that, so I changed the subject.

"Will you ever forgive Darren?"

"Oh, Aliyah. I already did, months ago. Moments after I found out it happened, in fact."

"I don't understand." There was an awful lot of that going around for me today. "Why aren't you back together, then?"

"Darren doesn't want that. He's not in love with me." He sniffled, tears welling up even after all that time. "Said he never was."

"Oh, Noah. I'm so sorry." I set the hot chocolate down and open my arms, reaching toward my brother. Ember moved out of my lap, peeping softly.

He put his down too, with Lotan curled around the ceramic, and we hugged. As we sat, rocking back and forth in time to the tears falling on my shoulder, I realized something.

Noah had been carrying all this hurt secretly, hiding it under a veneer of cattiness and social climbing. That was why he'd followed Charity last semester, becoming one of her most tenacious hangers-on. While I set fires, he'd upended his social life. So much of it made sense now. And so did one other thing, from this new perspective.

If Noah was this traumatized about Alex, Darren, and my default dating status, what would it do to him when he found out I was an extramagus?

He'll probably die of a broken heart. Or kill you.

I started crying too because that was the only possible response for the evil inside voice this time. Our combined weeping made a melancholy sort of music that filled the room, heavier than the air we breathed.

By the time we finished, the chocolate was tepid. We didn't mind. I sat with my brother in silence, finishing our illicit upstairs beverages. When the cups were empty, we headed back to the kitchen together. For now.

———

Dinner was at five-thirty that night. Grace was back in time and told me Hal was coming at eight for Nin to have an extraveterinarian visit, so after dinner, Grace and I headed out to meet Hal on Essex Street.

The door to Hawthorn Academy was right next to the Witch's Brew this time, so we got ourselves some Red Zinger tea and an extra for Hal. When he emerged alone, we were both ready. Grace and I both rushed over to the door because he was awfully teetery on the cobblestones.

"Thanks." His smile was dim tonight, which really said something because Hal Hawkins usually had the brightest smile of anyone I knew.

"We're just going to take a nice, slow stroll here." Grace linked an arm through Hal's. "Like we're a bunch of tourist looky-loos, okay?"

"That sounds great." Hal nodded.

Nin poked her head out of his jacket's collar, squeaking at Ember. She glanced down at Lune and flared her nostrils in greeting.

She didn't look so great either, but mostly in ways that made me think the little Pharaoh's Rat hadn't slept well. Totally understandable. When a magus bonded to a familiar got sick, the poor critter ended up dropping the ball big time on their self-care.

We made it all the way to Izzy's house before Hal needed to rest, which meant this was a better day than I thought for him. The break from classes must have given him some much-needed time off from using his magic. We sat on the front stoop outside the psychic shop, drinking our tea.

Izzy waved from the window, then held up a feather duster. Clearly, Abuela had given her some evening chores, probably because she wasn't around much during the day. At least she looked like she'd recovered from that intense soothsaying at lunch.

The cups were empty by the time Hal was ready to get back up again. We easily made the walk between numbers 10 and 11 and up the drive to 10-1/2. Instead of opening the door to the stairs that led to my apartment, I reached for the shop's latch. Bubbe was expecting us.

"Come along back now." The corners of my grandmother's lips turned up, although I knew for sure she wasn't really smiling. Hal's appearance must've really shaken her. The fact that this was a good day for him made me feel horrible about waiting this long to get him here.

She brought us right into the kitchen and let Hal sit at the table.

Nin jumped out of his coat and scuttled around for a bit on the blue and white linoleum.

"Yes, little one." She nodded at the Pharaoh's Rat. "We're all concerned."

"You can't understand her, can you?" Hal tilted his head.

"No, but it's obvious from her body language that she's deeply worried about you." Bubbe opened a cabinet and brought out a blood exam kit.

The kits were in boxes wrapped in blue fabric. They contained one of the blood tests I mentioned before that we'd be using on Hal, and also a set of instruments for examining the ears, noses, and throats of most familiars. These had lights and magnifiers on them.

There was also a bisected basin, designed to either take samples or provide food and water. Because Bubbe was not really doing an exam on Nin today, she dumped a handful of treats in one side and poured water in the other. After that, she placed it in front of the little critter.

"Peep?" Ember headbutted me on the cheek, then looked at Nin and Lune.

"In a minute, girl. Let her eat first."

When Nin was done, Ember joined her on the floor, but the Pharaoh's Rat was near exhaustion. Ember escorted her across the floor toward a corner near the radiator. Lune had already parked his tail there, but he made room. Nin settled down between the moon hare and the dragonet, and Ember put her wing over the lot of them.

"Thank goodness for friends." Hal grinned.

"Indeed." Bubbe had already pricked his finger and was smearing blood on the plate for the test. She looked up at the clock to check the time, then down at the sample again.

We waited a full minute before the plate changed color, going purple. I had no idea what that meant, but Bubbe didn't like it one bit.

"How long have you had your powers, Hal?"

"To the point I could use them for anything besides feeling magic energy? Less than a year."

"What about before that?"

"Oh. Almost three."

"And your mother's not a magus?"

"No. She's psychic."

"And that's all?"

"Yeah. Psychometry. Touching things and getting an impression."

"I see. And do her powers always work?"

"You know, I never thought about that. Give me a minute." Hal closed his eyes. And yes, it was close to a minute before he opened them again and gave us an answer. "No, not always. I remember she had a problem a few years back at Gallows Hill. She couldn't tell which student had vandalized the lockers, and the principal pulled her yellow slip. She almost got accused of lying about her status."

He meant the license all practicing psychics have, especially when they worked in institutions like law enforcement or education.

"There's one more thing I need to test, Hal. Is that okay with you?"

"Sure. I'm just so tired of not knowing what's wrong with me." His eyes looked dry, like they were cried out and had given up on making any more tears over this mystery illness.

"Just a moment." Bubbe left the room, heading down to the end of the hall where the supply closet was.

While we waited, I puttered around the kitchen, cleaning the basin now that Nin was done with it. I just couldn't sit still, this was so nerve-racking. Bubbe had definitely found something. Whatever it was, it was serious enough that she wanted more information.

She came back with a venipuncture kit and a vial with a serial number on the name section of the label. An anonymous test of some kind.

"I never knew you had these kinds of human supplies here." I almost dropped the basin I was drying.

"Up until now, you haven't needed to." She unwrapped the needle with its tubing apparatus, leaving the business end capped. "When you get into the business of helping familiars, creatures so closely bonded to other beings, you find yourself crossing the line once in a while. And while I'm not licensed to treat illnesses of extrahumans, I can certainly send samples out so they can seek the care they need from properly qualified professionals."

"You mean we'll have to wait for the results?" Hal watched her swab the inside of his elbow with alcohol.

"Not all of them, but let me get the sample ready first. The holidays are coming, and the night courier will be here in minutes. I don't want to miss this window of opportunity."

She deftly punctured Hal's vein and pushed the rubber stopper on the vial onto the spike. Blood fountained into it. When she was done, she asked me to put pressure on the wound and bandage it, then hurried out the door and toward the front.

As I taped up Hal's tiny injury, I heard her speaking to someone out there, probably the courier. When she returned, he was all bandaged.

"I want you to listen to me very carefully, young Master Hawkins. Aliyah, you and Grace ought to head down to the storeroom and fetch some multivitamins for Nin. We don't want him returning to campus empty-handed."

Grace stood, and I tossed the bandage wrapper in the trash. We didn't hesitate to follow her instructions because we knew Bubbe would do the right thing by our friend, except Hal didn't want privacy.

"I don't want to hear this alone if it's all the same to you, Dr. Morgenstern."

"It's your right to privacy were talking about here."

"I trust my friends with my life." His smile was faint but present. "They brought me to you in the first place."

I blinked, almost sagging against the wall. I could hardly believe what I was hearing. Even though he knew beyond a doubt that I was an extramagus, Harold Hawkins trusted me implicitly. Grace took things in stride much more easily than I did. She had an admirable handle on this situation.

We grabbed chairs, dragging them around to his side of the table so we could sit next to him. Once we were all set, Bubbe nodded.

"The sample I sent off will verify the reason for this, but the test I did right here in this room is practically infallible." She reached across the table, taking both of Hal's hands in her own. She held them gently, as though they were made of eyelash-thin blown glass.

"You mean the purple smear?" He nodded. "Okay, what's it mean?"

"You have pernicious magiglobular anemia, a rare disease without any true cure." She gazed at his hands. "Symptoms include difficulty conjuring magical energy, inability to absorb magic energy from this realm's environment, and extreme fatigue after engaging in magical activity. Therapies include direct infusions from magical wells in the Under, which is easily done on campus. Doctor Br—I mean, Zeke has centuries of experience with those."

"I'm getting them every day. Sometimes more than once." He sighed, flexing his fingers slightly. "But I'm on the Bishop's Row team. That must be why it's so bad right now."

"When your test comes back, either visit me or find a way that we can chat. I've got a few other ideas, the basis for things that researchers in Boston are working with. Palliative, for comfort measures, these are. And I believe you may be in a position to give one of them a try on your own."

"Thanks, Dr. Morgenstern."

"That's not all, young man." Bubbe looked him right in the eye. "You should not continue with Bishop's Row."

"But Doc, we've got a tournament starting on Monday night. All our strategies hang on my space magic. I can't sit it out."

"You participate at extreme risk. Your results will be back Monday morning, so if the alternative therapy I mentioned will work for you, there's time to try it before your game. It won't make playing risk-free, but your energy levels won't crash as easily for a few hours afterward. However, you'll sit out on Tuesday if my hunch is correct. You'll sleep the clock round. But it will give your team time for alternate strategies after you stop playing."

"If you don't mind my asking, what's your hunch?" Hal pulled his hands back, staring at the backs of them, at the veins standing out.

"There are other forms of magiglobular anemia. They're generally caused by diet or environment, and people with those live full lives using magipsychic medicine every day. But the pernicious kind is genetic, and those treatments don't work. The only possible way you can have it is if someone in your family tree is a Dampyr."

"I understand." Whatever conclusion Hal came to, he didn't share it, at least for now. The pressure was on for my friend.

"Do you have any other questions?"

"No. I'll be sure to get in contact somehow, although short of leaving campus, I'm not sure."

Oh, dear. There's nothing to be done. All this effort for nothing.

I closed my eyes and clenched my fists, deciding how to defy the evil inside voice this time—and there was only one way. Because there was something to be done, but it meant revealing one of my secrets. A tame one, thankfully.

"I've got a communication orb at school." I opened my eyes, gazing right into Bubbe's. "I'll arrange for Hal to use it sometime Monday afternoon."

"Excellent." My grandmother's smile warmed my heart.

"You could get expelled for that." Hal blinked. "Not that I'm going to tell anyone at this point, but wow. Thanks, Aliyah, you're saving my life here."

"She has a way of doing that." Grace put her arm around Hal, patting his shoulder. "Saving the world one magus at a time."

They looked at me, grinning; they got me. I couldn't protest or go on about how I was doomed to go mad and turn evil someday because of what I was, not in front of my grandmother. And they knew it. Maybe this was their attempt to save *me*.

"I've got to feed the animals and close up for Passover, so unless you young folks want to clean some litter boxes—"

"No, we're good." I stood, assisting Hal to his feet, along with Grace. The last thing I wanted was for him to insist on doing chores while he was this exhausted.

"Thanks again, Dr. Morgenstern."

"I'd tell you not to mention it, but..." She rummaged in a pocket, produced a bottle of vitamins formulated for small magical carnivores, and passed them to Hal. "Give her one per day with food."

Hal nodded, then beckoned to Nin, who came scuttling across the floor. There must've been vitamins in the treats Bubbe gave her because she looked better already. Lune and Ember followed, both stretching before coming along after us.

For the matter of that, Hal looked better too. A diagnosis can have that effect right after it's made. I'd seen it a million times in here when magi discovered what conditions their familiars had, even a few of the terminal ones. Knowledge was power, even when the only control you had was how to face death.

We headed down the hall, through the waiting room, and out the door. We took our time again strolling down Essex Street, steeped in the remains of the evening.

CHAPTER FORTY-SIX

Passover was the celebration of liberation, but I felt like a slave to my powers. And also to the evil inside voice, because it hadn't left me alone for a whole day the entire semester. Its constant presence, naysaying half my choices and putting down everything from my academics to friendships, was an albatross around my neck.

I wished there was a way to be free of it, but the problem with maladies of the mind was that you couldn't get away. There was no running from a bully inside your head. Even with distraction, there was always part of your brain working without your knowledge. Mine tended to run counter to what was healthy.

When we'd celebrated Yom Kippur, the weight of my stress had lifted, something I'd experienced before. But with Passover, it was all about appreciating the freedoms you had while remembering what it was like to live without them. The Seder plate literally symbolized fight and flight from oppression.

All I could see was the prison of lies I'd built for myself. I barely remembered what it was like anymore, being open with my family. My mind had slipped, and my heart was just as bad. I knew what I wished to be free of, but it was utterly impossible to break those chains. I'd never heard of anyone losing their extramagus powers.

So, because I couldn't cast off my solar magic, visit plagues upon it, or part a sea to drown it, the only possible course was confessing everything. Being honest had always been my fallback until this year. The yoke of dishonesty galled me, wearing holes in my resolve and fraying the fabric of all my relationships.

At least I wasn't going it completely alone, although I'd always wonder whether my school friends only accepted me because I kept their secrets. Despite that, it was a comfort that Grace knew and was with me that day as we prepared for our Seder. Bubbe baked downstairs, so I was in the upstairs kitchen with Noah and Grace, helping Mom and Dad with everything else. This included finishing the soup, roast, and brussels sprouts, but also making sure we'd gotten rid of all the leavened grains in the house.

"Are you really throwing this out?" Grace raised an eyebrow as she held up a bag of Bubbe's challah rolls.

"If you want to bring it back to school with you, go ahead. Just stow it in your luggage because we can't keep it in the kitchen." My mother nodded toward the stairs.

"Thanks. I've been craving this bread since Thanksgiving." Grace dashed up the stairs and returned in a few moments.

That was it for leftover leavened goods. Tonight, and for the next eight days, it'd be all matzoh all the time. Fortunately, there were several varieties, so there was plenty to bring back to school, and I wouldn't get bored with it.

During my long-overdue conversations yesterday, Mom and Dad had gone out to get the symbolic foods and all the special Kosher for Passover stuff they'd use this week. The most well-known was matzoh, but there were so many others.

From pasta to jam and everything in between, there was a version that was Kosher for Passover. That seemed sort of extra, but it was all because the ancient Israelites didn't have time to let their bread rise as they fled Egypt. Things like meats are specially blessed by a rabbi, but other more shelf-stable foods had substitutions for any leavened ingredient, and those got certified too. Nothing like croutons or breadcrumbs were in those items. Yes, we got that particular about it.

Most of the work was already done. All that needed doing now was setting the table. It was different from Thanksgiving because Passover had both religious and cultural significance. You didn't just yeet thousands of years of tradition without a good reason, so this night was different from any others.

One way was in how we arranged our seating. We sat upright at all our other meals, but on Passover, we got comfy. The *Haggadah*, that book of instructions for Passover, called it reclining. What that really meant was we could put our feet up or lean back or add extra cushions to the chairs. One year, Noah even set up piles of pillows on the floor, insisting he and I have our meal there.

We set up the Seder plate. This was the big symbol energy of the entire holiday, so it always went right in the center of the table. Ours was enameled wood, white with blue edging, with four sections ringing the sides and one in the middle. Remember when I said before that this holiday symbolizes escape from slavery in Egypt? Every item on that plate represented a different part of what our ancient forebears experienced.

I helped Mom put everything on it, just like last year. The only thing different this time was Grace watching over my shoulder. And Ember, perched on top of the refrigerator.

"What's that parsley in middle?" Grace asked.

"*Karpas.*" Mom added more. "It represents how the Israelites first came to Egypt. Joseph brought them."

"Who?"

"You know." I snapped my fingers. "Remember that musical we watched last week with the guy in the coat of many colors who interprets dreams? And for a while, it was good. Sort of like parsley when you first taste it."

"Raw parsley doesn't have a pleasant aftertaste." She wrinkled her nose.

"That's why we use it," Dad said. "Life in ancient Egypt was like that. Bitter later on. At one point, we'll dip it in saltwater because it got so bad."

"That actually looks good." Grace pointed as the paste of fruit and nuts. "What is it?"

"*Haroset.*" I spooned some on the appropriate section of the plate. "This is my favorite because it's delicious."

"What does it mean?"

"It's all about the labor," Noah answered. "The mortar we used, building for the Pharaoh. But this stuff's nasty." He wrinkled his nose and dropped a dollop of horseradish on the plate. "*Maror,* standing in for the bitterness of slavery."

"I knew people who had it with sandwiches on the regular." Grace shrugged. "But yeah, it's strong. Do you actually eat any of this stuff?"

This time, Bubbe answered.

"At one point during the meal, we mix the *haroset* with *maror,* because while labor can be sweet, forced labor is bitter. It gets pressed between two pieces of matzoh, just like mortar between bricks. And we eat the *karpas,* both before the saltwater dip and after. But two items on that plate, we don't eat. They're for contemplation."

"Right." I nodded. "The *zeroah* and *beitzah.*"

"The what and the who now?" Grace blinked.

"*Zeroah* is that lamb shank," Dad explained. "It symbolizes the Israelite's sacrifices and celebrations after reaching Jerusalem. And *beitzah* is this roasted egg. Any guesses on what it means, Grace?"

"Life and hope?"

"Egg-zactly." Dad chuckled.

Everyone groaned.

"But there's a little more than that to Passover." Bubbe patted my shoulder. "The egg reminds us that this too shall pass."

For me this year, that was an enormous truth, one so big that perhaps I hadn't been able to see it through all my inner turmoil and chaos.

The plate was finally done, so we brought it out and set it on the table. Noah followed with three pieces of matzoh covered in a cloth. Dad brought out the dish with saltwater for the parsley.

Noah headed back to the kitchen, then returned with an orange. This was something he did last year after coming out because an orange symbolized the social and emotional fruitfulness that comes with including everyone in our society. He set it on his right beside his plate, which was where we always put the items that represented liberation to us personally.

Grace had some of that shimmery copper fabric, the stuff that had been the overlay on her dress for Valentine's Day. Making her own clothes, stuff that rivaled a masterwork of tailoring, was an amazing accomplishment.

Bubbe had a carefully preserved photo of her father as a boy, standing in Trafalgar Square in London. He'd just arrived there as part of the Kindertransport program, rescued from certain death in Nazi camps.

Dad and Mom usually placed their wedding rings there because they always told us they'd saved each other, though never how. But this year, it was different. Dad had his diploma from Hawthorn Academy. I think because both Noah and I attended, working hard at school, he wanted to show us how important education was to living a free life.

Mom had a clipping from the Providence Journal. It showed a picture of her, one I never knew existed. She walked down the steps in front of the Extrahuman Courthouse downtown, cameras and microphones pointed at her face. She wasn't looking down, although the shot they chose for this piece was in profile. My mother faced whichever reporter or photographer stood in front of her, staring them down with a gaze as intimidating as any eagle's. The date was over the summer, only one week before she gave me the swimsuit.

The headline read *Estranged Hopewell sister testifies against extramagus brother.*

I felt strange that I didn't have something of my own this year. Usually, it was some paper or project from school I had done particularly well on, or something from Izzy or Cadence, symbolizing how important friendship is. But I had nothing this year because I felt caged.

Our readings came from the abbreviated *Haggadah*, which didn't take long. This was good because my stomach already grumbled, and

D.R. PERRY

Grace was in the same boat. We'd skipped lunch. Big mistake, but easily rectified.

My father recited the Plagues of Egypt in Hebrew, something he'd always done. After that came the Four Questions, which Noah and I took turns reciting. Reading them wasn't required because they were in our memories forever now. It was something we did together every Passover. Usually, it's the youngest child, but being only a year apart meant he only would have read them once in his life.

One of the best things about this part of Seder was that when we had guests, like Grace this year or Izzy and Cadence on others, they got to learn why everything was just so on Passover. Grace didn't even have to ask why this night was different, why we ate only matzoh and no bread, why we dipped bitter herbs twice, and why we got cozy seats.

The short answers were that we celebrated freedom, the Israelites had no time to let the bread rise, we needed to remember bitterness to appreciate sweetness, remembering tears helps us appreciate joy, and people needed time and space to rest and celebrate after going through trauma.

So that was Passover in a nutshell, but my dilemma was far from over. I had nothing to share because I felt hollow, as though I was the *beitzah* egg but just the shell. I sat staring at it, sometimes averting my gaze to the news clipping at Mom's right.

Bubbe's story about her photograph was part of family legend. Noah's explanation for his orange was the same as last year. Dad's was new but predictable. Grace said only one sentence, that with freedom comes responsibility to craft a life from what you've learned.

We all hung on Mom's every word. This was a story even Dad might not have heard in full. She'd offered to testify, wasn't responding to subpoena. She said it was her duty to go on record as saying that Richard's crimes were part of a lifelong pattern. That he'd never change or get better unless he admitted to his shortcomings and sought help on his own.

How could I be the daughter of woman this brave? One who summoned the courage to leave her oppressive family, then decades

410

later, spoke out against the worst and most dangerous of them? And she had done it all without a familiar; that was something I got from Dad's side of the family, not hers. The Hopewells were nothing if not supremacists, in more ways than one. They believed magi were above all other people and that magic creatures were there for our amusement, not as friends or even companions.

I wasn't sure how she bucked the odds, but as I stared again at the *beitzah* egg, contemplating that the one constant in this world was change, I felt something tiny but warm, like that first ray of sunlight hitting the icicle that forms every year outside my window. The one that brings it down, eventually.

Maybe I wasn't brave like Mom because that was not what I needed to overcome my circumstances. Maybe I needed my family and friends. Perhaps the best way to fight my inevitable descent into the madness too much magic brought was just love.

"Ember, come here, girl." I patted the empty space to my right, where my item would be. No material thing I possessed could represent this new faint hope for redemption.

"What's this, Aliyah?" Bubbe raised an eyebrow.

"This year, it's my bond with Ember that liberates me." I managed a grin as she swooped toward me.

As my dragonet lit on the table between my brother and me, I understood that the lies needed to stop, but not tonight. I'd keep my secret until after the game tomorrow because just like Hal, I'd let down our entire year if I had to bow out. All I had to do was make sure I didn't accidentally conjure anything solar during the game.

Piece of cake, right?

CHAPTER FORTY-SEVEN

On Monday, we were all back at school, finally. Faith didn't get in until the last train up from Boston on Sunday. Logan's flight was a red-eye, so he didn't arrive until early in the morning. He practically fell asleep in his eggs, so it was a good thing he wasn't on the team.

Alex kept his distance. Instead of following me closely as he'd done since the dance, he had his head down over his books and notes. Maybe he was behind on studying, or perhaps Ember made faces at him when I wasn't looking. More likely, he knew I'd spent the whole week in the same house as Noah.

The plan was to have a chat with him later today. For all I knew, he'd been as weighed down by guilt this year as I was. Or maybe not. The biggest takeaway I had this Passover came from Mom and also what she'd testified about Uncle Richard. Some people wanted to do better. Others weren't ready. If Alex was, maybe that'd help me decide how I felt about him.

We had a half-day of classes, which was the case all week because of the tournament. So, we went to homeroom and then Creatives, where we could all chat before heading to the locker room. Alex sat at a drafting table, sketching something. All my other friends hovered over a table in the middle, making collages.

"Aliyah, what's wrong with you?" Faith shook her head. "You've been stiff all day, almost awkward. I saw you drop your pencil like twenty times in homeroom. Are you nervous about the game?"

"No. She's carrying something important for me." Hal glanced at my knapsack, which looked heavier than usual.

It wasn't. I just put extra padding in there to protect the communication orb. Izzy had brought hers to Bubbe's office before leaving for school, so she could take Hal's call.

"Okay." Faith put her hands on her hips, tapping her toe and giving her boyfriend side-eye. "This is something to do with that stuff we talked about last night, right?"

"Yes."

I knew what the alternative therapy was, too, because Bubbe had let me in on it. She'd even given me a clinical description so they could try it before the game. Yes, I was going to use my contraband orb that could get me expelled right there in the locker room before a tournament game.

Grace had an idea on how to do that covertly. She offered to hide the orb and Bubbe's side of the conversation from casual view with umbral magic. Anyone walking by would see Hal but would think he held a more benign item. He'd be talking to it, so we'd need to cover his voice mundanely. This meant we'd need to shut him in the sauna without turning it on or sit in one of the showers with the water running.

We all agreed that the sauna was the better choice. It was a gender-neutral area, while two of the showers weren't. The entrance to the one gender-neutral shower we had was in a high-traffic area, while the sauna was off in the corner. Also, nobody used saunas before a workout, but sometimes folks showered before games to invigorate themselves.

We bailed on Creatives early, heading to the locker room. The headmaster let us go because it was our first real game. He must have assumed we were super nervous and wanted to be totally prepared, which worked in our favor. Hopefully, more than this would go right today, but I wasn't counting any chickens.

The wood-lined room was dry and warm; quiet, too. I bet the Night Creatures would have loved to use it as a studio if it weren't for the fire pit in the corner that supplied the extreme heat when the sauna was in use. Hal sat on a bench, and I got the orb out of my knapsack. Grace touched it, conjuring her magic to obscure its true nature. Once I set it in Hal's hands, the orb resembled a library book, at least unless you got closer than arm's length.

It would seem weird if anyone walked in. I mean, who read books in the sauna, especially when it wasn't even on. I figured other students might imagine this was a weird sports-related superstition. Coach Pickman would not be so easily fooled, so I positioned myself by the window as a lookout.

"Hello?" Bubbe's voice was tinny coming through the orb. "Am I speaking with Harold?

"Hi, Dr. Morgenstern," Hal replied quietly, nodding.

"Well, your results came back, and you definitely have Dampyr DNA. It's a significant amount too, so that means it's a very close family member.

"So it's my mom." Hal's voice was flat.

"Perhaps, but the only way to know for certain is if your parents take their own tests."

"Well, at least this can't make Easter dinner awkward since that already happened." Hal's words belied the gravity in his tone.

Getting hit with a secret identity out of left field was like being in a car crash. Everything slowed down. Each object in your field of vision was at an impossible angle, and when you tried to make sense of things, they moved again. There was nothing about the world that you could pin down in an immediate sense. The only thing that helped after it all stopped was time and distance. "And Hal doesn't have much of either."

"I don't have what now?" Hal blinked.

"Sorry." I shook my head. "Inside voice being a jerk."

Oh, you don't know the half of it.

I closed my eyes, leaning against the door, using my ears instead for my lookout duties. It was hard to focus on whether there were footsteps outside the sauna, though, not with Hal getting bleak for the first time where his friends could see it. I wouldn't lie to myself and pretend someone as ill as Hal hadn't despaired in private.

"Is there a way for me to find out if my dad's really my father?"

"I'd say he is. You resemble him quite closely when he was your age, in feature and build. Besides, space magic is quite rare. It's practically impossible that if your mother were unfaithful, she'd have found another space magus to carry on with on this side of the Atlantic."

"Nothing's impossible for magi." Hal's voice cracked. He cleared his throat and continued, "Pardon my language, but coincidence is a bitch, Dr. Morgenstern."

"I already checked the registry, Harold. There are no space magi besides you and your father on this side of the Atlantic Ocean. And you're pardoned in my book."

"That means nothing. Mom's on the registry as a psychic, not a Dampyr. There must be something more to this than even you found out. How do I look for it?" He sniffled. "You're the only person who's given me anything like a real answer about any of this, so what do I do now?"

"You try the therapy. You play your game." Bubbe's voice was too even, the way it got when she delivered the worst news about a patient.

"I'm talking about in the long-term, doctor."

"Get through this day. Come by anytime this week. We'll discuss that."

"Okay, but when I do, we're making a list of questions for my parents. They will explain this."

I stood with my back to the door, staring at Hal, my chin practically on the floor. I'd never seen him angry, nor even imagined it. And yet there he was, totally justified in it.

You've dropped the ball, Aliyah.

The evil inside voice sounded like it clicked its tongue even though it didn't have one.

The door hit me in the back as someone pushed through it. I tried leaning backward, keeping it closed, protecting my friends, but it was no use. My knees got weaker than a little door pushing should have made them. My head lighter too, so I knew who was trying to bust in.

"Get out of here, Alex." I turned, trying to push with my arms and get it to close, but his foot and his arm were already in the door.

"Why are you in there with the headmaster's son?"

"None of your business." I glared at him. "Shut off your poison immediately." He knew Hal was sick, and that room was small. "Or I swear—"

"Fire is a bad idea in there without the vent on, Aliyah." His chuckle was low and rolling. And entirely inappropriate in this situation. "So is poison. Which is the worse way to go, I wonder?"

Some folks would have been startled by a callous remark like that. Not me. Remember my first day? Yeah. Let's just say I wasn't reacting with a flight response here.

"I'm going outside, you guys."

I opened the door just wide enough to get out, physically blocking Alex from entering the room and pushing him out of the way. Even through the poison-induced haze, somehow, I found the strength. When Ember dropped down from the perch outside and above the sauna door, I understood.

My familiar channeled some of her strength into me. This was like that first day in the cafeteria, except I hadn't conjured any fire in my hands. It was all in my body, fighting the poison. I felt it burning out of me instead of through my veins, Ember helping me to use it as a purifying force.

"You are the pushiest person I know." I crossed my arms over my chest, blocking the doorknob with my body. "I can't believe you tried gassing a room with three people inside and then laughed about it."

"I'm shocked." He blinked. "I thought you'd have a sense of humor like my cousin. And ambition, like your uncle."

"Not really." I shook my head, finally getting the picture.

The evil inside voice had been right. Alex Onassis did admire me for being an extramagus. For all the wrong reasons. He was a bully but stuck with a subtle sort of magic, so he was looking for a partner with power, and he thought he'd found one.

But you're too kind. Such a shame.

"Not really," I repeated. "We're breaking up, Alex."

"That's sudden." He licked his lips. "Are you sure?"

"I should've talked to Noah sooner, and then it really would've been sudden." I snorted.

"Are you worried I'll cheat on you?" He rolled his eyes. "It won't happen again. If I'd known how powerful you were, I'd have kept my hormones in check around your brother's boy-toy."

"You never asked if I wanted to date you. You just assumed and followed me everywhere. Toxic City."

"Women want a man who takes what he wants." His chin was clenched, but his eyes darted from one side to the other. "I'll ask again. Are you sure we're breaking up?"

"You broke my brother's heart for kicks." I narrowed my eyes. "So yes, I'm sure."

"Aliyah, do you need help?" It was Faith. Her hands were shrouded in the faint gray of undeath energy, and she wasn't alone, either. Seth stood with all four of his feet planted on the tile, growling at Alex.

"Thanks for the back-up." I jerked my chin at Alex. "Maybe now he'll take no for an answer."

"Dumping me right before the game? That's classy." Alex smirked. "You're judging me for what happened on the first day. Honestly, I expected greater things from you."

"It's not something that happened; you made a choice." I shot a glance at Faith. "You knew Darren was Noah's boyfriend. You should have apologized and owned up. But instead, you act like you're too good for that."

"Wait." Faith blinked. "That was you? Jerk."

"I went to a great deal of trouble to keep my name out of that particular rumor mill." Alex looked down his nose at me. Or tried to, because we were almost the same height. "If it finds its way back in, be assured yours will join it."

"Wow." Dylan came around the corner, eyes in a constant state of motion between me, Faith, and Alex. "Did I just hear you threaten my friend?"

"Grow up, Khan. It's only quid pro quo." Alex dropped his hands to his sides. "If she doesn't want any trouble, my ex will fall in line. We'd better start warming up, getting prepared to play rough."

He walked away, but overall, I figured this was a victory despite his veiled threats. Sure, I ran the risk of having my secret outed before I was ready. Once I did, Alex Onassis and his rumor mill would have no power over me. I hoped.

"Is Hal in there?" Faith jerked her thumb at the sauna door.

"Yes, Grace too." I heard footsteps in the room behind me. "And they're done." I stepped aside and let my friend through.

Grace came out with my knapsack, packed up again. She handed it off, then headed toward the lockers, Dylan following. Faith went in to sit with Hal. When I peeked through the window, I saw them holding hands with their eyes closed, the paper with Bubbe's instructions on it beside them. They were doing the therapy, which involved using undeath magic to stabilize Hal's regulation of his space magic.

I stayed outside the sauna, guarding the door because the last thing I wanted was Alex learning even more secrets. He might know mine, having guessed correctly because he'd seen it before, but my friends shouldn't pay for my mistake in trusting him.

In about five minutes, the pair emerged, faces flushed and holding hands. The bond I always sensed between them was stronger than ever.

I walked with them to the lockers where we stored our stuff and changed. After that, we put on and tested our ankyr and cestus, including the new professional-grade ballistae. These were worn in televised tournaments. They added refinement to channeling so extra energy didn't escape our hands, making the conjure more efficient and less draining.

I realized that these ballistae might help the other types of extrahumans playing this sport. Part of the reason psychic energy and glamour were so hard to use for conjuring orbs was that they were more diffuse and harder to focus, but with gear like this that funneled as you channeled, maybe it was possible for them to really generate a good orb and throw it with accuracy.

Maybe that was how folks like Izzy could play. Precognition, telepathy, projection. Mentalist psychics, whose powers didn't otherwise manifest, now had a way to participate if they wanted to. Was this the big secret Izzy was keeping?

Coach Pickman blew her whistle. It was time for us to head out of the locker room and onto the court.

The first team we faced off against was my brother's. If it hadn't been for our conversation last week, this would have caused me no end of stress, but now there were no hard feelings, except the ones I carried inside, secret for now. I'd have to handle my confession delicately and do all I could to spare his feelings since my brother would always be important to me.

I stood behind Grace, waiting for Coach Pickman and the second-year team's Coach Ives to call for the coin toss. Noah caught my eye, nodding from his position as second defense. Our whole team already knew to watch out for his solar magic. He'd used it to blind other players before.

One reason this game was so exciting was that players could use tactics like that. As long as an orb was held in a defensive posture, moving around and letting its general effects just happen was perfectly within the rules.

Fortunately, we had Grace to counter that, and she excelled at staying on her toes. I fully expected this game to go long, potentially even for us to win since Hal's abilities were totally unknown to the other side.

The first defense guy was another air magus. They were pretty common, so it was no wonder the school had so many in attendance. He wouldn't be able to block my fire too well, so I could mostly ignore his defense and take him out as soon as I got the chance.

The other mid-players were both girls, earth and water, respectively. I wouldn't be able to do much against either of them, but Alex could negate both with relative ease. Considering his state of mind wasn't the best at the moment, I expected him to be especially fierce on the court. Hopefully, all the activity would take his anger down a notch or three.

Perhaps he could channel his anger at me into something constructive during this game. All the activity might even chill him out enough to reconsider the threatened vengeance angle. I might hope for the best, but I had no illusions about him apologizing anytime soon.

The person we really needed to worry about on the other team was their reverse point. It was Elanor Pierce, Logan's sister. I know, she didn't seem like the type to play competitive sports, let alone have any talent at it, but assumptions were bunk, so there you go.

She was uncommonly quick at conjuring her fire magic and throwing too. According to everything I'd read about her in the notes from last year, Elanor had also mastered the art of the fake-out. That meant she'd be able to conjure and misdirect almost everyone on our team. Part of team planning over the last month had involved me keeping an eye on her because I could sense fire energy. I'd be able to tell where she was actually aiming.

Other than that, most of what we'd do was protect Dylan. He had loads of stamina and could dodge most anything as long as we backed him up.

All we needed to do now was flip a coin.

CHAPTER FORTY-EIGHT

The coin toss didn't go in our favor. I watched Noah conjure, calling forth his solar magic with a smirk on his face, which meant almost everyone on the team squinted or otherwise tried shielding their eyes.

He was my brother, so I knew better.

I stared him right in the eye, watching them widen as he realized I wasn't falling for his shtick. I conjured fire right back, and although I'm slower than him, it wasn't enough.

He wound up with both hands spinning his ball of daylight-bright solar energy. I knew he wasn't really going to blind my entire team, so I tossed my own orb in the air, knocking his out of the way before it could hit Hal in the chest. He'd covered his eyes and didn't see it coming, of course.

Maybe it would have been better for Hal, in the long run, to have let Noah's throw hit its mark, but there was nothing I could do about it now. Alex was there, leaping toward the middle to counter a chunk of earth heading straight for Dylan. It pattered to the ground, then vanished as the court's wards banished the energy. But Alex wasn't paying attention to his footwork, so he slipped on some before it dissipated and ended up on the floor.

This meant Dylan had no protection except his own air orb. I was still conjuring and didn't have enough to counter the ball of water coming straight for him, not that my element was much good against that anyway. But he had it handled.

Dylan's orb spun like a tornado, so when he held it up in front of his chest and pressed forward with it, the water orb appeared to shatter, bits scattering everywhere. Once the orb's cohesion broke, none of the droplets could tag us out. I got hit with a few, and they were almost impossibly cold. That was a helpful side effect of the unexpected shower. It stopped Hal from spacing out.

I wracked my brain, trying to remember any details about the alternative therapy Bubbe gave us, and there was one that might have accounted for that. The therapy was only possible because Faith used undeath energy, but that particular brand of magic came with its own set of problems when used on the living. Hal was a little bit zombified, which ended up being a good thing.

Elanor did one of her fake-outs. I sensed it, but she was so fast I didn't have time to warn my teammate. Hal didn't need one now that his eyes were open. Whatever Faith did, it gave him crazy reflexes. He blinked to one side as the fire orb sailed by, bouncing harmlessly out of bounds.

The girl casting earth stood there flabbergasted, leaving her wide open for Alex's orb. He hit her directly on the cestus, which flashed red as she was tagged out.

I hear Kitty, Eston, and Logan cheering from the bleachers. Our three friends were so gung-ho excited that we scored the first out, and that was where Dylan's gregarious nature failed him.

Dylan Khan was my favorite goofball in the world, so of course, he smiled and waved at our friends. It was a natural thing for him, but this game was unforgiving, so Elanor took her opportunity to throw another orb.

It must have been all the performance art training that had built her speed to that degree. I could imagine that in order to be entertaining with fire magic, you had to summon and banish your element with extreme alacrity. It served her well here, but her orbs ended up small and not so powerful. It was the same for Lee with his wood magic. I knew exactly how to deal with that.

By being stronger.

Grace had to hold her action in case Noah tried a blinding move, so I leaped into the middle, holding up my own fireball. Because it was the same element, Elanor's didn't dissipate. Instead, mine absorbed it, and I found myself breathless at how fast it all happened.

Or maybe it was the giant fiery orb eating all the oxygen next to my face.

My power level was exponentially larger than hers. She was a candle in the wind, while I was walking on the sun, but finesse could still win the day if I wasn't careful.

Throw it already before you incinerate yourself.

"Thanks, broken clock." I rolled my eyes along with the orb. Nobody needed to know I was talking to the evil inside voice, but I was. It was right.

I threw at Noah. He was the most dangerous player besides Elanor, who was better protected. The last thing we needed was someone getting blinded.

Ducking wouldn't help Noah, and he knew it. He hit the deck, flattening himself on the floor. He was as nimble as Grace. My fireball almost hit the mid-player behind him, but she managed to hop aside in time because I wasn't aiming for her.

I conjured again. It felt different. Why?

Solar magic. That's why.

"Stop. Banish time."

Beside me, Alex chuckled. I ignored him and conjured fire again, my focus intense. Meanwhile, Grace blocked a throw from their second defense. It would've hit me.

"Thanks."

She nodded and conjured shadows again.

Noah recovered with another sunlit orb, and everybody expected him to throw it instead of blinding us. But he aimed at Alex—at his head, not his cestus. I understood. He was angry. As much as I'd like to see Noah get revenge, I needed to make this play count.

So I launched my off-color orb. I missed, failing to deflect my brother's attack. Alex ducked, laughing. He avoided Noah's orb easily but took mine directly in the gut, sneering.

He wanted you to hit him, foolish girl.

His cestus flashed red, and just like that, Alex Onassis was out.

I blinked. How did this happen? The team's magic got calibrated to our equipment last week, so it shouldn't have triggered an out. But as my energy faded into Alex's protective gear, I saw it.

My orb had been solar magic after all, masked by a thin veneer of fire, which meant I had conjured both elements at the same time, using one to hide the other. And magicpsychic equipment doesn't lie.

A blast from Coach Chen's whistle cut the air, stopping the game.

I just told you there are no breaks in Bishop's Row, but that wasn't entirely true. If there was equipment failure or suspicion of cheating, any coach could call time out.

He led both teams to the sidelines where Coach Pickman, Headmaster Hawkins, and the second-year coaches waited. All four looked over Alex's equipment, checking for tampering or malfunction. They found nothing, of course, since this was all my fault.

They're going to catch you.

The singsong taunt from the evil inside voice was more than I could take. Yes, I was being a stereotypical fire magus and losing my temper. Anyone might have at that point. I'd spent months dealing with that incessant voice in silence. Not since the solar magic showed up. I understood now. It had first chimed in when I started lying. It was time to stop this insanity, or at least give it less to plague me with.

I raise my hand.

"Headmaster, I've got something to say."

"Step forward, Miss Morgenstern."

All my friends stared at me, mouths open and eyes wide. Except for Alex, who glared poison darts. Looked like I had made another enemy. I took a deep breath and prepared to own my mistake.

"I'm sorry, everyone. I didn't lie exactly, but I failed to report some-thing. You have to disqualify me. Put Lee or Faith on the court in my place. This is my fault, not a malfunction."

"How?" The headmaster leaned forward.

"I thought I could control it just for one game. I was going to step down later. But now I have to say this in public."

"Say what, exactly?" Noah stepped forward. He was as pale as a vampire.

"Shh." Elanor put her hand on his arm, shaking her head.

"I'm an extramagus with solar magic." I raised my head, which felt weightless. "If that disqualifies me from Bishop's Row forever, I understand. If it's grounds for expulsion, I'll appeal through the proper channels with my parents."

"You're certainly not expelled, Miss Morgenstern." Headmaster Hawkins stood. "The athletic staff makes all the team decisions, including ability-related accommodations. However, I can't allow you to continue to play in this tournament."

"Somebody could've gotten hurt." Alex stepped forward. "If my equipment hadn't held up, I'd have second-degree burns by now."

"Not true." Coach Pickman snorted. "You were perfectly safe, Onassis. This court's got extra safety wards. I insisted after Morgen-stern made the team. I hadn't forgotten the cafeteria incident that first day. Had you?"

"She lied. Won't she be punished?" Noah's question shocked me.

But it made sense. He was hurt again. I had blown my chance to tell him over break about all of this, and only a person completely bereft of empathy wouldn't realize Hal, Grace, and Dylan already knew my secret. My brother always caught the feels.

"Wouldn't you feel punished if you got disqualified for the whole tournament? They've been practicing for months." Coach Ives, the fellow in charge of Noah's team, punched his shoulder. "I believe that's sufficient. At least, I'm satisfied on behalf of my players."

"It's settled, then." Headmaster Hawkins nodded. "Coach Pickman will retrieve a new set of equipment for Mr. Onassis and choose a reserve player to replace Miss Morgenstern, who will accompany me to my office."

"Father." Hal tilted his head, wringing his hands. "Please stay."

"I don't know what this development's about, but I'll grant that request, Harold. However, Miss Morgenstern sits with me, not on the reserves bench."

"Thanks, Dad."

The headmaster led me to the sidelines, then toward a section of unoccupied bleachers. It was far away and not at the best angle, but at least we could watch the rest of the game. Probably, he wanted to make sure I didn't hurt anyone. Ironically, I felt like less of a risk to the people around me now than before my hasty confession.

Coach Pickman tapped Lee to take my place. I'd been hoping for Faith since she might have been able to help Hal if anything happened and he ran out of energy. I understood her strategy, though. With Elanor and Noah both capable of fast conjuring, she needed someone with speed. Faith was pretty fast, but nothing like Lee.

It was a jungle out there, in no small part because Alex was even angrier now. He played with a ferocity that could only come from extreme rage. I was worried about how the rest of the semester would go, sitting in classes with him.

I used to think he was neutral, like Switzerland, and this whole year, I had felt like the only person living a lie. I had been wrong. While my secret was a condition beyond my control, Alex took actions of his own volition. He hurt other people on purpose.

I knew there was a difference, but contemplating intent didn't make this easier. I had still lied, and people I loved were still in the dark. I sighed.

"How long have you known?" The headmaster kept his voice low even though the roaring crowd obfuscated it from eavesdroppers.

"Since the first lab." I hung my head.

"You're not the first extramagus on campus, you know."

"What?" I froze.

"Your grandmother had a brother. Same elements and everything."

"I've never—she's never spoken of him. Not once. There aren't even pictures."

"And you haven't told her." His voice was as deep and gentle as a cup of herbal tea. "Am I correct?"

"Yes." I nodded, wiping the tear off my cheek. Bubbe would have understood, after all. "Do you think she'll forgive me?"

"Peep?" Ember put her paws on my leg, peering at my lap, a signal she wanted to sit in it. I moved my arms to make room for her.

"There's only one way to find out. I want you to go home this evening after dinner. Talk to your family."

"Are you sending Noah home too?"

"That's up to him. But if he chooses to, I'll give you a head start. It's your responsibility to tell your parents, not his."

"Headmaster, th—"

My expression of gratitude was cut off by something horrible.

The whistle blew. Hal collapsed.

I didn't remember us rushing to his side, but that must have been what we did because we were there like no time had passed. Faith arrived first, then the headmaster. I stopped to stand with my friends, unsure what good my presence would do.

There was a tension in the gymnasium, one that could erupt into panic at any moment. I couldn't do anything to counter it because I might have been one of the sources. What was scarier than a magus collapsing due to an unknown malady? An extramagus standing up and taking initiative, of course.

So, I stayed back and left it to someone else to pick up the slack. And just like on Parents' Night, Logan Pierce stepped up and saved the day.

He dashed down off the bleachers, stacking equipment chests and standing on them so everyone could see him. After that, he opened his mouth and let out a cacophony of sound. I'd never seen anything like it, but somehow, I knew what Logan was doing.

He was talking to everyone's familiars like Doctor Freaking Doolittle.

Magi were subject to mob mentality like mundane folk or any

other extrahuman. A group of us incensed or frightened could cause serious harm, but when you added magical creatures into the mix, especially nervous ones with their emotions magnified in the echo chamber of bonds with magi, you had the potential for epic levels of disaster.

The noises Logan made were soothing somehow, despite their alien nature. He'd mastered practically every critter call in the book: peeps and chirps, warbles and coos, barks and growls, howls and meows, even whinnies and bleats.

The critters paused. One by one, I saw them relax. The airborne ones landed, and the landbound ones sat or laid down. Some cuddled together like the best of friends, while others ignored each other in comfortable silence.

The calm spread, overtaking the sea of troubled magi in moments. Each found his or her familiar nearby. It wasn't entirely silent in here since that was impossible in a gymnasium, but there was enough time and space for everyone helping Hal to do their jobs. For him to breathe.

Nurse Smith and Zeke lifted Hal on to a stretcher, an oxygen mask covering the lower half of his face. Seth jumped up on it, cuddling up with Nin. Faith kissed his forehead, then returned to the court and put on her equipment. She'd finish the game for him.

But the headmaster wasn't staying, not in the middle of his son's medical emergency, so neither could I. I followed him, joining the procession to the infirmary.

Once Hal was in bed with the transfusion tube in his arm, Headmaster Hawkins finally took me to his office. Instead of sitting at his desk, he stood with his back toward me, leaning on one of the built-in bookcases behind his seat as though he and the school held each other up.

I remained standing too, with Ember curled around my neck. It just felt wrong to sit when he hadn't yet. He was the ultimate figure of authority at Hawthorn Academy, but he was only extrahuman. This was his first year in this job, and his son was gravely ill, maybe dying.

He's weak. Use that. Prove your worth.

"No."

"Excuse me?"

"I said no, but not to you, sir." I walked toward the desk, then past it. Once I was beside him, I spoke again. "What I meant to say was, how can I help?"

"There's nothing you can do. Everything's complicated by my ex-wife. It's enough that you've befriended my son."

"Are you sure there's nothing I can do?" I turned my back and leaned against the bookcase, looking up at him. "My grandmother's got all kinds of medical connections. I can ask for her help."

"I know about the anonymous test." His Pharaoh's Rat peeked out of his blazer pocket, holding a yellow slip in its mouth. It had a serial number on it, the one from Hal's vial. I'd seen slips like this before. The courier service used them. "The diagnosis, too."

"Oh."

Headmaster Hawkins was a space magus. Their power went beyond just moving things around. I should have realized he'd know where his son was at all times and be able to track something as personal to him as a vial of blood.

Now he'll punish you. Perhaps even make you vanish forever.

He did nothing of the sort, of course. Most of the time, that evil inside voice was the biggest liar in the world. Thank goodness.

"Thank you. But that's about the extent of what your grandmother can do. The divorce designated my ex-wife to handle Harold's medical care. He's supposed to ask her."

I thought about my mother—the clipping she'd brought to Seder, and how it represented liberation from her toxic family. She'd called out a wrong when she had the chance. My friend needed some of that energy now, but his father had to know the truth.

"Hal says his mother's kept him from medical care even after he asked for it." I clenched my fists. "Isn't that abuse?"

"That's not how she tells it." He sighed.

"So, ask him." I closed my eyes, remember helping Grace. "Sometimes the people who need help the most have the hardest time asking for it."

"I will." He cleared his throat, then turned to face me. "It's time you go home, Miss Morgenstern. I'll send a message ahead to your family. Professor Luciano will expect you in homeroom tomorrow morning."

"Thank you, Headmaster."

He clapped his hands, and just like that, I was on Essex Street outside one of the Ambersmith's shops with my knapsack dangling from my arm and Ember on my shoulder.

CHAPTER FORTY-NINE

Our team lost. Faith managed to tag Noah out, though, and Dylan didn't go down until it was just him and Elanor Pierce left standing. They all got to show the school that first years weren't fooling around when it came to Bishop's Row.

I got grounded, of course. That was what happened when you lied to your parents for months on end, doing everything you could to cover things up. That meant I couldn't stay at school on the weekends since I was responsible for all sorts of chores around the house. Seriously big messy ones too—the spring-cleaning kind.

"You should have told us." Mom set a cardboard box beside me so I had somewhere to put all the dust bunnies. "I understand waiting the week out to be sure, but you came home the first weekend and told us all about that Charity girl and the fires. So, what happened?"

"It was because of that incident when we walked in, Mom. The Hopewell business." I leaned forward, reaching along the side of the dryer. This was the one in the basement that Bubbe used for all her medical linens, so it was extra dusty. "I didn't want you to start being afraid of me."

"I understand. But Aliyah, it's dangerous to go it alone as an extramagus." She sighed. "I suppose we could have done a better job of informing you and Noah, all things considered."

"Thanks, Mom."

"She's the one cleaning, and she thanks me." She smiled. "See? You're a good kid at heart."

"Less chatter, more dusting." Bubbe set a basket of dirty towels beside the washer.

My family still loved me. As far as the heavy chores went, I'd earned them, so while I didn't do all of the work with a smile, I completed every task using my best effort. Sometimes I fudged it a little, using my magic to help.

Bubbe wasn't ready to talk about her brother yet, except to tell me Dad had named Noah after him and that he'd died during the Boston Internment. That had me totally curious, but between working at home and all the homework from school, I was too tired to snoop around or do extra work to dig up info on the other Noah. She promised to give me the scoop this summer.

School wasn't much different on the punishment front. I was on honest-to-goodness detention, which wasn't anything like Familiar Bonding, unfortunately. Instead, I painted the bleachers in the gym and re-shelved books for the Ashfords in the library.

I had time for meals, class, and studying, and that was about it. The one silver lining was Alex couldn't mess with me. Kitty even kicked him out of her Truncheons and Flagons game. Neither could Charity Fairbanks. I noticed the two of them spending an awful lot of time together in corners around campus. Mostly, they whispered and pointed. At least she'd graduate and be gone next year, so I'd only have to deal with the poisonous magus.

But one thing happened that got me worried.

I was outside the lounge when I saw them, so I stepped back to the side of the doorway. It was shadowy, an ornately carved pillar framing it. Even so, I worried they'd see me until Grace joined me. With a wave of her hand, we were shrouded in shadows, courtesy of her umbral magic. Our concealment was so complete, Faith almost walked right into us. I dragged her into the occluding bubble, making a zipping gesture over my lips.

"I mean it, Charity." One corner of Alex's mouth tilted up, his eyes narrowing. "I'll do anything to show them we're better."

"Academic probation is no joke, kid." Charity was shorter and still managed to look down her nose at him. "You'll be on thin ice, just like Morgenstern, but for different reasons."

"I can handle that." He snorted. "I'll pass the classes easily."

"Okay, then." She unslung her oversized Hermes bag from her arm, setting it on the chair beside her. "Tempe's in charge, but you'll do the grunt work."

"And that'll let me get direct comeuppance?"

"On her and those pathetic sub-races she calls friends." Charity wrinkled her nose. "Ugh. I can't believe they'll be all over campus next year. But you and Tempe will do the right thing with the new crop of students. Add them to our cause."

"Will that be enough?" Alex chewed his lower lip. "Half of next year's graduating class doesn't understand that magi are meant to be the masters."

"You'll have no trouble if you play your cards right." Charity dropped him a wink. "They scare easily and freeze up. If you keep them out of it, the right side will win. That's why I'm entrusting you with this."

She opened her bag and removed one of those paper shopping bags, the kind with handles. It was shadowy, so we couldn't see what was inside. At least not until Grace pointed at it and called up more of her magic.

It was the Slayer's garb, the costume from the Night Creatures concert. Now that I saw it like this, I knew it was authentic. The Fairbanks were dyed-in-the-wool magisupremacists, extrahumans who'd hunted their own during the Reveal and even before it since magi can pass for mundanes.

Faith hung her head. Grace clenched her fists and ground her teeth. I stared, watching my evil ex-boyfriend reach into the bag and stroke the fabric with more affection than he'd ever shown his familiar.

"Oh, yeah." Alex hadn't smiled this much since the dance. "I'll rule the school next year."

"Tempe will." Charity's smile could have curdled milk. "You're behind her throne, not on it. Stick to our agreement, or I will break your name. You've got so many nasty little secrets."

"Understood." His grin was too broad, eyes too wide. She'd startled him.

"Have a great summer." She slung the large handbag over her shoulder and turned her back on him, tossing a tiny wave in his general direction.

Alex Onassis blinked after her for a moment. Once she was gone, he sank into the chair, rubbing his temples. I almost felt sorry for him, but almost didn't count.

"We need to tell the Headmaster." Faith's voice was hushed, which was good because even umbral shadows didn't hide raised voices. "If we go now, he'll catch Alex with that." She pointed at the bag by his feet.

"No, he won't." Grace shook her head. "We only see it because of my magic. That's a cloaking bag, magipsychic. He won't even know it's there."

"You can show him, though?" I waved my hand at the shadows above our heads. "Faith's right. Let's go."

"Good point." Grace nodded, directing us toward the wall so Alex wouldn't see us when she dropped the cloak.

But Headmaster Hawkins wasn't in his office. We didn't end up seeing him for the rest of the year. Professor Luciano said he was away from campus, dealing with a legal matter, and I couldn't be angry about that since maybe it had something to do with Hal's health.

Noah stopped talking to me again. It had me down, but not in a funk. Part of this was because it was my fault this time. There was no wondering why or second-guessing. Nobody to blame but myself. I had to atone, which meant both apologizing and trying to make it up to him. If I worked hard and showed him I cared, he might forgive me by the time Yom Kippur rolled around next fall.

Even with all the extra work and responsibility, I finally felt free. I might be days late to celebrate liberation, but at least I was nowhere near a buck short. None of my friends at school or at home were angry. Lee, Kitty, and Eston treated me the same as ever. I called a meeting in town to tell Azreal Ambersmith. Izzy and Cadence pretended this was the first they'd heard of it for his sake.

"I'm precognitive." Izzy rolled her eyes. "Saw something big coming, should have guessed."

"I didn't." Cadence elbowed Azreal, who was trying to steal some of her French fries. "But everyone in both worlds has secrets. I'd better learn how to handle that, especially if I want to be a good reporter someday."

"It's no big deal to me." Az shrugged, sticking to the food on his own plate. "Variety is the spice of life. Anyway, we've known each other practically forever. If magic starts giving you brain gremlins, we'll notice and help."

"I don't understand." I shook my head. "Being my friend could get super dangerous. I appreciate it and all, but I have to ask. Why put yourselves at risk?"

"Because you'd do it for any or all of us in a heartbeat, Aliyah." Cadence reached across the table, patting my hand.

"Yeah, and we're your friends." Izzy nodded. "We love you, Aliyah."

The detention was done, along with all the chores at home a week before final exams and the end of the semester. I spent most of my time studying in the lounge with Dylan, Grace, Hal, and Faith. And Logan, of course.

He didn't feel like a third wheel, but sometimes I did. It was hard to stop myself from laughing too loud at Dylan's jokes or watching him from across the room to half the time. But either I managed to keep it at a respectful level, or Grace knew and understood. Maybe a little of both.

I almost felt like my old self again, the Aliyah who'd walked along Essex Street with her family on the way to campus that first day.

Except I knew more about myself. I was still afraid of my strength, but not nearly as much because I had backup. That was more important than I could have imagined that first time through the migrating door.

We sat for exams, and this time, I wasn't the first person done. Alex stood up and stormed out of the room after only twenty minutes. We had three hours. None of us saw him study. There was no way he passed that exam without cheating. I wouldn't put it past him, but probably he didn't. Nobody looked that angry if they thought they'd passed a final in record time.

After lunch, there was no Lab, just another meeting in the home-room, where Professor Luciano posted our exam scores and then met with each of us for five minutes in private.

I was utterly shocked to find that Alex failed this exam, putting him below the GPA needed to pass first year. Everybody else scored above average or higher, with Hal at the top of our class. Logan surprised everyone by getting the next highest score. He was one point ahead of me, even.

Faith and I got the same grade, an A-. Bailey's was lowest but still in the B- range. She'd bombed two of the labs by refusing to work with Logan. When she complained, Faith told her to check her attitude and try teamwork next year. I was proud of her.

We were all moving up to second year except Alex, who was being held back. At least we could avoid him most of the time in second year, but Faith thought it was bad news.

"There's going to be trouble." She shook her head. "Temperance is coming."

"There's no throne for us to fight at Hawthorn Academy." Dylan snorted. "I don't see how this is a problem. With a name like Temper-ance, she can't be that bad, right?"

"Does Charity's name have anything to do with her personality?" Grace elbowed him in the ribs. "Except for being opposite, I mean."

"Grace is right." Faith sighed. "We have to watch out. Charity's been telling him about Tempe. They could team up, or worse, become a power couple. If that happens, we're screwed."

"It might be hard next year, but we can handle anything they throw at us." Hal smiled. "Because we'll do it together."

"We have to make through the summer first." Faith frowned, and I didn't blame her. She didn't want to go home, of course.

"I get it." Logan patted her on the shoulder. "Parents should have to take classes and get a license, like professional psychics and magi."

"I'm staying in town again." Dylan shrugged. "I've got a job at Walgreens this time. It pays way more than the Willows, and Brianna hooked me up. There are jobs all over town if you need one."

"I'm way ahead of you there." Grace leaned down, reaching to scratch Lune behind the years. "The Ambersmiths offered me some summer work, textiles stuff. I'll be super busy but in town."

"My parents won't let me stay." Logan shook his head. "Gotta keep learning the family business in what they call my spare time, but I'm going to insist they let me focus on critter calls instead of stunts and dancing."

"Good call." I grinned. "That's a handy skill to know. And more importantly, something you actually like. What about you, Faith?"

"My parents think it's pointless for me to spend even more time in Salem. The only way I can escape for the whole summer is by going abroad, visit the cousins in Geneva." Faith leaned against Hal's chair. "But I don't want to go that far away, not now. At least if I stay in New York, I can take the train up once in a while."

"Why aren't there summer classes or something?" I scratched my head. "That'd give you all the reason you need. Overachieving parents can't argue with trying to better yourself academically."

"There used to be." Hal reached up, taking Faith's hand. "But Dad hasn't got the faculty for that this year, or the time since he'll be with me down in Boston during the week for most of the summer. Dad sat me down with Mom and a lawyer, and she signed off on my medical care. I get to make my own decisions on it from now on."

Everyone smiled at that. It was about time Hal Hawkins, easily the most responsible of our entire group, had the chance to determine how he dealt with his illness.

"You guys, guess what?" It was Kitty. She dashed up to us, dragging Eston behind her as Lee followed along.

"What?" We sounded like a Greek chorus, answering in unison like that.

"It's about next year." She dropped Eston's hand and clapped hers. "It's finally happening. We're finally having intramurals! Can you believe it?"

"You mean we're competing against other schools?" I blinked. "But how?"

"In all the ways, of course." She grinned. "Show them the paper, Eston."

He smiled, cheeks flushing, and handed over the flyer. It had the names of three schools on it. Hawthorn Academy, of course, but also Gallows Hill and Messing Prep.

"This is going to be interesting." Lee nodded. "In all the ways, of course."

Lee Young couldn't see the future, but Izzy pretty much confirmed his sentiment when I visited her the day after school was over. We sat at Engine House with Cadence and Dylan, almost exactly like countless times last summer. Except Grace was there too now, and so was Lee. He got an internship at the museum.

"We'll all be visiting your campus several times next year." Izzy took a sip from her soda. "All the competitions will take place at Hawthorn because you guys are hosting."

"What are those again?" Cadence scratched her head. "The different categories, I mean. I can hardly keep track of them."

"Bishop's Row for one." Dylan chuckled. "And we'll win that one if I have anything to do with it."

"Oh, yeah, Mister Star Athlete." Grace waved her hand dismissively. "As if I won't be up there stopping orbs from hitting you. There's no I in team, you know."

"There's a crafting competition, too." Izzy chewed her lip. "But that'll probably be a tossup between Gallows Hill and us."

"Not if I have anything to do with it." Grace shook her head. "Ugh. Now I sound like Dylan."

We all laughed at that, Grace included.

"Isn't there something cooperative? You know, so we get to try working together?" Cadence batted her eyes at someone out the window. By the time I looked in that direction, whoever it was had passed by. But there was a jet-black tuft of down settling to the cobblestones outside.

"Yes." Lee nodded. "It's a collaborative lab. Students from each school team up to build magicpsychic devices, and they get judged by a panel of professors."

"What else?"

"A talent show." Cadence smiled, her teeth shining like pearls. "That one, I definitely remember."

It certainly seemed like next year would be complicated. That was probably an understatement. I thought we could handle it, though. Friendship had a way of making just about anything possible, and I had some of the best folks in the world on my side.

The End

Thanks for reading Aliyah's adventures during her first year at Hawthorn Academy! Don't worry, her story continues with year two which you can find now at Amazon and through Kindle Unlimited.

Did you know there was another series set in the same world? Check out Providence Paranormal College to learn more about extrahumans on a whole different campus. You can find them, along with my other books, here: http://www.amazon.com/-/e/B0O06851HO

The story continues with Hawthorn Academy Year Two, available now at Amazon and through Kindle Unlimited.

PROVIDENCE
PARANORMAL COLLEGE

At Providence Paranormal College, class is about to start.

Who's enrolled? Students who are a bit different: vampires, were-wolves, changelings, shifters, psychics, and magi.

For one-hundred years, the college has taught and trained only psychics or magi, and for the first time, it's opening the doors to those not different: regular humans.

At this Ivy-League school, the students are expected to learn their powers and keep high grades.

Unfortunately, grades are slipping, but that's what happens when a mysterious villain is hunting you down...

Because someone is angry about this new admissions policy and they'll kill to stop integration. To defeat this rising evil, the students must band together and master their strange powers – because if they don't..

Well, it's pretty hard to graduate when you're dead.

Includes the first five books plus four brand new short stories inside the college.

"I spent more than a couple of late nights reading through these stories to find out what was going to happen to my new friends!" – Michael Anderle, Best-Selling Author of The Kurtherian Gambit

This series is for fans of Harry Potter, Jaymin Eve, and all academy books.

Get it today at Amazon and through Kindle Unlimited

AUTHOR NOTES

FEBRUARY 3, 2020

Hello, readers!

I'm so excited to bring you this series, Hawthorn Academy. It's been a couple of years since finishing the last book in *Providence Paranormal College*, but I knew there were still plenty of stories left to tell in that world. This is one of them.

Hawthorn takes place in Salem, Massachusetts, where I lived for a number of years. Writing in the PPC version of that locale has been a fun and engaging experience. Lots of little details come straight out of my time there.

I actually lived at 10 1/2 Hawthorne Street. The real-life building doesn't have an Extraveterinary office on the first floor, but otherwise, many of the details about it are based in reality. You can walk by the driveway and look up at the building, on the side of the street across from the Boys and Girls Club. But please don't disturb the residents.

The Witch's Brew isn't a real place in downtown Salem, although I designed it to look and feel a lot like the Front Street Cafe with more magic. I've spent many an afternoon there, writing poems and drinking coffee or tea. The biscotti and sandwiches there are delicious, so stop in if you're ever in Salem.

Aliyah Morgenstern is Jewish, like me. Part of the reason I wrote her that way comes from having read the *All of a Kind Family* series by Sydney Taylor when I was young. Finding representation like that is part of what inspired me to be an author. I'm paying it forward. While I only detail Yom Kippur and Passover in Year One, expect to see Hanukkah, Purim, and Sukkot in the next two volumes.

Finally, Hawthorn Academy is a school for magi only. I mention Messing Prep and Gallows Hill, schools for other types of extrahumans. Perhaps I'll write about those in the future if that's something readers express interest in.

You can contact me via my website, drperryauthor.com. From there, you can also find more information about the Providence Paranormal world, other series and books I've written, and links to my social media and Patreon.

I hope you have as much fun reading about Aliyah's adventures as I had writing them. Who am I kidding? I hope you enjoy them even more!

Thanks so much,

D.R. Perry

THANK YOU!

Thank you for reading! If you loved this book, please leave a review. You can find my other work by clicking the links below, going to **my website** or visiting my **Author Central page**.

Providence Paranormal College Volume 1
Providence Paranormal College Volume 2
A Change In Crime
Wiser Guys
The Longest Night Watch
Stardust, Always
Supernatural Vigilante Society
Challenge of Vircon
Poetry Collections

CONNECT WITH THE AUTHOR

Website: https://www.drperryauthor.com/

Join her newsletter!

Find more of D.R. Perry's books on Amazon.

OTHER LMBPN PUBLISHING BOOKS

To be notified of new releases and special promotions from LMBPN publishing, please join our email list:

http://lmbpn.com/email/

For a complete list of books published by LMBPN please visit the following pages:

https://lmbpn.com/books-by-lmbpn-publishing/

All LMBPN Audiobooks are Available at Audible.com and iTunes. For a complete list of audiobooks visit:

www.lmbpn.com/audible

www.ingramcontent.com/pod-product-compliance
Lightning Source LLC
Chambersburg PA
CBHW020229110726
47898CB00004B/1200

* 9 7 8 1 6 4 2 0 2 7 3 8 9 *